Torn

Bound Trilogy Book Two

Kate Sparkes

Sparrowcat Press

Torn

Formatting by RikHall.com
Cover by Cover art by Ravven

ISBN: 978-0-9938220-5-6

For Simon and Isaac

You can read it when you're older.

Prologue

Nox

(One Year Before)

They called me too late.

The grieving father handed me a burlap bag of onions and cabbage-heads as his wife wept over their daughter's body. My fingers brushed his, and he jerked them away.

"It's all we have," he said, and wiped his nose on the discolored sleeve of his shirt.

The child had been hardly more than a baby, dirty and thin, probably not especially well looked-after at the best of times. Her parents had sent their older son to fetch me early that evening. I hadn't been able to do more than ease her suffering as she left us, but they'd been grateful for that.

The poorer folk always waited too long. Their pride held them back. If they couldn't afford to offer a Potioner a decent fee for her services, well, they wouldn't take charity. Not until things got so bad that even I couldn't fix them.

Foolish people.

Their house reeked of weak cabbage stew and the effects of illness, but beneath that lay the lingering soap smell of the laundry the wife took in, their only source of income through the winter. A pittance, really, and likely abandoned when the child fell ill. Had it been up to me, I'd have told them not to worry about paying. My husband would expect me to bring something home, though. He'd have preferred coin, but I could hardly ask that from these people.

Instead, I expressed my regret over their loss and accepted the sack of vegetables.

Even when they needed me and after all the good I did for them, people in northern Tyrea were superstitious about Potioners, especially one like me. At twenty-two years of age I was too young and inexperienced to be considered trustworthy, but too talented for them to ignore my gifts. At least this man had the good grace to look embarrassed about his nervousness as he showed me to the door.

The wind pulled my breath from me as I stepped into the frigid night and found my way home, holding my lamp in front of me like Pourana, the woman of legend who guided spirits of the dead to paradise.

We saw so much death that winter. A terrible sickness had swept through the province, and though other villages lost far more than we did, the guilt over those who died still weighed heavily on me. Not everyone was as kind as that family, and many blamed me when I couldn't save someone they loved. But they needed me, and I tried to keep my resentment over their ingratitude and unending demands to myself.

There was no one at home interested in listening anyway, and I wasn't about to start muttering to myself.

I had been practicing forbearance for several years, silently weathering my husband's criticisms and demands, shrugging it off when he insulted me, quietly tending to my own wounds when the need arose.

Denn was the son of a local businessman, and accustomed to a certain lifestyle, of which I was an integral part whether I wished it or not. The folk of the village saw him as an upstanding citizen and hard worker, and they looked away from his many indiscretions. If they suspected what went on behind the walls of our little home, they never offered to help. I was an outsider from another town. Denn had charmed me into marrying him, and the consequences of that were mine to deal with. I didn't need anyone's help or pity.

A strong gust of wind ushered me into the house, scattering snow across the scratched and dented wood floor. I struggled to close the door and silently cursed Denn once again for building his home facing east, with its back to the town and nothing to protect us from the winter winds.

I crept across the floor and set my black bag on the kitchen table, careful to not let the glass bottles within clatter against each other. I kept meaning to wrap them properly, but the past week had left me barely any time to eat, sleep, bathe, or brew, let alone take care of small chores. My supply shelves covered the smallest wall in the kitchen with rows of glazed pots and glass jars. I refilled my bottles and returned them to the bag. Best to get it done, though my hands shook with exhaustion. Someone would need me again soon, and I had better be ready.

My workbench and equipment gleamed in the dim lamplight, a stark contrast to the filthy dishes in the sink, all of them covered in congealing gravy from the meal I'd been forced to abandon earlier. I turned my back on those and returned my attention to the shelves. My potions called to me, each with a purpose and personality that I loved more than any person I knew. A quick nip from an unlabeled bottle of pale-yellow liquid warmed me like bottled sunshine, though it was nothing more than a fermentation of fieldsun blossoms and torranceroot. Simple, but elegant and perfect in its balance.

3

The hem of my skirt dripped melted snow over my leg as I lifted it to examine my left thigh, where a purple bruise was fading to green. A pungent ointment from the top shelf eased the stiffness and encouraged bad blood to move on. Air hissed through my teeth as the tingling set in, bringing pain before blessed relief.

The bruise was a gift from Denn, a reminder that the work I did for the town should not interrupt his rest or come before his needs. Meals on the table, money in his hand, a potion to ease the morning-after pain when he'd been drinking. It had been days since he'd hit me, and before that he'd left me alone for weeks.

And that's what passes for good times, I thought. Not exactly the life I'd dreamed of when I was younger.

I scoured the pots, again keeping my curses to myself. It wouldn't have killed him to at least rinse the damned things. A lid fell toward the floor, and I snatched it out of the air before the clattering could wake him.

My careful silence was needless. When I peered into the bedroom, it was empty.

I sighed, as much from relief as from frustration at my husband's continued wanderings. *Let him take it out on a more willing body tonight.* Arberg was a small town and short on whores, but Denn could charm his way in anywhere he pleased.

I didn't bother undressing before I collapsed into bed and dozed off.

The door slammed open, then shut, and my stomach clenched. I lay with my eyes closed, listening to Denn muttering as he stumbled about the house, his ox-like body banging into furniture as he went. Something shattered, almost certainly the bottle of bitter-leaf I'd just finished preparing that morning. It would take me a week to do it again, and I was nearly out. Without the medicine I handed out to his conquests, the consequences of his indiscretions could be severe.

Idiot, I thought, but a fearful chill spread through

me. My emotions betrayed me when Denn was around, no matter how brave or contemptuous my thoughts when I was alone.

I rolled over and pulled my knees up to my chest, making myself small.

He eventually made his way to the washbasin to splash water on his face, then staggered into the bedroom. The straw mattress crunched under his weight as he sat to remove his boots, and he exhaled the stench of ale as he leaned over to study my face. I shifted slightly, as I might if I were asleep. He grunted and finished undressing.

He rolled toward me, pressing his body against my back. "Why're you dressed?" he mumbled, and tugged at the buttons on my shirt.

"Just got home. Need sleep." I crossed my arms over my chest and tucked my hands into my armpits.

He abandoned the buttons and reached for the hem of my skirt. "You get paid?"

"Well enough." I pushed his hand away and pulled the skirt tight around my legs. "I'll probably have to go out again soon."

He pulled harder. "Good thing this won't take long, then."

"I mean it, Denn. Stop." Tight as I gripped the fabric, his hands were stronger than mine. He pried my fingers open and rolled on top of me. "Denn, no."

He laughed and nipped at my ear. "Who the hell d'you think you are, missus?"

I drew on what energy I had left and tried to bring my knee up between his legs, but he had my skirt pinned on either side of me. He grabbed my wrists in one of his massive hands, fingers circling the scars he gave me mere months after our wedding.

"You think you're so damned special," he muttered, words slurred. With his free hand, he pinched the skin on the inside of my upper arm, and the sharp pain made me cry out. "You need to remember who's in charge here. Town should be grateful to me."

His face smelled of cheap perfume, and I had no desire to know what other parts of him smelled of.

"I say how and when you use your talents." He pressed his hips against me and struggled to maintain his balance as he yanked at my skirt. "All of 'em. You're nothing without me. Right? Nobody."

After a moment of fumbling, he growled. "You're not doing it for me tonight. Go to sleep."

His body went limp, and he rolled off me. I thought he'd passed out until one massive hand reached up to wrap around my throat. He squeezed, and mumbled some vague threat about what would happen if I ever left. One finger touched the white scar that ran from my left temple over my cheekbone. My potions never managed to completely erase the marks he left on me.

"You're mine, Nox. Mine."

Then his hand relaxed, and he began to snore.

For the first time, his drunkenness had worked out to my advantage. But how long would that last? He'd be at me again soon. In the morning he'd be sick, and angry about me accepting cabbage as payment for services. As he so often reminded me, I'd be out on my arse if I couldn't contribute to our income. Gods only knew how he'd decide to take out that anger after my potions gave him his strength back. If I was lucky, someone would come to call me out again before he woke.

And it will never end, I thought as I gazed into the darkness. If I left, he would find me. A Potioner as talented as I was would stick out in any town, if I could even find a place that would accept me. Unless I kept my gift to myself and watched people die around me, he would find me out and bring me back. So I would stay, and be silent, and do my work, and dread coming home.

Forever.

I slipped out of bed and went to the bathing room to wash up in the basin, feeling dirtier than I had any reason to. I ignored the warped mirror on the wall. The changes I saw there only made me feel small and weak. Where once I'd seen reflected a face I thought more beautiful than any in Cressia, perhaps all of Tyrea, I would now find my long, dark hair framing a pale-faced woman with dark circles beneath her eyes, a few scars to mark battles lost, and lifeless blue eyes.

Enough, I told myself. My mother hadn't raised me to wallow in self-pity. *Fix the problem, or bear up under it and go on.*

I swallowed back the lump in my throat, and reached for my comfort. Not a potion this time, but a memory. I saved it for my darkest moments and tried to forget it the rest of the time, lest the brilliance of my secret throw the rest of my miserable life into shadow.

My mother's words. My identity, shared when I told her at age sixteen that I intended to go to the city of Luid to study at the university, to embrace my talents and become more than I could ever be in Cressia.

She'd said no. It was too dangerous. Because of the secret, because of who we were, we could never go back there. And so I'd stayed, and I'd married Denn instead. Still, I never forgot what she told me. I'd long suspected I was different from the people around me, destined for greater things. The fact that I'd been right pleased me. And yet, what good had my mother's secret done me? I'd allowed life to wear me down. To defeat me. The secret was as useful as a jeweled crown sitting in a dusty box on a closet shelf, never to be worn.

You are better than this.

I gripped the edge of the washbasin hard enough that the metal rim drew blood from my fingers. The secret usually comforted me and brought assurance that I had more value than anyone knew. Tonight it felt different, and brought a feeling I hadn't experienced in years.

When I looked up, I caught a glimpse of something in the eyes of my reflection. Not hope, or anything so lovely, but even the hate that now warmed my insides was better than the nothing I'd felt for so long. Determination replaced fear, rage overtook apathy.

Never again.

I'd made the decision before I had a chance to think it over. I covered the distance to the kitchen in long strides and opened the cupboard under my workbench. A tinted glass bottle waited in the back corner, covered with a layer of dust and spiderwebs. The shriveled mushroom inside looked like a decayed mouse, curled in on itself. It had been a remarkable find, plucked from the graveyard on a humid summer night. I hadn't been sure I'd ever find a use for it.

I removed the mushroom with a set of small tongs, careful not to touch it directly. Its energy still hummed, perceptible only to a Potioner, indicating that its poisonous strength had grown after years in the dark. I ground a portion to dust and dissolved it in liquid. No chance of him spitting it out. Just the touch of it on his tongue would do the job.

I hoped it would burn.

Chapter One

Rowan

"Try to relax."

I opened one eye to glare at Aren. "I *am* relaxed."

"No, you're not. You're thinking about it too much. If you want it too badly, you're never going to get there. You've almost got it."

Irritation churned my stomach. He couldn't read my thoughts as he could most people's, but I shot him a look that told him to stop talking before he made things worse. He got the message, and leaned back.

He brushed his dark hair back from his face and waited. I forced myself to look away before my thoughts had a chance to stray.

My breath sent a cloud of vapor into the frigid air of the old barn as I slowly exhaled. The winter had been a long one on Belleisle, and places to work at the school were hard to come by. Though Aren been allowed to stay, Emalda forbade contact between us outside of these lessons, and always had someone watching us. He was never to use his magic with or on another person, and wasn't allowed in the main building except at mealtimes. Even then he usually ate alone, later, rather than bear her cold looks and the silence of the rest of the staff. It was the price he paid for killing Emalda's sister—a punishment he bore without complaint, if with obvious irritation.

So we had to find other places for these lessons, and after nearly four months we had yet to find one that was particularly warm or pleasant. Still, this barn's walls cut the wind, and blocked out distractions so that I could practice my magic.

I closed my eyes. *Magic.* For so many years I had dreamed about it, imagining it was something as beautiful as what I'd read about in old stories instead of the abomination my people told me it was. It was beautiful, truly, but there was nothing simple about it.

You wanted this, I reminded myself. *Did you think it would be easy?*

In fact, I had. Magic had proved to be a more mysterious and powerful thing than I'd ever suspected, and mine was a unique case. According to Ernis Albion, Aren's grandfather and headmaster of this school in Belleisle, I'd nearly lost my magic when I broke the binding that had held it inside of me for almost twenty years. I was fortunate that using it hadn't killed me. In fact, Aren believed the only reason I'd survived was that the dragon scale I'd carried in my pocket had absorbed or deflected some of the magical force. Even that had been a close thing. I'd wakened from a dream world nearly empty of magic. But now that I had it back—

"Rowan?"

"I'm thinking."

"Don't think."

"I swear, Aren..."

Much as I adored him and admired how hard he'd worked to be allowed to remain with me, his approach to tutoring left much to be desired. I hated feeling irritated with him, but had so few chances to see him in other settings.

I opened my eyes again to peek at the snowball on the floor that I was supposed to move using my magic. Aren was watching me. His gaze had strayed from my face to the place where my bright red hair curled gently into the open collar of my shirt. His face showed nothing of what he might be thinking, but a wave of heat washed over me as my own thoughts strayed. *Other settings would definitely be nice.*

I raised an eyebrow, and his green-flecked, brown eyes moved back up. No embarrassment at getting caught, though. He still wasn't comfortable with love, but he was fine with lust.

He smiled. "Whenever you're ready to try again."

"One more time." My eyes fell closed, and my breath slowed. I tried to remember the advice I'd been given so far. So many people here had it to offer. Albion, Aren, the teachers. Even the students, all of whom were younger than I, knew what they were doing. But then, they'd all grown up with full knowledge of their gifts and learned how to channel their power as it grew.

Open yourself to it. I focused on relaxing the muscles of my face and my shoulders, and rested my hands on my knees. *Come on, magic. This will be fun. Work with me.*

Magic welled in me, warm, smooth, and powerful as an ocean wave, lifting me. I pulled back from it, though I tried not to. Using magic wasn't an unpleasant feeling, but I found it so unfamiliar. So intimidating. I wondered, *what would happen if I did it? It might be amazing. Or—*

"Come on," I whispered. I needed to push through, do it once, get it over with....

The magic moved in me, but I didn't feel anything else change. When I peeked again, the snowball hadn't moved.

My frustration flared, and I leaped to my feet.

Energy flashed, and the snowball vanished into a puddle.

Fantastic.

"I give up!" I stomped on the puddle. Childish, but I had to take my frustration out somewhere, and

Aren had borne the brunt of it too many times.

He stood. "Rowan?"

The acrid scent of smoke filled the air, and I turned to see weak flames licking at a hay-bale behind me. Before I could react, a load of snow the size of a small pony floated in through the open door and melted over the flames, extinguishing them.

I turned to the girl sitting on the wooden bench behind Aren. She hadn't panicked. Hadn't even troubled to stand, or to stop petting the purring tabby stretched out on the bench beside her.

"Thanks," Aren said, and she nodded.

Celean was sixteen, but looked younger. Her wide, owl-like eyes peered out from behind thick, black hair and gave her a look of youth and innocence that suited her personality well. She was my roommate, my friend, and our assigned watch-keeper for the day. I'd nearly forgotten she was there.

"Lunch bell's ringing, anyway." She gave the barn cat one last rub behind the ears and went to the door. "I'm going to walk slowly. Try to catch up before I get to the kitchen so I don't get in trouble for leaving you." Celean's soft voice projected a quiet confidence I envied. She'd always known what she was, and expected to be respected for her powers. She knew her place in the school, her importance to the world.

I had been denied all of that by my people. Even though I knew they were wrong, some part of me still struggled to break free of their beliefs. I'd grown up hearing that people bought their magic from the devil. My own father, a magistrate in our small border town, had sentenced more people to death for using it than I cared to consider. He hated magic. They all did. I had realized months ago that it was my mother who had paid to have my magic bound when I was a baby, but I didn't know any details. Had she done it to protect me? To hide something shameful from the world?

Whatever her motivations, her actions had brought me a life of pain. A life I might not have had otherwise, if Aren was right about my people killing babies born like me.

At least the headaches were gone. In a sense, I was everything I was born to be—filled with magic, free of the binding. But it still wasn't right. I had power in me, and couldn't make it work. I couldn't even heal injuries as I had on a few occasions when my magic was still bound. That had been our first experiment in me using my magic, and it had turned out to be a painful one for Aren. That ability had been a weakness in the binding, nothing more. I'd lost it completely, and had found nothing useful to replace it.

After Celean left, I crouched on the floor and pressed the heels of my hands to my eyes. I wasn't going to cry. Not in front of Aren. Not over this. But the little frustrations kept building, and I felt ready to explode.

"You're getting there," Aren said.

"Am I?" I looked up at him. He held my coat in his hands, looking uncharacteristically uncertain. He never knew what to do when I was upset. When he was a child and showed emotions like this, he'd been beaten for it. At least he wasn't trying *that* on me. I sighed and stood. "Nothing has changed except that I'm causing more damage now."

"That's still progress," he said. "This happens to anyone trying to use her magic for something new. You get backlash. Unexpected effects. The problem is that everything is new to you, and you're dealing with a lot of power. There are going to be rough spots." He nudged the smoldering bale of hay with his foot. "Maybe the barn was a bad place to work."

"The barn's not the problem, but thank you. I guess moving stuff's not one of my natural gifts." The chaotic results were supposed to be less if one worked at a talent that was a strong gift. An encouraging theory, until one ran out of things to try out.

"We'll go back to things we've already tried," he suggested. "Maybe your magic simply wasn't ready before."

I stepped closer to him. The words came so easily to him. I wanted to believe them, to relax and have faith that the magic would settle into me, and I into it, but all I felt was pressure. His need to fix me only made me feel more broken.

During our early lessons, I accomplished nothing. My magic had been weak then, and we hadn't pushed it too hard. When it returned, though, it came in a flood. I could hold it back, but only when I wasn't trying to use it. When I did attempt to direct my power it ran wild, and trying to control it was like trying to catch a raging river in a tin bucket.

"It's going to happen," Aren said. "Just remember to focus your intentions, concentrate on what you want to happen, but—"

"But do it without thinking about it, I know!" I forced my voice lower. "Do you have any idea how little sense that makes to me? It's so easy for you."

He pressed his lips together, likely holding back sharp words. I'd have deserved them. I braced myself for a fight. Maybe clearing the air would help. It would be a release, anyway.

He looked away. "I don't know how else to help you. Maybe these lessons are a bad idea."

My stomach dropped. "What? They're all we've got."

"I'm not helping you. Every time we see each other, it ends with you feeling frustrated and me feeling guilty. I don't even understand why, but I do. I seem to be making things worse rather than better."

"I'm sorry for making you feel that way," I said. I should have been pleased he was willing to admit to feeling anything. That was progress for one of us, at least.

"I wanted to talk to you about something Albion mentioned yesterday. Something that might help."

"What's that?"

"He said in some places, people use words to focus their magic. Or wands."

"Spells? No. Absolutely not."

I crossed my arms. "What do you mean, 'no'? This isn't your decision. He said that they're helpful, that people use them to—"

"I know. It's a bad idea. All you need is time and practice. Those magical crutches are for weak people who can't use their power without them."

My eyes narrowed. "Yeah? Well, I don't seem to be doing so well on my own."

His eyebrows knit together, shadowing his dark eyes. "You can't give up. You're better than that."

"Am I?" Anger overtook frustration. "What if I'm not? What if the binding permanently crippled me, and I need something like that to help me control this thing? Will you stop caring then?" Tears prickled at my eyes, but I held them back. "Will you move on?"

His expression hardened. "You need to calm down."

"And you need to stop thinking you know what I need. You're so stuck on this idea of what I am that you can't even try to imagine things happening differently." I grabbed my coat from his hands. "Your way isn't the only way. You need to accept the fact that maybe I'm not good enough for you." I'd seen the way he looked down on weaker students, Potioners, and people without magic.

His upper lip lifted in a silent snarl. "You're fighting the wrong battle right now. I'm not your enemy."

My shoulders slumped. "I know," I whispered. "And I'm sorry. I'm just so damned frustrated. It's easy for everyone here, especially you. Your magic comes so naturally. It's beautiful. Mine fights me and frightens me. I can't control anything anymore. My feelings, my magic... my temper. I shouldn't take it out on you. You've been good to me. Better than I deserve right now."

He opened his arms and I stepped closer. I wrapped my arms around his waist, and he held me tight. "You say you're sorry too often."

"You've said it to me before."

"Only when it was important," he said. "People lose respect for you when it's a habit. It makes you smaller, humbler. A Sorceress shouldn't feel she has to apologize to anyone."

"Maybe not in Tyrea, but people do it a lot here. Good manners smooth things over. You should try it some time." I pulled him into a deep kiss that made my heart pound. I placed one hand on his chest and felt his heart doing the same. He tried to hold onto me, but I pulled away and offered a shy smile. "I won't apologize for doing that, though. Ever." I reached up to brush my thumb over his cheekbone.

"Any chance of you getting out tonight?" he asked. "Without Celean?"

"I wish I could, but I think they'll expel me if I get caught again. Maybe I'll see you in my dreams."

As if that could ever be enough. I wanted so badly to stay in the barn with him, away from prying eyes. We needed more of that. Every time he touched me, it left my body aching for more. We'd managed to share dreams on a few occasions since our arrival on the island, in spite of the fact that I slept in the main school building and he in his little apartment over the carriage house. The dreams were good, but that was all they were. The few times when we had managed to be alone, when I managed to sneak out to his rooms at night...

I forced my thoughts away from the memory of his touch. Thinking about it only made things worse.

I pulled my coat tight around me and stepped out into the bright sunlight that blanketed the school grounds. Celean waited for me by the old oak tree, and I hurried to catch up.

Fast as I ran, I couldn't escape my thoughts.

I had Aren, but thanks to Emalda's rules, we had to keep our distance. My magic was free, but I couldn't do anything with it. And somewhere behind me, my old life lay shattered. I'd had no word from my family since I left Darmid, though I'd written many times and Albion had assured me that he had reliable means of delivery. I worried about my parents, my aunt and uncle and their servants, my cousin Felicia...even Callum, the magic hunter who I'd agreed to marry, once. I wanted so badly to talk with him about everything that had happened. He'd been a good friend and could have been so much more. He deserved better than what I'd been able to give him, and as a hunter, he deserved to know the truth about magic.

Perhaps some day I'd get a chance to make things right with all of them.

Chapter Two

Aren

Rowan dashed out the door, hair the color of cherries flying behind her. The strange shade, a side-effect of the release of her magic, had deepened and darkened over the winter, leaving lighter streaks around her face. She'd never indicated whether she cared for it. I thought it suited her well, accidental though it had been. It also made her easier to spot at a distance—a place I was becoming far too accustomed to seeing her from.

It was my own fault. I'd done things in the past that harmed people. I hadn't cared who I hurt at the time, not as long as Severn rewarded me for it. The consequences hadn't mattered then, but they'd finally caught up with me. Because of a death I hadn't intended to cause, my grandfather's wife Emalda allowed me to stay at the school only if I obeyed strict rules that strangled me like a noose, growing tighter every day.

Whether the rules were intended to hurt me or only to protect Rowan and the other students, I couldn't say. Either way, Emalda had created the perfect torture for me. I was allowed to see Rowan, to speak with her, to hear her laugh and catch her warm glances and frustrated glares. But I was not to touch her, to whisper the things I longed to say, to help her forget her troubles. It broke me in a way that the other rules didn't, making me a prisoner even while I knew I was free to leave.

No matter how hard I worked or how trustworthy I made myself, there were some debts that could not be repaid. Nearly four months after my arrival at the island, Emalda kept as close a watch over us as she ever had.

If not for Celean's kindness, Rowan and I would never steal even the few moments we had—and that was for Rowan's sake. Not mine.

I leaned out the door as Rowan and Celean made their way toward the school. Better to let Rowan go without me. I'd sneak into the kitchen later and scrounge something to eat. I picked up a pitchfork and stabbed at the hay bale, from which wisps of smoke still rose. Magic and hard work kept the school safe, but a fire might still hurt someone—and the clean-up would certainly be my responsibility. I spread the hay out until it no longer smoldered, and the acrid stink of burned grass filled the air.

The end of a lesson and Rowan's return to the world of the school always left an empty ache in me, a space that uncomfortable thoughts rushed to fill. There was a time when I wouldn't have let anyone stop me from being with whomever I wanted, whenever I wished. I wouldn't have let Emalda talk down to me or give me orders. True, I'd been Severn's puppet then, but I'd had power. Position. Potential. Yet I'd just spent a winter mucking out the stable and doing odd jobs around a school in a land where I was no one, where I had no future.

I barely had a present. I had Rowan, but infrequently. We had our lessons, with their accompanying frustrations and everything that had to be left unsaid when our caretakers were less indulgent than Celean. We'd managed through luck or recklessness to have a few nights together. The last of those had resulted in Emalda cutting down the tree branch that Rowan had used to escape from her room, and a stern talking-to for me from my grandfather. Emalda's rules would hold, or I would be sent away. Rowan, too.

Time with my dear Sorceress was worth almost any trouble, but I wasn't willing to risk our banishment for it. I had nowhere else to go, and Rowan's prospects were no better. We were safe on the island, at least for the time being.

"*Nyaah?*" The cat Celean had been petting had a voice like a dying crow. It flopped onto its back and waved its white-gloved paws in the air. I ignored it.

I sat and rested my face in my hands. I'd already overstayed my welcome, and I wasn't helping Rowan with anything except getting in trouble. It was past time for me to leave, but every day we spent together made it harder to go. Though she and I were completely different people on the surface, it seemed that our roots grew more entwined with each day I stayed.

In truth, I needed Rowan. I hated to admit it, even to myself, but she had wakened a part of me I'd thought destroyed, something that had been resting far below the surface during the years I served my brother, Severn. What I felt for her went deeper than the frustrations and the disagreements, linking us even when more reasonable people would have given up and moved on.

Even on my worst days she made me smile, and even on hers, I couldn't help admiring her. Loving her. Wishing to be more like her.

The cat rubbed on my leg, and I shoved it gently away with the toe of my boot.

"Still having troubles, eh?" Ernis Albion stomped the snow from his boots as he came through the door at the far end of the barn, then wiped the snowflakes off his spectacles. He stood with one hand on his hip and scratched at his short, white hair as he watched the cat roll around in the hay. "It's sad. We have no respectable barn cats. Emalda babies them." He scooped the purring beast into his arms and cradled it there, scratching under its chin.

"How much of that conversation did you hear?"

He sat down beside me and set the cat on the floor. "Just enough to know that you're both getting discouraged. Certainly nothing I shouldn't have heard."

My grandfather walked a careful line between making his wife happy and trying to keep me around for reasons I still didn't quite understand. I liked the man. I'd come to appreciate the strength he managed to radiate while being what I'd once thought disparagingly of as "a good person." I'd always thought strength came through solitude, through cruelty and not caring, through creating fear in those who didn't show respect. Albion was different. He earned the respect of his students through his competence, his love for them, and his unwavering dedication to making the world better. I admired the man, but kept him at a distance. I wasn't like him, and didn't know how to be—or whether becoming like him would mean sacrificing everything I had been before.

"I'm running out of ideas," I told him. "Rowan's right. Magic always came so easily to me. Even when I couldn't do something, I pushed myself to learn. I suppose I never thought to appreciate the years when my magic was still small and I had a chance to learn control."

"Hmm." He rubbed a hand under his chin. "She knows how you pressure yourself. Even now, you're learning new skills. She sees that. Why do you think she's pushing herself so hard?" He didn't ask accusingly, but the words stung. I was a bad influence on so many levels.

"I think I'm holding her back. I try not to let her see how frustrated I get when I try to teach her, but I think she knows. I don't want her to see that."

"I assume your teachers pushed you mercilessly when you were young," he said softly. "Rowan knows that, and I think she understands why your expectations are so high. She wants to live up to your standard. She doesn't want to disappoint you, and that frustrates her."

"I know. None of this is easy for me, either," I said. It wasn't just the isolation. Emalda had strictly forbidden me using my powers to so much as look into anyone's thoughts, and I was forbidden to practice controlling minds. I considered myself fortunate that she didn't threaten to banish me every time I took my eagle form to fly over the island. I felt my skills atrophying, and could do nothing about it. "I feel trapped here, though I don't want to leave."

Albion smiled in his peaceful, quiet way. "I think Emalda is warming to you."

"She had me clean out the old cistern yesterday. Without magic."

He let the cat drop to the floor. "No one said love or heroism were easy. Or rewarding, for that matter. Walk with me?"

We stepped out into the early-spring sunlight and started toward the stables and the house beyond them. I snapped my fingers and produced a tiny flame. It had taken a good deal of practice over the winter, but I'd picked up the skill while my power hadn't been occupied with more familiar things.

So many people thought that a powerful Sorcerer should be able to do anything, not understanding the study and practice required, having no understanding of the risks we took every time we tried to use our magic for something new. I tried to tell myself that learning to create a flame was impressive, but when I thought of Severn's skills in it, my own seemed a pale imitation.

I missed being allowed to use my strongest gifts, missed the power filling me and pouring out, the sense of purpose and strength it gave me.

"I didn't come to speak to you about Rowan," Albion said, interrupting my thoughts. He handed me a letter. "I received this from Tyrea."

"Not from Severn?"

"No, nothing from him yet. This is from one of my 'eyes and ears' folks."

A dangerous position, as they were reporting to him against my brother's wishes. I scanned the neatly penned note. "He's conscripting Sorcerers?"

"And Potioners, yes. Forcibly consolidating magical talent in Luid. Do you know why?"

"Nothing that he ever mentioned to me." But then, my brother had never trusted me like I'd wanted him to. "Our father did something similar, bringing talent to the city, but he made them generous offers to enter his service. He didn't force anyone to leave their homes or work for him. He kept a close eye on those who refused, though."

"I suspect that your brother's hunger for power exceeds even your father's, and he seems to lack the temperance that made Ulric a good king."

"Hmm." A good king, perhaps. In his personal life, he'd been cold and cruel. I hadn't mourned when he disappeared three years before. Severn may have been ruthless, but at least he valued my talents while I let him use them. He'd offered me a position in his councils. I'd have had a bright future in his court if I hadn't thrown it all away for Rowan.

"Do you regret leaving?" Albion asked.

"Your wife doesn't approve of mind-reading, you know."

He waved that off. "Not a gift that I've tried to develop. Your thoughts are written on your face."

I'd have to watch that. A few months ago Rowan had been calling me a closed book, and I preferred to remain that way. The relative safety of the island had made me soft.

The lines on Albion's forehead deepened.

"You're not concerned he'll try to do the same here, are you?" I asked. "Steal your magic-users?"

He lifted his chin and squared his shoulders. "The

island has its defenses, and our magic is strong. I don't think he'd dare. He could certainly make life miserable for us, could harm us, but I think he knows he would never take us." His words were confident, but his voice less so. Belleisle had kept an uneasy peace with Tyrea when my father ruled there, but there was no telling what Severn would do to get what he wanted. "You know him better than I. Will he try anything?"

I watched the last of the students filing into the kitchen after riding lessons, and my stomach growled at the thought of the potato soup the cook had been preparing that morning when I went in. "You're probably safe for now. He has other concerns." *Rowan and I among them*, I added to myself. "You'd all be safer without me here."

Before he could answer, Emalda slipped outside and closed the door against the laughter that drifted out. She strode toward us, pulling a bright red cap over her silver hair. I adjusted my posture, standing straight and square, ready to hear about whatever I'd done wrong this time. Much as I hated her snide comments and complaints, I had become used to them. Her words could irritate me, but they'd lost their bite.

There was no anger in her expression, only a tightness that I didn't have to use my skills to know concealed panic. Albion stepped toward her. "My dear?"

"Tyrean ship approaching off Krota Head," she said, and shivered. She pulled her wool coat tighter around her thin frame. "Flying Severn's flag."

My stomach turned, and I dismissed the thought that we had summoned a demon with our words.

"A lone ship?" Albion asked, and Emalda nodded. "Messages? Emissaries?"

"No," she said. "Not yet, at least."

One ship, approaching boldly enough that we'd received word long before it reached shore, in daylight no less. This was no sneak attack. Severn felt I owed him a debt, and he'd come to collect. He wasn't going to leave until he had what he wanted. If I didn't go to him, he would come to me and deliver every bit of misery to the island that Albion seemed to think him capable of.

"Where are the students?" I asked. "Safe?"

"In the house," Emalda said.

"Good. Please keep them there."

I waited for her to order my immediate departure, to note that my indecisiveness over leaving may have placed everyone on the island in harm's way. She'd have been within her rights to be angry, and for once I wouldn't have blamed her for harsh words. Instead, she hesitantly laid a hand on my arm.

"What will you do?" she asked.

A mantle of calm settled over my mind even as my heart pounded. I'd hoped for more time, and expected less. The moment had come.

I offered a smile that I hoped looked more reassuring than it felt. "I suppose I'd better saddle up a horse and go see what Severn wants."

Chapter Three

Aren

After a short ride I reached Krota Head—a wide, grassy bluff overlooking the ocean to the east of the school. Probably a lovely spot in the summer, but on that day the cold, salty wind swept up from the ocean and cut to my bones, rattling through the dead grasses as it came. My horse shuffled and tried to turn his backside into the wind, and I pulled him back around to face the sleek ship that rocked on the waves below us, a black speck against dark water and blue sky.

Severn's personal ship, the *Nightfire*. It had never sailed without him on board. I'd had no doubt he would come, but seeing his vessel sent a shock through me, and I fought the urge to ride away. I'd neither seen nor heard from my brother since the night Rowan broke the binding that had held her magic within her, the night that its release almost killed Severn. In fact, I'd heard little *of* him, even through my grandfather's news-gatherers in Luid. All I knew was that he was alive, and undoubtedly angry.

Another set of hooves thudded over the grass behind us, and Albion brought his black horse up next to mine.

"Severn?" he asked.

"Yes."

"If you go to him, he'll—"

"I know. I don't see what choice I have."

When Rowan and I arrived at Belleisle and Emalda agreed to let me stay, I hadn't expected to be there for more than a few weeks before I left. I couldn't have defeated Severn on my own, but I should have gone back to Tyrea as soon as Rowan was settled. Then Severn would have tracked and followed me there, and he wouldn't be here now. The others would be safe.

It was one ship, not an army. Still, its presence in these waters meant nothing good.

The waves crashed against the rocks below the bluff, sending mist spraying into the wind, but the ship appeared to rest in a spot of calm. Someone on board was controlling the waves in a powerful way. This was not one of Severn's skills. He had at least one other Sorcerer with him. I regretted my decision to follow Emalda's rules and not practice my less pleasant gifts, which I would soon need.

A trio of dark specks floated up from the ship's deck, rising in the wind, spiraling up until they cleared the masts, then turned toward the shore.

Albion squinted. "Are those birds?"

I didn't answer, but handed him my horse's reins and slipped to the ground. A moment later my clothes fell to the grass as I changed into my eagle's body and flapped my wings hard until the wind lifted me. I flew into it, toward the intruders.

They might only have been messengers, but I wasn't about to take any chances.

The large hawks seemed desperate to reach land, but all hesitated when they caught sight of me. The one in the lead cut low to get around me. I dropped with talons outstretched. The hawk, from which I sensed strong magic, darted away at the last second. I stretched, turned, and managed to grip its thin neck with one set of talons. The bird twisted in my grip, nearly slipping free, but it was too small to fight me. I grabbed on, broke its neck, and released its body into the waves, nearly dunking myself in the process.

While I'd been occupied, the second bird had darted around us. I turned hard and let the wind push me toward land. The bird screamed as my talons gripped the sleek feathers of its back, sending several whipping away as we rolled through the air. The wind ripped its shrieks from its throat as I tore into its flesh, and it met the same fate as its companion, lost among the waves.

I had no way of knowing whether the magic was an enchantment placed on the animals, or whether they were Sorcerers and shape-shifters. I didn't have time to question them, or to care.

The third bird rushed past as I dropped the second body. I wheeled and climbed high, never losing sight of its rusty-red tail in spite of the sun's glare off of the water. When it flew in my shadow, I folded my wings and dropped. The hawk darted to one side and I clipped the edge of one wing as I passed, glancing off without grabbing so much as a flight feather. The hawk dropped on top of me, and we fell together toward the crashing waves with the smaller bird latched onto my back.

This is no regular hawk, I realized. It thought, planned, strategized. A Sorcerer for certain, but the thought changed nothing for me. He wasn't going to get to the island.

I twisted my neck and slashed out with my beak, and tasted hot blood. The little talons released my feathers. I picked up an air current before I hit the water and spiraled up. The hawk was still airborne, but hurt and struggling. I cut in front of him before he reached the cliffs, and he turned back toward the sea, toward the ship and safety.

I was trying to decide whether to let him make it when he turned back and shot toward me, darting around at the last moment. My own flight skills were no match for his. An older Sorcerer, then, more experienced.

I screamed a warning toward shore, but when I looked back at the top of the bluff, Albion showed no sign of concern. He stood holding the horses' reins, watching.

The Sorcerer would make land.

I'd nearly caught up when bright light flashed around him. The hawk screeched and shot backward. At nearly the same moment, I felt it—perhaps not as fully as he had, but a shock like lightning went through me, leaving me gasping for air but still aloft. The hawk didn't fare so well, and his body spun toward the water.

Words Albion said to me the first time we spoke of the island's defenses came to mind. *If you'd come with ill-will, you wouldn't have made it.*

No further threats had appeared, but still the ship rocked on the waves. Waiting, and I thought I knew for what.

Or whom.

I forced my stunned wings to push me higher and flew toward the black ship. The island could defend itself for a time, but the threat would remain until I faced it. Terror passed over me, chilling me from beak to tail feathers. I forced it away, leaving only the echo of fear and a feeling of cold, blind determination.

Albion yelled something, but the wind mangled his words. I wasn't about to stop, no matter what he said. If Severn wanted me, it was best that I go alone. I'd made mistakes in dealing with him before, but I would be the one to pay for them. Not the old man on the cliff.

Not Rowan.

I circled the ship, giving it a wide berth, and sized up the situation. I didn't recognize any of the men who stood at the railing. I approached cautiously, trying to feel for harmful magic. I couldn't see anyone's thoughts when I was in this body, and it left me at a disadvantage. My wings would give out soon if I didn't rest. I could normally soar for hours, but the shock of Belleisle's magic defenses had left my muscles trembling.

A cloaked and hooded figure emerged from the shadows, taking slow steps over the gently-rocking deck. The others stepped away from the railing as the black-clad form approached. Not one of them looked at him. He rested one gloved hand on the smooth, dark wood rail and beckoned with the other.

I kept my distance, riding the air currents, moving along the side of the ship, waiting to flee at the first sign of aggression.

Pale hands reached up to grasp the edges of the deep, heavy hood, and pulled it back.

My flight wavered. If not for the familiar magic radiating from him, I wouldn't have recognized my oldest half-brother. Where there had once been strength, health, and a face that had charmed the finest ladies in Luid, there stood a shadow. Gaunt, with skin as pale as mist. His white hair lay flat and lifeless. His blue eyes still glowed with power, though, as he once again motioned for me to come closer.

When the other men stepped back I landed on the railing, just outside of Severn's physical reach. He hadn't burned me out of the sky when he had the chance. I would trust him this much further. My only other option was to fly away and wait for him to attack later, perhaps when I was less prepared to meet him.

Unease made my feathers prickle.

"Well." He flashed the cruel, heartless smile I knew so well. "We meet again. Where's your whore?"

I couldn't answer, and I offered no reaction to his baiting.

He raised his hood again and turned away. "We'll talk inside," he called back over his shoulder. "The wind cuts through my cloak."

The other men on the deck watched him warily. Those who looked at me showed no indication that they would attack. I wished I could see what they had planned.

Severn turned back. "I didn't come here to hurt you. Merely to talk, and to make an offer that I think you'll find tempting."

And if I refused, I didn't like my odds of getting off the ship alive. Several of the sailors stepped closer. My survival instincts screamed for me to fly. Instead, I jumped onto the smooth deck and shuffled after Severn, as awkward on my feet as I was graceful in the air. Information first. If he wanted to talk, I would listen, and settle the rest later.

He held a thick wooden door open and stepped aside to let me by. The feathers on my hackles stood on end as I passed, and my muscles tensed, ready to spring into an attack at the slightest provocation. Severn kept his boots well clear of me, and I moved inside the ship.

We entered a large and well-lit room, with sunlight streaming in through large windows that framed a distorted view of the sea. A table had been set with a modest yet hearty meal of meats and bread, and two heavy-looking wooden chairs waited with wine glasses placed before them, ready to be filled from any of the three bottles on the table. A large bed filled an alcove to one side, with velvet curtains tied open to reveal silk blankets and plush pillows.

A room for a king.

Severn closed the door behind us and turned with a sweeping gesture that took in the entire room. "What do you think? I had it improved especially for this journey. I do find it hard to get comfortable since my encounter with your little Sorceress friend, but this bed is not unpleasant."

Had I been in my own body, I might have found it difficult not to smile at that. She'd hurt him that night, and worse than I had known. I hoped it shamed him to have been defeated by someone like her, a novice, untrained and unaware of her own power.

His eyes never left me. "Will you sit with me while

we talk?"

I shifted from one foot to the other, unable to answer.

"Aah. Let's see what we can do about that." Severn went to an ornate wardrobe and pulled out a few items of clothing, which he laid on the bed. His movements were smoother now, but a stiffness remained. Still, I couldn't rely on his physical weakness to protect me. I'd need to be on my guard.

"I'll give you a bit of privacy." He went to the window and stood with his hands clasped behind his back, watching the waves.

I transformed and slipped into loose pants and a shirt made from the richest fabric I'd felt against my skin since I left Luid. Though I'd never been as interested as Severn in what he called "the finer things," I couldn't help running my fingers over the blue flames embroidered in silk on the sleeve cuffs. I could do without luxury. That didn't mean I wasn't capable of missing it.

Severn turned. "That's better. Wine?"

"Will you be offended if I say no?"

"Yes."

"Then I suppose I'll have some."

"Excellent choice." He poured slowly, and green wine flowed into bright, clear glasses. "Sit."

He placed a thick cushion on one chair and settled onto it.

"You're looking well," I said, and took my own seat.

"I look like shit, and I know it." His voice was stronger than his body looked, and the words cut through the still air of the room. "I'm regaining my strength more quickly than any of the physicians or my Potioner expected. They say I'm lucky to be alive." He snorted, and sipped his wine. "Lucky? I hardly think so. Skilled. Powerful. Able to act quickly. That is what I am." He placed his glass on the table and reached for a knife, which he plunged into the roast. "I don't believe in luck. Are you hungry?"

"No," I lied. Everything looked and smelled delicious, and my stomach growled. "Why are you here?"

Thin slices of beef peeled away from the roast, arcing toward the plate in waves as he cut. Severn served the meat onto two plates.

"Eat. It's not poisoned." He took a bite of his own meal.

I did as he instructed. My head would be clearer if I had something in my stomach.

"Feeling at home yet?" he asked.

"No. Again, why are you here?"

"Your manners have suffered since you left us, brother."

Severn's power filled the space like a thunderstorm about to break. I held mine in check and looked out the window, careful not to let my unease show. "What were you doing with the hawks?"

"Testing. You made it past the island's defenses as an eagle, didn't you? It seemed worth exploring."

I didn't ask how he knew what I'd done. He'd never tell. "Neither you nor any of your men will ever land on Belleisle in any form. I think you knew that. So what brought you this far from home in your current state?" I probed gently, testing his magic with my own, reaching toward his mind. If his magic was weak, there was a chance he couldn't block me. His mind immediately resisted, and I pulled back before my actions angered him.

That would have been too easy. I only hoped it was his magic and not my own lack of practice that held me back.

"Much has happened since the night of my encounter with your dear friend," he remarked, and gestured toward his emaciated body. "We'll talk about that situation first. Clear things up between us. I want to understand."

"I thought you wanted me dead."

His lips curled upward in amusement. "I did. My temper has cooled, though, and there are other factors to consider now. Tell me, why did you do it? Why did you defy me?"

I didn't answer.

He leaned back in his chair. "Let me tell you what I think. I think you wanted an excuse to run, and she provided it. You tried so hard to be strong, but there's always been this weakness in you, Aren. Our father saw it. I saw it. I thought I could help you overcome it, but it ruined you in the end. Did you even fight it?"

"I tried to." I met his gaze, unwavering. "I kept my loyalty to you at the forefront of my mind until the moment I stepped off the ship with her."

"But underneath, your loyalty was weak. What part of you did she reach and exploit? Your need for acceptance? Kindness?" He shook his head. "You had so much potential. You could have had everything."

"Everything save for what I truly needed."

He snorted. "Need? Childish want, more like, and you threw a spectacular fit to get it."

"That's one way of looking at it." My words sounded confident, but his had shaken me. Here with him, my actions seemed so foolish. So weak.

"You've had your little rebellion, Aren. It has cost us both so much. But I still wonder whether our business is not finished."

I was certain that it wasn't, but suspected his ideas of how it would end didn't line up with mine. I took a sip of the tart wine. "I'm listening."

Severn's eyes narrowed. "Are you? Truly?"

I sat back. "Of course. This is unexpected, but I'm interested to hear what you have to say."

"Why?"

Careful. One wrong word would be the end of me. I lowered my gaze and tried to feel the truth of my words. "Things have not worked out as I'd hoped."

Severn chuckled. "Poor Aren. Do you miss your old life? Your home? Your freedom?"

I wouldn't have called working for Severn freedom, but I nodded.

"Are you tired of her already?"

"Truthfully?"

He waved that off. "Never mind. What's important here is that you've seen the error of your ways. I want you to come back."

My meal suddenly sat heavy in my stomach. Severn was many things, but forgiving was not one of them. There was something he wasn't telling me. "That is most generous."

"Isn't it?" He rolled the stem of his glass between his thumb and forefinger, sending beams of reflected light over the table. "I'm not willing to forget what you did. There will be consequences. But I find myself in need of someone with your skills and training."

"Is that so?"

"I should have told you more, sooner. Perhaps if you'd understood the gravity of our situation, you would not have abandoned the cause." He set the glass down. It tipped over, and he didn't bother to set it right even as the last few drops of wine dripped onto the table. "I was right, you know. About the magic. About ours being choked off by Darmid."

"How do you know that?"

He ignored my question. "If we can diplomatically convince young king Haleth of Darmid to keep his magic hunters in check, leave wild space in the North and cease their magic-killing near the mountains, it would allow magic to flow freely from our land across the isthmus, through their land, and connect to the Western wild-lands. It will increase our magic."

"You never seemed to be suffering for any lack of it. At least, before your accident."

His power pulsed, and a sharp prickling sensation covered my skin. "I could be stronger. *You* could be stronger, with more ambient magic to draw from. The fact is that we have fewer Sorcerers now than they had in our grandmother's time. There's even been a drop in the number of lower-level magic users. I'm unable to find as many as I'd hoped."

"Are you sure they're not simply hiding from you?"

He scraped his knife over the surface of his plate, producing a screeching noise that set my teeth on edge. "No, Dan is making sure they can't hide. The fact is that the Darmish are killing magic. Surely you noticed how weak we become in the desolate hole they've created beyond the mountains."

I had. Severn and I, like our father, carried more magic in us than any Sorcerers who had come before, and when that ran out, we were able to channel magic from the land around us. In Darmid, where I'd found Rowan, we had to rely on what we carried within us. Though some remained near the border and in wild places, they'd killed the magic in their cities. Tyrea would never become like that. As long as we used it, as long as we allowed the magical plants and creatures to thrive, magic would remain in our land. *Still...*

"It's an interesting theory," I said. "What happens if the king of Darmid refuses?"

"Then we resort to non-diplomatic means."

"And that's why you're forcing every powerful magic-user in the country to Luid? To prepare for war?"

Severn glared at me as he cut and chewed a thin piece of meat. "Don't tell me you care."

"My concern is for our people, not theirs. It's folly. The lack of magic in their land would make it impossible for a magical army to operate there. They know how to fight without magic. They'd slaughter us if we invaded."

"I've already considered that, thank you. Still, you're thinking." He pointed his knife at me and smiled humorlessly. "I miss this. You're the only person I had who wasn't afraid to second-guess me, even when you knew it would hurt you."

He spoke as though he'd forgotten how he relished my fear. Either he was hoping I'd forgotten, or his mind was failing as much as his body appeared to be.

He righted his cup and poured another serving of wine. "We'll figure out the obstacles before we move. The first step is to consolidate our power, see what weapons we have available to us. I have some things in the works in Darmid already. Do you see what I'm doing, Aren?"

"Tell me."

"I am doing what our father refused to for too long. He knew what they were doing in Darmid, and was content to let them have their way in their own land, not considering the potential costs to us. He was proud of the peace he maintained between Darmid and Tyrea, never understanding the value of keeping them afraid of his strength. And now I'm paying for it. We all are."

"I'm still not sure why I'm here. It sounds as if you have your plans made."

Severn glanced down at the table and tapped a finger against the dark wood, frowning. "You were once a member of my family. You're still a Tyrean, and the second most powerful Sorcerer we have."

"Assuming our father is dead, of course."

Severn's lip lifted in an ugly sneer. "Dead or gone, it makes little difference."

I'd long suspected that Severn had something to do with our father's disappearance, but he'd never seen fit to share that information with me. In truth, I hadn't cared. One tyrant or another made little difference to me personally. But the rest of the country wouldn't fare as well under Severn as it had under Ulric. My father had made my life hell, but he'd cared for his people. Severn cared only for himself and his own power.

"I could use you back in my council chambers," he continued. "Not as my Second. That's Dan's job now, and I hardly think it would be prudent to give you that much power after you've proved your disloyalty. Still, I had high hopes for you once. With a little redirection and supervision, you could be a great benefit to our cause. I've had problems with some small groups of people, particularly in the outer provinces, who aren't willing to contribute to our interests. Some who are actively resisting. I need you back at your old job. Make things right. Convince them to join me, or end them. Break their minds, if it pleases you. I just want them out of my way."

My mouth went dry and nearly refused to form the words I had to speak. "I'm not coming back."

He seemed more interested than angry, a reaction I immediately mistrusted. "No? You're not happy here. Do they appreciate your gifts as I do? Are they helping you become the great Sorcerer you're destined to be?" He smirked. "They must understand you so well. Your abilities. Your needs that go deeper than whatever they can offer you. Deeper than whatever it is you think you want." He chuckled. "I know you, Aren. I *made* you."

My silence was answer enough on that count. Much as I'd hated acting as Severn's killer puppet, I did miss the thrill of stretching my abilities to their limits, taking pride in my accomplishments no matter what they cost anyone else. The idea of being appreciated again, even feared, filled me with longing. *Perhaps if I went back, it could be different...I could change things.*

But the life that Severn offered hadn't been enough for me.

He cleared his throat. "You can bring the girl. The Sorceress."

My mind snapped back to itself, all thoughts of

accepting his offer gone. "She may not be as useful as you think. Her power is uncertain."

"Is it?" Severn picked up the knife again, and with a flick of his wrist flung it toward me. I ducked out of the way, and it stuck into the wall behind my head, vibrating. "Don't be coy with me. She's Darmish, but their magic is the same as ours, barring individual differences. I know intimately the power she had in her a few months ago. My researchers could learn much from a true Sorceress bred and born there. More about the nature of magic, where it comes from, what effects their meddling has had. We've only found pathetic, lower-level specimens so far."

"I see." I ignored his actions and my own racing heart. With every word he spoke, I became more convinced that my brother's sanity was slipping. I needed to keep him talking until I saw a way out. "And she'd be well cared-for while they were researching, I'm sure."

"Naturally. You know, I think I feel like some fresh air after all. Walk with me."

"Are you so energized by my presence?"

He gave me a thin smile and turned away. "That must be it."

I pulled the knife from the wall and concealed it under one of the shirt's long sleeves, then followed him back onto the deck.

I adjusted my stride to the rolling surface beneath me. Many of the sailors had disappeared. I made eye contact with the others as they looked up, testing them, sensing their thoughts. I found it difficult after so many months of letting my talent stagnate, and sensed vague impressions rather than sharp images and emotions. Still, I managed to pick up a few things. Fear or uncertainty, mostly. Some of them despised me and wished me harm, but at least they didn't seem to have planned a coordinated attack. It would be impossible to watch all of them, but I maintained my awareness of their movements.

"What of the island folk?" I asked.

Severn looked toward land, where the great Sorcerer Ernis Albion and our horses still waited, dark specks on the bluff. "He caused your mother's death, did you know that?"

I tensed, as I always had when he spoke of her. "No. You did that. Their communication was harmless."

He chuckled. "You assume so much. In any case, I'm surprised to see you allied with him. Even if he is your grandfather."

"How long have you known?"

"Far longer than you." He tipped his head back and let the hood fall to his shoulders. The wind lifted his hair, blowing it in a bright halo that he smoothed down and tucked into his collar. "Information is power. I want to know what you know about this place, these people. I want to know their weaknesses. How to bring them over to our side, by whatever means necessary."

"No."

His jaw muscles clenched. "No you don't know? Or no you won't tell me?"

"You said it yourself. Information is power."

"Power is also power." Pain cut into the scar on the back of my right shoulder, the one he'd given me when I was a child. It washed over my body and left me sweating in spite of the chill in the air. "Join me, and perhaps I won't need to involve them. We can do it on our own. We'll take Darmid back, free the land. If you can prove your loyalty to me, we'll call this incident with the girl a foolish misstep, a learning experience. I'll let you rule Darmid as my governor."

"And if I decline and leave now?"

"You won't." He nodded over my shoulder, and heavy boot steps approached. I slipped my hand free of the sleeve and spun, plunging the knife into the throat of the burly sailor before his hands could close over my arms. He stumbled away, taking my weapon with him.

The pain in my shoulder left me, replaced by a chill that froze my muscles in place. I tried to transform and fly, but nothing happened. Cold panic gripped me as a sailor with ragged scars on both cheeks above a bushy, black beard stepped into view.

Severn grinned. "What do you think? I found him in Cressia, fighting dragons. This is his only talent so far. It's limited, but useful."

The magic's owner paced between me and Severn without looking away from me.

"Fantastic," I replied through gritted teeth.

The Sorcerer smirked and crossed his arms over his narrow chest as he raised his gaze to meet mine, unafraid.

His pride was his undoing, as mine had been for me so many times. His attempt to project confidence left him open. As soon as his eyes locked onto mine, I pushed into his mind. My skills hadn't dulled after all, but had simply needed dusting off. They were back and restless after a long season of disuse. A thrill coursed through my body in spite of the danger. This was my element, my gift, and using it felt so right. My enemy shrieked and closed his eyes, but he couldn't protect himself. I gripped and twisted his thoughts. He released me, and turned on my brother.

He believed Severn was his enemy now. I would leave them to fight it out. I didn't like the stranger's chances against Severn's magic, or my own chances if I stayed to find out how things went. I transformed and took off, narrowly avoiding a kick from another sailor as I pushed off from the deck.

I left the turmoil behind me and flew hard for the shore.

I will fight, Severn, I thought. *But not for you.*

Chapter Four

Rowan

The school buzzed with whispers. Not one of the seventy students seemed to know what was happening. All our instructors told us was that they needed to meet about something, and that we should take our work to the library for the afternoon.

No one was to leave without an instructor. We were to focus on our work, and they would explain later.

We gathered, and brought our work. No one left. That was all we could promise, though. Speculation was the order of the hour, not work. Though I kept my ears open, most of it floated past me in little wisps that I could barely hear. The large room filled with tiny conversations muffled by rows of bookshelves and soft leather chairs, interrupted by the occasional thud of a dropped book hitting the floor.

No one directed their words at me. Though I had a few friends at the school, I was still an outsider. Too old to be a proper student, too ignorant to be worth talking to, and too involved with someone they weren't supposed to trust for me to be anything other than the subject of gossip. I did my schoolwork, my chores, and the tasks assigned to me as part of my job in my library, and kept mostly to myself.

Celean was a friend, as was Bernard, Albion and Emalda's son. He sat in the corner now, occasionally shushing students who got too loud, but mostly letting the whispers flow. Shutting us up now would be a losing fight, especially since most students didn't listen to him any more than they would to me. As the son of a Sorcerer and a Potioner, Bernard had no magic. Even here, where the students were encouraged to accept their gifts with grace and never lord them over those with lesser talents, those of us with less skill felt the distain of those who had more. Bernard and I had bonded over that, and it was nice to have a friend who was interested in talking about things other than magic.

I tried to focus on my work. I seemed to fall further behind every day, and couldn't afford to slack off even now. Not only did I have the seemingly insurmountable problem of my magic to deal with, there was also the ignorance that seemed bred into my bones. Magic theory was fascinating, but completely foreign to me. I had thousands of years of history to learn, covering multiple countries, languages, cultures, even species. Everyone said that magic was supposed to help me pick up information and skills more quickly than I would have otherwise, but I'd seen no evidence of it.

I hadn't mentioned that little problem to Aren. He didn't need another reason to be disappointed.

I pulled a map from my history book, a piece I'd been working on for months. Drawing things out helped cement them in my mind in a way that reading or listening couldn't. The outline of the map looked much like one that Aren had once drawn, but with more detail. I'd labelled cities in Darmid, Tyrea, and Bellisle, as well as the names of great forests, mountain ranges, lakes and seas. At the top I'd written in flowing script the word *Serat*.

I hadn't known this land as a whole had a name. My people had never acknowledged that our country was a part of something larger than itself.

Someone whispered Aren's name, and I gave up

on trying to focus on anything else as I strained to listen. Something about a ship. My stomach clenched. At the mention of Severn's name, a chill came over me.

Who the hell am I supposed to pray to here? I wondered, and sent out a silent apology to anyone I might have offended. My people's God, who was said to hate magic and who I'd never felt a particular attachment to? Aren's gods or the great unnamed Goddess of Tyrea, who I hardly knew anything about? The spirits of Belleisle, who the students and staff spent time with in silent contemplation each Seventh-day?

I tapped an un-inked quill against the map. Aren could take care of himself, if he were involved in whatever the trouble was. He always did.

The thought didn't ease my worry in the slightest.

The door to the corridor opened without a sound, and all eyes turned toward it. My breath caught in my chest as Aren slipped in, apparently unharmed. *Thank you, whoever.*

Conversation ceased. As far as I could tell, the students' attitudes toward Aren ranged from opposition to romantic speculation from a few silly girls who thought him a tragically misunderstood figure, though possibly dangerous. Few showed the unattached acceptance that Celean did.

Bernard walked toward Aren, who ignored him and stood beside the table where I sat alone.

"Do you need something?" Bernard asked.

I tensed. I liked Bernard, and loved Aren, but the two of them together were impossible. Always wary, always on the verge of fighting. Blood might have connected them under other circumstances, but their differences made them rivals.

They certainly didn't look related, though Bernard was technically Aren's uncle. Bernard was deeply tanned and kept his hair short, whereas Aren's skin remained pale even after months of regular outdoor work, and his dark hair hung to his shoulders in the Tyrean style he refused to change. Both had inherited Albion's height and slim build, but the physical similarities ended there.

The only other thing they had in common was the fact that they hated each other with a passion born of envy—Bernard's for Aren's power and the attention he received from Albion, and Aren's for the way Bernard was welcomed in the school and community, and his friendship with me.

Aren slowly turned his attention to Bernard. "I only need to speak to Rowan. Thank you."

The *thank you* took me by surprise, as it seemed to catch Bernard. He opened his mouth to speak, and closed it.

"It's important," Aren added.

"Please, Bernard," I whispered.

He frowned, but nodded. "I'll be right back," he said, and left the library.

I watched him go, then turned to Aren. "You didn't just..."

"No. He made that decision on his own." He ran a hand through his hair and sank into the chair next to me. "How's the work coming?"

He took my quill and dipped it into the ink pot, then scrawled, *Everyone's listening* across a fresh piece of creamy paper.

I took the quill back. "Fine. Having some trouble with geography."

What's going on? I wrote.

"Anything I can help with? I was good at that subject." He took the quill back. *Severn came. I spoke with him. He wanted me back in Tyrea, but I left.*

The students continued to watch us, but the whispering picked up again.

I forced a smile, and pulled out a charcoal pencil. "I get the feeling you were good at every subject." *We can't talk here. Let's go before Bernard comes back.*

The corners of his lips twitched as he wrote, *Your rooms or mine?*

Not funny.

Much as I appreciated his attempt, I couldn't joke with him. Not when hc looked so weary, disheveled, defeated and uncertain. I packed my papers and books into my shoulder bag and led the way toward the door.

The whispers turned to murmurs. I ignored them, and took Aren's hand to pull him down the corridor.

"Albion went—" he began, and I shook my head.

"Not yet. We need to get away."

We rushed through the empty corridors of the school, a beautiful old building that had been Albion's family home until he'd returned from some adventure and founded the school. On any other day I'd have taken deep breaths of lamp-oil-scented air, or examined one of the complex paintings on the walls. Today it was all a blur, and my focus was on avoiding the staff as we escaped.

Aren pulled me into a dark classroom. A moment later Derrian Surgess and Qurwin Black, two of the regular instructors, passed by.

"Thanks," I whispered. I hadn't heard them, but Aren had sensed their presence. It seemed he'd opened up whatever cupboard his skills had been locked in for so long.

Minutes later, we'd left the building. "Where to?" Aren asked.

I took in a deep breath of fresh air. "Beach."

We walked in silence through the woods. Though we'd made it away, my heart refused to stop racing. Whatever he wanted to tell me, it was bad news—perhaps news I'd been dreading since our arrival, since he made the agreement with Emalda that he would leave as soon as his presence on the island became a threat.

My eyes stung. *You will not cry*, I told myself.

Whatever happened, I wouldn't make him comfort me. This had to be far harder for him.

"Albion and Emalda went to town," Aren said at last, "to tell the governor what happened."

"And what did happen?"

He explained as we walked, told me about Severn's ship and his wretched appearance, his plans for Darmid and the offer he'd made. I suspected Aren left out a few details about his escape, but what he told was harrowing enough. I stopped and wrapped my arms around him.

"Were you afraid?"

"Yes. It didn't really catch up with me until I was back on the island, though, and safe."

We continued down the riding path until we reached the edge of the woods, which opened onto a grassy field and cliffs that sloped down to a rocky beach. It was a favorite place for students who wished to get away from the school to relax with friends. Or so I'd heard. I came alone, myself. The water calmed me, even as it reminded me of my seaside town in Darmid and the troubles I'd left there—troubles my family would still be dealing with, many of them my fault.

Fog had rolled in, dressing the grassy hills and the beach at the bottom of the cliff in a cloak of cloud. An abandoned watchtower stood high on one of the arms of land that encircled the harbor, a dark shadow in the bright haze. On the tip of the other arm sat a tall lighthouse. As I understood it, this had once been the island's main harbor. The people had since built a new one closer to the city, leaving this one for the students and nature to take over.

We climbed down the cliffs.

"You weren't invited to the meeting?" I asked.

Aren snorted. "Have I ever been?"

He'd been as good as imprisoned at the school. If most of the students mistrusted him, the people in the city were worse. Aren had been allowed to attend one town meeting, where he assured them he meant the people of the island no harm. They'd thanked him politely and ordered him to stay out of their town and their business.

He didn't seem to blame them for their attitude, but I knew he found his situation nearly unbearable.

I stepped onto the pebbled beach and closed my eyes, taking deep breaths of the salty air. The breeze picked up and tossed my hair into a wild tangle, and I pulled a ribbon from my pocket to tie it back. The ceaseless rhythm of the waves filled me, slowing my breath and my heart.

When I opened my eyes again, Aren was watching me. "It's good to see you relaxed," he said.

A smile I hadn't realized I was wearing faded from my lips. "Celean keeps telling me that worry brings pain and accomplishes nothing good, that we should accept what comes with grace. I'm trying to let go."

"Is it working?"

My chest tightened again as I looked into his eyes. "Not completely. Walk with me?"

The only thing left to talk about was the future, and I wasn't ready for that yet. Aren seemed to be in no hurry, but clearly had something he wanted to say.

"Have you heard about the shipwrecks?" I asked.

He raised an eyebrow. "Can't say I have."

"Just a few around here, a long time ago. Sometimes I look for treasure here on the beach. You never know, right?"

His faint smile crinkled the corners of his eyes. "I guess not."

Such a different response from what he'd have given when we first met.

"I've found treasure here before."

"Rowan—"

"You're leaving, aren't you?"

He looked away. "I don't think I have a choice. I leave at sunrise."

An unexpected calm came over me once the words were out. He'd be safe for one more night, at least. I sank to my knees and dragged my fingers gently through the pebbles. Searching.

"I knew you couldn't stay forever," I said. "I didn't want it to be like this, though. I thought you'd leave and go somewhere safe. I—" I paused. "I didn't think you'd be leaping from the island straight into Severn's path."

He sat beside me and watched as my hands moved through the rocks. "Not straight into it. He's sailed for Luid. He'll be back, but not right away." He shook his head. "I waited too long."

"Because of me?"

He didn't answer.

"Where will you go? Are you..." I bit my lip. "I don't know how to ask without insulting you."

"I'm not going to challenge Severn for the throne, if that's what you're worried about."

I reached for his hand. "You understand that it's not that I don't have faith in your abilities."

That faint smile again, though less amused this time. "No, you'd be right to worry. Severn is hurting physically, but his magic is as strong as it's ever been, and that's the only legitimate way to challenge a king. I'm not sure my skills are suited for that type of combat. Not yet, anyway."

"What, then?"

He looked out over the water. "I'm going to bring my father back."

My jaw dropped. "He's alive? I thought..." My words trailed off as I realized I didn't know what I thought. Aren hated to speak about his family, and his father's disappearance had seemed so final.

"After speaking to Severn, I feel certain that he is." Aren rubbed the back of his neck with one hand. "I'll visit my uncle Xaven. He's not fond of Severn, and might help me if he has any idea where my father was traveling before he disappeared. If my father is still alive somewhere, if I can find him, he has every right to take the throne back. We have until early summer before he's declared dead and loses his claim."

I shivered, though not from the cold. "Are you certain he's the lesser of the evils your family has to offer? The way you've spoken of him, he sounds horrid."

Aren frowned. "He was a terrible father, no question. But he kept Tyrea safe for over a century when he ruled, and it's taken Severn less than three years to begin to destroy everything. Ulric might not be the ideal ruler, but he's better for the people than Severn is. Wiser. More just. More fair."

His voice cracked as he spoke. His father had been anything but fair in his dealings with Aren. Cruel, cold, unforgiving of anything he perceived as weakness.

Yet Aren thought this was the best thing.

"That's settled, then," I said. The words felt flat, foolish, but there was nothing else to say. I shifted my weight and dragged my fingers through a new patch of beach, and scooped a pair of shining treasures into the palm of my hand.

Aren's shadow fell over me as he leaned in. "Find anything there? Gold? Priceless jewels?"

I held my hand out toward him. "See for yourself."

He looked down at my treasure, two pieces of glass. One green, one brown, both with edges smoothed and surfaces dulled by the rocks, sand, and water. He looked back up with eyebrows raised. "That's the treasure? Garbage?"

"It's not garbage."

"It's broken glass that somebody once threw away, or that floated off one of those shipwrecks you mentioned. It is the very definition of garbage."

Amusement touched his voice, and I realized that he was as glad to have a brief change of subject as I was. Everything else would catch up with us soon enough.

I stood and walked farther, pausing to pick up a few more bits of glass, and handed a clear, freshly broken piece to Aren. "No. This is garbage."

He turned it over in his hand. Some student had broken a bottle here and left the remains behind. Aren closed his fist around the glass and winced. When he opened his hand, blood welled up from a puncture in the center of his palm.

I frowned. "I can't heal that for you."

"I know. You don't need to. It's only pain." We watched as the bleeding stopped. His magic could handle small injuries, even larger ones if they didn't kill him too quickly. It didn't make him invulnerable, though.

"This," I continued, and placed another piece of glass in his hand, "is treasure." Another piece of glass, but amethyst-colored, turned lilac by its pitted surface. The sea had worn the edges so smooth that aside from its color, the glass was indistinguishable from the round pebbles that littered the shore. "I suppose it was garbage once, but after a while it becomes beautiful. Do you see?"

He rolled the glass pebble between his fingers, and nodded. "No one's ever going to mistake it for a gemstone."

"No. No chance of a dragon stealing it."

His smile widened slightly, and he looked from the glass to me. His eyes softened. "It's beautiful like the rocks. Like the forest, or driftwood." He cleared his throat. "I don't see those things like you do."

"You're learning."

He turned back to the water. "It reminds me of you, a bit. The people in Luid, the ones I grew up with, had this cut and polished kind of beauty, like diamonds. Bright, but boring before long, and all the same. You're like..." He studied the purple glass I'd given him. "You're like this. It gets lovelier the longer I look at it. More interesting."

Sharp pain spread through my chest. "I know what you mean."

He stooped and picked up a shard of green from the ground near his feet. "What about this one?"

I took the glass and looked it over. "Almost there. See how this edge here is clear? It's just broken recently. The ocean needs to work on it a little more. It's a shame, the color is good."

Aren moved away and sat on a weathered piece of driftwood that had landed above the tide line, a bleached log covered in swirling patterns. I followed, and we watched the waves as they crashed gently over the pebbles.

The future wouldn't stay away forever. Much as I tried to remain in that moment, thoughts of losing him crept into my mind. True, things had been hard. He was miserable, we almost never had time together, our lessons were a constant source of frustration that ended in us fighting more often than they did in me accomplishing anything. But I loved him. That hadn't changed.

My breath hitched, and he reached for my hand. I threaded my fingers through his and wiped away a few tears that escaped in spite of my commands that they stay hidden.

I looked at the unfinished glass in my hand. We were safe here, or we had been until today, but neither of us were getting anywhere. We weren't making any progress, weren't moving toward our destinies. We were both stuck, afraid of making things worse, afraid of hurting each other.

I released Aren's hand and walked toward the water. I pulled my arm back and threw the glass in an overhand toss that sent it spiraling though the air and back into the ocean.

When I turned back, Aren stood with his arms held open. I hurried back and held him tight, pressing my face against his shoulder. "What if we don't get washed back up on the same beach when this is all over? I can't lose you."

"I'll come back, I swear. Not even death could keep me from returning to you." He released my hair from the ribbon and trailed his fingers through it. "Maybe you'll be the one who discovers you want something else once I'm gone."

I shook my head. "Never."

"Don't worry about me. Focus on learning what you can while I'm gone. I hope you'll be able to stay out of this, but you need to be prepared for anything. You got rid of Severn once. Maybe you'll do it again."

"I surprised him that time."

He chuckled softly. "You surprised everyone that time."

I kept one arm around his waist as we turned to walk back toward the cliffs, the school, and the inevitable future. As we reached the base of the hill, a handsome red fox face peered down at us from the long grasses at the top. *Albion.*

"I think our time's up," Aren said, and tried to give the purple sea glass back to me. I closed his fingers over it, instead.

"Take it with you," I said.

"I don't need anything to help me remember you." He spoke softly, either to keep Albion from hearing, or to hide the emotion in his voice. His expression was as unreadable as I'd ever seen it.

"Then take it as a gift. It's all I have to give."

He nodded, and slipped the glass into his pocket. "Thank you."

When I looked at the top of the cliff again, the fox had disappeared. We were alone, at least for the moment. Aren pulled me close, and I stretched up on my toes to wrap my arms around his neck.

"I'm going to miss you," I whispered.

I kissed him hard, fiercely, trying to force every word we hadn't spoken, every opportunity we'd been denied, and everything we'd miss after he left into a single gesture and moment.

His magic surrounded me, cold and dark, as familiar to me as my own. I always noticed it in these moments, when our bodies and hearts entwined. He said mine was like sunshine, bright and warm and filled with promise. I found his no less beautiful for its chill, and wished I could keep it with me after he left.

Albion waited for us at the edge of the forest in human form. While Aren had to be careful about transformations because he lacked the ability to form clothing after he changed back, his grandfather had no such difficulties. Aren had told me that it took Albion decades to master that difficult magic and form the dark brown robes he always wore, but it obviously still troubled him that he couldn't figure it out. He had such high expectations of himself, and so much of his identity was wrapped up in his abilities.

No wonder he'd been miserable when he wasn't allowed to use most of them.

As we walked, Aren explained his plan to Albion, who listened and nodded and made suggestions for routes and methods of travel. I listened, and tried not to worry.

"You'd better get back in there," Albion said to me as we reached the school.

"Am I in trouble for leaving?"

He smiled kindly. "No, but please pretend you are. Emalda won't have a bad example set, you know."

I thanked him and hugged Aren again. "Don't you dare leave without saying goodbye," I whispered.

He released me. "After everything we've been through, you don't trust me?"

I forced a smile. "Not at all."

I walked back into the school, past the library and the classrooms now filled with teachers and students, and went straight to my room.

One more night, I thought, and laid down to rest while I still could. *He's safe for one more night.*

Chapter Five

Aren

That evening, I flew.

I soared over the island toward a waterfall that was all but inaccessible on foot, clutching a bar of soap in my talons. A warm bath would have been more pleasant, but I didn't feel patient enough to prepare one, and there certainly weren't any servants in my apartment over the carriage house to do it for me.

Best to get used to hard living, I thought. Gods knew what I'd find ahead on the road.

I supposed I was fortunate that I had an evening to prepare for my journey, that they hadn't forced me to leave as soon as Severn's ship departed. Instead, I would leave at dawn, at which time I would leave myself open to whatever ways Severn had of tracking me, at least for long enough to convince him I'd left the island. He would be searching, and he had found me before.

I hadn't mentioned that part to Rowan. She would worry enough.

Moonlight glinted off the water as I landed on the flat rocks next to the river at the bottom of the roaring falls, and transformed. The frigid air hit my skin like a slap, and I hurried into the water to get it over with, slipping over smooth, algae-covered rocks as I went. Perhaps coming all this way to freeze my bones had been a stupid decision, but it had felt important that I get away from the school. Flying cleared my mind, and physical discomfort would help me focus on the important things.

I gasped as the water covered my body, and took a deep breath before stepping under the waterfall. The cold chased all thought from my mind, and I emerged with a string of curses on my lips. *Stupid decision, indeed.*

At least I had no reason to worry about freezing to death. My magic protected me from that fate as much as it did death by injury—not perfectly, but far better than someone without magic could manage. It worked without direction from me, and seemed to prioritize its work based on what would best keep me alive. Had I been injured, my magic would have focused on that even if I nearly froze while it worked, and even if the injury were too severe for my magic to heal it. As I was in good health for the time being, I was free to suffer through the icy river beating down over my head. My magic didn't make me comfortable, just as it didn't protect me from pain or exhaustion, but I would survive.

These involuntary uses of magic used up a disproportionately large amount of power compared to anything I controlled, but I had no fear of running out. There was plenty here to draw from.

I'd planned to use the time to think over my options concerning my new mission, but found my thoughts returning to Rowan. She had great power in her. Not only was it evident in the destructive effects she caused when she tried to use it, but I'd felt it myself. She'd healed me on several occasions, back when she was able to. The sensation had been uncomfortable to me at first. Now I only wanted to feel her magic flowing through me again.

If only she could break through whatever was still blocking her and use it for her own purposes, she would go down in history as one of the great ones. I felt it as much as I knew it.

I didn't realize I'd become lost in my thoughts until my legs turned numb and the current dunked me underwater. I hurried to climb out of the river and braced myself against the cold until I had dried enough that my feathers wouldn't be soaked when I transformed. The soap had drifted away. Small loss.

I flew hard on the return journey, and my muscles warmed as they worked. Still, I looked forward to a warm fire and one last night in a soft bed before I set out. There were so many things that I failed to appreciate until they were gone.

My clothes and my key were at the edge of the woods where I'd left them, and I hurried to dress before anyone should happen to pass by. I walked around the outside of the carriage house before I climbed the stairs to my door, as was my habit. I felt nothing out of place, and no one around.

I tried to light the logs in the fireplace using magic. It didn't take the first time. The skill was familiar enough now that I could usually avoid any unexpected effects from using the magic, but I still had trouble directing enough power to generate more than a tiny flame. I cursed again. Hard-won as this skill had been, I still expected more from myself. Expected to be more like Severn.

But he had been born with fire in his blood. I had not, and so I fought for every flame.

On the second try, the fire caught on the rough bark. Still not good enough, but it was something. At least I wouldn't have to worry about packing a flint for my journey.

I'd just finished laying out clothing to take with me when I heard a soft tapping noise. I stretched my awareness, then hurried to unlock the window and help Rowan over the ledge.

"I have a door," I reminded her, and took her into my arms. Her damp hair smelled faintly of flowers. She felt natural in my arms, like an extension of my own body. I pushed down the physical ache that rose in me at the thought of leaving her behind. I still resented the way these new emotions sneaked up on me, seemingly outside of my control.

"You do have a door," she said, "one that faces the school. I'm not taking any chances tonight." She looked up and grinned. "Besides, where's the fun in that?"

I looked out to where she'd climbed up a downspout onto the roof. Her idea of fun was often rather different from mine.

She stepped back and sat on the edge of the bed next to my clothing and the other supplies I'd laid out earlier. She left her long jacket buttoned, leaving only her knees exposed over the tops of her boots. "You're really going."

"Looks like it."

She picked up a sheathed knife and turned it over in her hands. Her dark eyebrows knit together. "You'll be careful?"

"As much as I can be and still get this done."

At least she didn't ask how long it would take. I wasn't prepared to think about that, myself.

"I have complete faith in your abilities," she said. "I still can't help worrying. You're going to be out there on your own, with no way to contact us if you need help. If something happens..." She set the knife down. "I could come with you. I know my magic's not useful most of the time, and does more harm than good. But I could watch out for you while you sleep." She looked up and forced a sad smile. "I know. I'd just be one more thing for you to worry about."

"And somewhat distracting," I said, noticing the bare flesh at her throat, her uncovered collarbones when she turned and her jacket fell further open. I forced my gaze back to her eyes. "At least if I only have myself to worry about, I can escape danger by flying."

"True. I guess that makes me feel better. You will, right? Fly? Flee?"

"I have nothing to prove. I'll do whatever it takes to get where I need to go in one piece."

"Good." She went to the fireplace to poke at the logs. "Could you stay that way? Aquila would be less conspicuous. As a person, you're recognizable. Even people who have never met you can't help seeing that you're not an average person."

It still made me smile when she called my eagle form by the name she gave it before she knew who I was. How things had changed since then. "It would make basic survival easier, too, but I can't. Sorcerers who have animal forms and stay in them too long get strange in the head."

"What do you mean?"

"They take on more animal characteristics, even when they return to their proper bodies. There are stories about Lyloch, a Sorcerer who lived in Luid during my grandmother's time. He learned to change into a wolf-dog, and by all accounts he used his skill well in the queen's service, spying for her, traveling through the winter and finding his way into enemies' homes when compassionate servants let him in. They say he would go weeks at a time before changing back. He became vicious as a dog, and then mean as a human. He began to prefer the company of dogs, snarled at people who got in his way. Started to run with wolves."

"What happened to him?"

"They caught him ripping a whore's throat out with his teeth."

"You mean—"

"In human form, yes."

She paled. "Okay, so don't try that. But I'm still glad you have the option. Will you promise me one more thing?"

"I might."

"Don't be afraid to accept help."

"I'm not afraid."

Rowan rolled her eyes. "Fine. Don't be stubborn about it, then. If Severn is causing trouble for people, you might find support out there. There must be people who want your father back."

I packed the single bag I'd be taking with me, rolling my clothing to fit, adding knives and food and other necessities. "So be cautious, but be trusting? Sounds perfectly logical."

She crossed her arms. "It worked for us on the way here."

True enough, but that had been when I had her faith in people to balance my skepticism and natural mistrust. I wasn't sure I could manage the same on my own.

"And you do have friends out there," she added. "I'm not saying you'll run into any merfolk while you're crossing Tyrea—"

"But it's a big world, and stranger things have happened?" I offered a smile to soften the hard, disbelieving edge I heard in my voice. Her optimism was easier to stomach now than it had once been, but I couldn't share it.

She shrugged. "My point is that you made friends with them once. Maybe that was a different time, and you were a different person. But you did it. There have to be more people out there who won't hate you on sight."

"You did."

"You changed my mind, though." She slipped a hand into a pocket in her coat and pulled out a pair of vials. "Courtesy of Emalda. She said there's not much she can do for you that you can't do on your own with magic, but these will help you stay awake and aware if you find yourself in a situation where you need them. For emergency use, not for every night." She produced another tiny flask. "And this will speed healing if you apply it directly to a wound."

I accepted the gifts and tucked them into an outside pocket of my bag. "Please tell her I said thank you."

"She's warming to you."

I snorted. "You're the second person who's tried to tell me that today."

"It's true. She doesn't speak badly of you now, and she does want to see you succeed and survive. I don't think she's forgiven you for things that happened in the past, but she finds you useful, and I think she's stopped worrying about you using certain talents."

I sighed. "That really doesn't make me feel better. A young dragon is less fearsome if its fire is doused and its teeth pulled, too. I have no intention of becoming a lap-pet to her or anyone."

Rowan tilted her head. "You still have your claws, though." She stood and pressed her body against mine, grinning in that way that drove me half-mad. I rested my hand on her hip and gripped the fabric of her coat. It slid without resistance against the smooth skin beneath.

She leaned forward to whisper in my ear. "I like your claws."

I wondered what she'd think of me if my fire returned, if I went back to looking into people's minds, bending them to control their thoughts and actions. She hadn't been too keen on it when we first met, and still seemed overly concerned any time she thought I might have used it. I'd given it up for her as much as for Emalda's rules.

Those thoughts fled when she pulled me into a deep, long kiss. Her hand slid over my chest and around the back of my neck as her lips pressed against mine, warm and real. Occasional shared dreams were pleasant, but were no better than pretty illusions compared to this.

My body instantly became more alive, and her touch made me shiver as it chased the night's chill from my flesh. She laughed deep in her throat and kissed me again. I wanted more, but the talk of dragons reminded me about the gift.

"I have something for you," I said.

"I bet you do."

Instead of answering, I went to my coat and pulled a cloth-wrapped bundle from the pocket.

She gave me a curious look. "What's this?"

"Open it. I didn't know I'd be leaving when I had it made, so it's not a farewell gift. I just thought you'd like it."

Rowan gasped when she pulled the cloth open. "It's incredible!"

"You don't mind? Celean helped me get it from your room."

She held up the necklace, a silver chain with a flat, ruby-red pendant hanging from the bottom.

I'd found the dragon scale cracked after her binding broke. Rowan had decided to keep the pieces hidden deep in her closet in case she ever needed a reminder of the incredible power within her. The silversmith hadn't been able to put a hole through the teardrop-shaped remnant to hang it. He'd had to meld silver to the edges and do it that way.

"Of course I don't mind," she said. "It's incredible. I wonder what Ruby would think of it."

"You might find out some day. We still owe her a story." The dragon had released us on the condition that we return and tell her how things turned out for us. It had to be the strangest way anyone had ever escaped from a dragon's lair, and I doubted anyone but Rowan could have done it.

She lifted her arms to hold her hair up behind her head, and I reached behind her neck to fasten the chain. Her hair fell back around her shoulders in heavy waves as she rubbed her thumb over the pendant's surface, admiring it before opening a few more buttons on her jacket and letting the scale settle against the bare skin over her heart.

She faced me. "What do you think?"

"Perfect," I whispered, and she smiled. I think she knew I wasn't talking about the necklace.

"The story's not over, though, is it?"

"Not remotely."

She left the necklace on all night. Maybe it was a mistake. Maybe her coming to my room only made it harder for me to leave the next morning. I needed sleep before a long journey, but I needed her more. She didn't have to use words to tell me she felt the same.

I saddled a good horse and started out long before dawn, after Rowan left to sneak back into her room. There was no one else I needed to say goodbye to. Albion would understand if I left quietly. I rode through the remainder of the night, and reached the bridge not long after the sun crept over the horizon.

Over the winter I had grown accustomed to keeping my defenses up, to doing everything I could to keep Severn from sensing my precise location. As I dismounted and led the horse across the narrow bridge, I dropped those walls, opened myself to whoever might be looking for me, and hoped that by staying that way as I rode deeper into Tyrea I would draw his attention away from the island.

My odds of success were slim at best. I wouldn't endanger the people of Belleisle by hiding—not until I knew I'd drawn the danger away.

I mounted the horse again and reached into my pocket to touch the smooth pebble of purple glass, my small reminder of everything I wished to return safely to when my journey was over.

The sun cast the horse's shadow and mine long on the road as we headed west into Tyrea.

Chapter Six

Rowan

Dawn came with brightness that seemed cruel in its cheerfulness and beauty. I kept my eyes closed against the sunbeams that streamed through the window and wrapped my arms tighter around the feather pillow next to me. I wasn't ready to face the day.

"Rowan?" The end of my mattress sank as Celean settled there.

I buried my face in the pillow and inhaled deeply. I'd taken it when I left Aren's room, and it smelled like him. My memories stirred, bringing back sensations and images of the previous night, opening an aching crevasse in my chest. Being with him in real life was far better than any dream, but every moment had been marred by the invisible clock ticking in my mind, counting down the time until he was gone.

Gone, my mind echoed, snapping me to full consciousness.

Celean waited as I struggled to lift my heavy eyelids. My exhausted muscles refused to obey orders to sit up, and I settled for rolling over onto my back. Emptiness settled onto my chest like a contented cat.

Celean poured me a glass of water.

"Thanks," I whispered.

Celean was a quiet person, wise and practical beyond her years. She often made me think of my cousin

Felicia. They looked nothing alike, and in their mannerisms and attitudes they couldn't have been more different, but they were both the best friends I'd ever had and exactly the people I needed at different times in my life. I thought about Lecia a lot, and about my family. Not knowing what might be happening at home tore at my heart, but it wasn't something I talked to Aren about. He had little enough reason to care about my family, and too many problems with his own for me to want to trouble him.

A lump formed in my throat, and I took a sip of water to soothe the ache. Once again I wondered what was happening. Did everyone in town know my secret? Were my parents suffering for it? Endless questions, always circling, never answered.

Celean had been teaching me to quiet my racing thoughts in those lonely times, to focus on nothing—or if I couldn't manage that, at least to pray for my family's well-being, then set it aside and focus on the present. It was good advice, but as of sunrise, the present offered just as many worries as my past.

"You okay?" she asked, and rubbed my leg through the blankets. "You were out longer than I expected last night. How did you get back in?"

"Kitchen door. Dora was up making bread, but I don't think she'll say anything to anyone. Thanks for letting me sleep."

"I told Emalda you weren't feeling well this morning. I think she thinks you're just sad about...you know." Celean was three years younger than me, but in this it felt like the age gap between us was far larger, as though the weeks I'd spent searching for a cure for my binding had been a lifetime. She understood that I was sad, and she was sad for me because she was my friend, but she couldn't truly understand what I'd lost.

Just sad couldn't describe the dark pit inside of me.

"I'm going to stay in bed for a while, if no one minds."

Celean's heavy brows pushed together over her dark eyes. "You can't mope for too long. Sadness becomes a habit. I don't want to see you give up on everything you've gained here because—" She pressed her lips together, cutting the thought off. "You care for him, I understand that, and you're probably worried about him. But this is for the best, and life will go on as it's meant to. You'll see that someday."

"He's going to come back."

"I'm sure he will."

Was that pity in her eyes, in her voice? I'd have been angry had I not understood that she didn't know him like I did.

For all they talked, no one at the school knew him. There would be more gossip now if I let anyone see how Aren's leaving affected me. I thought about getting up and going to class, and the idea exhausted me. Better to let them think I was ill, or even to draw their own conclusions, than to have to hold back my raw emotions in front of them.

"Give me one day," I said. "Let me be until tomorrow morning."

I couldn't ask for longer. Ernis and Emalda were allowing me to work instead of paying tuition because they saw potential in me and wanted me as a student. I was there to learn, not to grieve. I also had no desire to have anyone pity me. I got enough of that over my background and my struggles with magic.

Celean gave my leg one more pat, then stood. "Take what time you need, but there's a beautiful day waiting outside. Florizel is allowing us to take the horses into the woods if we wish, after classes are done."

"I'll think about it."

After she left, I got out of bed to use the toilet down the hall, but couldn't find the energy to clean my teeth or brush my hair. I pulled the bedroom curtains closed against the bright sun, burrowed under the blankets, and cried.

One day, I told myself. One day to nurse my aching heart, and then I would do what I came to the island for.

* * *

I made myself comfortable in sleep, nested there for the day and much of the night. I dreamed of Aren, and wished I were dreaming *with* him. When wakefulness threatened I forced myself back into the lighter realms of sleep, where dreams were under my control and reality was no concern. I woke each time Celean came in the room, then slept again.

I knew it was cowardice. Surely Aren wasn't out on the road tucked into his bedroll, heartbroken over leaving me. He might even have been glad to be away from this place. But I had lost much in the previous months, and never properly grieved any of it.

Celean came in well after midnight, likely having done her evening's schoolwork in the library instead of our room. After she got into bed and closed off the lamp, I lay awake and thought about the sleeping princesses in the stories I'd once loved.

Is this how they slept, those princesses? I'd always imagined that their sleep looked like death, that they were either unaware of what was happening or trapped in their own minds as I had once been. Perhaps it was more like this. Maybe they kept waking and discovering that their prince hadn't showed up yet, so they forced themselves back down, preserving themselves in sleep until he came to make their lives complete and show them the way to happily ever after.

Ugh.

Certainly not the fate I'd choose. I would figure out who I was without my prince, find my magic and stand on my own.

I sat up on the edge of the bed and reached for my clothes, trying to be quiet for Celean as she'd been for me. Still, when I turned around, I found her watching me. "Where are you going?"

"Library. I think I've slept enough."

She closed her eyes again.

I wondered what she dreamed about. As far as I could tell, Celean had few troubles. Good student, gifted in magic and skilled in its use, a highborn young lady who had never had to work for much, but who was kind and calm and had many friends. Nothing ever seemed to bother her, but there had to be things I didn't see below the surface. After all, my own life had seemed nearly perfect, once.

I slipped out of the room and made it to the library without running into anyone. We weren't strictly forbidden to wander the halls late at night, but it would have raised questions if anyone had seen me heading in to work in the dead of night.

Entering the library felt like going home. The air seemed to tremble under the weight of accumulat knowledge, and I took a moment to enjoy it. The sm dust and aging leather were as much a part of th as the books were, or the paper and ink lin shelves near the door. It was like every librar up with—my uncle's, the one in my homet once worked—and yet not. This one fe solemn. More consequential.

I lit a lamp and carried it w between the tall shelves, not cer for. Albion had already foun situation, and had helped written in languages I ha about looking for child those of Belleisle were fr against it. Similarities wou and differences would only remind me of how far away I was.

I settled on *Magical Theory for Beginners*. My lessons had already taken me beyond the basics, but it would help focus my mind on the one problem I had any control over.

I set the lamp and the heavy, leather-bound book on a round table and sat with my eyes closed, feeling my magic. Its energy burned warm within my core, a feeling like elation, though more subtle.

It frightened me a little when I let myself feel it. So much potential, and so many ways I could mess it up. In the stories I wasn't supposed to read back home, people wielded magic as if it were an extension of themselves. Orphan boys who learned they had great magic in them found it easy to use it to complete whatever quests they were given. I thought it should be the same for me, but it wasn't even close.

A few pages in the center of the book reminded me how lucky I was to have my magic at all. I'd expected a section called "magical maladies" to concern itself with curses, but it turned out to be about ways a person might lose magic. Breaking bindings wasn't listed, but over-use and draining of magic were.

Think of magic as a flame, the book suggested. *When a flame burns low due to lack of fuel, it might be* *rought back if more is provided. Once burned out, the* *me is gone unless one finds a way to re-ignite it. Even* *ny flame may be brought back, but left on its own, a* *ll flame will burn out, and a large one may well* *out of control. We are indeed fortunate to have an* *supply of fuel, but over-use of magic has on rare* *ns led to its loss.*

My flame had nearly burned out. Emalda brought ith some brilliant potions, but according to ad been a close thing. And now I found myself e wildfire side of that spectrum.

I paged through the book as the night went on. As I reached the final pages, the red sunrise at the windows brightened to yellow, illuminating the dancing dust motes that thrived in the library no matter how often we cleaned. I was about to close the book when an entry caught my eye.

Acceptance, listed under "Cures and Concerns."

Magic does not tolerate those who do not accept it, and will rebel against rejection and disrespect.

I smiled to myself. No one truly believed that magic was an entity, that it was self-aware any more than life itself was, or the energy in a lightning strike. Still, folk spoke as though it were, the way one might accuse a stuck wagon wheel of being ornery. These older books were especially taken with phrasing things that way.

I had accepted my magic. I knew what I was. I spent my days struggling with my power and trying to keep it from hurting anyone, trying to become more like the other students. More like Aren.

But are you happy about it?

Of course, I answered myself, and shoved away the idea that it might be otherwise. *Who wouldn't be? This is what I always dreamed of. I just need time, that's all.*

I closed the book and turned my thoughts to other things as I re-shelved it. I'd need to hurry if I wanted to be dressed and ready for breakfast before classes. They started early at Albion's school.

I'd heard a rumor that we'd have a new professor soon, someone who stayed at the school when not on missions to Tyrea and other lands. Whether the trips were diplomacy or spying or something else, I didn't know, but I had been interested to hear that this Beaumage person was an illusionist, among other things. It wasn't something I'd seen or tried myself, and books made it sound like an interesting type of magic. I'd have to ask about that.

The school was quiet when I entered the hallway, and I shook my head as I remembered that today was what they referred to on Belleisle as Seventh-day. Most of the students would be attending a brief time of reflection and prayer this morning, after a decent sleep-in. I'd gone a few times, but was under no obligation. It was never exactly free time for me, though—any time I sneaked out of the building, another student or a staff member would find they had business near wherever I headed.

I needed company, needed to talk things out. But who could I go to? Grateful as I was to Emalda for agreeing to let Aren stay, her insistence on our near-constant separation chafed me like rough cloth, and had led to me keeping my distance from her. Even when Aren was leaving in order to protect us, she wouldn't have let me be with him for the night before he went. Albion would be asleep, or already deep in his meditations.

I couldn't think of anyone else I could talk to, even if they were available.

At least, no human.

I hurried back to my room to grab my coat and headed toward the kitchen door. A few early-rising and bleary-eyed students gave me strange looks as I passed. I must have been quite a sight with my un-brushed hair and wrinkled clothes, but it didn't matter. Florizel wouldn't notice. I grabbed a couple of apples as I passed through the kitchen and stepped into the cold.

She would be around somewhere, enjoying the clear skies and a day without classes. The riding mistress and I had more than a few things in common. Both of us were far from home, separated from our families. She was a quiet sort who had never revealed all of her history to anyone, as far as I knew. Still, I saw her as a friend, and she wasn't someone who would judge me for my loyalties as even friendly humans did here. She seemed to have had an understanding with Aren, too. If they weren't particularly friendly, they'd shared their silence comfortably enough. Perhaps that had something to do with their common love of flying.

No use checking the stable. She didn't spend much time with the horses, much as they accepted her as one of their own. I watched the skies and walked toward the back fields. It felt strange to look up and only watch for one familiar silhouette.

I approached the paddock, a peaceful place of flat ground, lush wintergrass, and bare trees that would provide plenty of shade when the summer sun came to the island. I leaned against the whitewashed fence and watched the horses. Of all of the surprises that had met me on my journey through Tyrea, they were one of my favorites. I'd grown up around horses that were lovely, but had not a speck of magical lineage. These creatures, though recognizable as horses, still surprised me when I looked at them. The stocky beasts were stronger, able to travel farther and longer than horses I knew back home. The long hair on their lower legs and their thick manes looked like they should weigh the animals down, but they moved with surprising grace. They tended to be highly intelligent, if somewhat stubborn because of it, and though suspicious of strangers they were loyal to those humans they chose to trust. The only difference I'd really had trouble getting used to was their mouths. Heavy jaws held sharp teeth that allowed them to eat meat, and I'd thought I was seeing things the first time I watched a horse crunch through the bones of a coyote that the herd had caught in the paddock.

A thudding noise sounded behind me, followed by a heavy snort and hoofs crunching over the thin snow. I smiled and turned toward the riding instructor. My journey to Belleisle had taught me to accept friends where I found them, and in whatever form. Even if my new friend happened to be a flying horse.

Her cloudy gray coat turned darker at her points and faded to a light, speckled pattern on her rump, while her mane, tail, and wings were a rich, creamy white. Though as tall as many land-bound horses, she appeared far more delicate thanks to her thin legs and fine-boned face. I thought her one of the most beautiful creatures I'd ever met.

She folded her massive wings at her sides and waited for me to speak.

"Did you see him go?" I asked.

"I did. I told him to take Harryson—Aren can handle him better than the students here can, and he needed a strong and swift horse. He didn't say where he was bound. Is it to Luid? Will he challenge his brother?"

"No, he has other plans."

"Ah."

We walked on, Florizel picking her way carefully over the icy spots. Her dainty hooves made her less sure-footed than a land-bound horse. She managed well enough over grassy fields and on roads or trails, but was really built for the air. She was the only one of her kind on the island.

"Did you bring me something?" she asked. I'd once found her words difficult to understand, coming as they did from a horse's lips, but had quickly become accustomed to her speech.

"You know I did." I slipped the apple from my pocket, and she stopped to crunch it, juice dripping from her lips. I bit into mine, and we kept walking.

"Thank you. So what now?"

"Life goes on as it should, I suppose," I said, remembering Celean's words.

Florizel snorted and tossed her head. "Nothing is as it should be. Life will go on, but for now we settle for things as they should not be, or we strive to make them right." She paused. "I should have taken him. I might have helped, even if he wasn't going to Luid."

"May I ask why it's so important to you?" It was clear from the way her ears laid back at any mention of his name that Florizel hated Severn. She'd never spoken about why, though, except to say that he'd harmed her herd in some way.

She arched her neck and looked back toward the house, as though making sure no one was listening. "I don't mind telling you, but please don't let anyone else know. I don't need humans talking about me. Feeling sorry for me." She shook her head. "I'll accept help, but pity seems a silly and useless thing."

I silently agreed.

"Do you know how I came to this island?" she asked.

"No. Just that you arrived a little over a year before we did."

"I come from the mountains far west of here. I should have been happy to spend the rest of my life there. My herd lived in a green valley near the foothills— lower than many of our kind, but the grass there was sweet and the river's water clean, and we had room to run and to fly. We made ourselves too accessible, I suppose, but we'd never had human threats to deal with before.

"The men came on a spring night several years ago, passing through our valley on their way west. They surrounded us in the night and frightened us into confusion. It was magic, of course. Everything seemed wrong, turned around, and I couldn't remember which way to go to find the sky. One of our stallions—Murad is his name, and a finer horse you could never wish to meet—shook it off. He should have flown away when he could, but he went instead toward the source of the magic. He found Severn there, and a few other Sorcerers."

She snorted, and her breath rose into the air as hot mist. "I don't know exactly what they said to one another, but they reached an agreement. Murad went with them, carrying Severn where he wished to go, never to return to us. Severn holds him still, by magic and by the promise Murad made to serve him in exchange for the freedom of the herd. All Murad told us before they left was that he'd entered into this slavery willingly, and would not be free until his master's death."

"That's horrible," I said.

She shook her mane and snorted again. "The herd's safety was the important thing. Murad behaved in the most honorable way a stallion can, saving us all. I don't doubt the men would have killed us or taken us into captivity. As I've heard it, Severn doesn't make empty threats."

I shivered and reached out to lay a hand on her strong neck. "No, he doesn't."

"No. But I couldn't let go of the memory of Murad, the thought that something had to be done. It destroyed me to lose him. A year later, I and a few others went against the leadmare's wishes and we took off on our own to find him and bring him home. We'd nearly reached Luid when a great wind came up from below us. It blew hot and dry, and though we fought against it, we were separated. I heard my friends screaming, and saw one fall to the earth. When the wind pushed me again, I let it carry me away. I landed not far from here, on the mainland. Emalda found me wandering when she crossed the bridge to search for her herbs. Here I stay, waiting for the day when I can go back and take what is owed to my herd by those who stole from us."

There's little emotion in a horse's voice, only odd inflections and a strange rhythm, but I heard her pain. "Have you thought of going back to your herd, getting more help?"

She lowered her head. "I disobeyed the leadmare. It was my idea to go. If my companions died, and they certainly did, their blood stains my feathers. I'll not be welcomed back home unless I return with Murad. Even then, I don't know."

I understood, then. This stallion had been worth risking her life and losing her home for, in a mission doomed to fail.

"You'll get him back."

"If he lives, I will try."

A memory tickled at my mind, nearly escaping before I grasped it. "I'm certain he's alive, or was in the autumn," I said, excited to be able to help. "Severn said something about flying on a horse the first time I saw him. He must have been referring to Murad!"

Florizel stared at me. "Aren never mentioned it to me."

"Did you tell him all of this?"

"I—no. We hardly ever spoke, except to discuss things related to the horses here. I find some humans intimidating. He doesn't enjoy conversation, you know, and I think he might have thought me beneath him, being a horse."

I'd have told her she was wrong, but I couldn't be sure. Aren had lost many things since he betrayed his family, but his pride wasn't one of them.

Florizel twitched an ear forward and back. "I should have been more willing to tell my story. Nothing to be done about it now. But this gives me hope, thank you. Perhaps there will still be an opportunity to take Murad home. Until then, I'll hope that whatever Aren is doing, it will somehow lead to his brother's death and Murad's freedom."

I didn't want to think what that might cost. "We can both hope for everyone to return home safely."

"Ah, little one," she said, and nudged me again. "Would that I could make it so. I think I need to fly now. Will you join me?"

I stepped back. "No, thank you. I'll walk."

She nickered—a horse's laugh. "I'll get you into the air some day, you foolish thing."

I grimaced. "Not today, at least." High places

made me nervous, and the mere thought of flying sickened my stomach.

She laughed again, stomped the snow beneath her hooves, and took a running start, pushing off the ground with her powerful hind legs, beating her wings hard to pull herself into the air. It was beautiful, but it was not for me. I watched her for a minute, then turned back toward the school.

I'd spent enough time moping. Everyone around me was moving forward, looking to the future, making plans. My answers had to be in that school somewhere. It was time that I found them.

Chapter Seven

Rowan

I hadn't known what to expect when Beaumage contacted me to set up a private lesson three days after Aren's departure. An hour into it, I still felt uncertain.

The lamps dimmed, flames burning low, allowing gloom to creep into the corners of the classroom where light from the large windows couldn't reach. The faint glow glinted off the polished surface of ten rows of wooden desks, separated by a central aisle, all empty. A breeze whispered past my ear, and a pale apparition appeared at the doorway. Smoke at first, nearly invisible, but solidifying into the form of a bright-green dragon. Every part of it was beautiful, from the arch of its snake-like neck to the angles at which the light reflected from its overlapping, metallic scales.

The creature came closer, neck and back arched, nostrils flaring, steam leaking from its mouth. Bright yellow eyes locked on mine. It lifted a foreleg to paw at the air, and took a few more steps, until it stood nose to nose with me where I sat frozen on the professor's desk at the front of the room. The scaled lips rolled back, baring vicious fangs that dripped with venom.

"Can I touch her?" I asked.

"Give it a try," said a soft voice behind me.

I reached out, and my hand passed through the steam unharmed. The dragon snapped at me, and its teeth passed through my wrist without resistance. The dragon's flesh looked as real and solid as my own, but I felt nothing.

"Incredible," I whispered.

The dragon winked as it disappeared back into the smoke it had appeared from.

The lights brightened, and my new teacher stepped into view. Tall and olive-skinned, trim and imposing, radiating confidence and power, she was the kind of Sorceress I could only dream of becoming.

"She's not bad," she said. "Any suggestions? I've heard you have some experience with dragons."

Griselda Beaumage was born on Belleisle but had traveled widely to study magic, and her voice dripped with the influence of the places she'd visited. Griselda had a magical gift for picking up languages, and had seen more of the world than anyone I'd ever met.

"Suggestions? I don't know," I said. "It looked perfect to me." I thought back to my one, brief meeting with a dragon. Griselda, who insisted that her students call her by her first name, was a strange sort of teacher, one who questioned more than she answered. It seemed she expected me to come up with something now.

"The one dragon I've met glowed all on her own, just a bit," I offered. "The light in her cave came from her scales. It wasn't reflected from any other lights."

"Maybe I'll try that." Griselda leaned against the desk next to me, leather-clad legs stretched out in front of her, knee-high boots crossed at the ankles. Even in the classroom she dressed like she was ready to take off on an adventure, but today she had left her blond hair loose instead of pulling it into the messy ponytail she'd worn since her arrival two nights before.

She'd made a dashing figure, riding up the drive in the moonlight as I watched from a second-story window, stalking the halls and speaking in hushed tones to Albion, who appeared concerned by whatever news she brought. Such news wasn't for students, though, and I no longer had Aren around to tell me what he'd heard from his grandfather. So Beaumage had remained a mystery save for what she'd disclosed in the classroom over the past few days.

She tilted her head to one side. "You want to try? Your records indicated that you hadn't attempted illusions yet." She reached behind her for a leather-wrapped file that already strained to hold the notes and forms that had been stuffed into it, in spite of my short stay at the school. "That, or conjuring."

"Everyone thought those were too difficult to start with."

"We won't know until you try, will we? Perhaps you'll try them, and it will be so easy. Like breathing."

I smiled. "That would be a change for me. How do you do it?"

"Practice. Great focus and will. An intimate knowledge of the subject is essential for it to be convincing. It isn't a simple skill, though some look down on illusion as a pretty little party trick. One usually starts with copying, you see. Makes an image based on a real object, unmoving and unchanging. Then you try a copy of something that moves. A double of a rat, animated but following its every move. Maybe, if you have a natural gift for it, you create something based on a memory, which follows the actions you remember. To create something like my dragon, which moves at my command, is much harder."

"I would love to be able to do that."

"In time you may, Sorchere."

"Sorchere?"

"An old word for a Sorceress and friend."

"Oh? Thank you."

Griselda smiled, revealing perfect teeth. I'd learned that Sorcerers and Sorceresses tended toward beauty not because they manipulated their appearances, though some certainly did, but because their magic cared for their bodies so well. Scars tended to be short-lived unless caused by magic, infections rarely became a concern, broken bones healed quickly. It was certainly not a perfect protection, but it helped.

"Never doubt what you are." She rested a hand on my arm. "There is magic in you. I sense it, though you hold it close. Albion feels its strength. This is why I agreed to these private lessons."

"Thank you," I repeated. I wasn't sure what else to say.

She pulled a few pages from the file and narrowed her eyes. "I missed so much while I was gone. Aren Tiernal, here. A new Sorceress. Bound magic. I knew about the problems between Severn and Aren, of course, but I had only the other side of the story."

I swallowed hard. "You've been in Luid these past few years?"

"I have, as Belleisle's ambassador, and Albion's ears."

"Did you ever meet Aren?"

She raised an eyebrow. "I did. He kept to himself, and went away frequently. I did track his comings and goings, of course. This was of particular interest to Albion."

"I wish you could keep an eye on him now." The words were out before I had time to consider keeping them back. I looked out the window and pressed my lips together, holding back expression of the fear and uncertainty I now felt whenever I thought of him.

Griselda shuffled through her papers again. "It's all right, you know," she said, her voice soft. "Emalda told me that you and he were close. *Are* close, I should say. I should like to hear the details of your journey together someday. It all seems so contrary to what I know of Aren."

"That's what everyone seems to think."

82

"Hmm. People change," Griselda said.

I looked up, surprised. "You believe that? About Aren?"

"You seem to. Albion does. I'll withhold judgment, as Aren is not here to speak for himself."

I had to ask. "What was he like, when you met him before?"

Now it was her turn to look away. "As I said, I didn't know him well. But he struck me as arrogant, above everyone. Didn't mind if people were afraid of him and gave him his space, at least most of the time."

I waited for her to go on. There was so much I'd never asked him about his past. He'd revealed more to me than I suspected he wanted to, but an outside perspective could have told me so much more.

Griselda cleared her throat. "I think it's best we not speak of the past though, eh? Especially when those we speak of aren't here to object. And we do have an assignment. I have some ideas about your troubles, but first I need to get a sense of your magic. Try something simple."

My heart skipped. "I'm afraid nothing is simple for me. Things go wrong."

"I can take it. Show me. Try to duplicate this in an illusion." She picked up a half-filled glass of water from the edge of the big desk and placed it square in the middle. "Picture it in your mind. Will it into being."

I studied the glass. Simple shape, flared near the rim. I imagined a second glass beside it. Ripples crossed the surface of the liquid. I thought I saw a flicker of shadow next to it, though perhaps it was only because I wanted to see it. A cold draft passed by my cheek, and I clenched my fists to keep from trembling.

Just let it happen. It wants to work.

I felt the power rising in me, strong and frightening, a force that could overtake me if I let it. I clamped down, suppressing it.

The glass shattered, spraying water and glass shards into the air. I gasped and ducked, and heard Griselda's sharp intake of breath behind me. When I turned, a thin trail of blood ran down her cheek.

"Oh, I'm sorry," I whispered.

She wiped her face with her hand and looked at the bloody smear next to her thumb. "No harm done. That was promising. There was something there with the water. This is what always happens?"

"Not always glass shattering. I can't predict what it will do. No one can. I've flooded two classrooms, burned Aren, made a rash appear on Emalda when she walked by one of my lessons. The magic is there, but I can't make it do what I want."

"Hmm." She ignored the mess on the desk and walked the perimeter of the room, drumming her fingers on the low bookcases under the window as she passed, eyes on the floor. "Well, it's too strong. That's your biggest problem."

"Aren mentioned that. Albion, too. I think I agree."

"Hmm. And you're afraid of hurting someone."

"Always. Ever since I burned Aren. I was trying to see his thoughts, but..."

"It was bad?"

"It wasn't good. It could have been a lot worse, I think, if I hadn't been holding back. Then I tried to heal that and made a mess of it." The loss of that skill broke my heart. I'd developed such high hopes for becoming a healer, but could barely heal my own scratches as any Sorceress should have been able to without thinking. My magic didn't seem to help with that any more than it did with my classwork.

Griselda spun on one boot heel and came back toward me, walking between the desks as her dragon had. "You can't afford to hold back. But I understand. It's hard to master a skill when your energy is focused on trying not to kill anyone."

At least someone understands, I thought. "So what do I do?"

"We'll keep working together. Try some other things. Tell me, how does your magic feel to you?"

I closed my eyes and felt it again. "Like warmth? Like a tiny sun inside of me."

"Compared to what? Or whose?"

I looked up. "Well, Aren's feels—" I stopped myself when I caught the knowing smile she tried to hide behind her hand. "What?"

She shrugged one shoulder. "As I hear it, you only began to experience magic in any form a few months ago, when you came to the island."

"True."

"Did you feel his magic before then? Did he use it on you?"

"No, I wasn't aware of it at all until I woke up here on the island." My face grew warm as I realized where she was going with this. We magic users were able to sense power in others, but there were only a few ways to become familiar with the specific feel of another magic-user's power, with its signature. It could happen if a Sorcerer used magic directly on someone, as I had on Aren when I'd had the ability to heal him. It often came after spending years together, as in a family or a close working environment. Aren suspected that was how Severn had located him before.

Or it could come from great physical and emotional intimacy, from moments of complete unguardedness. The nights when I sneaked out of the school to be with Aren had opened me to that until his magic felt familiar to me, until I felt I carried a piece of it with me. Even now, if I concentrated, I could feel its cold depths.

If I hadn't felt his magic before I broke my binding, if he wasn't supposed to be using it on anyone on the island, and if he and I weren't supposed to be seeing each other outside of classes...

Griselda seemed to be following my thoughts, amused by my discomfort. "I thought you and he weren't supposed to be sharing such closeness now."

"Well, I—" I stammered. Not that we could get in trouble now that he was gone, but..."You won't put that in my file, will you?"

She laughed, a deep, joyful sound. "No, Sorchere. Your secret is safe with me. No need to speak further of it. Though I wonder."

"What?"

She shook her head. "I was going to ask whether he's ever tried to take some of your power into himself, to ease your burden."

"Is that possible?"

"It's not completely unheard of, but it wouldn't have worked unless he had a skill for stealing it. You see, if his magic was fully replenished, he'd have no way to take yours on. And yours would have recovered." She shrugged. "Now tell me, have you given any further thought to trying a wand or spoken-word direction? I saw in your notes you discussed it with Albion. It might help you channel this excess power, take some of the pressure off."

The change in direction caught me off guard, as did her willingness to keep my secret. "I've thought about it. I think I'm going to keep trying without."

"Oh?" No judgment in her voice, but some surprise.

"I know it might be easier that way, but..." I sat on a student desk and twisted my fingers together on my lap.

"Is it because of Aren? He seemed to have quite rigid ideas about what qualifies as real magic. You're afraid he'll think less of you?"

"Not that, exactly. It's more the fact that even

after all this time, he still thinks I'm capable of doing this on my own. When he was here I felt pressured, like I wouldn't be good enough for him if I took a shortcut. But now that I've had some space and time to think about it, I agree with him. Not that I should be ashamed of needing help, but that I am strong enough to do this on my own, if I can figure out how."

"Ah. So you're saying he was right, but he was being too much of an ass about it for you to see that?"

I laughed then for the first time since Aren had left. "Something like that. He's what we call a hard case back at home, but I—" I paused. "Well."

Griselda's smile disappeared. "I know. It wouldn't be appropriate for me to tell you I'm sorry for what you've lost, as I'm your teacher and claim no knowledge of any intimate relationship, as we have not discussed that here today. But I understand." She leaned in and bumped me with a shoulder. "If you need anything, you come to me. Privately, of course." The clang of the massive bell in the yard filled the room, and my stomach rumbled in response. Griselda ignored the bell. "The other thing I notice is how you speak of your magic as though it's separate from you."

"Is that wrong?"

"Not wrong, exactly, just odd. Describing your own magic should be like describing how your blood feels when it flows through your veins, unless you're specifically calling on it. I wonder if there's a disconnect between you and your magic. Between that and the size of it, I can see where you'd be having problems."

"That's good to know, I suppose." I'd never spoken of that to anyone. I hadn't thought to. I still had so much to learn.

The lunch bell clanged again. Griselda stood and stretched, then slipped into the leather jacket that hung from the back of one of the desk chairs in the front row. "We'll figure it out. We Sorceresses must stick together.

For what it's worth, I think you're making the right decision about the wands and such. We'll meet soon and try illusions again. Something simpler. We'll see if there's anything to what happened with that water, too. Have you had success there before?"

"Not exactly."

"Your natural talents may just need time to manifest. Things will improve once you connect with your magic a little better." She reached out and patted my shoulder. "You'll get there. We're already making progress."

I gave her a few minutes' head start. The fact that I was getting private lessons from the professors wasn't a secret, but some students weren't pleased with a foreign stranger receiving what they considered preferential treatment. I didn't want to rub it in their faces.

I stepped into the space the dragon had occupied so recently and inhaled deeply. The classroom's smell of old books and wood polish hadn't changed, but I felt magic lingering in the air.

I reached deep inside of me again. She was right. I felt my magic as something living within me. Not an unwelcome guest, but not-me nonetheless. I ignored my hunger and focused, not comparing my magic to Aren's, but feeling it as a part of me. The longer I stayed there, still and silent, the more familiar it became, and the less aware I felt of it.

My awareness of it returned as someone in the corridor called my name. *Celean.* I opened my eyes, and grinned.

I still had a long way to go before I could solve my puzzle, but something told me that we'd found one of the clues.

Chapter Eight

Aren

Three days after I left the island, I still hadn't encountered danger. Under other circumstances this would have pleased me greatly. Now, it only made me wonder why.

I had opened myself as well as I could to Severn. Where once I'd built walls around my thoughts to keep him out and kept my magic quiet in case he was able to sense it from afar, I now shouted my presence. As we rode on through the woods and over roads toward Luid, I transformed. I made flames. I experimented with unfamiliar magic in case that somehow drew attention. When we passed a farm I had once spent the night at, I stopped in and made it clear who I was.

They asked me to leave.

Luid was not my true destination. Far from it, in fact. My uncle's home in Stenbrach, in the province of Durlin, was farther north and west of there. But Severn had to think I was coming for him. As soon as I knew I'd been spotted, I would change course and hide myself.

The plan was far from perfect, but it seemed the only way to be certain that Severn would leave Belleisle alone. There was a time, mere months before, when I wouldn't have been so concerned. The island had defenses. They could all take care of themselves. Yet here I was, riding through the vast wilds of Tyrea on an obstinate horse, adding days on to my journey, in order to draw the danger to myself.

Time to move on. Either he's seen you, or he's not going to.

I made camp that evening far from the road. I transformed and hunted while the horse foraged, then lit a fire to cook the partridge I'd caught. The cooking was unnecessary, as I could have eaten the meat raw in eagle form, but the fire was pleasant, and warmed me long after the food was gone. I took the purple glass pebble Rowan gave me from my pocket and held it tight in my hand. I didn't look at it often, not wanting to turn into a sad, sentimental fool. But the glass was a reminder of her, and of the fact that she was safe at the school. It felt good to have something to be thankful for even as I doused the fire and the cold night pressed in on me.

I missed her like I'd never missed anything before—at least, not that I could clearly remember. I wanted to think of her, and yet the memories pained me. It was like missing a limb, or my heart, and I hated it. *No wonder my father thought love was weakness,* I thought, and tucked the glass away. *Look what it's turned me into.*

I transformed again to sleep. The ground was far too cold and wet to be comfortable, and my feathers kept me warmer than clothing did. Though magic might save me from freezing, I still found it difficult to sleep while I shivered. It was easier to stay alert to danger that way, as well. No chance of falling into dreams. If my eagle's brain was slower to strategize, to sort through human ideas and the consequences of actions, it was the price I had to pay.

I understood the appeal of this lifestyle to someone like the legendary Lyloch. Traveling as an eagle, without the worry of a horse and human concerns, would have been far easier. But the warnings and legends of my childhood, as well as cautions from tutors and elder

Sorcerers, kept me from spending more time as an animal than I had to.

A faint sense of unfamiliar magic woke me near dawn, followed by voices. My mind and body snapped to alertness instantly.

They were already too close. I didn't have time to transform and dress, and I wouldn't let them catch me naked and unarmed. Instead, I moved into the shadows of an evergreen's branches, and waited for them to pass.

I pushed away my frustrations with my own limitations. The inability to make clothing or to read human thoughts while in eagle form would still be there later to taunt me. For now, I focused on the situation as it stood.

I looked for the horse, hoping he wouldn't make any sound, and found that the clever beast had slipped his halter during the night and wandered off.

Another problem for later.

The voices grew louder, distorted by a swirling wind that had picked up overnight. They came closer, and I found them. Three men, one with magic, and that was all I could know without being human.

They stepped into view. Soldiers, unmounted and wearing gray uniforms that identified them as belonging not directly to Severn, but to the province of Artisland. No sign of other humans in the area. Something about that thought troubled me, but I couldn't think why.

"He's here somewhere," said a young man with a chin so weak it seemed to disappear into his throat.

"No shit," muttered the oldest among them, a rough-looking fellow with one eye and a massive white beard. He kicked at the remains of my fire. "Shut up."

They stood with their backs to one another, searching first the ground, then the treetops.

They're looking specifically for me, then. Severn had sensed me, or someone had. That was one problem solved.

I looked to the ground. My clothes and a pair of daggers my grandfather gave me were safe enough under the shelter of the tree I rested in, but they might as well have been back on Belleisle for all the good they did me now.

The young man who had spoken first spotted the horse's saddle and my bags under another tree and looked through my things. I remembered my promise to Rowan, and resisted the urge to attack.

"You think it's them?" No-Chin asked.

"Don't know," said the third man, one with a weathered face and gray hair. "Could be."

Them, I thought. Severn assumed Rowan was with me.

"Watch yourselves, boys," the bearded one muttered. "He's dangerous, and she likely is as well. Kill her on sight. Severn wants him alive."

The young one scratched at his nose. "I thought she was ours to do what we wanted."

Gray-Hair shook his head. "You are new at this, aren't you? She'll kill you before you lay a hand on her. You heard what she did to Lord Severn."

The young one mumbled something about magic being ineffective if a person were unconscious, and my talons gripped the branch tighter.

"You have fun trying it," replied Gray-Hair.

My idiot horse chose that moment to return from his foraging. He stood there, blinking at the men, shaking snow from his mane when it slid off of a tree branch he bumped into.

I might have tried to escape, to creep as well as I could along the ground under the pine trees' skirts, where they couldn't see me. It would have been wiser. But something deep inside of me told me to attack. I could blame the eagle's hunting instinct, but I knew better. They'd have harmed Rowan. I didn't need any more reason than that.

I moved slowly out into the light while the horse had their attention, careful to make sure I had clear space for my wings. The men didn't notice me until I exploded from the tree.

The youngest man screamed before I grabbed his throat in my talons and ripped it out. I used my feet to push and my wings to pull me away from the body to avoid the hot spray of blood that would have matted my feathers.

The other two spun to face me as I landed in a bare oak tree. The one-eyed soldier one held a dagger in his hand, blade flashing in the thin afternoon sunlight. I leapt at him. He ducked, protecting his neck, and I swooped over his head, turning in the small space, gaining what altitude I could before aiming for the other one.

The gray-haired man appeared startled, and didn't snap out of his daze until I was on him, battering his head with my wings as I held fast to the front of his coat with one foot. He spun around and tried to throw me off, but I held on and slashed at his face with my beak.

There's something completely inhuman about biting an enemy. Still, he had a knife, and I didn't. It wasn't an unfair fight, and I wouldn't have cared if it was. I ripped at his eye, and slashed at his throat and pushed off as he fell to the ground. Bright blood spread over the snow where he lay, gloves pressed to his face. He pushed himself up onto his hands and knees and crawled a few paces, then collapsed.

I couldn't say I was sorry. It felt incredible to be fighting again, to feel my blood coursing through my veins, to be reminded of the power I'd been forced to suppress for far too long. The world came into sharper focus when I fought, every sensation heightened and every pain dulled.

Gods, how I missed this.

I flew to a higher branch in the oak tree and looked down on the gray haired one.

"It's true what they say about you, then," he called up to me. "Severn himself warned me how dangerous you were in either form. Perhaps I didn't communicate that to the others clearly enough." The other man made a choking noise, but the older man ignored it.

I prepared to attack again. There was only one left. *I might transform, take him off guard—*

Footsteps crunched through the trees, and my adversary smiled. "It's about time you showed up," he called back over his shoulder. Though I searched with my mind and my magic, I felt nothing, even as six more men entered the clearing, all wearing the scarlet and gold uniforms that identified them as Severn's soldiers, likely sent from Luid at the first sign I'd left the island.

Severn was gathering power from all over Tyrea. I hadn't known anyone before who could hide a group of people from me, but that didn't mean that such power didn't exist. One of these men had managed it. As he lifted that defense, I felt magic burning in all of them.

I flew. Rowan had been right. I took too many chances, let my confidence lead me into trouble. Though it shamed me to retreat, I saw no other choice. I couldn't win against seven men, and gods knew what sorts of magic hidden among them.

I made my way further toward Luid and opened myself for just a moment in the hopes that Severn would believe I was still coming for him, that the men would follow. Late that night, under the cover of a clouded-over sky, I returned to the camp site to see whether I could salvage anything, intending to resume my true course toward Durlin and my uncle's home.

They'd taken the horse, as I'd expected. My bags were gone, and with them all of my food, my gold, my bedroll, my maps, and the potions that Emalda had sent for me. The sun had melted the snow in the trees, leaving my clothes soaked from the runoff, but at least they were still hidden. I dressed, shivering at the touch of frozen cloth against my skin.

I had my daggers. I had my wits, though I was beginning to lose faith in those. Best to stick with a human brain as much as possible, I decided, and struck off through the woods.

I had my magic, too, though the thought of using it to get more supplies gave me pause. True, I'd felt a rush of pleasure when my long-unused skills came back to life on Severn's ship, and I'd have happily broken the minds of those men if I'd been in human form when they came for me. But where I once would have used my skills to manipulate anyone, months with Rowan had made me doubt my actions. Her look of horror when she realized what I did to people and how I used my power was burned into my mind, as were my grandfather's suggestions that I find better ways to use my power, and the school's strict rules about using magic against anyone.

They're wrong, I told myself. I wasn't going to hurt anyone. A little manipulation would allow me to get the supplies I needed without harming a soul—or a body. And I had good reason for doing it. If I succeeded, the people would have their rightful king back. Surely the prize was worth the small price.

Something crashed in the trees to the east. I tucked my soaked cloak under my arm, put my daggers away in easy reach, and ran deeper into the dark forest.

Chapter Nine

Rowan

After a few more private lessons, I'd had no more success with Griselda than I'd had with Aren. I hadn't expected miracles, but I wished I could contact Aren to let him know that it wasn't him who had been holding me back.

It was just me.

Still, I wasn't going to give up. I'd used magic. True, my most impressive feats had happened while my magic was still bound. Everything I'd done recently had been harmful or destructive, but at least things were happening. And what choice did I have but to go on?

"Hey, you with me?"

I blinked hard and looked up. "Yeah, sorry."

Bernard grinned and brushed back the blond hair that had fallen over his eyes. "You walked right through a mud puddle back there."

I glanced down at my boots, which were, indeed, filthy. "Sorry. I was thinking."

The smile disappeared from Bernard's face. "Don't worry about it. You know he'll come back."

I hadn't been thinking about Aren, but asked, "How do you know?"

"Guys like him always show up when I don't want them to."

"From your mouth to various gods' and

goddesses' ears," I said. "No offense."

"Yeah, sure." He forced a smile and gave me a friendly elbow bump, almost sending me stumbling into another puddle.

Bernard and I frequently worked together—he helped me in the library, and I assisted him with the manual labor that paid for his room and board and kept the school running smoothly. He was busier now that Aren wasn't picking up the slack. We'd developed an easy way of conversing, skimming over anything of any real importance. As long as we stuck to easy and everyday topics, our friendship flowed smoothly.

No talk about Aren. No talk about Bernard's desire to marry a Sorceress so that his children would carry her magic as well as what he carried in him, dormant, from both of his talented parents. Certainly no acknowledgement that he'd ever thought of me that way, no matter how briefly that might have been. No awkwardness.

Today we were to move hay bales into the new barn.

We rounded the corner of the huge, red building, and Bernard stood with his hands planted on his hips as he took in the sight of heavy bales stacked in teetering towers high over our heads.

"Little shits," he muttered.

"What, the delivery men?"

"No, the kids. One of the students did this. They think they're so damned special."

I looked behind us and around the corner of the barn, but saw no one hanging around to watch. "Should be easy enough to figure it out. There can't be too many who can use magic to move objects, right?"

Bernard waved the idea off. "Maybe a handful here, but I'm not going to let it bother me. Some people who have a lot of power think they're better than everyone else, you know?"

My shoulders tensed at the obvious sideways dig at Aren. "Some of them are at least learning better, if people would give them a chance."

"As I said, I don't let it bother me. We should get started." He stepped toward the closer pile.

"I don't think that's stable—" Before I could finish speaking, Bernard laid his hand on the stack, and the two bales on top pitched forward. "Bernard, get away!"

The bales fell, and Bernard stood frozen as the heavy blocks plunged toward him. He threw his arms over his head and crouched. I threw mine forward, not knowing what I was doing, and felt power explode out of me.

Move, I thought, and willed the heavy bales to fall to the ground behind him. I saw it in my mind, and felt a push of magic. The bale exploded into a grassy cloud with a force that sent me stumbling back.

"Bernard!" I screamed again, and raced through the chaff that floated in the air, tickling my throat as I breathed it in.

I stopped. Bernard was still crouched in the same position as he'd been moments before, arms covering his head, trembling slightly.

I grabbed his shoulder and shook him, and he opened his eyes, then stood. He reached out and pulled a piece of hay from my hair.

"What did you do?" he asked.

"I'm so sorry! Are you hurt?" I reached out and touched him again to assure myself that I hadn't blown any holes in him. He felt solid enough.

Bernard grinned, then laughed until he sat in the mud, hands clasped around his stomach. I began to worry that I'd saved his body, but broken his mind.

"What? Bernard, say something!"

He wiped his eyes. "I'm fine! It's just...I don't even know. That was terrifying. I thought I was in for a snapped neck, and who saves me but the broken

Sorceress herself, the mistress of mayhem?"

I punched his arm and sat beside him, suddenly shaky-legged and out of breath with relief. "I guess you're lucky I didn't set you on fire. I wasn't trying to make it blow up. I was trying to push it away."

Bernard swallowed hard and stopped laughing. He took my hands in his and squeezed. "Rowan, you saved me. That thing didn't hit me at all. I didn't feel anything. You did it! You used your magic, and you saved my life!"

"But I did it wrong."

"So? You did something good. Enjoy that."

I leaned forward to rest my forehead on my knees. True, it hadn't been what I expected. But when I didn't have time to worry about hurting someone, when I didn't over-think it, my magic had accomplished something.

Bernard leapt to his feet and held out a hand to pull me to mine. "Come on, we're going to tell Father." He pulled me into a massive hug, and I squeezed back.

Wait until I tell Aren, I thought, and felt a flash of heartache as I remembered there was no way to do that.

Then Bernard grabbed my hand to pull me back to the house, and I tried to enjoy the moment.

Aren would want me to celebrate.

Chapter Ten

Aren

I moved onward as quickly and quietly as I could, trying to remember my maps and the location of the nearest town. Branches whipped at my face as I moved through the dense forest, leaving shallow scratches on my cheeks and forcing me to close my eyes as I pushed through thickets. I cursed the trees, and the roots that tripped me where they arched up from the ground, sending me stumbling if I tried to move too quickly. Still, there was no time to waste. When I didn't appear in Luid, Severn would send parties out to search for me.

Artisland wasn't a densely populated province, but near the Durlin border the towns were closer together. I would find something if I kept walking. When I came to a river, I followed it downstream. If I recalled my maps correctly, it would lead me back to the road and a nearby village.

Exhaustion caught up with me toward morning and weighed down my limbs, my eyelids, and my mind. Emalda's potions would have helped at that point, but they were gone. I hoped the man who took them would drink every drop and find himself never able to sleep again. He deserved the insanity.

When I reached the road I continued along beside it, staying close to the shelter of the forest. The creak of carriage wheels reached me, and I crouched in the thin brush to watch a party of merchants go by. They were talking, but too far off for me to hear their words or get a clear sense of their thoughts. They watched the woods carefully, but whether they were watching for me or for bandits, I couldn't guess.

Best to be cautious, though. I let them go on, and followed them until I reached the outskirts of a village.

I pulled my cloak on and raised the hood to cover my face, though the streets were nearly empty as the thin sunrise stained the eastern sky pink. There were no signs stating the name of the town, only a posting at the crossroads that indicated the way to other and presumably better places. The gravel roads were well kept, the log-and-plank buildings plain but tidy. The houses had little ornamentation save for their front doors, which people had painted with scenes of daily life and legends, all in bright colors. Some were little better than the scribblings of children, but one spectacular piece caught my eye.

The double doors of a temple of some sort stood out against the whitewashed building and depicted a group of men in brown robes raising their hands before a white dragon—not attacking or defending, but holding up offerings of food and white gems. It brought to mind a story I'd heard as a child, the legendary tale of the Dragonfreed Brothers. I was never clear on their origins, but had heard they were a religious order of unassuming men who lived austere lives, devoting their days to prayer and meditation. They'd offered care and counseling to the people who made the long journey to visit them, often fugitives and outcasts, or those in need of healing.

Perhaps that much was true, and this building belonged to some tiny remnant of that movement. But the Dragonfreed Brothers of legend were also warriors, skilled in non-magical combat both on the battlefield and in the streets, able to approach and kill a man before he knew he wasn't alone. They were assassins, and far more subtle ones than I had ever been, skilled with weapons and famous for not needing them. They proclaimed themselves independent from any kingdom that rose or fell around them, offering no loyalty or service to kings or lords. They worked for themselves, and in the service of the Goddess. Beyond that, their motivations were a mystery.

There was no indication of that part of the story in this painting. Still, the artist had captured a certain grim dignity in the men's faces in just a few simple brush-strokes. I'd have been interested to look for longer, but time was passing.

A general store sat with its product-cluttered porch bumped directly against the street, without the garden spaces out front that had defined properties in the residential area. I climbed the steps and passed a life-sized woodcarving of a wolf on my way to the door. Someone inside was already awake and bustling about. Mumbled words drifted out of a cracked-open window.

No chance of breaking in and taking things quietly, then. She was alone, though, as far as I could tell. The thought that the Sorcerer who had blocked me might be there crossed my mind, and I opened the heavy door cautiously.

I saw no sign of anyone but a plump, middle-aged woman, and as soon as I caught her attention her mind was open enough that I'd have known if she were hiding anyone else there. She had a hint of magic herself, so slight that she was likely not aware of it. Not enough to protect her from me, surely.

Still, I would use caution. I stepped in and closed the door tight behind me, and slipped the deadbolt lock silently into place.

The shopkeeper gave me a wary smile. "G'morning, sir," she said, and smoothed her apron down over the skirts of her blue, floral-print dress. "You're out and about early this morning." Her nervousness filled the air. I'd long since learned not to let other people's emotions affect me when I sensed them, but it still made for an unpleasant experience. I wanted to shake her, to yell at her to control herself. I might have taken control of her mind then, but still my grandfather's admonitions and Rowan's fear held me back.

And there was her magic to consider. Small though it was, I wasn't about to take unnecessary risks sooner than I had to. Not when I was exhausted, and so out of practice. For now, I would just watch.

I smiled to put her at ease. "I'm just passing through town. How fortunate for me that you're an early riser, too." Her shoulders relaxed at the warmth in my voice and expression. "I only need a few things."

I listed off a few items as I saw them on the shelves, nothing that might take her to a back room and break the tenuous connection between us. Clothing, food, a new pack, a blanket, and a full bag of fresh water covered the counter, and in moments when her attention was on her work, I found my way deeper into her mind, careful not to alert her to my intrusion. Her magic was weak, indeed, though I felt it as it pushed back against me. I retreated slightly, and it quieted. I moved in again, and it remained still.

Her thoughts drifted frequently to the news that had arrived late last night, news of a fugitive that had kept her awake and led to her opening early this morning since she wasn't getting any sleep, anyway. Each time her thoughts tended in that direction, I nudged them gently away, toward the task at hand.

She marveled inwardly at her uncharacteristic calm and focus.

My intervention kept her from making the dangerous connection between me and the fugitive, and I was careful not to probe too deeply into private thoughts, even when her attention strayed to my appearance, and then toward her slob of a husband who had been gone on a hunting trip for the past two weeks. Her thoughts moved toward suspicion again when she remembered something about a fugitive of some sort, and she decided she was glad her young daughter was safe, sleeping at her grandparents' house that night. They'd protect the girl from danger.

I turned her thoughts away again. *Definitely best to not let this one out of my sight.*

"Anything else?" she asked, and looked over the items before her, tallying up the purchase in her mind, hiding her glee at the thought of the gold she expected. I wondered whether Rowan would still be as horrified at the thought of stealing for survival as she had been when we stole horses. Funny how that had become a pleasant memory.

But I couldn't be distracted by it. Not now, when I was so close to making my escape.

She scratched out figures on a sheet of paper and gave me a total. I slipped deeper into her mind and gave her the image of me handing her the money with a smile. I wasn't sure where she would put the money, so I didn't address that. The memory would be imperfect, and confusing for her when she couldn't remember what she'd done with the gold, but it would have to do.

"Thank you," she said, but her eyebrows pulled together in confusion. A thought rushed forward, a warning about me. I shoved it away, and she blinked hard. Her magic pushed back, harder and stronger than before, attempting to push me out.

Not yet.

"I'm sorry," she said, "I'm not feeling well. Will you need help with those things?"

"No, thank you." I stuffed everything into the bag, maintaining my hold over her the whole time. She was going to make the connection as soon as I released her. Aren Tiernal, former prince and current wanted criminal, in her store and taking her things. The town would be after me. I would have to go in again, twist her mind until she believed I had never been there. I reached deeper.

The door to what I took to be the back rooms or living quarters creaked open and a red-headed girl of perhaps seven years stepped into the shop. She wore a green dress and a curious expression. "Mama?"

Gods damn it.

The shopkeeper's eyes widened, and she sucked in a loud gasp as even I couldn't keep her from understanding the danger. Her mind fought back, and her magic surged forward hard enough to take advantage of my momentary distraction. It tried to force me out, pulling and pushing until it caused a flash of agony in my brain.

I forgot where I was and what I was doing. Everything was confusing, and I lost myself. I pushed back with as much force as I could, not sure what exactly I was trying to accomplish, knowing only that I felt trapped, panicked. My magic expanded, and hers went out like a light.

The woman shrieked, and her mind went blank. She dropped to the floor behind the counter, sobbing. I recovered myself and looked around. Nothing had changed, save for the fact that when I reached out tentatively to take in the woman's thoughts, there was nothing there.

The child turned her huge brown eyes on me, and her chin quivered.

"Shh," I whispered. "She'll be fine." I couldn't know that. In fact, it seemed likely that the woman's mind and magic were lost forever. Most folk did not recover easily from magical attacks. But the lie came easily enough. I slung the pack over my shoulders and backed toward the door.

The child continued to watch me as she stepped closer to her mother. I considered changing her memories, but couldn't bring myself to do it. Whether it was the influence of the people I'd been spending time with or some bone-deep shred of humanity I had never had reason to discover before, I had found the limit of what I was willing to do, and to whom. And I couldn't risk another disaster.

"Go away, bad man," the girl said, speaking in a calm and matter-of-fact tone.

I obeyed her command. A skinny gray horse was tied up in front of the shop, saddled and warm from carrying the girl home. He shied when I came close, perhaps sensing something of the storm of thoughts and emotions I couldn't keep from raging through me. Despair battled with fear for the top spot as I managed to mount the horse and calm him. Not fear for my life or fear of being caught, but fear of myself.

What have I done? Who am I?

For once, I couldn't shut the feelings out. All I could do was ride.

Chapter Eleven

Rowan

My next lesson with Griselda took us back to the beach where Aren had told me he was leaving. It looked different on a clear day, all sparkling water and the derelict elegance of the decaying buildings on the cliffs. Bernard joined us. While he couldn't offer advice from experience, he'd spent his life among the school's students, and I wasn't about to turn down his offer to observe and assist.

Florizel flew overhead. She remained convinced that I would love flying, and had suggested that I only needed to escape the cares of the grounded world for a while. Her shadow passed over us, broad wings and a strong body, circling lower, and I shuddered. She meant well.

"Again," Griselda called. "Remember, Sorchere. Do not focus on the tool. Think only of the outcome. Ignore the magic."

I turned to the water and concentrated on calling it to me, attempting to clear my mind even as I focused on my task. The aim was to separate a small portion of the sea, not more than a handful, and make it flow over the stones toward me. Not so different from the snowball experiment, but there was nothing to catch on fire here save for driftwood.

Don't think about it. Just do it.

Seconds passed, and minutes. Nothing. I felt the magic in me, swirling and growing, eager to make something happen, but every time it tried to leave me, I held back.

I'd escaped a life of confinement in Darmid and found the adventure I'd always dreamed of, only to find myself stuck again. Useless. Bound.

Griselda shrieked, and my eyes snapped open. She stood nearby, drenched. Behind me, Bernard burst into laughter.

I turned to him. "Stop!" Then, to Griselda, "I'm so sorry."

"It's fine," she said, but shot an irritated glance over her soaked clothing. Bernard looked away as she slipped her shirt off and wrung it out. "At least it was something," she said.

"I didn't even get my target right." My own clothes were perfectly dry.

"No, but the water came, didn't it? That's more success than you've had with other things. This is worth exploring." She shivered. "Bernard, be a dear and pass me a towel."

Bernard complied, then stood with his hands in his pockets. "Maybe we should start dropping things on my head, see what happens."

"Don't even joke," I said.

"No, really." He bent and picked up a pink shell and tossed it into the air. It bounced off of his head, and he winced. "You're supposed to save me."

"Save yourself."

Griselda clicked her tongue and tilted her head to one side, watching us. "It's not dangerous enough. Every time you've used your magic effectively, someone you care about has been in danger."

"Aww, shucks," Bernard said, and I rolled my eyes.

"I didn't particularly care about Aren either time I

healed him," I reminded her.

"Perhaps your magic responded to his the first time, eh? In any case, it was an emergency. You felt compelled to act, to take control. Bernard isn't wrong. It could be that these theoretical exercises are too safe to push you into action. Your people did harm to your mind, didn't they?"

"I suppose so." In fact, I knew so. Though I'd dreamed of magic since childhood, shame still burned deep within me when I considered what I had become and what I was doing. Leaving old ideas behind had proved harder than I thought, even if I'd always doubted them.

Griselda placed her hands on my shoulders and looked squarely into my eyes. "I'm going to suggest something strange, even frightening. I don't want you to feel pressured."

I took a deep breath. "Go ahead."

"The binding."

My chest constricted, and a chill that had nothing to do with the ocean air crept over my skin. "Yes?"

"It controlled your magic."

"Far too much. It almost killed me." I stepped back, and she released me from her gentle grip. "I'm not going back to that."

"I know. And I would never suggest such a thing." She watched as I sat on the stony beach. "What they did to you was wrong. I only mention it because there may be lesser forms of a similar process. Temporary solutions that can place limits on your magic. Emalda may know something about it. I don't think anyone has the formula anymore, but I've heard there are substances that can—"

"No. Please. I can't risk that pain again. There has to be another way." I hated the way my voice trembled. I thought Griselda would be disgusted. Surely she never showed weakness. But when I looked up, her brow was creased with compassion.

"I'm sorry, Sorchere. It was merely an idea." She wrung out her thick hair, releasing a narrow stream of water onto the pebbled beach. "Well, let's try again, and then I think I need to get out of this cold air. I don't miss much about Luid, but the weather there is vastly preferable."

She passed the towel back to Bernard, ignoring his suggestion that he swim out to see if a sea serpent would attack him and provoke my protective instincts.

"Rowan!" called a voice from above us. Emalda hurried along the edge of the cliff, holding her gray skirts out of the way with one hand, waving an envelope in the other. She climbed down to the beach, arriving breathless, and handed the letter to me. "This just came, marked urgent."

My heart leapt into my throat and lodged there. Was Aren in trouble? Had he found his father already?

I reached for the paper with trembling hands and was surprised to see that it had been marked by the Belleisle postal service as having arrived from Darmid via Tyrea. I didn't realize until that moment that I had given up on hearing from my family.

I tore into the envelope and pulled out two pieces of thick paper, one cream and one pure white.

The note on cream was from my mother. Tears blurred my vision at the sight of her precise, elegant handwriting, and further at her words.

My darling Rowan,

I hope and pray that this note finds you well. We were all so relieved to receive your letters, though I will confess that I never stop worrying about your safety.

There are so many things I wish to tell you, but Callum is here waiting to take the letter. He's offered to have this delivered along with one he's sending to you, which seems a kind gesture, but does put some pressure on me! To answer your questions, your father and I are in good health. Things have been difficult, but it's nothing you should concern yourself over. Your sisters are well. Willow and her husband have moved to a town a day's journey from here. It has been difficult, and I miss the children, but it's for the best. Laurel and her family are considering doing the same.

As for your brother, he misses you terribly. Ashe's health has been poor these past months, since not long after you left. He was injured while out searching for you, and has contracted some form of blood poisoning that our doctor has thus far been unable to cure. Fever, chills, frequent confusion, and this wound on his hand that won't heal...He wouldn't want me to trouble you about it, but it seems wrong to keep it from you. You were always closer to Ashe than to any of the rest of us.

I haven't spoken to your uncle recently, but as far as I know your aunt Victoria's situation is unchanged. I don't know whether they told the poor woman you'd gone missing. She's lost so much already. Ches has been staying closer to home; whether this is by choice or not I couldn't say. Things may be difficult for him in Ardare now.

Callum tells me he must be off, so I'll bring this letter to a close. Please keep your brother in your prayers, and know that you are in mine. I hope we'll meet soon, and that there will be time for me to explain everything.

Until then I will remain,

Your loving Mother

I wiped at my eyes with my sleeve. *They haven't disowned me.*

Fear that had been wrapped tight around me for months loosened. But poor Ashe...and things had to be bad for Willow to have moved away. She and mother were more like sisters than mother and daughter, and I doubted they'd spent more than a few weeks apart in all of Willow's twenty-four years. It was good to have news, but I needed more.

The paper had been torn in a neat line across the bottom. That was typical of my mother. Waste not, want not. I flipped the letter over, but she hadn't written anything on the back.

The letter on white paper was, indeed, from Callum Langley, the magic hunter I'd promised to marry before I learned what I truly was. I'd never expected to hear from him again. I assumed he'd received the letter in which I told him about my magic, and the follow-up in which I told him I was safe and pursuing the use of the power I'd been born with.

I unfolded the letter slowly, and read.

Rowan,
Please forgive me for not replying sooner to your messages. I searched for you after you disappeared, sent men into the mountains to search, took every professional tracker my father could spare. Your letters brought relief, though no small measure of surprise, as you can imagine.

I have stayed in contact with your family this winter. They are eager to see you, and I myself would like to sit with you, to see that you are, in fact, as well as you say. Though we no longer have a future together, I think that we can still be friends, as we once were. If nothing else, I wish to hear more of your experiences in these past months. Though I would never say as much to my father, I have long held suspicions that we're not told the full truth about magic. As I am a low-level hunter, he doesn't share his secrets with me. If, as you say, this is something you and others are born with, that the lost children are...well, that's too unpleasant to speak of here, but I wish to know the truth.

However, I can't risk further correspondence. My father read your other letters. It would be best if you didn't respond to this one.

Your disappearance was difficult for your family, as was the aftermath. Your mother will have told you about your brother's terrible illness, and I know it would help them to see you. I would be pleased to meet you at the border and assure your safe passage through Darmid to visit with them. Again, discretion would be of utmost importance, but I feel that this is something I owe to you, and to myself.

If there's any way you can make it, I will be at the Boar's Head Tavern in Archer's Point next month. My father is allowing me a bit of time away from my duties, and I've chosen to vacation in the mountains alone. It would be an ideal place for a quiet meeting, and from there I can take you to meet your family in whatever location they choose. I'm afraid it won't be a long visit, as we must all value our safety, but surely it's better than nothing. If you're able and willing, please meet me at mid-day on the twenty-second.

C. Langley

I folded Callum's letter, slipped it back into the envelope, and handed my mother's to Emalda. The crease between her eyebrows deepened as she read.

"Foolish Darmish folk," she muttered, without apology. "They destroy the magical plants in their country and then complain when they can't find the cures they need." She shook her head. "There's no need for such suffering."

"So you know what it is?"

"I'd say barb-vine slipped through their defenses there in the mountains, and he took a scratch while they were thundering through the brush. Simple enough to treat. I can give you a list of herbs, but even if you send the recipe no one in your country will know how to brew the potion and administer it properly. I doubt they'd be able to find the ingredients."

"So I guess I have to politely ask you to brew it for me and deliver it myself."

Emalda handed the letter back and crossed her arms over her chest. "I hardly think so. I know you want to see your family and are concerned for your brother, but this is a bad idea."

"Will Ashe die if he doesn't get treatment?"

She held my gaze. "Perhaps."

"Emalda?"

"Probably," she admitted. "But you're not ready, and I'm not willing to sacrifice one of my students for this. We might consider it in a few months, if your training goes well enough that you can defend yourself should something go wrong. As of right now you'd be killed out there if you went alone, and we can't spare anyone to escort you across Tyrea."

I turned to Griselda. "What do you think?"

She looked from me to Emalda and gave an apologetic shrug. "I don't know. We should speak to the headmaster about it. Rowan may need to get out on her own and try her magic in the real world, you know? Take some chances. Force herself to learn. But then, we are making progress here. Stopping may be a bad idea. I can't say."

"She'll be killed," Bernard said. "This is a worse idea than the sea serpent." His mother raised her eyebrows, but didn't ask. "Griselda's right. She's starting to make progress. She can't just leave."

"Bernard," I said, "I'll come back. It's just a little break." I remembered the book's words on acceptance, and my attempts to allow my magic to become a part of me. "Maybe I just need to need it more."

Bernard squared his shoulders. "I could go with you, if you need me."

"No," I said. "Thank you, but they need you here."

Florizel landed, sending beach rocks clattering over each other in her wake. "Am I interrupting?"

"Not at all," I said. "We're talking about me leaving the island. Going back past the mountains, to Darmid." My stomach froze as I spoke. There was only one way to go if I didn't want the journey to take weeks. "You said you'd been feeling restless..."

Her ears pricked forward. "Are you going to help Aren?"

"Not yet."

She flexed her wings, and a wave of nausea swept over me. *For Ashe*, I reminded myself. Maybe for Darmid, if I could get Callum to understand the truth about magic.

"This is crazy," Emalda said. "We'll talk about it with Ernie later. He won't allow it. He won't. Perhaps if Aren were still here, he could...Damn it." She picked her skirts up again, and hiked back up the cliff without another word.

A bemused expression crossed Bernard's face. "Did my blessed mother just say 'damn'?"

"Probably not the first time she's paired it with Aren's name," I said, and Bernard snorted.

"So we're going?" Florizel asked. "Soon maybe?"

"Sounds like we might be."

A shiver rippled over her gray hide, and she pawed at the beach. "We'd have to fly," she said, and her lips twitched in a horsey smile.

I looked up into the clear blue sky. "I know. God help me."

Chapter Twelve

Aren

The horse fought me until we left town, only accepting my authority after we'd gone some distance at a hard gallop. Perhaps he was simply too tired to fight anymore.

The main road served us well for a time, but I turned off onto a smaller one heading north before we ran into any other travelers. As we rounded its first curve, voices came to us from the main road, shouting over the noise of pounding hooves. The horse tried to go back, and I turned his head forward. We kept on, still moving more quickly than I suspected he liked.

The small road led to another which was little more than the ghosts of wheel-ruts in the earth, with grasses and tiny shrubs springing up between. It looked quiet, and it led away from town. That was all I needed at that point. The path twisted and turned between massive boulders and around marshy dips in the ground, leading ever deeper into what I recalled my maps showing as a massive blotch of trees. Not much help there.

We didn't stop to rest until the sun shone high overhead. The horse took a drink at a small pond fed by a brook that was barely a trickle even at this time of year, then stepped into the water to snap at an early frog and chew on the tops of lily pads. Not a dietary preference I'd seen in a horse before, but if he could look after himself, so much the better. I kept him tied on in case he decided to wander, and closed my eyes for a moment's rest.

When I opened them again, the light had shifted. I cursed under my breath. I'd slept too long. I couldn't regret the dream I'd been having about Rowan, though, except to wish it hadn't ended so soon. I collected the horse, tightened his saddle and adjusted the bridle, and rode on.

The path disappeared completely, but I had no desire to turn back. Though I'd never developed any magical skills that would help with finding my way through the woods, I knew a few things. Mosses grew more heavily on the north side of rocks and trees, and the sun traveled east to west. We continued north and west, going around steep rises and boggy hollows, weaving between the trees. I considered taking flight to get an aerial view of the land around us, but couldn't risk being seen. A mountain eagle here would be a clear give-away of my location, and would be far too visible in the clear blue sky.

The light dimmed as we moved into an older part of the forest, where pines ten times my height branched high up to filter the sunlight. Few other plants grew in the shadows between the widely-spaced trunks, leaving plenty of room for us to pass. It made for easy riding, but the quiet woods felt wrong. Eerie. A few birds chirped overhead, but I suspected prey would be scarce if I decided to change and hunt later.

Pine needles covered the forest floor, dulling the sound of the horse's steps. We went slowly and carefully over the unfamiliar ground, but made good progress.

After a while, everything began to look the same. Still, I was certain we were still heading the right way, though we had to adjust course frequently to avoid trees and bounders. I brushed my fingers over a strip of moss decorating the side of a tree and turned slightly to my left, correcting to travel north-west past a gigantic willow covered in strange purplish leaves, the only one of its kind in the otherwise all-pine forest.

A quarter of an hour later we came to the willow again.

I dismounted and tied the horse to a low branch so I could look around on foot. A closer-set pair of trees to my left caught my eye, and I went to take a look at them. I judged direction based on the moss on one, and walked to the other.

The moss pointed in a different direction.

So much for that plan.

The light in the woods was fading further, and I decided I had no choice but to fly. I made the horse comfortable near the willow, the only potential source of food besides pine bark and moss. He stripped buds off the slender branches as I moved a good distance away to undress and transform.

The forest was easy to navigate until I reached the canopy overhead. I forced my way through, climbing and breaking branches that left tiny droplets of sharp-scented sap on my feathers. Above, the sky was pink and fading to purple, with a few stars showing themselves in the east. I pushed off toward them and flew higher. The pine forest stretched below, broken by the brighter branches of the willow tree and parted by a wide and shallow river. I followed it upstream.

A freezing gust of wind ruffled my feathers, and I cursed Severn for not having the courtesy to wait until later in the spring to upset things. Night darkened the landscape, and a curious owl flew too close, so silent that I didn't notice it until it was nearly on top of me. I whipped my head around and snapped my beak at it, and it veered off into the darkness.

I was in no mood for company.

I continued up the river, and a flash of light caught my eye. Another joined it, then a series of four, all together, remaining lit. Windows. I changed my course to investigate. If it was a town, I would stay clear. But I didn't recall any on the maps, unless I'd strayed farther off-course than I suspected. Something else, then. Something uncharted. Maybe even something useful.

The forest thinned beneath me and the silhouette of a long building with tall spires at each corner stood stark against the twilight sky. I circled it at a safe distance, coming closer with each pass. In my poor night vision it looked to be an ugly thing, constructed of dark stone that could have sprouted from the ground, brick by massive brick. The spires rose high over the surrounding forest, and the slate-shingled roof slanted sharply up toward a row of ornate iron spikes that ran along the top, like the spines on the back of a dragon. A few dark outbuildings surrounded the massive structure, all surrounded by a high stone wall.

It was impossible to see into the narrow windows, and I didn't dare pass over the outer walls of the property, not until I knew what this place was. I turned back and saw that the lone willow among the evergreens wasn't too far away. I'd return with the sunrise to investigate further.

Though the trees sheltered us from the wind, the night was still too cold. I changed for long enough to remove the horse's saddle and secure my blankets over him, then slept in eagle form, roosting high in the branches. Nothing moved in the woods all that night, and I managed a few hours of broken sleep.

I ignored the damned moss in the morning and trusted my instincts instead. We reached the strange building at sunrise—or at what would have been sunrise had the sky not filled with heavy clouds overnight. They hung low and dark, and lightning flashed far to the east as we reached the edge of the thick forest.

The horse snorted as I tied him to a tree next to a pitted and poorly-kept road.

"I'm sorry," I said. "I'll try to come back soon. We may need to leave in a hurry."

When did I start talking to horses?

Rowan's influence again. I closed my eyes to try to remember the feel of her magic, the sound of her voice and the touch of her lips, but she felt so far away. It was for the best, really. Perhaps I could forget her entirely until this mission was over.

A memory of her laughing eyes flashed through my mind, and I decided to keep her with me.

A rooster crowed as I transformed and flew to the top of an elm that reached over the thick stone wall of the compound. The main building was indeed unusual, but less hideous in the light. The long, tall building had a spire-topped tower in each corner and narrow buttresses along the sides, and all of it dotted with statues of strange creatures. What had seemed at night to be rough and rugged stone turned out in daylight to be ornately and carefully carved. I wouldn't have called it beautiful, but it was certainly impressive.

I'd never seen anything like this, not in real life. But a memory of an old story book simmered deep in my mind, one that I couldn't quite reach while in my eagle body. Something important, something having to do with the town I'd just left.

A small, thin man, clean-shaven and dressed in a rough, brown cassock emerged from a side door of the main building and came toward the wall. I shrank back, though he didn't appear to be searching for me. The frigid ground didn't seem to bother him, though he wore nothing on his feet. A flurry of clucking and crowing greeted him as he stepped into a wooden outbuilding, carrying a pail in one hand.

"Yes, yes," he called, and closed the door behind him.

Lightning flashed, closer than before. Thunder boomed a few seconds later, and somewhere behind me my horse let out a nervous whinny. The rooster crowed again. The door to the outbuilding opened, the rooster

Kate Sparkes

was unceremoniously turned out to make his noise in the open air, and the door slammed shut.

At least the man hadn't heard the horse.

Lights moved about behind the heavy, leaded windows in the large building, but still I could see little else. I studied the robed man when he appeared again to return to the side door, and forced my eagle's brain to make connections it wasn't designed for. Brown robes, rough material, belted with a green rope that hung down nearly to his knees, otherwise unadorned. A deep hood hung down his back, which he didn't pull up against the cold. I searched for the word that would have been immediately available to my human mind.

Ascetic.

A religious order. Still that deeper connection niggled at me. I gave up and returned to the horse to change and dress. At times my eagle brain seemed deeply connected to my humanity. At others, it was absolutely useless at recognizing things it hadn't seen with its own eyes.

The horse startled, eyes white-rimmed and feet shuffling, when I landed and changed in front of him. He reared when I tried to quiet him, but I managed to dart in and release him from the branch I'd tied him onto. He calmed, appearing comically surprised as he recognized me.

"Well, you're no good to me if you kill yourself," I told him as I dressed.

Dragonfreed Brothers. The answer clicked into place, but seemed impossible. They had been mere legends even in my father's time, stories once based in fact but embellished over the years to make them something that resembled the truth no more than Rowan's beloved fairy tales did. These men had to be something else. If the order did survive, it was as a harmless shadow of the dangerous assassins I'd heard about.

Still, I would approach with caution.

The sound of galloping hooves drifted toward us from the road, approaching the heavy iron gates at the front of the building, and I crept closer to watch. A quartet of horses passed not far from me, puffing and blowing, lathered with sweat. Their riders looked little better off, harried and unkempt-looking in spite of the scarlet-and-gold uniforms they wore.

One reached out and pulled a heavy, tasseled rope that hung from the gate. The horses paced as the men waited for an answer. He pulled again, harder, and an ornate wooden door swung open at the front of the building. The man who appeared was taller and broader than his brother who had fed the chickens, dressed similarly but with a white rope at his waist. Grey stubble covered his broad jaw. He raised his eyes to take in the scene before him, but did not hurry to open the gate. His steps were slow, measured, composed.

"Come on, man," a rider called. "We've been riding since midnight."

The lead rider glared at the speaker and motioned for him to be silent. "My apologies, Brother Phelun," he called. "My companion is out of sorts."

The ascetic tilted his chin upward. "And what is so urgent that it has brought you here, riding so hard? Plague? Flood? War?"

"A message, brother, from the king."

The monk raised one thick, silver eyebrow. "Is it, now? I thought he'd disappeared some time ago." He looked down at his keys as he flipped through them, then slid one into the lock on the gate. "Has Ulric returned, then?"

I couldn't help liking the man just a little for his obvious lack of fear in the face of Severn's men.

The lead rider frowned. "From the regent, then, though it'll not be long before he's king. Will you speak to us?"

The monk offered a reserved smile. "Of course. Please, do come in."

The riders passed single-file through the gate and rode directly around to the back of the building, while the monk went back through the wooden door, his pace unchanged.

I leaned against a tree and waited, but there was no sign of the men, or anyone else coming out of the building. I considered leaving, but there was too much I might learn here.

The wind picked up, and a light snow began to fall. At least the lightning had moved off for the time being, but I shivered.

An hour or more after they entered the building the riders reappeared, accompanied by the one they'd called Phelun. Another of the brothers brought their horses around, and the riders mounted.

"We'll be in touch if we see or hear anything of the fugitive," Phelun said.

The leader nodded. "We'll have someone come back to check on things, of course."

A mysterious smile flickered over Phelun's face. "I think we can handle anything that comes our way."

The rider's expression hardened. "I have no doubt, brother. But we have our orders."

"I'm sure. You are welcome at any time."

Phelun let them out, but instead of locking the gate, he stepped through, closed it behind him, and pocketed his keys. He closed his eyes and turned his face toward a patch of sun that broke through the storm clouds, spreading his arms out as though to gather the weak rays to him. When he opened his eyes again, his expression was serene.

"If you're here, you can come out," he said. "I would speak to you, Aren Tiernal, before they get their hands on you." His voice was low and smooth, and his words came with a strange and unhurried cadence. He walked a few steps farther down the road, away from the safety of his gates. "The Dragonfreed Brothers are no friends of Severn, or of those who would do you harm. You will be safe here, if you wish to rest. All we ask in return is information."

He appeared harmless. But then, the man stood in the middle of the road in his bare feet, unarmed, open and waiting, knowing what I could do to him. Perhaps the more far-fetched stories of their skills weren't inaccurate. It would be best if I moved on.

A tiny, sharp object bounced off my head, followed by another. Hail. The wind was picking up, too, and the rays of sunlight were swallowed up as the clouds closed.

"Late storm," Phelun called, and turned toward the gate. "You'd do best not to stay out in this."

A memory surfaced. Rowan's voice, and the fierce look she wore every time she put me in my place. *There have to be more people out there who won't hate you on sight...don't be afraid to accept help.*

It hadn't sounded like Phelun intended to help Severn. I reached out, but he was too far away for me to sense his thoughts, and I felt nothing of his emotions. No magic, either.

I focused on my magic, which gathered inside of me, coiled like a snake waiting to strike, strong as it had ever been. I would remain on my guard, though this man didn't seem to be any threat. Simply a religious man kept separate from the world, only half of what the stories had claimed. I would have a warm place to wait out the storm, and if they were so keen on information, perhaps they'd have some about my father. They'd had their eyes on this land and its people for longer than my family had been in power.

Phelun raised his eyebrows and smiled as I stepped onto the road, leading my horse. As I got closer, I felt calm radiating from him. Peace. Satisfaction.

He reached into his pocket for his keys. "And I thought She had run out of surprises."

Without another word, he turned and walked toward the gate, and I, filled with apprehension, followed along behind as the hail bounced and piled around our feet.

Chapter Thirteen

Aren

"Leave the horse, we'll take care of him," Phelun said without slowing his steps. I tied the reins to the saddle and patted the horse's neck. He snorted and wandered off to nose at the sparse grass as I followed Phelun into the building.

The heavy door swung closed behind us on silent hinges, and Brother Phelun led the way into a great hall where a fire blazed in the largest hearth I'd ever seen. Simple wooden tables and benches, enough to seat a hundred men, stretched in a single line down the middle of the room, dwarfed by the space around them. The ceiling arched high overhead, stained dark in patches by the lamps below. The scent of roasted meat and vegetables hung heavy in the air, mingling with smoke and floor wax.

A spiral staircase at the far end of the room led to a second-story mezzanine that stretched back toward us on the left side of the room. Closed doors behind the bulky balustrade would lead deeper into the massive building. To my right, the wall was broken by two levels of windows that let in faint, distorted light from outside. Otherwise the dark walls were bare, and far less ornate than the ones on the outside of the building.

Phelun and I were not alone, and yet it felt like we were. Dragonfreed Brothers stood around the hall, all clad in the same brown robes as Phelun. Some appeared to have been at work clearing dishes from the tables, others just passing through the room. Every one of them stood still as a statue with his open, empty hands pressed against his hips, former task abandoned. All had their hoods raised, shadowing their eyes and leaving only the expressionless lower halves of their faces visible. Not one of them spoke or moved as we passed, and I didn't get the sense that any were watching us. They might have been statues for all I felt.

The sound of my boots echoed through the hall, bouncing off the wooden rafters high overhead.

I risked a look back over my shoulder to glance at the round window over the doors, which depicted a scene similar to the painting on the doors in town. Men, white dragon. She looked fiercer here, though.

My companion climbed the staircase, and I followed. We passed through a door into a well-lit corridor, and I heard the clink of plates below as the men returned to their work.

Here, away from the fire, the air felt as cold as it had outside, and my breath came out in puffs of white. Identical wooden doors lined the walls at uneven intervals, each of them a pointed arch with iron fittings. Ornately sculpted iron torches burned on the walls, tiny flames giving off more light than they had any natural right to.

Phelun knocked softly at an unmarked door, spoke to someone inside, and closed it again without comment to me. He motioned for me to follow as he continued down the corridor.

We walked for what seemed an impossible distance. Phelun finally stopped after we'd turned several times through the corridors and gone up another tight spiral staircase, this one enclosed and constructed of stone. He unlocked and stepped into a room, empty save for a narrow bed, a small table and chair, and a simple wardrobe made of the same dark wood as everything else in the place. He opened the cupboard doors, pulled out robes identical to his own, and laid them on the bed.

"You'll be warmer if you put that on over your clothing," he said. "I'll excuse myself for a moment. Are you hungry? I missed breakfast, myself, and it must be near dinner time."

"I am, thank you."

"One moment, then."

The door clicked softly as it closed behind him. I went to it and tried the latch, which lifted without resistance. The door swung open a crack when I pulled. Satisfied that I was not being kept prisoner, I slipped into the robes and sat on the bed to wait.

I rose to answer the door when Phelun knocked, then returned to the bed, offering him the chair. He set two bowls of stew and two cups of wine on the desk, then motioned for me to choose which I preferred.

Phelun closed his eyes and clasped his hands in his lap, and I followed suit as he said his silent thanks. He pushed his hood back, revealing short, gray hair that could have used an encounter with a comb.

We ate in silence, and I understood what he was so thankful for. The brothers may have had little in the way of material comforts, but someone among them understood the magic of flavor, and had elevated a simple spiced-beef stew to something resembling art.

"Do you eat this well every day?" I asked, and Phelun grinned.

"Don't tell anyone," he said. "We'd prefer not to be overrun. Do you think that's selfish of us?"

"If the gods had wanted the masses to enjoy this, they'd have sent your cook to a city instead of to you. I think you're safe to enjoy your gift as you all see fit."

He took another bite and nodded. "Indeed. I'll certainly not argue with that, except to say that we consider the Goddess herself our benefactor. We don't concern ourselves with lesser deities here."

The food warmed my body in a way that my clothing couldn't, and the chill left the small room as we sat. Phelun continued to give off a sense of calm, touched with only a hint of wariness and curiosity. He obviously saw no need for small talk, which suited me.

"Talented cook, indeed," he said as he stacked our empty bowls on the table. "I suppose we'd have to watch out for your brother, too, wouldn't we? He seems to be taking talent from all over this country, whether it wants to be taken or not. He might not mind a fine cook."

"Is your cook a Sorcerer, then?"

"Not in any traditional sense. He was here, you know. Severn."

I leaned forward. "He came here himself? Why? And how did he find you?" Severn had never spoken to me about the Brothers. He'd always considered legends and such stories unimportant—or so I'd thought.

Phelun's lips narrowed in a smile that didn't reach his eyes. "He sought guidance. Answers."

"About what?"

"The nature of magic, and power."

"So not moral guidance, then."

Phelun chuckled. "Not exactly, no."

"Why here? Why you?"

He shook his sleeves over his hands and clasped them beneath the fabric. "This is what we do. We worship the Goddess. We seek to know her through the natural forces at work in our world. Magic included, though we don't possess it ourselves. We are passionate yet unbiased students of Her laws, and this gives us a perspective on magic that is not the same as that of a Sorcerer, or your learned men in Luid who are surrounded by its effects every day."

He paused and shook his head slightly before he continued. "I didn't trust your brother. Even without magic with which to read him, I could see there were things going on below the surface of his mind. Dark things. His gaze is unnerving. He sounded tortured when he spoke."

Tortured, I thought. Had I ever seen Severn that way? I'd seen him as brilliant and cruel, worthy of my hatred even as he earned my respect. He had closed his thoughts to me since the day he suggested I learn to manipulate minds, had set up his defenses before my first lesson. Lacking the ability to see into him, I'd stopped looking. Perhaps I had come to rely so much on my magic that I'd neglected to see what was in front of me.

Phelun cleared his throat. "Now, as to your presence here."

"I did not seek you out. I wasn't aware this place existed. Severn obviously paid better attention than I did."

"Few people find us, even if they're searching. The would-be king has resources available to aid him, but you?" He shook his head again. "You wouldn't have made it here if you had tried."

"So the stories of you aiding the ill and the wrongly accused are untrue?"

"Not at all. It simply seems to be the Goddess's will that those who find us are the ones who are truly in need."

"And my brother."

"Exactly. Though perhaps his need was greater than he realized. We may have done more good than we know. That is not for me to judge."

So it seemed the stories were half-true. Phelun didn't strike me as a trained assassin, and my belief that those stories were all fiction grew stronger. But his words reminded me of the less far-fetched stories from my childhood, the soil of truth that the more fanciful tales were rooted in.

I took another sip of the wine, which was finer

than most I had tasted. "And what good would you do with me, Brother? Why did you invite me in?"

Phelun leaned back in the chair, lifting its front legs off the floor. He scratched his chin. "That is the question, isn't it? It could be that She wanted nothing more than to save you from the storm, but there's likely to be more. Perhaps if you told me what brings you here. From the beginning."

"Forgive me, Brother, but how can I know you're not reporting to Severn? You might be keeping me here until his men can return, or collecting information that he'll use against me later."

Phelun closed his eyes and rested his chin against his chest for so long I thought he'd fallen asleep. "I suppose you have little enough reason to trust strangers," he said at last. "You've been taught from an early age that those outside of your family are not to be trusted, is that so?"

"I suppose."

His eyes opened, and he regarded me from beneath his bushy eyebrows. "Hmm. So it has been with your family for generations, I think. But you have learned to trust others, or to mistrust your family, or else you would not be here."

I thought of the servants who raised me after my mother's death, until Severn took me on. I thought of the merfolk I'd known, who had helped Rowan and me on the strength of old friendship, in spite of the person I'd become. There was Rowan, whose magic had taken me by surprise, who had fought for and won my respect. A person I would trust with my life, without question, though I'd known her for only a season. I'd once trusted an old Wanderer to give me advice. I had allowed my grandfather to become a confidant, though on a much shallower level than Rowan.

Not one of them were the family I'd been raised to serve, and yet I trusted them. They were who I would fight and die for if it meant keeping them safe from Severn.

"There are people who have earned my trust," I admitted.

"And?"

I reached out again and felt his mood unchanged. I didn't try to probe into his thoughts. The storm was still building outside, and I had no desire to be tossed into it if he felt my attempt. Still, I thought his openness was sincere. "And sometimes it's instinct that makes me trust people. My mind is always suspicious, but occasionally something inside of me overrides my better judgment. It's the opposite side of the sense that tells me a situation is dangerous, even though I have no reason to believe it is." Experience had honed my alertness to danger since my earliest childhood. I had barely begun to learn about the other.

"What do you feel now?"

"I feel safe enough, but I don't trust it. It's a feeling."

"The sense of danger is also a feeling, and yet you trust that."

Hard, icy snow rattled off of the window and gathered on the sill outside. I shivered. "I've had more evidence that my instinct for danger is reliable."

And yet I continued speaking, my words punctuated by the wind gusting around the corner of the building and the snow tapping at the window. I explained my mission to him, why I thought I needed to find my father. I spoke cautiously, offering only the barest information. He listened, and nodded.

He asked why I'd been to Belleisle. To explain that I had to go back to when I met Rowan, and what I'd been doing for my brother before then. I skimmed over parts of the story. Some things weren't mine to tell. Still, it was far more than I'd expected to share with him. Patterns became clear to me, choices that changed the course of our journey. As I spoke, I found it became easier to tell more.

"Is that what you wanted to know?" I asked.

Brother Phelun tilted his head back and closed his eyes. "Perhaps. There are so many threads to follow in your story. So many that you haven't thought to tell, or that you've left out intentionally. The binding interests me." He opened one eye. "Did you know that the formula and technique for that were stolen from us?"

"I didn't."

"By your grandmother, in fact. That was a carefully guarded secret. I'm sure you can see why we didn't want it getting out."

"I can now, yes." Even the imperfect version performed on her had crippled Rowan's magic, containing it until it nearly killed her. "Dangerous thing."

"It can be, depending on whose hands it's in. I was relieved when your father stopped using it. It disturbs me to hear that it's in the hands of people who hate and fear magic as the Darmish do."

"I suspect that if their king and magic hunters had the formula, we'd know by now. Their magic hunters aren't binding magic. Not yet."

"Hmm. Nothing we can do about it for now." He sat up straight and tilted his head slightly to one side. "I can't help you find your father."

"I didn't think you would. That would have been too easy. Too much of a coincidence."

"And yet I still believe there's a purpose to you being here. Tell me more about this mind-control."

Magic was always difficult to explain, like trying to describe the mechanics of walking to someone unfamiliar with the concept, but far more personal. It's instinct, habit, and intuition. He seemed less interested in how I did it than in the results, though, and I explained what I could.

"You use this frequently?" he asked.

"When I need to. For years I used it to carry out assignments that Severn handed to me. It was the easiest, cleanest way to get information, or to get rid of his enemies."

"Clean, you say?"

I looked down and studied my hands. It had kept them clean, at least, whatever that was worth. I heard the echo of the shopkeeper's screams, the blank stares of a bystander whose memory I'd once cleared too much of.

"Since I left my brother's service, I've made an effort to not harm people if I can avoid it. But in the past, I've used my magic to twist people's minds, to plant ideas and control their actions long after I've left them. People have died because of it. Others have been saved. I've collected information and left people unaware that I'd done so, eliminating the need to dispose of them after they'd seen me. I've made it so people don't have to lie when they're questioned about me or about things that have happened."

And if it doesn't always work, I added to myself, *that's a small price to pay.*

"This is why my brothers closed their eyes when you passed," he said, "lest anyone ask whether they saw anything unusual."

"And this?" I asked, and turned my hands palm-up against my hips.

"To show you they were unarmed, and welcomed you in peace."

"So you understand, then."

"No." Phelun's gaze turned cold, and I felt as though it were boring into my soul, if indeed I still had one. "Are you familiar with the concepts of dark and light magic?"

"The idea that some forms of magic are inherently bad and others good? Killing versus healing?"

"Just so. What do you think of it?"

My shoulders tightened. "I think that it's a lie. I

think that magic is magic, and it's how we use the gifts we've been given that is dark or light."

"It is so for many things," he said. "Your brother's gifts concerning fire might be used to light flames that keep a family warm on a cold night, saving them from certain death. The same gifts may also be used to kill, or to torture."

"Just so," I said, echoing him. I'd seen it myself.

"Something like this, though. Is it possible to know that you don't harm anyone when you manipulate their thoughts?"

I pushed away the memories of the previous morning. That was an anomaly, and therefore irrelevant. "I don't see how it could have harmed the people at the hotel where Rowan and I stayed. All that changed was that they remembered a couple who looked quite different from us passing through the night before we actually stayed there."

"There is always a cost to great magic," he said softly. "Either to you or to someone else. What about when they found signs that their memories were false? You can't have covered your tracks so well. Unaffected people must have seen you. There would have been signs that someone had been staying in a room that they thought unoccupied on that night. I imagine these people began to question their own sanity."

"It would be temporary."

"It took away their free will, my son." His gaze was compassionate now, but with steel in it. "The greatest gift the Goddess has given us. This is the essence of the talent you've so carefully developed. It's magic of the darkest sort, and I don't see how it could be seen as anything else."

I stood and paced as well as I could in the tiny space. "What would you have had me do? Let them find us and kill me? Let Severn take Rowan back to Luid and keep her a prisoner while his researchers experimented on her, then do whatever he wished with her after they had used her up?" I tried to keep my temper in check, but he was digging into the very center of who I was and telling me that it was evil. Worse, something in his argument rang true.

"There must have been other ways," he said, his voice calm. "And you don't know for certain what would have happened."

I thought I did, but didn't bother to say so.

"Would you give this up if you believed me?" he asked. "If you knew for certain that what you did was wrong?"

"I don't know. No." Right or wrong, it was a useful skill.

"What else do you do? What other skills can you use to bring good to the world as you continue on your journey?"

I had a few gifts that I'd worked hard for years to strengthen. Mind control and transformation were the two that I used most frequently, but there was also the awareness of things happening around me, and my mostly-successful attempts to keep Severn from locating me. There were little things I'd picked up along the way that were useful even with my imperfect skills, like shocking a lock to pop it open, or my newly acquired ability to spark a flame. It all took some time to tell.

"There's something you're not telling me," he said when I'd finished. He took a sip from his carved cup. "What else?"

"It's nothing. I haven't done it since I was a child."

He waited without speaking, and I reluctantly continued. Perhaps my mind-control would seem a brighter thing to him in comparison. "When I was young, maybe seven years old, I had a dog that I loved. I was often alone otherwise. My brothers were too old to want anything to do with me, and my caretakers were trying to keep me away from them anyway. The little girl I played with when I was small stopped coming by around the time my mother died, and the other servants kept their little ones away from me, so the dog was my one friend. My brother Wardrel killed her."

"Accidentally?"

"No. He enjoyed hurting things. Still does. He cut her throat enough to let her bleed out and then watched her crawl around the room trying to find me until she died. He made sure he was there when I found her. He'll take whatever kind of pain he can get. I was sad and angry, and more than anything, I wanted her back. I didn't know what I was doing."

"You brought her back." He shuddered and took another long swallow of wine, emptying his cup.

I shook my head and looked away. "Not her. She was gone. But her body moved. It stood and walked, slow and shaky at first, and then it got stronger."

"Your skill grew that quickly?"

"Yes. It terrified Wardrel. That would have been satisfying for me under other circumstances, but I was too upset to really notice. I called my dog, and she didn't come to me. Her eyes were blank. I told her to come, in my mind, and she did. She wagged her tail when I told her to. But she wasn't really there. I let it go and buried the body in the garden."

"Is that the only time you ever did it?"

"I experimented on a few other animals, but never got better results. I never tried to bring people back, if that's what you're asking."

He shuddered. "No, that's good. The effects of that sort of thing on you would have been horrifying had it continued. There's a reason no one develops that skill. This thing that you did, it's—"

"Dark magic, I know."

"It should never have happened."

"I didn't try to do it. It's not like transformation. I

had to study that for years before I could so much as attempt it. If I have a natural gift—"

"This is not a gift. It's a curse."

"Did the Goddess curse me, then?" I turned to face him. "You put such stock in her will. Why are you so sure that this is not a part of it?"

Phelun frowned. "Instinct. I've had longer to hone mine than you have. Dark magic is one of the unanswerable questions, but we have some understanding of it. Never have I seen it so clearly." He unclenched his fists, which had tightened around the folds in his robe as I spoke. "You were right to let it go. If you stop going into people's minds, this is not something you should take up as a replacement."

"I know. I took quite a beating when my father found out about the dog. Even my family knows better." We were silent for a few minutes. "What exactly are you trying to make me realize, here? That I should give up on using talents I've worked hard to develop, that have served me well for so long?"

He leaned forward and rested his elbows on his knees. "I'm not trying to do anything. You seem to want to leave your family's ways and your brother's lessons behind and move on, perhaps to be a better person, to stop hurting people. I would suggest that you look deeper into your own heart and see whether you really think it's acceptable for you to continue doing this. Killing people isn't the only way we hurt them. You're a powerful Sorcerer. I hope you will use your gifts for good, even if it means starting over in some places and rebuilding different abilities that you can use for better purposes.

"To a certain point," he continued, "I think you are correct about magic being neither good nor bad, only the way we use it. But these things you've done, interfering with people's free will and raising the dead...these things are ultimately never worth their cost to your spirit, or to the world."

My upper lip curled. "You have no idea. I believe that you're educated, that you know much about magic. But you're sheltered here. What do you know about the world I have to survive in?" Every conversation I'd had with people who disapproved of my skills crowded in on me, fueling my anger. "You can't possibly—" A wave of dizziness hit me, and I sat down on the bed. "What did you do?"

He didn't respond, but sat and watched me as he traced his finger over the rim of his wine cup. I glanced at mine.

Cold sweat broke out on my face, and a violent shudder wracked my muscles. "You son of a—" `

The world went black.

Chapter Fourteen

Aren

I woke feeling like I'd been knocked out by a hit to the head rather than a potion, and through the lifting haze of pain I cursed Phelun and wished on him every imaginable torture.

The sun shone in through the window of my little room, and someone had pulled the gray wool blanket up to cover me. I blinked hard, trying to clear the grogginess that made the room swim, and pushed up to sit on the edge of the bed. Pain flared over the top of my skull, then shrank to a single aching spot at the crown of my head when I stopped moving. The blanket crackled with static as it pulled away from my robe. I pulled that off, too, and tossed it in the corner.

Phelun was gone, as were the dishes. Judging by the light, I guessed it to be mid-morning. I'd slept almost an entire day and night.

Every muscle in my body tensed, and my body temperature shot up as my pulse increased, making me light-headed. I took deep breaths, attempting to control the rage that churned inside me and made the pain worse. It hardly helped.

This was what trusting someone got me, what following my positive instincts brought. Severn had been wrong about many things, but he'd been right about this. *No one wants to help out of the goodness of their heart.*

Everyone wants something, and will do whatever they're capable of to get it. Gods, I'm stupid.

I wondered what Rowan would say to that. *Trust people*, she'd said. A fine idea. What would she do now? She'd once talked her way out of a dragon's cave. If these people had ways of protecting themselves from me, I could do worse than to follow her example.

Certainly she wouldn't be overcome by her anger. She'd be upset, let that out, and then think things through. She'd look at things from a perspective that didn't involve the desire to destroy everyone who opposed her.

I could try to calm myself, at least.

When I'd slowed my visceral reactions and calmed my muddled thoughts, I took stock of the situation. My strength was quickly returning, my head clearing, and a cursory inspection revealed that I'd apparently come to no physical harm while I was knocked out. Panic gripped me when I thought that they might have tried to bind my magic, or the parts of it that they considered evil, but everything felt as it had before. Having no minds to control or dead bodies to animate left me unable to test those powers, but I thought they'd left me alone. I held a shaking hand in front of me and managed a weak flame.

They wouldn't dare anger a Sorcerer as powerful as me, I thought, and could have laughed at my own hubris. Obviously they weren't afraid of anything if they'd done this.

I stumbled to the door and tried it. Locked. I slammed the palm of my hand against the lock and directed magic into it. The components groaned, but the lock held, protected by its own magic. I was about to try again, with the force of my frustration along with the magic, when someone knocked at the door.

I slid open the iron panel that sat slightly below my eye level. Brother Phelun's brown eyes came into view, the only things visible aside from his unkempt brows. His eyes revealed no fear or trepidation.

"How are you?" he asked, as though we were old friends meeting after a long absence.

"I've been better," I replied through clenched teeth. "Am I a prisoner, then?"

"Nothing of the sort, I assure you. Is it safe for me to enter? We should speak."

I stepped back from the door. "I suppose you're taking your chances. I'll try to control myself." And I would, I decided. Though my nerves and my temper remained on edge, I wanted to hear him try to explain this.

He stepped away and spoke to another person standing in the hall, and after some struggle the key clicked the lock open.

Brother Phelun stepped in, carrying a breakfast tray on one hand, and jiggled his key to work it out of the lock. "Seems to be stuck. Did you do that?"

"I did."

"Hmm. Just as well I arrived when I did, then."

"I thought you didn't use magic here."

Phelun tapped the door with his fingertips. "This building is centuries old. We don't direct magic ourselves, but that doesn't mean it's not useful."

"You drugged me."

"I did. Will you allow me to explain?"

I motioned for him to sit in the chair.

"To be clear," he said, "if you try anything, I will have you on the floor before you can blink."

"Understood." I would believe him, at least for now. I'd already misjudged him once. "So the stories are true about the Dragonfreed Brothers? All of them?"

"The stories don't tell half of it." There was steel in his eyes today, and determination emanating from him that I needed little magic to sense.

I returned the hard look. "I'm afraid I

underestimated you."

Phelun adjusted his robes as he sat, and I remained standing, ready to run or fight as soon as I needed to. But I wanted an explanation, some reason to believe I hadn't been as foolish as I suspected I'd been.

"You did," he said, and met my eyes without fear. "But I'm glad you didn't leave before I had a chance to explain. What we did was for your protection."

"I hardly think drugging me and locking me up was in my best interests. In fact—"

"The messengers came back with armed soldiers while you slept."

I shouldn't have been surprised. "You knew this was going to happen?"

"We suspected." He looked out the window, where drifted snow sparkled on the outside ledge. "I'd hoped the storm would keep them away. They know our reputation for assisting those in need, even if it's not in their interests, and they knew you might be in the area. It stood to reason that they would come back to check."

"Why didn't you warn me?"

He pushed a bowl of steaming oatmeal toward me. I didn't move, and he smiled. "Can't fool you twice. There's nothing in it except oats and a little sugar. We only needed you out for the night."

"Why? I could have left, instead."

"And been caught, or died in the storm. If they'd seen you leaving, it would have been our necks on the block as much as yours. This was not a risk we were willing to take."

"I could have remained in this room, disguised as one of you."

"No one would have felt the magic in you?" He shook his head. "They have a Sorcerer traveling with them. Perhaps not someone you know, but he would have known that you were out of place here. Your magic had to be invisible when they came."

My skin grew cold for reasons that had nothing to do with the chill in the air. "You bound my magic."

"Silenced it temporarily with a potion prepared by Brother Roched. It's a far more nuanced thing than what happened to your friend."

He watched my face carefully as I struggled to accept his words. I had been powerless. Helpless. Had my stomach not been empty, I'd have vomited.

"We have not survived as long as we have by taking unnecessary risks." He arched an eyebrow. "I'm sure you understand."

"You left me defenseless with enemies in the building? Against my will?" I felt as though I'd been robbed, stripped and humiliated. "Did you not think I would object to this?"

The corner of his mouth twitched. "Why do you think I slipped it into our wine instead of asking politely?"

"You had no right."

Phelun watched my hands close into fists. "I can feel that, you know," he said. "Your magic. The way you're pulling it to you, ready to attack. I can well imagine how it feels to another Sorcerer. To anyone who knows you."

I made no effort to contain it.

He rubbed a hand over his forehead. "Let me put it this way, then. How is what we did to you any different from what you've done to anyone else? Are you angry that we gave you no choice, that we manipulated you to suit our purposes?"

My breath left me in a rush. "I told you, I—"

"You had to, I know. When you did those things, you were protecting yourself and the woman you care so much for. Brother Roched and I were protecting the men who are our family, and an institution that existed long before your family took the throne. Before Tyrea existed. Is this less noble?"

"You would condemn me for what I do, yet do the same to me?" My heartbeat sounded in my ears, and every muscle tensed.

He stretched, arching his back against the hard chair, and met my gaze again. "The world is complicated. Take what you will from this. Is this a reminder that no one can be trusted?"

"Yes." The word came out in a growl that didn't seem to faze Phelun.

"Or might it be an opportunity for you to understand what you do to other people when you use your magic against them? True, I acted against you, and I did it for reasons similar to ones you claim. To protect my brotherhood, but also to keep you safe." He leaned forward, and his gaze held me captive. "Remember how you feel right now. Violated. Confused. Now imagine if you had no idea what had happened to you. Imagine that we hadn't had this conversation, that you woke in an unfamiliar place, or that people told you you'd done things last night that you had no recollection of. Imagine that reality doesn't match up to memories that are clear and fresh in your mind. Imagine you think you're—"

"Stop."

"Insane."

My stomach heaved again. "You could have done anything to me when I was in that state."

"True. Unpleasant thought, isn't it?"

I wanted to choke him until he turned purple, to punch him, to break his mind until he shut up, to turn him into a quivering shadow of the man who sat before me, calm and apparently confident that I couldn't hurt him.

He stood and turned toward the window, leaving his back exposed.

I lunged, and he spun around, moving faster than any human I'd ever seen. Before I could react, he had me pinned against the door with his forearm at my throat, pressing ever harder as I gasped for air. My magic screamed within me for release, but as he met my gaze with his own, I felt nothing. His mind was a wall of marble, impenetrable and unyielding.

I had access to my magic, and it was useless.

He released me, and I dropped to the floor, gasping.

"Who are you?" I whispered.

"I think a better question might be who you think you are, Aren. Powerful? Undoubtedly. Intelligent? Possibly, though inexperienced, and your pride gets in your way. But what else? You're not a prince anymore, if your brother has anything to say about it. Assassin? Killer? What will you use your magic for now? What would you be without it? Is there more to you?"

"How did you block me without magic?"

"Our potions master is quite good, isn't he?" Phelun crouched on the floor in front of me. "You don't understand as much about this world as you think you do. You have been given great gifts, and you squander them. You use them for selfish reasons, to harm and kill and destroy. Do you think this is what the Goddess intended when she blessed you so?"

He offered a hand. I ignored it, instead pushing myself up from the floor by pressing my back against the door and forcing my shaking legs to straighten.

"I don't know," I answered. "Was it her plan for my father and his mother before him to arrange their marriages to produce the strongest children? Was she at work in his bedroom when I was conceived, or Severn? And where was she when my father and my oldest brother turned me into what I am? Where was she when my mother died, when my caretakers were killed, when I lost the only friends I'd ever had? Did she expect me to rise from the cesspool of hate and mistrust I was born into, to turn my back on the advantages of belonging to the wealthiest and most influential family in the world?

To betray them for a deity who's never given a shit about me?"

"You did betray your family, in the end."

"Not for her. You said yourself that the magic I use is dark, and not her will. Yet you also say it's a gift from her. Which is it?"

He stayed where he was, crouched at my feet. "I don't know. But I don't believe she would have sent you to us if you were beyond redemption. There's hope for you, Aren Tiernal."

"So you believe you've done good here?"

"It's possible. The results of our actions are often not immediately apparent. I trust in the Goddess, based on my experiences and what my brothers have learned over the centuries."

"And I trust in myself." I crossed my arms, looking down at him, seething with hatred.

He looked back, but with compassion. His eyes became wet as we stared at each other, reflecting the pain that I didn't often allow myself to feel.

There was a time when I would have called it weakness and turned my back on him. It still made me uncomfortable, but I'd learned from Rowan and my grandfather that my father's ideas on what made a person weak were not the whole truth. Not by far. And though I had no desire to turn my back on *dark magic* for the Goddess' sake, perhaps Phelun was not entirely wrong. Maybe, if I wished to be the hero Rowan deserved and the man my grandfather thought I was capable of becoming, I would have to make some sacrifices.

Gods, it will hurt.

I extended a hand. Phelun grasped my wrist to pull himself up.

"I won't thank you for what you did," I told him.

"Nor would I expect you to." He returned to his chair as though nothing had happened. "We did what we thought necessary. I do not control your response to it."

"So you went through all of this, risked much to help a stranger who you suspected to be dangerous, only because you believe it was the Goddess's will? How do you know she wanted this, that Severn isn't her chosen darling? You might be working against her right now." I was beginning to suspect that the man was mad, though I'd seen no other evidence of it.

He turned slightly toward the window, and a smile flickered over his face. "The Goddess plays a larger game than any of us can imagine. We can't know the purpose or effect of anything we do. We simply play the moves as we are able. Some of us see more, as we remember better how things have played in the past."

"And what will your next move be?"

"To evict you. They found nothing last night, but that doesn't mean they won't be back. I'm afraid you're too dangerous to keep here. Brother Roched is gifted, but our eggshell stockpile is too low for him to keep everyone safe from your magic, should you choose to use it."

"Does he need so much? You have many chickens."

"Dragon egg."

"Ah." I'd met a mother dragon once. I could imagine how difficult it would be to get into a nest and take shells, even when they were no longer in use. "I'll let you save that in case Severn does show up, then. I hope..." I trailed off. I hated the man, and at the same time, I didn't. Even as my blood continued to boil, I understood his need to protect his people. And he'd done no permanent harm to me, as I had to so many.

"I hope that whatever happens, you will be safe here," I said, "and that if we meet again it's under better circumstances."

A mysterious smile twitched at the corners of his lips. "Perhaps we will, at that. The Goddess's will is a mystery."

Chapter Fifteen

Rowan

The less said about my flying lessons, the better. Florizel couldn't fly with a saddle, but she consented to having a thick rope of fabric twisted around her barrel and chest that I could brace my feet against, and I held tightly to her mane when I rode. It was unlike anything I'd ever experienced, smoother than riding a regular horse once we were in the air, but with no control—and with the added danger of falling from cloud-height to my certain death.

At first, I held on so tightly that my arms and legs cramped and my fingers turned white at the joints. But I learned to relax, to feel Florizel's muscles moving beneath me and anticipate her movements. I even opened my eyes after a few lessons, though looking down made me nauseated every time.

Emalda, Albion, and Griselda saw us off on the morning of our departure, a cold day with an unwelcoming, cloudy sky. I pulled my jacket and cloak tighter and adjusted my pack as we stepped out of the school. Florizel waited on the circular carriage path by the door, tail twitching, eager to be off. I wished I felt so enthusiastic.

It hadn't been easy to convince Albion of the wisdom of my journey, especially when I confessed who I would be meeting at the other end. Truth be told, I wasn't entirely certain about it, either. Callum had sounded sincere in his letter. I had never known him to be unkind or cruel, or as devoted to his work as his horrible father, Dorset Langley. Still, I wondered whether I could truly trust him. I wanted to see Callum, to tell him more about the truth of magic, to make him understand that it wasn't evil. Perhaps he'd be able to bring about change within the ranks of the magic hunters, and from there it might spread further.

It was a dangerous proposition. He was still a magic hunter, and my leaving had to have hurt him. In the end, it was for Ashe's sake that I went. Though Emalda and Albion counselled me to stay on the island, they allowed me to go as long as I promised to return as soon as Ashe was safe. Darmid was no place for a person like me.

I would meet Callum at the tavern in Archer's Point as he had suggested, deliver Ashe's medicine to my family, make sure they were all safe, and come back. A simple enough plan, but my stomach turned each time I thought of it. *But Ashe*, my mind would whisper, and I would decide again that it was worth the risks.

Albion offered a grandfatherly hug and pressed a small bag of coins into my hand. "Come back to us soon. And if you happen to see my grandson, you tell him the same."

"I will, thank you." I forced a smile and ignored the ache in my chest. I wished he hadn't mentioned Aren. Thinking about the dangers he faced made me more anxious than thoughts of my own near future. We'd heard nothing. Severn hadn't come looking for him here again, and for all we knew, he'd already captured Aren.

Enough. You don't know anything.

Emalda gave me a few bottles of the potion she'd prepared for Ashe, and a packet of dried herbs with detailed instructions in case something happened to the bottles. "It won't turn out the same without a Potioner's skill," she said, "but it'll be better than nothing." She also gave me a silver flask filled with something to calm my stomach, which I promised to ration carefully.

"Thank you," I said, and was surprised to see tears in her eyes. "Emalda, I'm sorry if I've made things difficult for you by—"

"Hush." She smiled. "We have differences of opinion regarding some things, but you have your reasons as much as I have mine, and you may not be entirely wrong about him. It doesn't change the past, but I do hope you both come back safely." She shook her head. "I never thought I'd say that."

Albion chuckled. "I knew it."

I hugged her, and she let out a surprised wheeze before returning it.

Griselda spoke quietly to Florizel, then turned to me and shook my hand. "Remember that you have power waiting to be used if the need arises," she said. "Trust the magic, even if you don't trust yourself. It will come in time."

I mounted Florizel before my trembling legs could collapse and waved to my teachers, trying to look as though I deserved their confidence.

I can do this, I thought.

I would do it for Ashe, and I would warn Callum about the possibility of Severn attacking Darmid. Maybe it wouldn't make me a hero, but it was all I could do. That, and attempting to change an entire country's beliefs about magic.

No problem.

My stomach clenched as we spiraled away from the ground. I forced my knees to relax and leaned closer to Florizel's neck as the air became colder and thinner. She paced herself so as not to tire, as she could have so easily when carrying an adult human on her back, but we crossed the strait to Tyrea late that morning.

I passed the hours by taking deep breaths of the

thin air, trying to relax my muscles enough that I wouldn't stiffen after we stopped. I focused on my magic, on letting it become a part of me, and found that it felt as separate from me as it ever had before.

No matter, I told myself. I was taking a step toward my destiny, toward finding my place in the world. Taking it alone frightened me, but it also filled me with a sense of purpose and strength I hadn't felt at the school with everyone watching my every move. The rest would come in time.

We stopped to eat and continued on for a short while longer, staying within the cover of low clouds. The forest spread below us as we veered away from the road, trees covered in bright-green buds.

When we landed to make camp, I found that I remembered the place. Though I didn't recognize landmarks, I had seen and felt these hard-barked trees once before, when Aren and I were on our way to Belleisle. The stone forest, though we had to be near its western edge by now. The memories brought back the uncertainty I'd been feeling then, the hope of a cure mixed with confusion about the way he was pulling away from me.

I gave my head a shake and focused on building a small fire, trying not to think about Severn, about the pain, about how close I'd come to losing Aren that night. How close I'd come to dying, myself. We'd saved each other's lives many times on that brief journey, only to end up separated again.

He'll be fine, I reminded myself for what felt like the thousandth time. *And so will you.*

Here on the mainland, the hardiest plants were already sprouting from the ground, providing ample forage for Florizel. I, however, was stuck with rationing what I'd brought with me. I ate enough to keep my energy up, and packed the rest of the dried meat and fruit away. The temperature dropped with the sun and with the dying of the fire, which I didn't dare keep feeding after dark lest someone see the light and investigate. I lay close to the comforting pulse of the glowing embers as I pulled my blankets tight around me, but still I shivered.

Florizel took her time as she settled her big body next to me, forelegs curved on the ground near my head. She spread one of her wings over me. "We could share our warmth," she said.

"Thank you." Her wing smelled like horse and dust.

"We do this with the foals on cold nights back home," she said, her voice nearly a whisper. "Helps everyone. Comforts everyone."

I craned my neck to look up at her. "You've been lonely, haven't you?"

Florizel answered with a nicker and a shuddering sigh. She closed her eyes and turned her neck to rest her muzzle on the ground. Unsure of what else to do, I nestled into the warmth of the feathery cave she'd created for me and drifted off to sleep.

I woke the next morning soaked in dew, my nose and toes frozen, but I'd passed less comfortable nights before.

Florizel didn't speak as we prepared to leave, but I'd dealt with reticent companions before, too. I packed up my blankets and made sure the fire was fully out before I searched for a rock tall enough to use as a mounting block.

"Florizel?" I asked before I climbed up.

"Hmm?"

"Thank you."

She stepped closer and rested her chin on my shoulder, pulling me into a horsey hug. "No, thank you. I'm glad to be doing something again. This may not be what I set out to accomplish when I left home, but it's something. Perhaps there's hope for my mission yet."

I wrapped my arms around her neck. "Of course there is. Always."

We crossed the country far more quickly than I could have on a land-bound horse. It felt like cheating. The journey that had taken me and Aren weeks even with magical help took only days with Florizel. A part of me was glad to be missing out on the dangers below, but I couldn't help wishing I could be down there with Aren, journeying again, just the two of us. It would be so different now that we didn't have to spend most of the trip disliking or mistrusting one another. I'd missed that on the island, too, I realized. Our love was forged in danger, not in safety and dull routine.

I became increasingly comfortable with flight, and even began to look down and appreciate the beauty of the land below us. On my first journey across Tyrea I'd learned about the things that made it different from Darmid, the magical plants and creatures that populated it, and a little geography. From above, I could see so much more. Distant lakes, meadows, tiny towns, and cities larger than any Aren had taken me through. We stayed far enough north that I didn't get a glimpse of Luid, and we didn't pass Glass Lake, where we'd met Kel.

I made a few trips into unfamiliar towns to buy food, thankful for Albion's foresight in giving me Tyrean coins to spend. Anything from Belleisle would still have been gold, but it also would have raised more eyebrows than I cared to deal with.

"Are we near your home?" I asked on our last night in Tyrea, as we settled under thin tree cover. The mountains were visible in the distance, an imposing wall of rock.

"We were a little farther south, but nothing is really far on the isthmus."

"Will you go back while I visit my family?"

"I hadn't thought about it. I suppose I can't go with you. I might have time, if you'll be gone to your family..."

"I won't go to Lowdell to meet them," I said. "It's too dangerous, even with Callum there. But I'll probably be a few days, even if they're meeting me half-way."

I waited as she thought it through. She was an intelligent creature, but it took her a long time to process decisions that didn't involve listening to a herd leader or were not small, day-to-day concerns.

"No, I think not," she said at last. "I wouldn't like to be chased away if I went to them. If I return to the herd, it will be with Murad." She dug into the dirt with a fore-hoof and looked down, shy. "I can see how it might be difficult, but I thought perhaps I'd stay with you. I'm not sure Emalda would ever forgive me if I left you all alone, and Griselda told me we should stay together."

I stroked her neck, and she shivered. "I can't take a winged horse into Darmid, especially if I have to go near a town. They'd kill you, or do God knows what with you." I looked over the massive wings, folded tightly over her back. If not for those, she could pass for a particularly fine-boned horse of the kind my people favored. I smiled. "If you want to stay with me, we'll come up with something. A disguise, perhaps?"

Florizel snorted, and nodded. "We'll stay together. That will be best."

She found a snow-speckled pass between two rounded summits, and we entered Darmish territory by passing high over a quiet border guard station that sat near the Tyrean foothills. The mountain range was narrower than I'd always thought, really just a few lines of worn-down old mountains. Not at all the great protection we'd been taught they were. From our great height I could see nearly from one end of the isthmus to the other at its narrowest point. The sea glinted to the north, while mists shrouded the south, where my family lived.

We could just go to them, I realized. *Forget*

Callum and fly to Lowdell. I almost told Florizel to turn, but decided against it. Without a magic hunter on my side, I'd be an easy target for any others who spotted me. At least Callum could warn them off. And I had no idea where my parents planned to meet us. We might miss them completely.

So Callum it was. I tried to bring his face to mind, and had trouble. So much had happened since I'd last seen him.

As we landed on the Darmish side of the mountains, I felt the magic surrounding us lessen. Not my own magic that I carried with me—that would be safe enough as long as I wasn't using it. But something changed, something I could feel deep in my bones, the way a person feels a storm coming.

But this wasn't a building storm. This was a dissipation of energy, and returning to my homeland filled me with dread and a sense of loss. Florizel sniffed at the air as we landed on the trader's road that led toward a cluster of Darmish mountain towns. "I don't like it here. The feel is bad."

"I know. Do you want to leave?"

She shook her head, and walked on.

We had landed well away from the village of Archer's Point, and left the road as we drew nearer, before anyone could spot us. Callum wasn't due to arrive at the inn there until the next day, and we'd have to make camp again. In the meantime, we needed to figure out what we were going to do about disguising Florizel.

I tried tossing a blanket over her back, but it made her look lumpy and suspicious. We needed more, and I thought I might have an idea. I stayed out of sight and watched for an opportunity to present itself.

A carriage passed, pulled by a pair of dirty white horses, and then nothing for hours. I'd sent Florizel off to forage on her own when a small group of soldiers marched up the road, passing directly beneath the heartleaf tree where I rested on a thick branch. I held my breath and hoped I would be well-enough hidden if any of them looked up. They didn't, though they turned their heads to scan the forest on either side of them, on high alert.

We were luckier with the travelers who passed by as the afternoon light grew dim, traders returning from Tyrea. They spoke in quiet voices, but seemed in good spirits. A brunette woman laughed and said something about cold ale and songs, and a few other people muttered their approval of the plan. There were five of them, riding and leading several large packhorses, their baskets and carriers nearly empty save for a few burlap-wrapped packages. They all stopped short when I stepped out onto the road ahead of them, scarf wrapped tight around my head and hood pulled up to hide my hair. My dark eyebrows wouldn't trouble them, but the bright red locks would give me away.

"Pardon me," I said.

"Well that's unusual," said a man whose thick mustache trailed down past his chin. One of his companions shushed him.

"Good afternoon, my love," said the woman, and the familiar phrase and accent of my home country warmed me to her immediately. "Are you all right?"

"Fine, thank you," I said. "I came alone. My friends and I didn't want to frighten you. I do need help, though. Would you be interested in selling the pack carrier off of one of your horses?"

The mustached man raised his heavy eyebrows. "Why? Have you found some treasure you need to carry down from the mountains? Because I'm sure we could help with that, for a share."

I chose my words carefully. They were Darmish, but that didn't make them friends. Not to me. Not anymore.

I pasted a bashful smile on my face. "No treasure.

Not unless you count wood and tree bark." I patted the tree I'd been resting in earlier. "We can't find heartleaf near my home anymore, and my mother needs the inner bark to help with her pain." I lowered my gaze to the ground. "I know it's illegal now, but..." I thought of my brother, and when I looked up at the riders again my eyes had filled with genuine tears. "It's the only thing that helps."

"Oh, my dear," said another man, this one sporting a black beard peppered with gray, with a face underneath that looked like he'd been smacked with a broad board. "We'd be happy to help you carry it ourselves. Are you going to Archer's Point? We're passing through there."

"No," I lied. "We thought we'd look around here a bit more, and then we're going south. You can't spare anything?"

The three who had spoken glanced at each other. The other two, a man and another woman, waited in silence behind them.

"I suppose that depends on what you can offer," said the mustached man.

"Davis," said the woman, a soft admonishment in her voice. She looked tired and ready to be in a warm bed, but she didn't act as if she was in a hurry to be away. I liked her for that.

"What?" he said. "It'll cost us to get another made. If she can pay us that much, we can talk. How much do you have, girl?"

"I—I don't know exactly," I stammered. I had no idea what that might cost. "I don't have the money on me. I can go ask, if you tell me how much we need."

Davis narrowed his eyes at me. "Are you hiding something, dear?"

The woman smacked his arm. "She's being careful, you idiot. Doesn't want us to rob her."

"Hmm. Eighty, then, if it's a frame and baskets

you want and not a saddle. That'll get us fixed up when we get back to Ardare. We'll just have to hope we don't come across a good opportunity along the way that we might've needed that pack for."

"His generosity never ceases to humble me," the bearded man said, and winked at me. "We'll wait."

I went back into the woods, careful to make sure that no one followed. I estimated how much Tyrean coin would equal seventy Darmish goldens. They likely expected to barter, and I couldn't afford to spend more than was absolutely necessary. As it stood, this would leave me with few coins, and hungry if Callum didn't pay for my meals on the road. But it would disguise Florizel if I couldn't convince her to hide herself or leave me.

Davis hemmed, hawed, and groaned about taking a loss for a stranger. I protested in return that I had nothing more to offer and agreed to take their oldest rig. In the end we made a deal for a rickety set-up and a few baskets. He counted the foreign currency carefully and without question, and motioned for the woman who hadn't spoken to remove a pack horse's things.

The lightweight, wooden frame had ribs to strap the baskets to, and had been made for a horse significantly larger than Florizel. I accepted it with thanks and hauled it back to the woods, politely refusing their offers of help. I stopped out of sight and listened to them leaving, speaking a little more loudly now, pleased with the deal they'd made.

I didn't make the straps tight, but we tried the frame and my bag on Florizel before we lost the sunlight. It wasn't perfect or comfortable for her, but the large size meant that there was room for her folded wings underneath. I arranged the blankets under the frame to cover her wings and her rump, where feathers protruded. It would have to do, and I would have to walk while she wore it.

We moved farther from the road, and I removed

the frame. Florizel stretched and flexed her wings. "I can't say I like it. Makes me think of being tied up, unable to fly. Do we have to tighten the straps?"

"Not if you can balance it, I guess. We're in trouble if it falls off, though."

"It won't."

I placed the frame back on her. "Show me what happens if you rear up."

She did, and the contraption slid to the ground. She hung her head. "Is that bad? We can do the straps."

"No. Please listen." I stepped closer, and her ears pricked forward. "I think things will be fine, but there could be danger." I swallowed back the trepidation that filled my throat. "If something should happen to me, I need you to do exactly what you just did. Free yourself, and fly."

"Griselda said—"

"Stay with me, I remember. But you've done enough, and you getting caught won't help. If something bad happens tomorrow, fly away. Go back to Belleisle and let them know what happened. And stay safe. Please."

She let out a long, shuddering breath. "I will. I only wish I were braver."

I put my arms around her strong neck. "I couldn't have come this far without you."

We followed the evening routine we'd established over the past week. My dreams that night were filled with the people I knew, people I hoped to see, those who I missed, those who I worried about. It was a lot to dream on.

I woke exhausted, but excited to be moving again. I dressed in the only skirt I'd brought with me. It was ankle-length, loose enough that I could still run if I needed to. Much as I wanted to look presentable, my safety was a greater concern. I made Florizel's disguise as perfect as I could. She plodded convincingly behind me as we made our way up the road to Archer's Point, and none of the few people we passed gave us more than a quick glance.

The tavern was a dark little place at the edge of town. Florizel went into the woods to wait. She'd made me agree that if all went well, if Callum played fair and seemed open to accepting magic, she could accompany me to Lowdell. The idea still troubled me.

I tied my scarf tightly around my hair before I entered the building, and kept my hood up until I found my way to a booth in a back corner. The place was busy, and I barely made it into the seat before someone else had a chance to take it.

A young barmaid approached and nodded over her shoulder at the crowded room. "You could sit at the bar if you're alone, miss."

"I'm waiting for someone, thank you. A young man. He'll find me."

She chewed on her lower lip and tapped her shoe on the dirty floor. "Not a handsome fellow with long hair and a mean look to 'im, is it?"

"No, why?" And then I realized why Archer's Point sounded familiar to me. Ashe had mentioned it when he told me about the dangers of magic, about Aren's involvement in a magic hunter's death.

He'd been here, back when he was the Aren I feared. I shivered.

"No reason." She gave her head a hard shake and smiled thinly. "Soup?"

I couldn't refuse, and decided to spend a coin on a meal. I'd nearly finished the thick squash and potato stew with fresh bread when Callum entered.

He didn't see me at first, sitting as I was in the back of the room. He looked good. Obviously losing me hadn't been as hard on him as I'd worried, and I was glad of that. His sandy-brown hair had grown out a little longer than it was when I last saw him, though it was still well within the limits of what the Darmish considered fashionably acceptable. Everything else was the same—Prince Charming good looks, broad shoulders, confident stride when he entered the room. He spoke to the barmaid, who nodded toward me. I stood and he hurried over, a slight smile touching his lips.

"Rowan." His smile widened as he clasped my hands in his own. He looked me over, taking in everything, and I was glad I'd covered my unnatural hair. Better not to let him see a visible reminder of how I'd changed. "You're really alive."

"I seem to be," I said, and grinned back with relief. Perhaps I'd worried for nothing. "You're looking well."

His blue eyes searched mine as we sat. "I'm so sorry."

"Callum, none of this was your fault."

He leaned back and waved to the barmaid. "I didn't keep you safe as I promised I would," he said after he ordered his drink. "I should have accompanied you. Maybe I could have done better. Maybe..." He studied the foam at the top of his glass. "Did they...I hope no one hurt you. I tried to get you back, you have to believe that. I rode out as soon as I could, but you had vanished."

"We were hiding from Severn. Aren helped me escape less than a day after the attack, before their ship sailed from whatever port we were in. We traveled through the mountains to Tyrea, and on to Belleisle."

Callum nodded. "I got that from your letter, and it frightened me. That must have been horrible for you, being abducted by someone like that."

"It was fine," I told him, beginning to realize how awkward this situation was. When I wrote to Callum I'd left out most of the details of my relationship with Aren, not wanting to hurt him more than I already had. "It was my choice to go with him. He didn't hurt me. He helped me. Saved my life." I lowered my voice. "About the rest of that letter…"

"Yes." His brow furrowed, but his expression opened again before he continued speaking. "The magic?"

I looked around to make sure no one was listening. Even this close to the Tyrean border, people were funny about magic, especially in humans.

"I didn't know what to think about that," he admitted. "I was angry. I thought you must have known, that you'd lied to me, but I talked to your mother about it."

My heart leapt. "What did she say?" I still didn't know anything about my early childhood, how and when my magic had been bound.

"She had it done not long after you were born, and she acted alone. You had some accidents when you were younger, before it really took, and they sent you to live with your aunt and uncle to keep anyone from noticing."

"Thank you for not arresting her over it," I said.

"I couldn't fault her for trying to protect you from magic. And if she went about it by illegal means…" he shrugged. "Sometimes you have to fight an enemy with his own weapons. I haven't reported any of it, officially."

Not yet, I thought. But the threat would always be there.

"She said that she'd never told you about it," he added. "She thought it best that no one know. She thought you'd be angry and demand that she somehow undo it, even if it meant risking your own life. I suppose she was right, in the end."

I started to reach across the table to take his hand in a gesture of comfort, but stopped myself. I didn't want to send the wrong message, and something about him seemed wrong. His words were kind, as was his voice, but I sensed tension in him. *Careful, Rowan.*

"The binding was causing my headaches," I said.

"It was killing me. My life was in danger either way, and I wanted answers. It's not like everyone thinks, you know. Our people are wrong about magic being evil. It's a tool, not a curse, and can be used for so much good. It doesn't happen the way we thought. All of the people who—" I hesitated, but decided to push on. There was still a chance he would listen. "All of the people your father and the king and the other hunters have killed over the years were born with magic. They didn't choose it."

He studied my face, then smiled sadly. "You look different. I can't place what it is, but it suits you."

"Thank you." My unease grew. I ran a finger over one of my eyebrows, and stopped myself before I could pull a lock of far brighter red hair out from under my scarf to twist in my fingers. Instead, I folded my hands on the table.

"We'll get rooms in Renton tonight," he said, "half-way between here and Lowdell. I've sent word for your parents to meet us there tomorrow morning. You came alone?" He had surely scouted the building and asked around outside before he came in, but his eyes still darted to the windows.

"I did," I said slowly. "I have a horse, but otherwise, it's just me. Callum, can we talk about the magic?"

"He's gone, then?"

I crossed my arms. "He's not with me right now."

Callum nodded. "I see."

"I'm sorry, Callum, but I think we have more important things to discuss. You said you wanted to talk about my experiences with magic."

His jaw tightened. "Yeah. I'm sorry, too. It might be easier for me to take if you hadn't left me for someone we've been watching for years, who is a danger to us, who hates our people. But what does that matter, right? Magic, and all of that. Who wouldn't wander off with a known enemy, a killer, for a chance at that?"

I felt my magic moving within me, and I pushed it back. I had no idea what it might do if I set it free. Letting it out could kill everyone in the place if I wasn't careful. "Aren's not like that. He was, but he's changed."

Callum raised an eyebrow. "What? He changed for you?" He shook his head. "I'm sorry, I don't believe it. But you're here now, and that's good. Maybe it's not too late for you."

"I'm fine," I said again, my voice harder.

"Obviously." He drummed one thumb against the edge of the table, deep in thought. "This is hard for me, Rowan. I thought things were settled between us, thought we were going to be happy."

My magic settled, as did my anger. Perhaps he'd been hurt more than I realized.

"And then you left," he continued, "and I was so angry with myself for failing you. When your first letter came, I was relieved to hear you were safe. Part of me didn't believe it. I recognized your handwriting, but I thought he might have forced you to write it, to make sure I wasn't looking for you. Then your second letter came, delivered from Belleisle. By a bird, no less. I believed it then. After I got past the anger, I wanted you to come back."

"Callum, I—"

"I wanted you to come to the city, to see the people at the university who have been working on your problem. They're close to having a cure that doesn't involve binding magic, but removing it completely. In the meantime, we could control it. It's the beginning of a new era."

He said it as though he were offering hope instead of insulting me and everyone like me. I felt myself hardening to him again. *This was a mistake. He'll never listen.*

I stood and gathered my cloak close around me. "I don't need a cure. It's been nice to see you, Callum, and I hope this ends things for you. I'm going to leave now. I can find my way to Renton on my own."

"Please sit down," he said. Not threatening, but his voice had gone flat. "I'm not finished. I was going to say that I see you now, and I understand what you are. The life you and I were going to have together would have been good, but it's not the right thing for you anymore. I'm not going to try to convince you that it is." He rubbed a hand over the light stubble on his jaw. "You're not the woman I asked to marry me, are you?"

"No," I said, softly.

He nodded. "I'll be happy to take you to meet your parents, and I'll tell you on the way what's happening with your brother. If you really don't want any more help, if you want to go back to that other place, I'll even see you back to the border. Now that we've talked things through, I think I can move on. I want what's best for you."

He sounded like he meant it, but the words came too easily. I still didn't trust him. He couldn't help what he was any more than I could. "Thank you," I said, "but I'm not sure you know what's best for me."

Or anyone, I added to myself. A feeling of fairy-wings fluttered in my stomach, and my legs ached to run. If Florizel and I flew now and kept out of sight, perhaps I could find my family on the road before Callum did.

He looked down at his hands and tapped his thumbs together. "I hope we can forgive each other for everything that's happened, in light of our past together."

"Callum, did you hear what I said? I can't go with you."

"I heard. I'll walk you out. Dinner's on me." He put a few coins on the bar as we passed, and held the door open for me. "Rowan?"

"Yes?"

"I really am sorry."

A semi-circle of ten men stood outside of the

door, soldiers in their blue uniforms among them, weapons drawn, blocking escape. I called on my magic, and felt it filling me. It grew stronger, ready to act, if only I knew how to let it out. *I don't care what you do*, I told it. *Just get me out of here.* The magic seemed to agree as it burned brighter and hotter than I'd ever felt it before. I lifted my hands, unsure of what I was doing.

A flash of pain flared at the back of my head, and the world disappeared.

Chapter Sixteen

Rowan

The barmaid's screams sounded far away at first, coming to me as they did through a wall of black fog that muffled everything. I wished she'd shut up. My head throbbed, and as the sound drew nearer it pierced my brain like shards of glass. *Just let me sleep...*

But I wasn't sleeping. Not really. Even with my eyes closed the world came into focus around me, the feel of a hard bench under me and my cheek pressed against it. They'd tied my hands behind me, and my shoulders were stiff and sore. Someone walked by, close enough that the breeze of their passing made a loose lock of my hair tickle my nose, and I held back a sneeze. We were still in the tavern. The air smelled of spilled ale and old wood polish, and faintly of vomit. I didn't think the latter was mine, but it was a possibility. I remembered nothing after I saw those hunters.

Though I tried, I couldn't think of a magical solution to the problem. Any other Sorceress would surely have been out of the ropes by now and in the woods, calling for her trusty steed and making a dramatic exit. Anything I tried left me with the risk of burning the place down around me, and I assumed Callum would leave me there to die.

I settled for trying to undo the knots without drawing attention to myself.

If only the damned noise would stop. The screams faded to sobs, with Callum's reassuring voice interspersed.

"She's fine," he said. I opened my eyes slightly. He stood next to the bar, behind which the young woman stood, trembling. "She'll wake up soon, and we'll get her out of your way."

"I need a new job," the barmaid whimpered. She wiped her face with a bar rag and squared her shoulders. Callum placed a small bag on the bar which clinked as the coins inside rubbed together. My coins. The barmaid picked it up and slipped it into the pocket of her dress. "The hell with this place."

Callum crouched beside me. "Good morning, sunbeam." He brushed my hair back from my face, frowning at the bright strands that tangled between his fingers. I winced as he pulled back, taking several with him.

My tongue stuck to the roof of my mouth when I tried to speak, and I found my voice had left me.

Callum pulled the hairs free from his hand and let them drift to the floor with a look of disgust. "It's so obvious now, but God, you hid it well. Even my father didn't sense magic in you. I still don't know how that Tyrean knew what you were. But he did, didn't he?"

I didn't say anything, and he reached out again and gave my hair a sharp tug.

"He did," I croaked, and cleared my throat. "Before I knew, myself. He saved me."

"Did he?" He sneered. "I'd like to see him try that again. Come on, we're leaving." He grabbed my wrists, holding both between the fingers of one hand, and pulled me to my feet. I stumbled, and he jerked me up before my knees could hit the floor.

I caught the barmaid's eye on the way out, and she looked away. She wouldn't want to help someone like me. No one in my country would.

The world seemed to move around me rather than me through it, though I felt my legs and Callum's force pushing me forward. I felt the sun warm on my shoulders and breathed the forest-scented breeze, and took no comfort from either.

Stupid, I thought. Too trusting, just as Aren had always warned me. I had felt guilty over leaving my family and Callum behind, and had so desperately wanted to make things right with them that I had actually believed it was possible. I had remembered Callum as I knew him before, kind and trustworthy, ambitious and clever, and had trusted my hopes over my instincts. In my excitement over the idea that he might learn from my experiences, I had forgotten one thing that was now perfectly clear.

The moment he learned what I was, Callum had stopped thinking of me as Rowan, the woman he'd once wished to marry, and had started seeing me as a monster to be brought down.

What have I done?

Callum untied my hands so I could ride the plodding gray mare he provided for me. Six soldiers in royal blue uniforms surrounded me, accompanied by four more men in dark grey clothing, each wearing a copper medallion on his chest. Magic hunters. I'd only seen them dressed that way when on official business such as bringing a prisoner to court, never while hunting. I supposed they wore them now to warn folk not to approach us.

Callum rode slightly ahead, with my horse tied to his. Florizel had disappeared. I hoped she'd taken off as soon as she caught wind of trouble. She wouldn't have been able to do anything against these men.

As we rode, I fought to pull myself from the shocked daze that had clouded my thoughts since I woke in the tavern. I studied my captors, watching for some sign of sympathy, and found none. They wouldn't even look at me. Not until I let my magic well up in me again. The moment I turned my attention to it, Callum rode closer. I didn't have a chance to do more before he quietly said, "I can feel that."

"What?"

"Trust me," he muttered, "you don't want to try anything. You're surrounded by magic hunters, and the best ones in Darmid at that. We're trained to know when there's magic about, when you're going to use it. If these boys so much as get a hint that you're about to attack, I've given them permission to kill you."

I straightened my shoulders. "How do you know I don't have skills to protect me?"

He chuckled, and the sound turned my blood to ice. "Try something, and we'll find out."

My magic might help me heal if I were badly injured, might even create a diversion to help me escape, but here on the open road I'd have an arrow in my back or a dagger through my throat before I could make it more than a few paces. I wouldn't survive that. I forced my magic back inside me as I had so many times before.

Callum smirked. "Good choice."

Maybe it's not too late, I thought. *If I can just make him see me as the person he used to care for, make him see that I didn't choose this...*

The landscape of my home country unfolded as we descended from the mountain pass. The borderlands were as I remembered, though I'd never passed this way before, tiny towns embracing the road every so often, each of them huddled around a crossroads and surrounded by farmland that held the dark and dangerous forests at bay. We didn't stop, and were not permitted to speak. Callum refused to even look at me. I tried to calm my racing heart and mind, to organize my thoughts into a rational escape plan, but my mind had been rattled. I reached up to the back of my skull and felt a lump there, covered in dried blood that caked in my hair.

At least it's a different type of headache, I
thought, and fought to keep myself from dissolving into
lunatic laughter. I'd escaped this dragon's cave only to
run directly into its jaws, and not for the first time.

We went left at a sign indicating that we were
turning toward Ardare, capital city of Darmid and home
of the king and his magic hunters. My stomach turned.
Though I'd visited the city a few times, I'd only heard the
vaguest rumors about the prisons there. Certainly I'd
never heard anything from anyone convicted of using
magic. They never got a chance to talk about them.

I tried not to think about how right Aren had
been. I was too naïve about the darkness in people I
thought I knew. *I'm sorry*, I thought. He'd have accepted
an apology this time. I'd certainly failed badly enough.

So fix it, I told myself. *You still have your life,
your wits, and your magic if you keep your eyes open
and spot a chance to use it. Don't give up yet.*

The sun broke through the clouds that afternoon,
bathing a green-dotted field in golden light. "Lovely
weather for persecuting innocent people," I commented
to the soldier beside me. He didn't look over, but
frowned.

"Rowan," Callum muttered, and shot me a dark
look over his shoulder. "Don't make this worse."

"It can get worse?"

He didn't respond, but untied my horse from his
and dropped back, still holding the rope, so that I rode
beside him. He looked over at me, and the muscles in his
jaw flexed as he clenched his teeth. He waved a hand at
the hunters riding beside us, and they fell back, leaving
the two of us alone.

"You could have let me be," I said. "None of this
had to happen. I was in Belleisle, for God's sake. I wasn't
hurting you or anyone else in Darmid. You made the
effort to write to me, to trick me, to gather this crew to

meet me. Why?"

"Why?" He shook his head in something between anger and bemusement, and kept his gaze fixed on the road ahead. "Where shall we start? Perhaps it's because I lost a lot of credibility when everyone found out what you are. Can you imagine what people thought? Dorset Langley's son, on-track to become the next great magic hunter in the family, finds this wonderful girl and falls in love. Too bad he didn't know she was exactly what he's supposed to be hunting."

"I didn't know, either," I said, careful to keep my tone soft and reasonable.

His lip twitched. "It doesn't matter. There are still whispers about me. Gossip at parties. How funny that this should happen to Callum. How the mighty have fallen. He should have chosen someone from his own circle in the city to marry, not a girl from the borderlands."

"If I'd known—"

"And you got away, that's the other problem," he continued, as if I hadn't spoken. "In any case, I have orders. Even if I'd been willing to let all of this go, my father wouldn't have been. He disliked you, you know. Didn't trust you, though even he didn't know why. You can imagine his rage when he found out what he'd let slip through his fingers."

"Who."

"Pardon?"

"*Who* he'd let slip through his fingers. I'm a person, not a monster." He looked away, and my heart sank. "But you know that, don't you? You asked me to come to explain this to you, and you already understand it perfectly. You know we're born this way." I looked back at the others, a few of whom watched us with great interest. "You all know."

Not one acted like he'd heard me.

"I knew," Callum whispered. "There's a lot you

don't understand, Rowan. You think that because you are what you are, because we keep this secret, that you're right and we're wrong. There's so much you don't know."

"Then explain it to me. Make me understand how what you're doing is noble and good."

He was silent for a few minutes, and I thought he was going to ignore my request. It hardly mattered, really. I had little hope that letting him say his piece would make him more open to hearing mine, but I wanted to know how they justified it to themselves. Perhaps he would hear in his own words the mistake he was making, or I would learn something helpful.

"You're clever enough to remember your history lessons," he said at last, "even if you've never had all the details. Hundreds of years ago our people lived under the boot-heels of Sorcerers and Sorceresses in Ferfelle."

In fact, I'd never heard the name of that old land. We weren't even allowed to know that much. I kept my silence and waited for him to continue.

"They used their power to control those without it. Those who had no magic, no matter how clever or strong or otherwise talented they were, lived as slaves or servants to those with magic. When they overthrew and destroyed the oppressors, they fled the land and vowed never to let such a thing happen again. They thought that as long as there was no magic among them, they would be safe."

"But more magic-users were born?"

He frowned. "Things would have gone right back to the way they were if the magic-users were allowed to live. Our ancestors had to take precautions, rid their new land of magic however they could so that even if magic-users survived, they'd have less power. They said that magic was evil, that it was a sin, that it was a choice made at the cost of a person's soul. They taught the children to fear magic and anyone who used it, to report friends, neighbors, even family who used it. And for hundreds of years and many generations, we've worked toward the complete elimination of magic. It's the only way to protect those who don't have it."

He looked at me like I was a venomous spider in the shadow of his boot. "People like you are a threat to our freedom."

"You truly believe that?" I asked. "You think that every poor farmer you've executed for raising crops by magic, every person who's used his gift to locate water for a drought-stricken village, every innocent baby you've had killed for showing signs of magic was planning to overthrow the king?" My voice grew louder, harsher. I didn't hold back. "What about the helpers? The Potioners who would heal the sick, the Sorcerers capable of doing the same? The farmers who could help prevent famine, the—"

"It's too much of a risk. They'd have realized soon enough that they could take power if they banded together. Tell me, are things better in Tyrea? Do they not rule by magical force?"

I opened my mouth to answer and realized I didn't know. Severn certainly didn't sound opposed to using magic to get whatever he wanted, and their throne went to the strongest Sorcerer. It *could* happen. "I haven't spent much time in Tyrea," I said, choosing my words carefully, "but I think they've had good kings in the past who ruled fairly. Belleisle isn't under anyone's thumb. It's not ruled by magic at all, and Sorcerers and non-magical folk live in peace. They have for centuries."

He snorted. "It won't last forever."

I shook my head. His mind had been made up for him long ago. "So why not let everyone in on the secret? Gain support from the people instead of lying to them?"

"The regular folk don't understand," he said, and shot me a sideways glance before looking out over the massive pit-quarry we approached, an open wound on the land where a few men loaded squared-off blocks of stone into wagons. "You should know that as well as anyone. I saw your drawings of dragons and such when my father went through your things after your letter came. He had me help with the investigation. Let me try to prove myself. I saw your illustrations of those stories, and Felicia told me all about your obsession with forbidden things. Think of how easily you were swayed by the words of an enemy. Too many people might have that kind of sympathy toward magic, especially those who have lost children. It's better this way. Fear is more effective than enlightenment. It's for everyone's own good."

"The people you've killed might disagree with that assessment," I said. He didn't reply to that. "So who does know the truth?"

"Magic hunters learn it after we pass training and initiation. The old king knew. I don't know whether my father has enlightened King Haleth yet."

"What about historians?" I thought of my uncle Ches, who spent so much time in Ardare, working for the king. He had married a woman with suspicious gifts relating to plants, had lost two children under mysterious circumstances, and had never taken his family to the city where others might have seen that they weren't normal. Not the actions of an ignorant man.

"Some," he said. "Most of that information isn't available to scholars. We're now being even more careful about that, removing old documents from private collections and libraries."

He seemed so relaxed in giving me this information. It gave me hope that perhaps his attitude toward me was softening. *No*, I realized. Not softening. It simply didn't matter to him. My breath caught in my throat as I realized that he felt comfortable telling me all of this because I would never have a chance to share it with anyone. He planned to see me dead, and as far as I could tell he had no problem with the idea.

He gripped my horse's lead-rope tighter. "You're never going to understand, are you?"

I decided I wouldn't let him see my fear. "I doubt it. Callum, would you ever have told me all of this if we'd been married?"

"I hoped I could. You seemed so open-minded, and I thought you might understand. Support me. It seems I was wrong on that, too." He shook his head, slowly and sadly. "Things are changing, Rowan. If you could see the danger, we could help you." His eyes filled with concern. "We could take this burden from you, remove the magic. You could be an example. Give the land hope. Think of the babies that could be saved if we make this work."

It shamed me that a tiny part of me wanted to hear him out. I could live. I could see Aren again if I made it out of Darmid alive, though I wouldn't be the person he'd grown to love. I could have a long life instead of a few miserable days in some dank cell. And all it would cost me was a gift I'd never asked for. That and my integrity, and the world that had opened up to me when I learned what I was.

My magic twisted inside of me. I thought of Aren, of Griselda and Albion, people who had given so much to help me become my true self. I pictured the magic-users killed by these hunters, the faces on wanted posters in Lowdell. My lost cousins. I would not turn my back on them, no matter what the cost.

"I'm not interested."

"You'd rather die than become a normal person?"

It was my turn not to respond. His gaze turned to a glare, his lips compressed to a hard line, and he signaled for the others to rejoin us.

We stopped for the night at an inn in a small town. Everything there was built of brick or stone, and it gave the place a cold feel that I immediately disliked. The inn was a busy place, but they made several rooms available and served hot stew and fresh bread, and didn't ask questions. I imagined that Callum's gold went a long way toward all of that. I forced myself to eat, though my stomach protested. If I escaped, it might be a long time before I had another good meal.

There wasn't a single sympathetic face among the men at the table, and I gave up searching. I located all the potential exits, then kept my head down and sopped up the last of the gravy in my bowl with warm bread.

"I heard it was a blummin' massacre," said a voice in the corner, and I turned my attention to the conversation.

"You can't trust the news from over the border, though," responded a rough-voiced fellow.

"Still, if it's true, that's a shame. I mean, not that I care for Wanderers meself, but I never minded that lot when they came by. They'd almost made it over the border, too."

I glanced over in time to see the rough-voiced one, a dirty fellow in a faded brown shirt, nod toward the magic hunters. "They'd have had no peace here. Not with that lot around."

I turned to ask these strangers what Wanderers they spoke of. Surely not the group who had helped me and Aren. Callum grabbed my arm and squeezed until I turned to face the table again. "Mind your business," he muttered.

I looked around the room. There had to be some way out. Some way to use the crowd. Griselda could have created an illusion, frightened them into confusion. Aren could have bent their minds, started a riot and slipped away. My magic wakened. *Perhaps I could...*

Callum didn't stop his conversation with the hunter on the other side of the table, even as he pressed the tip of his dagger into the soft flesh beneath my ribs. I turned my thoughts back to non-magical means of escape, and my magic quieted.

And then it was time to go to bed. We'd be on the road again early in the morning.

My hands remained unbound, but Callum held tightly to my right wrist and guided me up the stairs. He stopped to let me use a windowless toilet room before turning in to a small bedroom filled with a large bed, a washing basin, and an opaque screen in the corner. The only window was high on the wall and too small to climb through.

Callum folded his arms over his chest and watched as I scanned the room. He closed the door, then sat on the bed to remove his boots. "Keep those clothes on. I don't have anything else for you to wear."

"You—you're staying in here, too?" I asked, trying to seem unconcerned.

"Funny, isn't it? If things had gone as they were supposed to, we'd be married by now, and you'd have been sharing a bed with me since midwinter, at least. Now you're with me against your will, and I can't risk leaving you alone to piss without worrying that you're going to disappear." He stood and walked barefoot toward me, and I stepped back until I hit the wall. He reached out to cup my face in his hand. "You should have been mine. Sweet Rowan." I wanted to look away, but I couldn't. He rubbed his thumb over my cheekbone, tenderly, then pushed me toward the bed. "Get in."

"No."

"You're not in a bargaining position. I know what you're thinking, but you have nothing to worry about. You assume too much about your own appeal if you think I'd defile myself with a magic-user. We're only sharing the bed so you don't get any ideas about leaving. Don't make me angry, though. You'll regret it."

I stood there for a minute, deciding whether I believed him. In the end, I sat down and took my boots off, then slipped under the uppermost blanket. He left the room, telling someone outside to keep an eye on the door.

Callum returned a few minutes later and closed off the oil lamp. Silence followed, and then he climbed into the bed. My muscles twitched as the lumpy mattress shifted under his weight.

"Go to sleep," he muttered.

I didn't think I would, but I must have drifted off. I woke to the feeling of a hand running from my waist down over my hip and resting on the outside of my thigh before retracing its journey back up to my ribs. Callum sighed, then rolled away from me.

I lay in the dark, eyes wide open and unseeing, waiting, but he didn't touch me again.

A few silent tears fell onto my pillow before I could convince myself that it wouldn't help to lose control. All I wanted was to be back in Belleisle. Memories of my last night with Aren burned vivid in my mind. I remembered sleeping with one of his arms thrown over my body, holding me close, and drew comfort from that even as the memory deepened my regret over leaving the island.

At some point I drifted off again, and Callum shook me awake as the sun rose outside of that tiny, useless window.

"Move," he said, and I did. If I was going to escape, it wouldn't be there or then. I'd have to wait and see what came next.

Chapter Seventeen

Aren

After I left the Brothers I tried to forget everything Phelun had said, to let go of the way I'd felt when I woke. Betrayed. Confused. Enraged. I couldn't examine my own feelings without remembering how Phelun had connected them to the way I hurt others, and so I refused to think on any of it.

I managed to forget while on the road, where the physical tasks necessary for survival distracted me. But in quiet moments of the evening, after I'd put away the maps the Brothers gave me, when I lay on my back, looking at the stars, I couldn't help but remember. Phelun's words crept into the corners of my mind, into my bones, drawing me to the conclusion he hadn't had to state aloud.

I am a monster.

I focused instead on my plans. Travel to the town of Stenbrach in Durlin, locate my uncle, and see what he knew about my father's disappearance. Perhaps it would be nothing, but I had nowhere else to start.

Even when I tried to think of more pleasant things, I found I couldn't escape. The only memory of Rowan I could bring to mind was the look on her face when she realized the full extent of what I could do to people. She'd been horrified, heartbroken, because by then she'd had feelings for me that didn't line up with that reality. Then the words of Mariana and Arnav, the mer elders, came back to me. *You will have to learn again who you are, decide for yourself what it is you value, what you live for when your family isn't all you have and are.*

So who am I? I wondered.

I'd spent several months not using my most powerful skills, but I'd still known they were there, available whenever I chose to defy rules that only bound me because I allowed them to. And I had been miserable. Even when I took the task more seriously and genuinely tried to reach the potential Rowan saw in me, I had felt like half of myself. I couldn't live like that, denying my nature and my gifts. True, I'd hated myself for things I'd done while in Severn's service, but at least I'd felt alive then, and useful. I'd been doing what I was born for, though it had hurt people. And I couldn't regret hurting people who deserved it.

But not everyone did. Had I stayed with him, Severn would eventually have sent me against Albion. I would have gone, not knowing that the man was my grandfather, not caring that he was kind, or that he spent his life educating young magic-users, or that he would never use his power against me the way I would have against him. I'd have done my job.

I rolled onto my side and used my arm to block out the moonlight, but still sleep wouldn't come.

Perhaps I wasn't the best judge of how my power should be used. Maybe Phelun was right, and it always did harm, no matter how careful I tried to be. I'd thought I wouldn't harm the shopkeeper, hadn't I? Just a little push, enough to get me what I needed and leave her unharmed. Though I'd be more cautious about small magic in the future, I couldn't say it wouldn't happen again.

But to give all of that up would mean losing myself, turning my back on the things that made me feel most alive. Was it possible for a man to draw moral lines in the dirt and refuse to cross them when he'd already been leagues past? And if so, did I want to?

In the end, I changed into my eagle body to get a respite from the questions, and slept. We travelled through the day, and I spent the next night the same way when late snows blanketed the ground in a thin layer of white.

I found the road to Stenbrach early in the morning of my third day out from the monastery, and soon after topped a hill above the town, which spread before me in a shallow valley. I glanced up at the sky, where clouds gathered again, higher this time. I urged the horse forward, toward what I hoped would be shelter and safety.

That would depend entirely on whether Severn had convinced our uncle that I was the enemy.

There weren't any people out that I could see. Smoke rose from several chimneys in town, smudging the gray sky. No wheel tracks over the fields, though a few cut through the already-melting slush on the roads. I had never visited my uncle, but it was easy enough to identify his estate on the outskirts of town. I found his house at the end of a long, winding drive, a white stone building with large windows and a welcoming porch. I tied my horse to a hitching post and climbed the wide steps to knock at the front door.

There was no point sneaking around. Either he'd help me or he wouldn't.

A well-dressed servant answered the door. He looked me over, taking in my rough clothing and the shaggy horse I'd left in the yard.

"Xaven Tiernal?" I asked for my uncle.

"May I say who's calling, sir?"

"I'd rather not."

"Who is it, Stanwold?" A young, female voice.

The doorman turned to answer. "He won't say,

miss. I don't believe your father is expecting anyone?"

A pretty face appeared beside him, bright-eyed and framed by brown hair that curled over her shoulders, probably a few years younger than I.

"Good afternoon," she said. "You have business with my father?"

"I have. Is he here?"

"It's all right," she said to the servant, and he stepped aside. She turned back to me and smiled. "Won't you come in?"

"I'll alert your father, then, and have someone see to the horse." The doorman walked stiff-backed up a wide, curving staircase.

The young woman watched him go, then turned back to me with a friendly smile and clasped her hands in front of the full skirt of her blue dress. "You seem familiar to me."

I gave her a pleasant smile. "I'm sorry I can't say the same."

She narrowed her eyes slightly, but seemed more curious than suspicious. I saw enough without prying to think she meant me no harm. *Not that that means much...*

"Follow me, please." She led me into an elegant parlor where a small fire burned in the hearth. A few chairs covered in striped fabric sat in the center of the room, arranged for conversation.

"You must be cold," she continued. "Shall I call for tea while you're waiting?"

"That's kind of you. Thank you."

"We do try to be hospitable."

My cousin leaned out the door and spoke to someone, then came and sat down beside the fire. Hard as I tried, I couldn't remember the names of any of my uncle's children, whom I had never met.

I took the seat opposite her, facing the door. I reached out with my magic, trying to sense any other presences, anyone hiding, any possible traps. There was nothing. I settled back into the chair, but kept myself ready to act if necessary.

My cousin seemed completely at ease in the company of a stranger who, I realized, must be looking fairly rough after several days on the road. I wanted so badly to take a look inside of her mind, to see what was right there on the surface, but couldn't bring myself to do it.

Damn you, Phelun.

Her relaxed attitude told me she believed she could handle trouble if I caused it. But then, any man who had survived growing up in my father's family would make sure his children were as competent as he. Though I remembered my uncle as a kinder man than my father, he'd had great strength in him. I wondered what it would be like to grow up with a father like that, competent but pleasant. It didn't seem to have hurt this woman.

"My name is Aren," I offered.

"That's why you seem familiar, then," she said, and nodded.

"Have we met?"

"No. But you remind me of your father."

A maid entered, carrying a tray with a pot of tea, three cups, and a few sweets and sandwiches. She wore a black dress and a neat white apron—nothing odd about her appearance, save for the faint blue tone to her skin. I didn't stare, or ask. She left us alone again. The scent of hot tea and fresh ginger-bread drifted from the tray, and I realized how hungry I was.

"I'm Morea," my cousin said.

"Pleased to meet you. You know my father, then?"

"Oh, yes," she said, and poured two cups of steaming tea into delicate floral cups. Her posture was perfect, her motions elegant. A well-bred young lady. I was glad her father hadn't sent her to live in Luid, as other wealthy families did with children they hoped would make powerful connections there and marry well. It never failed to ruin them.

"We visited Luid several times when I was a child, and your father came here...oh, a few years ago. Before he went away. Is that why you're here?"

"That's part of it. Do you know where he was going?"

The cup and saucer felt ridiculously fragile in my hands. I waited for her to sip her tea before I tasted mine. It was strong, prepared the way they did it in Luid, with a spice mix and warmed milk already added. I did miss these little luxuries.

"I didn't speak to him," she said. "He was quiet. Kept to himself, except when he spoke with my father."

That didn't sound like the Ulric I remembered. He was loud, powerful, commanding. Intimidating. Not quiet.

"My father will be here soon, I think." Morea set her cup and saucer on the table and leaned back in her chair. "Do you need anything else?"

I wanted a bath, a shave, and a good meal, but said, "No, thank you." Accepting hospitality was one thing. Demanding it was quite another.

When my uncle entered the room, he looked just as I remembered him from at least a decade before. Tall, gray-haired and thickly bearded, he wore a perfectly tailored vest to accommodate a prominent belly. The man had little magic in him, but it seemed to be enough to keep him healthy.

"Aren," he said, and offered a friendly handshake. "It's been too long. You've grown."

"You haven't," I replied, and he laughed.

"I hope not." He patted his stomach. "But I don't expect this is a social visit."

"No. You've heard about what's been happening with me, with Severn?"

Xaven poured himself a cup of tea. Morea stood

and moved to another chair so he could sit next to the fire while we spoke. "I've heard many things," he said. "We received word months ago that we were to alert Luid if we heard from or saw any sign of you. The explanation was simply that you'd been convicted of treason and were to be returned for sentencing."

"Should I be prepared to leave in a hurry, then?" He wouldn't have told me about the order if he planned to obey it. Still, I did another quick check to make sure no one was listening in.

Xaven waved his hand through the air, dismissing the idea. "Not at all. I'll confess that I'm curious as to what happened, but your brother..." He shook his head and added a heaping spoonful of honey to his tea. "Things have not been good. I don't know what you did, but I'm choosing to stay out of it, either way."

"If you don't tell him I was here, you've already become involved. Probably on the wrong side." I didn't know how much he knew about the situation, and didn't care to share more than I needed to. "He didn't lie to you. I betrayed him. Disobeyed orders. Stole from him, I suppose."

"The girl."

"So you do know something about it?"

"There were rumors. Where is she?"

"Somewhere safe. For now, at least."

"Hmm." He didn't have to ask why I'd have saved someone from my brother. "So you left, you've stowed this other person away somewhere, and now you're back here. Why? I'm afraid if it's shelter you're looking for, I won't be much help. I'm happy to let you stay overnight, but it's too much of a risk to myself, my family, and my household to let you stay longer. If Severn knew—"

"I know. I wouldn't ask that of you."

Morea stood. "I'm going to speak with Stanwold. He'll tell everyone that we have not had a visitor today."

"Thank you, my dear," Xaven said.

"She's a good girl," he told me after she left. "Helpful, too."

"Gifted?" I hadn't felt magic in her, but it would have made sense given her lineage.

He took a long sip of tea and raised an eyebrow over the edge of his cup. "Not a Sorceress, no. A Potioner, and talented enough that Severn would drag her off to Luid if he knew. Gods know how he would use her."

"You're right to keep her out of that, especially now."

"Indeed. You wouldn't remember her, I suppose. Your father and I had very different ideas about raising children, and we kept all of you apart when my family went to the city. It's nothing personal against you. I hope you understand that."

"Of course. Even if it were personal, I would understand. My family is a terrible influence. On anyone, actually."

He nodded.

"I'm not here to request aid," I continued. "I only wanted to ask whether you had any idea where my father might have gone when he disappeared. After he left, no one could find any record of his plans, and he didn't send word. If Severn knows, he never told anyone."

"You don't think your father told his advisers?"

"If he did, it didn't matter. I think most of them were working for Severn before Ulric's disappearance, and those who didn't support Severn are long gone."

Xaven frowned. "It's a terrible thing. My brother and I were never close, especially after he took the throne, but it saddened me to have him go missing. All things considered, you know."

"You don't have to hold back. I think we have the same thoughts on these matters."

"Very well. Especially with your brother next in line. Is that why you're searching for your father?"

"I don't see any other realistic way to take the

throne from Severn. Something has to be done. He's planning a war with Darmid. He's turning many of his own people against him, and I don't think things are going to improve. I thought I knew what was going on in his mind, but I'm starting to see how wrong I was. So I'm left with finding my father, if he lives, and soon."

We sat in silence for a few minutes, eating. I was still famished when the food was gone.

"Tell me," Xaven said, "what do you know about your father? He's only been gone a few years. I assume you remember him well."

"Well enough. He didn't have much time for me when I was a child, especially after my mother died. When I grew up, it was Severn who worked to develop my abilities, not Ulric. I saw my father in council meetings, though I wasn't a member at the time. They allowed me to sit and watch proceedings there, and when he held audiences. It was all much less exciting than I'd expected it to be. I remember him being efficient. Cold. Hard."

"He'd settled down by then," Xaven said. He rose from his chair and prodded the logs in the fire with a long iron. "If you'd seen him when he was younger, and I mean by a century or so, you'd see where Severn gets his headstrong and power-hungry nature from. Ulric was much more reasonable about his foreign relations than Severn is, but he didn't like to be told what to do, either."

"Do you think Severn will mellow with age?"

"Perhaps. But I don't think there will be time for that."

"Then you agree that I should find my father."

Xaven breathed out hard. "It's not the worst thing that could happen, I suppose. Unless you can think of anyone else who might be interested in taking the position."

"Absolutely not." I was neither interested nor qualified, in spite of the strength of my magic.

"It was only a thought," my uncle said. He leaned on the mantel and watched the flames flickering behind the iron grate. "Yes, I think bringing him back is a good plan, if he lives. You know, your father was a hard, cold man, but there were a few years when that wasn't so."

"Because of my mother?" My heart skipped, though I couldn't say why. Anything I thought or felt about that part of my past had been long since walled away. It didn't matter anymore.

"Hmm." Xaven turned his attention back to me. He seemed troubled. "You know about their situation?"

"Little enough, I suppose. Were you there when she lived in Luid?"

"No, I never met her. I heard things later, some from your father. He cared for her quite a lot."

"If he cared for her at all, he wouldn't have killed her, would he?" I said, more harshly than I meant to. It seemed everyone I spoke to on my journey had a way of opening old wounds. But I wouldn't let the walls crumble.

Xaven cleared his throat. "He didn't kill her."

"Fine. He wouldn't have had someone else do it, then."

My uncle raised an eyebrow. "No, I mean he didn't."

I struggled to make sense of his words. Surely he didn't mean...

His eyes searched mine, and then he sat down and pulled his chair closer. "I don't know whether he told anyone but me. I think I only know because he got too deep into the wine cellar when he last visited. He probably didn't remember that he'd said anything."

My skin prickled. "What did he tell you?"

"That he sent her away." He paused, observing my reaction. I realized my mouth had opened, and closed it. "Her and your sister. He knew that his position was in jeopardy if he didn't get rid of them, and he couldn't let the throne pass to Severn then. He was only a boy, impulsive and irresponsible. So your father sent them north, to the dragon-occupied country. Cressia."

My stomach dropped, and I felt glad I was already seated. I'd never questioned the fact of my mother's death. It had devastated me at the time, and I'd fought to leave it behind me. My father's insistence that no one speak of her had been so complete that I'd thought perhaps he felt some measure of shame or pain over killing her. This was too much.

It can't be true.

My uncle rested a hand on my arm, and I realized my hands were shaking.

"It's a lot to take in, isn't it? I'm sorry I didn't tell you sooner. Your father would have had my head, and you seemed to have moved on. It wasn't my place."

I barely heard him, trapped as I was in my own reeling thoughts. It seemed an odd question to have to ask. "I have a sister?"

"Twin sister. She was a well-kept secret. No detectable power at birth, or before they were sent away. What did they call her, now? Ava? No. Avalon, it was. Family name, though I don't expect there's any official record of her birth. Our family is superstitious about twins, did you know that?"

I shook my head to rattle my thoughts into some semblance of rational order. "Something about power being divided?"

"Doesn't seem to have been a problem for you, but your father couldn't afford rumors."

My pulse pounded in my ears. *I lost so much. Grieved so deeply. Lived a life of emptiness and pain in Luid, and she was...* I fought back the bile that rose in my throat. It should have been good news. It was. But all I could understand in that moment was what I'd lost.

My heart slowed. *Focus on the issue at hand. Nothing else matters.* "So my mother is alive?"

"I don't know. All I know is that she was, and your father deeply regretted sending her away."

"You think he went to find her."

"It's a possibility. I don't know, though. Perhaps he didn't. Perhaps he did, and died on the way. It seems he'd have come back by now if he could have." He sighed. "I'm afraid it's all I have to offer in the way of information."

"It's more than I expected. Thank you." My voice sounded like it came from someone else.

My uncle nodded. "I'm glad I could help a little. You look..." He leaned in closer. "Will you be staying with us tonight? You look like you could use another meal, a hot one, and a long rest."

"I think I will." I rose and shook his hand.

Morea returned to show me to a guest room. She chatted amiably as we walked up the stairs, but I found afterward that I couldn't remember a single thing she'd said.

What's done is done, I reminded myself as I lay on the bed. *You can't change it. Eyes on the future now.*

If only I could dam the flood of memories. My walls had been shattered. All I could do now was try not to be crushed by them.

Chapter Eighteen

Rowan

My captors were in high spirits after our night at the inn, chatting and laughing with each other as they tacked and loaded the horses outside of the stable. Not one of them so much as looked at me until I loosed my hold on my magic, if only slightly. That earned me suspicious looks as a few hands went to weapons.

I quieted it again, and found it obeying me more readily than it had before. Perhaps my attempts to connect with it were helping something, after all. I wouldn't know until I tried to use it.

We rode through the morning, passing through a vast and quiet forest. The men watched carefully for danger from outside of the group now as much as within. Callum wasn't speaking to me. I couldn't say I minded, but there were a few things I still needed to know.

"What about my parents?" I asked after lunch, quietly enough that no one else heard.

Callum frowned at me. Dark circles ringed his eyes, and I took comfort in the thought that his night had been as wretched as mine. "They're not expecting you."

"And my mother's letter?"

"That was genuine. I offered to have it delivered for her, but that's the only contact I've had with them recently. She sealed her letter in an envelope with a suggestion in the postscript that you be cautious of me. I removed that, of course."

The ripped page. "Of course you did."

"I doubt they'd have welcomed you. Do you know how much pain you've caused them? If this has been hard for me, imagine how much worse it's been for them. No one believes that they didn't know what you were. And your father a magistrate, too."

"I didn't—"

"I know you didn't. You didn't think about what your little adventure would do to anyone here, did you? You just met tall, dark and evil and followed him out of the country, not once thinking about your family. Or me."

"That's not fair, Callum." A few soldiers looked at us. Callum waved them off, and I lowered my voice as we mounted our horses. "It's not as if I had a better option. The magic would have killed me if I had stayed and married you. You'd have lost me either way." I'd have said more, but I wasn't going to get anywhere by aggravating him. I turned my thoughts forward, toward the city.

"What about Felicia?" I asked. "You said you spoke to her." I'd sent her a letter as well, and not heard anything back. I didn't want to drag her into this, but if it came to me needing a friend in town...

Callum shrugged. "She's living on Pine Hill in Ardare now. Nice part of the city, in a pretty blue house like she says she's always wanted. She's expecting a baby, but keeping it quiet for now."

My heart leaped in spite of my own circumstances. It had never been something I wanted, but Felicia had always desired a large family. She was her parents' only surviving child, and she said she wanted to spoil them with grandchildren. I closed my eyes and prayed silently that the child wouldn't be like me. It would meet an early end if it was. Nothing would change in Darmid, and Felicia had married a magic hunter. No child of hers would be safe.

"It's too bad about Robert, though," Callum continued. "Bad business."

He didn't provide any more information, so I had to ask. "Her husband? What's happened to him?"

"A dragon happened, that's what."

I resisted the urge to reach under my scarf and touch the pendant that hung there. I only knew of one dragon in Darmid.

"We went hunting it, and it killed him. This was nearly two months ago. Felicia's holding up well, though I'd say you'd find her changed. She's being taken care of, anyway."

"That's terrible." I swallowed back the lump in my throat. "Had it been attacking people?"

"Close enough. It was attacking livestock, eating or stealing cows and horses, carrying some of them away. We had to stop it, of course, and we knew it had young hidden away somewhere. We were searching in the mountains, following what trails we could find, and it attacked us from behind. Most of us survived. Robert was caught. We couldn't save him."

I thought of Ruby's massive claws and curving teeth, and felt ill. She wasn't what I'd call a friend, but I'd spoken to her, and I'd seen her three dragonlings. She was an intelligent creature and devoted to her young. If she'd thought that humans were a threat to them, she certainly would have attacked.

My heart broke for Felicia. She'd been so happy when I last saw her, bubbly and lively and excited for her beautiful future. "What did it look like?" I asked, just to be sure.

"Big. Terrible. Red as hellfire. Hideous."

I hadn't thought Ruby hideous. Terrifying, but her glowing scales were beautiful, and there had been an odd grace to her sinuous neck and body that I'd noted even as I feared she would eat me. But it was certainly her.

"Is she—is it dead?"

"Not yet."

In spite of the terror the dragon had brought me when we met, and the fact that I'd nearly met the same fate as Robert, I felt relieved that she still lived. One more piece of magic surviving in Darmid, fighting back against the hunters.

"What about Ashe?" I asked. "Have you seen him?"

"He's with your parents. No change in his condition." My heart sank. Even if I could have trusted Callum to deliver it, I'd lost Emalda's potion when I left Florizel. Everything was probably in a heap on the forest floor, or wherever she'd dumped her disguise.

He watched me, monitoring my reactions. I took a lesson from Aren and tried to keep my expression neutral.

"He wasn't aware of much when I was there," Callum added. "It's probably a blessing. He was as upset as I was when you disappeared. I think he blamed himself for what happened after. Thought he should have been able to stop you."

I closed my eyes and tried to digest the idea that Ashe might be ashamed of me and suffering for what I'd done.

No, suffering for our people's beliefs about magic. I couldn't let Callum make me blame myself. That would get me nowhere.

There didn't seem to be anything else to talk about after that. I watched the road, noting landmarks and how the landscape was changing around us. Though we passed through a variety of landscapes, no opportunity for escape presented itself. As the sun crossed the sky, I felt an invisible noose tightening around my neck.

Act now, part of me whispered. *You're dead if you don't.*

And dead if I do too soon, I answered. Surrounded as I was, my only hope was to somehow release a blast of magic that would kill them, as I'd done the night my binding broke, and I had no way of knowing whether I could manage it. If I failed they would kill me, and the thought of success filled me with cold horror. I couldn't kill, even if they were willing to do the same to me.

Coward.

We kept going until evening and stopped at another inn, this one quieter, with dirt-tracked floors and with the sharp stink of burnt meat in the air. The room the innkeeper showed us to had a large window, and my mind raced as I made my plans. But Callum shook his head, and the innkeeper led us to a garret room with only a tiny window that let in barely a stream of light.

Killing Callum seemed like a potential plan, but I knew I couldn't do it. Magic was too uncertain, and if I missed my first chance, I wouldn't get a second. Even if I succeeded, the guard outside the door would be on me before I could make another move.

I wished I'd had time to work on some kind of physical fight training at the school. Surely Griselda knew something about it. Or Aren could have, had we been allowed more lessons and not had to focus so much on magic. Too late now.

I took my necklace off and tucked it into the toe of my boot when I had a moment to myself, then wrapped my body in a blanket, cocoon-like, before Callum joined me in bed. I lay awake for hours, waiting to be sure he was asleep, heart pounding every time I thought of moving. When his breathing became slow and deep, I propped myself up on my elbow to see where he'd stored his dagger. I spotted it clenched tight in his fist.

Damn.

When I turned my attention to his face, his eyes were open, watching me. He smiled and motioned with the knife for me to lie down. I did, and had no sleep that night.

We reached the outskirts of Ardare the next morning, and my heart crept into my throat at the sight of the stone walls. I closed my eyes and fought for calm. Narrow streets, if I remembered correctly. Alleys. A marketplace. Though I was hardly familiar with the city, I had to hope it would provide some opportunity for me to slip away and hide.

I tried to bring the name of Felicia's street to mind and felt a flutter of panic as I realized it had slipped from my exhausted mind. It had been an option of last resort, true, but if it came to that... *Elm? Birch Path?*

Callum let out a cough, and I opened my eyes. "Whatever you're thinking, stop now. They'll go easier on you at the prison if you cooperate."

I could have made a good guess at how full of excrement that statement was, but I didn't speak. My voice would have trembled.

The capital was the largest city in Darmid, the jewel in our culture's crown. No danger of dragon attacks here. Though I'd noted the decrease in magic before, it was nothing compared to what I felt as we neared the city. It seemed to disappear completely. The fields outside of the walls showed a faint haze of green overlaying rich, brown dirt, but everything felt empty and lifeless. And I had never felt it. I'd been so cut off from that part of myself that I hadn't been aware of the land's ambient magic at all, or noticed it in other people.

Anger flared in me, hot and sharp. *They've already taken so much from me. They won't have my life, or my magic.*

I shivered, and nudged the fragment of dragon scale with my toe. *Remember what Griselda said.* My magic felt constrained here, held back in a way I never managed on my own, but it was there, and strong. Its time would come soon, whether I was ready or not.

"Cover that hair," Callum ordered. "Drawing attention to yourself will make things worse. We'll reach the complex soon enough."

"And then what happens?"

He shrugged as though it didn't matter. "That's for my father and the magistrates to decide, I suppose."

"You're going to let them kill me?" Even now I hoped he might change his mind.

Callum's eyes grew colder than I'd ever seen them. "That's the penalty for using magic here."

"My magic is only here because you brought me back. Do you really hate me that much?"

A look of uncertainty passed over his features.

"Callum, please."

He only shook his head as his expression closed off again.

I wrapped my scarf around my head and pulled my hood up. Callum nudged his horse toward the city, and mine followed. Callum's magic hunters left us at the gates, leaving only the soldiers.

Ardare is a city of winding roads that intersect each other at odd and seemingly random angles. I doubted I'd be able to find my way out even if I had the opportunity. If I didn't try, though, I was as good as dead. I'd never have a chance to master my magic. I'd never see Aren again, or Florizel, Celean, or Griselda.

I noted landmarks, but the tall buildings all looked the same to me, and I found the street names difficult to remember. Nothing in this section of town was familiar. I tried to track our direction by the sun, but lost track as we turned through the streets. I broke out sweating, and my heart raced faster with every block.

Don't panic. Eyes open.

We headed down a narrow side-street with the men leading their horses single-file and me riding. My heart continued to pound, but with excitement. I was no longer surrounded. The soldier directly behind me had his sword drawn, but he kept letting it fall to his side as he scratched at a red rash on his neck. A weak link in the chain.

Now.

"Callum?" I called, letting weakness come into my voice. "I'm going to be sick."

"No, you're not," he said.

"Give me a minute. I need to throw up." I swung my leg over the horse's withers and slid to the ground, gagging for emphasis.

The soldier behind me looked away, disgusted.

"Stay there!" Callum yelled. He let go of the horse he was leading, but it backed up beside mine, blocking the road. I lost sight of him. "Rowan, don't you dare move! Steef, grab her!"

The big soldier hesitated, and that was all the time I needed. I ignored the fearful pounding of my heart and focused instead on the flame of magic within me, on accepting it as a part of me. It flowed through my body, concentrated and growing.

A cistern sat not far away, filled with rainwater. I had no time to think what I could do with it. As long as my magic did *something* and didn't kill me in the process, I would be happy. Magic flowed more easily than it ever had before, flashing through me like a river, tingling through my muscles and over my skin.

Not the oneness that Griselda had described. I didn't care. It was beautiful.

The barrel burst, spraying my horse and Callum's with freezing water. Mine reared and cut off Steef's approach, and I bolted down the long alleyway next to me.

"Rowan!"

The street behind me erupted in confusion.

Heaps of rubbish crowded the alley, and I nearly tripped over a skinny black cat that hissed as I passed. A wooden gate blocked the end of the alley. I scrambled over it and kept running.

I crossed the tiny yards behind the buildings and entered a wider alley that opened onto what I took to be a main street. A few pedestrians gave me odd looks, but I kept moving, trying to look like I belonged in the crowd despite the unfashionable clothing I wore and the hood I held tight to my face. I cut through side streets at random as I came to them, running when no one seemed to be looking, not bothering to try to remember where I'd turned. I was already lost. It didn't matter where I went, as long as I didn't turn back.

They would expect me to run toward the gate we'd come in. They wouldn't find me there.

Yelling and clattering sounded behind me, several streets away. I found another narrow street criss-crossed by clotheslines and packed with carts and boxes. I wound my way past them and emerged on another wide road.

I leaned against a dirty wall for a minute, catching my breath and gauging my surroundings, then walked on. The buildings that surrounded me were built from soot-stained stone. Large windows lined the walls at street level, and shops displayed their goods behind them. Hats, candies, fruits, even a store devoted entirely to toys. The scent of fresh-baked bread and something sweet reached me as I wandered down the street, and my mouth watered.

I moved past the bakery and crouched in an alley around the corner of the building where the smell wasn't so strong. I rested my head in my hands for a minute. *Calm. Focus.* I expected my magic to feel greatly diminished, but when I reached for it, I felt little change. But then, my entire body was abuzz with fear and the rush of physical exertion. I'd have to take stock again later, after I found a way out of the city.

But how to escape? I couldn't get back to look for Florizel. I had no money to send a letter, and even if I did, no one from Belleisle would get to me before the hunters tracked me down.

I knew where Felicia's parents lived, but they wouldn't help.

Felicia would. She'd been my best friend once, and if we'd grown apart a little as our interests changed, that had never affected our love for each other. I hated to drag her into my troubles, especially if she were grieving her husband and expecting a baby, but where else could I turn?

Of course, Callum would think to look there. But if I could find her, beg for clean clothes, maybe a little gold and a good way out of the city...

A door opened beside me, and the bakery smells came wafting out stronger than before. "My dear?" asked a female voice, filled with concern. "Are you all right?" The large woman had a kind, deeply lined face, and had styled her silver-gray hair in a pile atop her head. Her pink dress and white apron were spotted with flour, but her hands were clean.

"I don't know," I said, deciding to be as honest as I could afford to be. "I'm a little bit lost."

She dumped a bowl of food waste into a small bin and held out a hand to help me stand.

"I'm looking for..." I hesitated, trying to remember. *Come on...* "Pine Hill." I couldn't help smiling in relief. "I came to visit my cousin, but the traders who brought me only came this far, and they're gone now. I don't even know whether I'm going in the right direction."

"Oh, poor dear," she said, shaking her head. "Who gave you to traders? Not the most trustworthy traveling companions."

"No one, I'm afraid. I don't have any family left back home. My cousin's not expecting me, but I didn't know where else to go."

"Oh, my." She looked over my dirty clothes. "You poor thing. Are you hungry?"

"I am." I'd been too nervous to eat that morning, and it wasn't helping me think any more clearly.

She held the door open and I entered the kitchen, where she poured me a cup of tea and cut a thick slice of white cake. Not the most sustaining meal, but I wasn't going to complain.

"I don't have any money left," I said, and she shook her head.

"I could tell you stories, my dear, about how strangers have helped me, but I don't think it matters right now. We're all human, we all care for one another, eh? We're not heathens."

"No, ma'am." I seated myself at her worktable, and she passed me the food.

"Will you take off your cloak, dear? I must say, it's...most unusual." She didn't recognize the Tyrean style, thank goodness. It was the one Aren had given me the day he took me off the Tyrean ship, charcoal gray wool lined with dark pink. I reached under the deep hood to make sure my hair was still tucked away beneath my black scarf and inside of my dress, and lowered it.

"Is that—" She raised her eyebrows toward my scarf.

"Mourning, ma'am," I said, and lowered my eyes. "I don't suppose it's the fashion here in the city?"

"No," she said, and leaned on the counter, "but it suits you well. Don't leave your hometown's traditions behind on our account. No one will think you rude for it."

"Thank you for all of this. I suppose I should get out of your way, though, and let you get back to work. You said you know where Pine Hill is?" I tried to maintain my table manners, but found it hard not to shovel the cake into my mouth. I'd never tasted one with such a balance of heavy texture and light sweetness. I let the icing melt against the roof of my mouth.

"Oh, that," she said. "You're not too far. I could—" A bell rang in the front of the shop, and my heart skipped. My hostess excused herself, and my leg muscles tensed as I prepared to dart out the back door.

She returned a minute later. "Trouble," she said, and frowned. "Escaped prisoner. Magic, even. Can you believe that?" I shook my head as I finished the strong tea. "I don't say that sort of person will go unnoticed for long. Anyway, I'll be locking my doors more carefully until I know they've caught him." She shuddered. "The very notion. Magic. What was I saying?"

"Pine Hill?" I made myself sound calm and pleasant. Inside, I was screaming.

"Oh, yes. Would you like me to have someone escort you? You need to be careful with criminals about."

"Not if it's close, thank you. I don't want anyone to go to any trouble."

She opened the door to the front of the shop and watched the people passing by outside the windows. She seemed to forget about me as her attention turned to the threat she assumed was outside.

"Miss?" I prompted.

She turned back. "Well, you turn left here, go eight blocks and turn left again, then the first right, and that street's called Pine Hill. It's only the one street. You have an address?"

I nodded. I had "blue house." It would have to do.

I thanked my hostess again, and she took a rag, dampened it, and used it to wipe a smudge of dirt off of my face. "That was bothering me," she said with another kind smile. I hated to think how that smile would disappear if she knew what I was.

She made me promise to bring my cousin back for tea, then wished me well and waved goodbye. I walked quickly and with purpose, ignoring the people I passed. When I looked back over my shoulder, the baker was leaning out the door, looking up and down the street, motioning for a younger woman to come over to speak to her. I pulled my hood back up and kept walking, counting the blocks and repeating her instructions in my head. Eight blocks, left, first right. Blue house. I listened, but I didn't hear any indication that anyone was following me.

I didn't know whether I had any real chance of escaping, but I was going to try.

Chapter Nineteen

Rowan

Pine Hill was much as I'd pictured it, a cobblestone road bordered with evergreen trees, curving slightly as it climbed a low hill and lined with fine-looking houses. Not all were large, but each of their owners clearly took pride in them, as evidenced by fresh paint and neatly trimmed hedges. People who lived in houses like these could afford to hire others to do the maintenance for them. Felicia had done well. It was everything she'd wanted.

Or it would have been, if not for Robert's death.

Most of the homeowners on the street had elected to paint their houses in sombre shades of brown or gray, a fact that would make my search easier. I walked up the hill and stopped on the road beside a slate-blue cottage with ornate white trim under the eaves. An elderly man came out with a little girl holding his hand, and the girl waved at me. I waved back and kept walking.

I listened for the sound of hoofbeats charging after me, and heard nothing. Perhaps Callum thought I wouldn't be so foolish as to come here.

I nearly missed a house tucked behind tall shrubbery, but I caught a glimpse of the upper level from across the street. Its light and cheerful blue paint seemed outlandish on this pretty, yet dull, street. I crossed and stood at the gate, but saw nothing to identify the house's owner. Just a neat garden and white curtains shut tight. When I looked back, the old man and the girl were standing at the end of their path, watching me. I reached in to unlatch the gate as though I belonged there and hoped they'd forget about me.

The bell at the door made a pleasant tinkling sound that reminded me of the cave fairies I'd once met. Felicia herself opened the door, dressed in a loose, lavender-striped dress with lace at the collar, and wearing thick wool socks on her feet. Her hair, once the envy of all who met her, hung in limp, golden ringlets over her shoulders. Other than looking a little tired, there was no sign she was pregnant. Not in that dress.

She clapped her hands over her mouth and stared at me, wide-eyed with disbelief. "Rowan?"

"Hi, Lecia," I said. "Mind if I come in?"

She looked past me to the street, then stepped aside. Her brows knit together, emphasizing lines in her forehead and around her eyes that hadn't been there a few months before.

"Rowan, I...I didn't expect to see you here. What's going on? Wait, let me have Sally put on water for tea. Sit in the parlor, you look exhausted." She hesitated, hand laid over her heart, then reached out to squeeze my hand. "My God," she whispered, and hurried off.

"I really can't stay for tea," I called after her. She didn't seem to hear.

I made my way into the room she'd indicated, an open and airy space decorated in light gray and cream. A scallop-edged patch of dark paint over the mantel indicated that something had once hung there and kept the paint from fading. A mirror, perhaps, or a painting. There were few other decorations in the room, and nothing that showed off the vibrant personality of the house's owner. This was a grown-up house.

I passed by the pale couch, not wanting to stain it with dirt from the road, and sat instead on a stiff, pewter-colored chair. I kept an eye on the door and an ear open for boots on the porch, but all was silent and still.

Don't relax, I reminded myself, even as I sank back into the chair and stretched my legs out to take the pressure off my aching feet.

Felicia returned with a teapot and cups on a silver tray. "I told Sally to take the evening off. I thought you might appreciate some privacy." She sat on the sofa, as close to my chair as she could get, and leaned in. "Rowan, I thought you were dead until I got your letter, and then I just...I didn't know what to say. Thank God you're here. Is it all true?"

"It is," I said, and took the scarf from my head. The room was too warm for it, and I didn't see the point in hiding anything from her. She tensed when she saw the unusual color of my hair, but didn't comment on it.

"I won't stay long," I said. "I don't want to bring trouble. I just need—"

She placed a hand on my knee, though only for a moment. The easy familiarity we'd once shared was gone, but her smile was as kind and welcoming as it had ever been. "Don't even think of rushing off. We'll get you set up with whatever you need, but please. Just tell me what happened. I've missed you."

I smiled. "I've missed you too, Lecia, and I have so much to tell you." I explained briefly what had happened since I received Callum's letter, leaving out the part about me flying to the border on a winged horse, not mentioning the small bit of magic I'd used in escaping. She knew what I was, but I didn't think she'd want to be reminded of my association with magic more than necessary. She listened quietly, shaking her head and murmuring her shock at the appropriate places, refilling my teacup when I emptied it.

"I heard about Robert," I said. "I'm so sorry."

Felicia twisted the amethyst ring on her left hand and took a shaky breath. "Thank you. He died doing what he felt called to do. I suppose that's more than most people can say. And there's the baby coming."

"I heard that, too. I'm so happy for you. You'll be the best mother."

She smiled and wiped her eyes with a white handkerchief that she pulled from the sleeve of her dress. "I hope so. It won't be easy, but if all goes well I won't be unmarried for long." She didn't have to say that *if all goes well* meant the baby being born normal. If she proved she could bear healthy children who were unaffected by magic, she'd be back to having her pick of the best suitors in town, if perhaps more mature ones than she was accustomed to flirting with at parties.

"As to your problem," she continued, "I don't know what to tell you. You can spend the night here if you want, but you won't stay hidden for long. Callum comes to visit sometimes."

"Does he?" He'd seemed familiar with her situation. I hadn't realized they were that close. She didn't seem to notice how my gaze moved again to the door. I wanted to run, but still needed her help.

"I think Callum feels like he owes it to Robert to look after me, especially since he has no—" She stopped herself. "He has time for that, when he's in town. He's been good to me since Robert died. It was difficult for him, too, but he's been nothing but kind and helpful. Rowan, are you certain you didn't mistake his intentions in bringing you to town?"

I narrowed my eyes slightly. Had she been listening at all? "I'm sure."

"Oh." She sipped at her tea and frowned again. I had never seen her so subdued. But then, I had never known Felicia to have a care in the world outside of keeping up with fashions and choosing which fantastic future she wanted. She was bearing up well, all things considered, but it broke my heart to see how she'd lost her joy.

"Would you like to see the house?" she asked. "I've been waiting so long to show you everything."

"I really can't, Lecia." I spoke slowly. "I need to borrow some clothes that will help me not look so out of place. Maybe a few coins, if you can spare them. Do you have a horse? If anyone asks, you can say I stole it."

She gave her head a little shake. "Of course. I don't know where my head is today. You have no idea what this does to your brain." She made a vague circling gesture toward her stomach. "Tell you what. I'll show you around, and we'll grab some things from my room."

Her mood improved as she pointed out all of the modern conveniences and pretty additions she'd made to the decor. The house wasn't one of the larger ones on the street, but it had a good-sized kitchen and four bedrooms, an indoor toilet, and a small library. No signs of preparations for a baby. There wouldn't be any for a few months at least, perhaps not until after the birth. Our people were superstitious about babies, with good reason. She helped me pack some bread, cheese, and fruit into a bag in the kitchen, and led me upstairs to find some clean clothes. She chattered the whole time.

"I'm sorry," Felicia said. "Listen to me going on when you must be exhausted. I've been rather short on visitors lately. Let's go sit again, and we'll get something cold for supper before you sneak off. I'm afraid I'm still not much of a cook." I sat in the chair again, and she went to the window and looked out toward the street. She cleared her throat and let the curtains fall back into place.

"I don't think anyone followed me." I leaned back and rested my head against the chair. "I'm sorry for coming here, Lecia. I didn't know what else to do. I should go."

"No, you did the right thing," she said. "Absolutely. Rest for a few minutes. Eat. We'll get you back on the road after dark. It will be safer."

"Thank you, Lecia."

She smiled and settled in her chair, though her back remained stiff and straight. "Have you been in contact with your family?"

"I heard that life has been hard for them since I disappeared. And for Callum. I hope you've been spared that."

The lines reappeared on her forehead as she frowned. "No. It hasn't been as bad for me, but people found out that you were my cousin, and it did make things unpleasant." She sat beside me again and looked straight into my eyes. Tears gathered in hers, and she gripped her skirt tight in her fingers. "Robert was so angry when it all came out. I don't think he believed me at first when I said I hadn't known. He wanted..." She hiccupped and brushed her hair back over her shoulder. "He wanted to break off the engagement quietly, but I found out I was pregnant that day. We should have been so happy."

The bitterness in her voice shocked me, not because it was inappropriate, but because I had never heard it coming from such a deep place in her before. And it was my fault.

Apprehension prickled at me. The change in her tone was too sudden.

She ran her hands over her belly, which showed roundness when she pressed her dress against it. "Do you know what it does to a man to find out that the woman carrying his child has magic in her family?"

"I didn't realize anyone acknowledged that it ran in families." I didn't want to hurt her, but surely she could see how inconsistent Robert's reaction was with what we'd been taught about magic.

She scowled. "Don't be stupid. It's not about the babies that we lose. It's a great shame, having a heretic for a friend and a cousin. Makes people look at me sideways. You're like this red mark in our family's ledger.

There's no hiding it. There's this idea that once there's someone like you in the family, there will be more."

I stood and paced the room, unable to sit still as my heart fluttered with panic, unwilling to run out into the streets if I might be safe. *No. Run. Trust your instincts for once.*

I picked up the food she'd prepared and the clothes I hadn't yet changed into. "Do you really believe that I've sold my soul to become what I am now? Hated and feared?"

"I don't say you wouldn't have." Her eyes flicked to the window again.

Panic stabbed at my heart at the echo of footsteps on the porch, and a knock at the door. My blood froze. "Felicia, what did you do?"

"What I had to. This is for the best." Her eyes were dry now, and angry. "You are not my cousin. My Rowan died on the road to Ardare, killed by Tyreans."

"Lecia," I pleaded, but she wouldn't look at me. Tears stung my eyes. This hurt far more deeply than Callum's betrayal had. "I'm still the same person I always was. The only difference is that now I know who I am. The binding was killing me. I had no choice in this. I—"

"I don't know who you are. I hope you've enjoyed your magic." She darted past me to open the door.

I started toward the back door, but looked back over my shoulder as several men stepped into the house. I froze.

I expected to see Callum, and instead found myself facing a man who was taller, though not as broad, heavier-browed and sharper-eyed. He looked much the same as the last time I'd seen him, right down to the disapproving scowl on his face.

He'd almost been family, once.

"Thank you, Felicia," he said. His deep voice filled the room, though he spoke softly. "It's good to know who's loyal to the throne. The king will hear of it."

"Thank you," she said, then looked back to me. "Rowan, I believe you've met Sir Dorset Langley."

I couldn't move. *Go*, I told myself. *Figure out where later.*

I ran toward the back door, knocking over a spindle-legged table and a lamp on the way through. It didn't slow Langley, and he grabbed my hair before I could get through the kitchen. I yelled as he hauled me back and clapped a hand to my mouth.

"Greerson! Sedative! And restrain her!" he called, and several sets of footsteps pounded toward us.

I kicked and struggled and bit his hand, but he could have been made of stone for all he responded to it. He was a trained fighter and likely weighed twice as much as I did, and he kept me pinned easily. They forced my arms behind my back. My magic roiled within me, and I sent it out again. *Just get me out of here*, I begged it.

One of the hunters near the door flew backward as though he'd been hit by a charging bull, and his head slammed into the doorframe. He fell to the ground in a heap, and blood flowed from his head. Felicia screamed and ran up the stairs.

A hard slap to my face distracted me and sent stars spinning across the room. The hands holding me gripped tighter.

"Sedative, I said!" Anger filled Langley's voice, and I gathered my magic again. It felt weaker now.

Damn this city.

Something stabbed into my arm and a feeling like ice water flowed over my skin, then deeper into the muscles, up my arm, and into my body. Pain hammered in my head, much as it had every day when my magic was bound.

As the world whited out around me, I heard the magic hunters moving around.

"He's dead," someone said. "Add murder to the

list of charges."

And that's how it gets worse, I thought.

Chapter Twenty

Aren

The horse stumbled into a dip in the ground hidden by long, matted grasses, nearly tossing me over his head. I cursed and righted myself, and decided once again that my wandering thoughts would be the death of me. I'd never find my father if I couldn't stop thinking about the past, about the what-ifs and the if-onlys.

I wished Rowan were there. Talking to her would have put my thoughts in order, and her perspective would have been helpful. She saw things differently from me. I longed to hear her laugh again, to feel the warm touch of her hand.

I hoped she was finding the situation at the school improved. Perhaps she was making progress now that she didn't have the pressure of me watching. Much as I missed her, I couldn't deny that she was probably better off without me.

At the top of the next hill, the world opened before me. A wide river marked the divide between Durlin and Cressia, the dragon-lands. I saw no immediate difference in the landscape, but knew from a single dragon-hunting trip when I was young that the farther north I went, the rockier the ground would get. Folks from Luid had little to do with the province, save for trade. Cressia was mining and sheep-herding country, a rough and difficult place to live. We wanted their goods, and they needed our food. It was an effective, if mistrustful and perhaps lopsided, arrangement, favoring Luid as all such negotiations did.

Perhaps that was why my father had sent his wife and daughter there. No one would recognize them, or care enough to turn them in even if they did.

The spring melt in the lower reaches of the mountains had raised the waterline, making it impossible for the horse to ford the river. The road led us to an old ferryman sitting in a wooden hut, picking his gnarled fingernails with a knife.

"Heh? Wharra ya warnt?" he inquired, pleasantly enough.

"Crossing, please."

On another journey I'd have thought nothing of altering his thoughts so I could save the coins my uncle had given me for a true emergency. It had worked before, at least for long enough for me to escape.

For the sake of all the gods, you idiot, do it. This is your power, and your right as your father's son. Take it.

Instead, I handed over a silver coin, and the old man limped to the ferry and helped me load my horse. He examined the coin, letting the sunlight bounce off it. "Can givvanuthn back."

"That's fine. Just try to remember me in case I need your services again."

He squinted at my face and snorted, then began the crossing, pushing us along with a pole while a rope spanning the river kept us on-course. Magic could have been helpful there, but the man did well enough without it, as so many people did. He tipped his hat to me as I mounted on the other side, and I set off into Cressia.

There were no dragons in those first days, and no towns or roadside inns. I let the horse forage where he could, and did my hunting as an eagle when I spotted game. I slept in that form, too, finding it more comfortable on every level than trying to sleep as a human. I considered the situation as I transformed and dressed on the morning of our third day in Cressia. There was no danger of that form hurting me as long as I changed back during the day. I'd spent far more time in that body when I first met Rowan and felt no ill effects, unless I could blame that for my decision to turn her in to Severn.

No. That was nothing but me being a stupid ass. I'd changed since then. Perhaps there was hope for me, after all.

In any case, spending more time as an eagle did wonders for keeping my head clear, at least while I remained in that form. As soon as I changed back, the hurricane of thoughts and unwanted emotions began again.

Late that afternoon, the horse and I reached a large lake of uneven shape, dotted with islands. White clouds reflected on the wind-ruffled surface, creating a peaceful scene. The land sloped toward the water, covered in grasses and low shrubs. I removed my things from the saddle and let the horse loose. We had settled into a comfortable routine, and he no longer tried to wander.

"Perhaps the dragon infestation claims are overblown," I said to him. He looked up, twitched an ear, and went back to foraging. He moved closer to the water, then in up to his knees, searching for his preferred treat, and I turned to put my things down.

A flash of movement caught my eye, and I spun back to the water in time to see my horse pulled under, his neck caught in the jaws of a massive, black water dragon. The dragon stayed near the surface, watching me from eyes placed high atop its head as the horse thrashed, then stilled. A moment later, both shapes disappeared into the depths of the lake, leaving only reflections to hide what lurked below.

"Well, shit," I muttered.

We'd been making good time. Now I didn't know how long it would take for me to reach civilization, if a Cressian town could be so named. I stripped off my clothes and stowed them in my pack, hid the lot next to a rock, transformed, and pulled myself into the sky to get a better look at my surroundings.

The lake was larger than I'd realized, an uneven shape snaking out into the surrounding land at several points.

The flickering light of a campfire appeared on the shore of a deep inlet, and I wheeled toward it.

As I came closer, a woman yelled something I couldn't quite understand. A lower voice answered, and the woman laughed. Water splashed, more gently than it had when the dragon took my horse. I dropped low over the trees and landed as smoothly and quietly as I could in a sturdy birch tree.

The woman wore green pants with pockets on the legs and a brown sweater that fit close to the curves of her body. Her movements seemed familiar, but I couldn't place her. Not someone I'd seen in my eagle's body, then. She turned toward the fire, but thick waves of dark hair covered her face. She prodded the wood with a long stick, sending a spray of sparks into the air that surrounded the spitted fish she was roasting.

A naked man with warm, brown skin emerged from the lake and walked back toward the fire. He shook out his short, black hair and wandered around the campsite, poking around in bags and laying out bedrolls while he dried in the cold air.

I needed to get closer. I couldn't think of names, but I knew these people. They were friends. I tucked in my wings and fell toward the ground, pulling up at the last second into a reasonably neat landing on the flat rocks.

The woman gasped and reached out to grab the

man's arm, nearly toppling him as he struggled into his trousers. He turned toward me, and his mouth opened into a wide grin.

"Well, I'll be a great whale's left stone," he said, and the woman slapped him. "What? Aren's heard worse."

"That kind of language is becoming a habit for you," she said, and turned back to me.

I remembered then, and would have smiled had I been able to. She was Cassia, and he was Kel, and they were merfolk. They stood there, and I sat on the ground, glancing back and forth between them.

"Kel, get him some clothes." Cassia shoved her brother back toward their things.

"As if he's got anything you haven't seen before." He removed clothes from a pack and dropped them in a pile beside me.

"He's only human," she said. "They care about these things."

She turned away, and I changed back into my human body and dressed as quickly as I could. With the change came a flood of emotions. Relief dominated, and happiness at finding my oldest friends alive. Kel waited until I dressed before he clasped me in a huge hug, and Cassia followed suit, molding her voluptuous body to mine and inhaling deeply as she buried her face in my neck.

I tried to ignore how good that felt.

"Where have you been?" I asked, and Cassia released me.

"Everywhere?" She smiled. "Feels like it, anyway. I'm so glad to see you. Are you hungry?"

The fish's skin had burned while we were talking, but it was the most enjoyable meal I'd had in ages.

"Did your mission go as planned?" I asked, and they exchanged a glance before answering.

"It was as we expected," Cassia said, and muffled

a dry cough with the back of her hand. "The merfolk we visited in Darmish waters feel we should be doing more to help them. Humans are making their lives difficult. There's little we can do, really. We're not going to war with humans."

Something Severn had said came back to me—*I have some things in the works in Darmid already.* "Humans go to war with humans, though," I said. "Did they mention Severn?"

Cassia picked at the fish bones. "They did, actually. They were taken aback when he reached out to them, but I think they're considering his offer. He gets rid of the Darmish people who are persecuting them, and the mers down there help him do it. Combined naval attacks, that sort of thing. They'd be an asset to his cause if he really is thinking of attacking."

I frowned. "He is. And they would be." Perhaps he wasn't as unprepared as I'd thought.

Kel crossed his arms. "There's a reason we keep our business separate from humans. We need a neutral king on the Tyrean throne again."

"I couldn't agree more," I said.

"How's Rowan?" Cassia asked, apparently ready to change the subject.

"*Where* is Rowan?" Kel added. "What's happened? We spoke to her parents on our way down. Horrible situation."

"Why?"

Cassia shrugged, a gesture that was both casual and strangely elegant. "Her family's not holding up well. The mother invited us in, wanted to hear about Rowan. She couldn't offer us any help on the binding issue, but obviously felt horrible over what happened. She blames herself. We didn't see the brother Rowan seemed so fond of. Her father wanted nothing to do with us, told us he had no daughter, and said we had to leave."

Not news Rowan would be pleased to hear, but I

hadn't hoped for any better.

"Her mother told me privately that she did what she thought necessary to protect Rowan after she was born with...what did she call it?"

"The condition," Kel offered.

"The condition, right. They don't even like to say the word 'magic' there."

My jaw tightened. The merfolk didn't often judge another person's decisions, but I would. I knew how being abandoned by her parents had hurt Rowan and how much physical pain the binding had caused her.

Cassia placed her hand on mine and squeezed. "She did what she did because she loved Rowan. You can't fault her for that."

"Maybe not for trying to protect her. But for giving in to those people? They could have gone somewhere else. Taken Rowan to Tyrea. Someone would have given a gifted baby a home."

"Easy for you to say now," Cassia said, though not harshly.

"The binding's not an issue, anyway," I said, after an uncomfortable silence. "Rowan broke it herself."

I told them what had happened since we left the Grotto, up until I'd left Rowan safe on Belleisle, though I was becoming tired of repeating the story.

Cassia grinned. "Good girl. I knew I liked her. I hope you're not a bad influence on her, Aren."

I smiled back. "I'm a fantastic influence, believe me."

"I bet."

Kel rolled his eyes at us. "So she's alive, her magic is free, and her headaches are gone, but she can't actually use her magic?"

"Right. It's there, but it's not doing much right now except frustrating her."

He narrowed his eyes. "Is that why you're here now and not there with her?"

My shoulders stiffened. "You mean did I leave her there because I didn't want her anymore?"

"Ah." Cassia nodded. "I see. Because she's not what you thought she was, or what you thought she had the potential to be. Dropped. Just like that."

"No, that's not it. Nothing's changed with that. I still..." I forced myself to relax. They were teasing, trying to get more information than they would have otherwise. "Rowan has been frustrated, and I haven't been able to help at all. Maybe I've been holding her back. That's not why I left, though. I'm trying to find my father."

Kel gave a low whistle, and Cassia arched her eyebrows. "No kidding?" she asked. "That's new. I was under the impression that you didn't care whether you ever saw him again."

"He might be the lesser of the evils available to us right now."

The siblings exchanged another meaning-filled glance. "You want some company for a few days?" Kel asked. "We're heading back to the sea, but this is important. You have a horse?"

"I did," I said, and nodded toward the lake, where a pair of eyes had appeared, barely visible above the surface.

Cassia shuddered. "Better your horse than Kel, I suppose."

"You suppose?" Kel asked in mock outrage, and Cassia laughed.

"A horse would at least have been useful." The smile fell from her face. "There are other dragons around here, though, land and sky. Besides your water dragon, we've only seen smaller ones so far. We've picked up a few tricks along the way, flares and such, but I think we'll all be safer together."

"Are you sure?" I asked.

She sighed and looked north, toward the mountains and the ocean beyond. "Much as I want to get home, it's in our people's best interests to see Severn removed from the throne. If that's what you're doing, our Elders would want us to help."

"Thank you," I said.

Cassia flashed me a wicked grin. "Besides, we've missed you. It'll be like old times."

The thought of those old times sent a pleasant shudder through my body. "Maybe not exactly like old times."

She shook her head. "You humans, I swear." But she smiled as she said it. We'd spoken about this before. She might not make it easy for me, but she'd respect my loyalty to Rowan.

I walked back to retrieve my things and hurried to re-join the mer siblings at the fire. Whatever waited over the hills of Cressia, I felt better knowing I would be facing it with them.

Chapter Twenty-One

Rowan

White mist surrounded me, letting through only the shadows of voices and vague awareness of movement. My body rocked from side to side, and I felt myself spinning through space. The frozen sensation in my arm turned to burning, a bright and sharp pain that seemed to move independent of my body. I struggled to wake, to force my eyes to open, but I'd lost the connection.

My surroundings gradually returned, and my thoughts took form again. Dorset Langley had taken me down, had done what Callum couldn't. My body was rocking. No, the hard, damp surface beneath me was rocking, and my stomach wanted no part of it. My head pounded and churned with a deep ache that echoed the nausea in my stomach.

I wanted nothing but to lie still, but a quick sideways motion made me heave, and I lifted my head to vomit. That caused a fresh dose pain to fill my skull, which sent another convulsion through my stomach. Someone cursed, and a boot moved away from my head. I laid my face back down. At least this floor was cold. I opened my eyes. Darkness. Thank every god for that.

Someone nudged my leg, but I refused to move.

"Stick her again." Dorset Langley's voice.

I opened my mouth to beg them not to do it again, to tell them I'd be still and that I was incapable of escaping. A sharp pain sliced into my shoulder, and the fog descended again, closing over me completely this time.

I gradually became aware of dim light, and the fact that the ground was no longer rocking beneath me. My head felt full of bricks that rubbed together in a painful clatter when I tried to move, so I left it resting on the soft surface that my cheek pressed against. The scent of strong cleanser prickled at my nose. It reminded me of spring cleaning at my mother's house, ages ago and a world away.

I wiggled my toes. They'd left my boots on, and my necklace had slipped beneath the arch of my foot. I moved my fingers, taking in the rough wool blanket that covered me. When I slipped my hand beneath it, I found that I still wore my travel clothes, though they'd taken my cloak. I lay on a straw-stuffed mattress, thin and narrow.

After a few deep breaths, I eased my eyes open. Lamplight reflected off blue stone walls that swayed as I struggled to focus on them. Another long breath, and I rolled onto my side, facing the nearest wall. I touched the stone. No, not stone. Metal, perhaps, and cold. I pressed my chilled fingers to my eyes, and the pain receded a fraction.

No matter how this ends, I thought, *it was all worth it not to have to live with this every day.*

I rolled onto my other side. I lay on a cot that sat on a gray flagstone floor. The rectangular room, a little larger than the classrooms back at the school, was empty save for the lamps set into the walls and a privacy screen set up at the opposite end. The clean space wasn't exactly what I'd expected from the prisons in Ardare, but I had no doubt about where I was.

I shivered. The dank chill in the air was as I had expected.

"Hello?"

No one answered. I sat up slowly, ignoring the darts of pain behind my eyes. The stabbing sensation had gone from my arm and shoulder, and when I looked them over I saw a pair of holes in my sleeve, smaller than I'd expected.

No windows in the room. There was a door, though, in the wall halfway between my bed and the screen. I pushed myself slowly to my feet and shuffled toward it, keeping my hand braced against the wall.

I felt empty. Ill. Terror flashed through me, overwhelming every other thought.

My magic.

In my panic I pulled into myself and nearly collapsed with relief when I found it, small and compressed though it seemed. I remained aware of its comforting presence as I continued my inspection of the cell.

The door was made of wood, polished smooth, but each board had an inset panel of the same blue substance that the walls were made of. A small metal square in the middle looked like it might slide open from the other side, but there was no response when I knocked.

"Hello?" I called again. The nearly empty room amplified the tremor in my voice. "Is there someone out there?"

I waited and listened, but heard nothing from outside the door. I took my hand off the wall, and the feeling of emptiness eased slightly. When I touched it again, the emptiness returned, as though my magic had retreated.

Strange.

I continued my circuit of the room. The privacy screen had birds painted on it, herons or cranes, but the pattern was faded and chipped. I found another bed behind it, identical to mine except that it had been made with soft blankets, and a worn, wooden storage chest sat by the foot. A three-legged stool sat in the corner, and a small table beside the bed held a few books, piles of paper, and a round glass pitcher filled with water.

Glass could be a weapon. I reached for it, and my heart sank as I felt its weight. My mother had made similar items in her shop and kept them around when her children were small. The glass was treated to break into harmless pieces if dropped. Nothing that would make a threatening weapon.

The blanket on the bed was rumpled near the top, and one of the books had been set down in a hurry, with a page bent beneath it. I picked up the volume, titled *Evils of Magic*, and shuddered. Why would anyone imprisoned here be reading such a thing?

I flattened the page before I set it face down on top of the stack again.

On my way back to my bed I looked more closely at one of the lamps affixed to the blue stone, set deep in a recess behind metal bars. Oil, encased in glass. More blue wall behind the lamp. The light made my eyes feel swollen and heavy. Painful. I returned to my cot and collapsed onto it, legs shaking.

What did they do to me?

I closed my eyes against the light and went back to cooling my hands on the wall and pressing them to my eyes and forehead. I thought about prison, about mistakes, about never hearing of anyone escaping from this place. I thought about Aren, and found that it calmed me. I knew I shouldn't feel self-pity, or focus on missing him. Instead I made promises to myself about what I would do when I saw him again, but found that such thoughts only brought black despair when I realized how remote that possibility was.

I had ruined everything. He would succeed in his mission, I was certain. He'd return to Belleisle to find me, and—

A low click echoed through the room, and

another. I pushed myself up as the door swung open.

"Stay where you are," ordered a guard in a brown uniform. Her tightly pulled-back hair amplified the severity of her expression.

When I didn't move, she stepped back and the door opened further. An older man entered, dressed in black slacks and a featureless, gray shirt. He had a thick mane of silver hair and deep creases around his eyes. A handsome fellow, but with an air of cold disinterest.

He glanced at me, but went straight to the other end of the room and behind the screen without speaking. The guard left us, the door slammed closed, and a pair of locks clicked. Silence followed until the sound of pages turning drifted out from behind the makeshift wall.

At least he's friendly, I thought, and gritted my teeth. I was accustomed to having a roommate, but Celean had been somewhat less frightening to share a space with than a man I knew nothing about.

I didn't know whether it would be better to reach out to him or take a cue from him and ignore his existence. He solved my dilemma when he sighed loudly, came out from behind the screen, and crossed the room, carrying the stool with him. He placed it near my bed, at a respectful distance. Non-threatening, at least.

I sat up, rested my back against the wall, and pulled my skirt down over my feet. He crossed one leg over the other with his ankle resting on his knee and folded his hands. His gaze was unsettling, dark eyes under stern gray brows.

"I thought we should meet," he said.

"Where are we?"

"They call this the compound." He plucked at the leg of his pants, straightening a wrinkle. "It functions as government offices and a prison for special people like us. They use it for a few other purposes they don't want the general populace to know about." He rattled the words off as though he'd spoken them many times before. "Though he resides elsewhere, the king has chambers here, and offices. He tries to be present for executions and very much enjoys telling me about them after. In great detail, in fact." A look of distaste crossed his face, erased as quickly as it appeared. "We are underground, in a secure cell reserved for prisoners of a magical nature. These walls are made from a rare substance that inhibits magic. An alloy, actually. They've found a method of combining their magic-inhibiting drug with silver and iron, and used it to make these lovely blue walls we're currently enjoying. It's effective within a limited range, but there's only one cell of this sort, so I'm afraid you're stuck with me."

"So there's no way out?" A strange calm settled over me.

"Not that I've found, and I've been here for years. When they remove you from this room, you'll be shackled with the same substance. They'll inject it into you if you misbehave—the drug, not the alloy. Quite unpleasant. I don't recommend it." He leaned forward, taking in the glaze in my eyes. "Or maybe you knew that."

"Is it like binding?"

His eyebrows crept upward, cutting deep creases into his forehead. "I wonder what you would know about that. But to answer your question, it is and it isn't. They don't have the formula for that nor the skill to apply it, but they have found ways to mimic the effects temporarily. Their version, however, does have the advantage of working even on a person who is resisting. With a binding, submission is required, and likewise with the..." He paused, and his lip curled into a sneer. "The experiments they're doing to remove magic. Cure it, as they say. I don't think they've had many strong volunteers, and it's stalled their progress somewhat. They can't take what's not freely given. At least, not yet."

"Removing magic? Forever?" So Callum hadn't been exaggerating.

A corner of his mouth turned up. "Horrifying, isn't it? They offered to let me go if I would submit to their experiments. If I'd let them cure me." He shuddered. "I preferred to rot in here."

We sat in silence for a minute, and I massaged my arm.

He looked off into a corner of the room behind my bed. "I don't want to get to know you well. I've had other people come and go before. Doesn't do to get attached. But we can't very well sit in silence. I think that would be unfair to you, and I wish to hear any news you have from outside."

It seemed preferable to silence, and to being left with my own thoughts. "News from when?"

"Oh, I think my last temporary cellmate left two months ago, if I'm counting correctly. It gets confusing in here. At least meals and relief breaks are regular. You can count by that."

My mouth went dry. "We never get out for air? Where did you come from just now?"

"They wanted you to have the room to yourself until you woke up. You might get out to see the place soon. You'll get a trial."

"I think they held my trial without me. I confessed my magic in letters to people I thought I could trust."

"I see. Well, we all make mistakes. Some more than others. I don't know what they'll do with you, then, but you shouldn't be here too long. You'll be called before the king. I'm not sure what happens after that. No one has come back to tell me. So you are Darmish?"

That casual way he mentioned the disappearance of previous cellmates shook me, and it was several moments before I answered. "I am, but I was elsewhere for a while. I shouldn't have come back."

He looked around the room. "Evidently."

"What about you? Who are you?"

"No one. I made the same mistake as you, in a way."

Pain slashed at my skull, retreated, and returned in a familiar pattern. My cellmate stood. "I should let you rest."

"No, it's fine." I had too many questions. Why hadn't they executed this man? If he could stay alive when cellmates came and went, I needed to know how.

Bile rose in my throat, and I lay down with my eyes closed against the light. I hadn't seen any handy buckets, and didn't wish to embarrass myself.

"It will wear off," he said. I thought I detected a hint of irritation in his voice, though the words were kind enough. "We'll speak later, if they don't take you away first."

That's so helpful, I thought. I opened my eyes, ready to object, but he was already on his way back to his corner.

"What's your name?" I called.

He didn't answer.

Chapter Twenty-Two

Aren

Cassia hitched her pack higher on her shoulders and squinted into the sun. "So where exactly are we supposed to be going?"

Overnight, I'd explained to them about my mother and my sister, news that surprised them as much as it had me, though not with as great an effect. We'd set off early in the morning, and for now they were happy to accompany me wherever I needed to go.

"I'm not exactly sure," I said. "According to my uncle, the village Ulric sent them to is called Trint. It's west of the lake, though I'm not sure I trust the map." My uncle had disagreed with it on a number of points and had marked several corrections in his own province. He was less able to help with Cressia. "I suppose we look for signs of humans and ask them for directions." I rubbed the back of my neck, which became tense every time I thought about the search for my newly discovered family, and what I'd do if I found them alive.

"And if we find your mother?" Cassia asked.

"Then we find out whether my father came this way and keep searching. I very much doubt he's still here after three years."

"That's it?" Cassia coughed, and stumbled. I caught her around the waist before she hit the ground, and she leaned into me. "Thanks. So you're hoping to find your mother, who you haven't seen for twenty years, and the twin sister you've just learned about...and you're going to say hello, and that's it?"

I waited for her to re-gain her balance, and kept walking. "I don't know, Cass. I have no idea how this is supposed to work. Are you all right?"

"Fine. It's just the air. It's rather dry, and we've been up here so long. I need a swim."

Kel frowned, but said nothing.

We didn't pass any signs of human habitation that afternoon. Far-off mountains to the north guided our journey westward, their unchanging forms making it feel like we were hardly making progress. The landscape didn't help, with all of it looking the same after a while. Grass, shrubs, an occasional clump of trees huddled together against the wind, ponds in the hollows, and rocks everywhere.

I was examining a set of massive claw-marks carved deep into the bark of a bare trunk when Kel grabbed me and Cassia by the arms and pulled us into the shelter of a patch of trees. Seconds later a huge, dagger-shaped shadow swept across the ground, bending and warping with the rises in the land, circling around and passing over us several times before continuing toward the mountains.

My heart raced even after it had disappeared. "Thanks."

"No problem," Kel said. "Just keep your eyes open. I'm sure he's not the only one around."

We walked through the day, asking questions about each other's journeys as they came to mind, but mostly in silence. Cassia had decided not to take her natural form the night before, so she went to swim in a small lake that we stopped at well before sunset. Kel and I sat on the shore, watching for trouble. I sharpened the hunting knife my uncle had given me on a stone Cassia had in her bag.

"So, what's going on?" he asked.

"I think I've told you everything."

"No." He shook his head. "You've told me the things that have happened. I want to know why you're not acting like yourself. Last time we saw you, you were going through a bad time. You thought you'd lost everything and expected to die soon, and you still seemed happier than you do now. I wouldn't have said you were happy then, mind you, but compared to this you were dancing on rainbows."

That made me smile. "Is it that bad?"

"Nearly. Is it because Rowan's not here?"

"No," I said, honestly. "I miss her. I wish she wasn't so far away, and that I could go back and see her, but I'd rather have her there. She needs to learn more, and I need to be out here. Time apart might be good for us, anyway."

"Hmm. I can see that," he said. "There's been a lot of—" he laced the fingers of both hands together. "*This* lately, I suppose? Not much time to figure stuff out on your own?"

I clasped my own hands together. "Not as much of *this* as I'd have liked."

Kel chuckled. "Sorry to hear it."

"You must think I'm terribly weak, needing her like this." Merfolk didn't usually form attachments as we did, though on the rare occasions when they did, it was for life. Most of them had friends, and gods knew they had lovers, but not the damnably complex thing I was still trying to figure out with Rowan.

"You think that, not me," he said. "I don't understand it, but I'd like to some day. So what are you so melancholy about, if not her? You're on track for finding your father, or at least you have more of a chance now than you thought you had before. You just found out that he didn't kill your mother, which must be a relief for you. You have a sister, if she still lives." He looked out over the water, and a gray tail flipped out of the water, followed a moment later by Cassia's head as she somersaulted to the surface. "It's not so bad having one, I guess."

"I doubt a sister of mine would be anything like Cassia."

Cassia turned toward us when she heard her name, and Kel waved her off.

She delivered an impressive view of the top half of her body as she raised her arms over her head and arched her back to dive under again. I smiled to myself and looked away.

"So what, then?" Kel asked. "Why so morose? We're worried about you. You seem to be a different person every time we meet you."

"Maybe that's it," I said. "Tell me who I am right now."

Kel rose and walked a few steps toward the lake, shielding his eyes against the sun that reflected off of the water. "Damned if I know."

"You should." Merfolk were known as excellent judges of character, and for good reason. "What do you see in me now?"

He walked back toward me. "Look at me." He looked into my eyes for a minute, squinting slightly, expression unchanging. It should have been uncomfortable, but we'd been friends for long enough that it didn't bother me.

"I don't know," he said, "and neither do you. You're confused. Everything inside of you down to your core is in turmoil. You're lacking something that in the past has been critical to you."

"What?"

"Confidence," Cassia said. Kel and I both looked up. She stood before us, already dressed in damp clothes that stuck to her skin, wringing the water out of her thick hair. "And purpose. You should have asked me. I saw that as soon as Aren started talking about himself last night. Also, I caught a fish just now, if you're hungry." She sat cross-legged on the ground in front of us and noticed our stares. "What?"

I fought the urge to grab her and hug her again. She was an odd person at times, but extremely likable. "It's nothing," I said. "I think you're right, that's all. But now might not be the best time to go into all of that."

"I think maybe it is," Cassia said. "Kel, go get some firewood?"

"What did your last slave die of?" he muttered, but he went off into the woods, leaving us to talk.

"I noticed it before, the last time we saw you," Cassia said quietly, regarding me with her sea-colored eyes. "Even when we met you as a child, when you were in your brothers' shadow and your father ignored you, there was still this confidence in what you were. You knew you would grow up to be as powerful as your father, and you had this amazing drive to prove everyone wrong for overlooking you. When you came back to tell us you wouldn't be coming to the lake anymore, you'd changed, but all of that was still there. Maybe more so, because your hatred for Severn sharpened your sense of purpose."

I'd nearly forgotten how I'd hated him then. Over time I'd forced the emotion deep inside of myself, unfelt and unacknowledged. I'd ended up working with him instead of against him.

"It was different when you and Rowan came to the Grotto," she continued. "Kel told me that when you were at the lake house, you were single-minded, determined to keep Rowan safe and help her with her problem. But when I saw you, when you were safe and there was nothing for you to protect her from—"

"And when there was absolutely nothing I could do to help her with the binding."

Cassia nodded. "Exactly. You were lost. Less

composed than I'd ever seen you. Like you didn't know what you were supposed to be doing."

"I didn't. I still don't."

There might have been no one else in the world I could have talked to about it. Even though I knew Kel was as unlikely to judge me as his sister was, I opened up more to her. "Cass, I don't know what's happening. I'm supposed to be looking for my father, and I am, but I don't know what I'm going to say to him if I find him, or whether I even want him to come back. I met this monk who made me think that prying into people's minds and changing them was dark magic and I shouldn't use it. I've poured so much of my life into learning how to do that."

"You know our thoughts on that," Cassia murmured.

The merfolk had never approved of that skill. If I had returned to the lake to visit after I learned it, they'd have turned me away. It was only because of Rowan that they'd allowed me back the last time, and then only with strict warnings about not using my talents.

"That," I said, "and dead-raising."

Cassia's eyes went wide at that. There are some things that even a mer doesn't see when she looks into a person's heart. "You don't, do you?"

"No. But I can. And I have, without practice or study."

"That's..."

"I know." We sat in silence for several minutes.

"Well," Cassia said, "do you think that's part of the problem? Your magic has been who you are for most of your life. The Aren I know would never let someone else's opinion of his gifts affect him like this, which makes me think that maybe you were having the same thoughts, and this fellow merely confirmed them for you."

I winced. I'd nearly forgotten how the mers' insights could sting. "Do you think he's right?"

She held her hands out, open but empty. "I'm not going to say that he was wrong. If you think there's enough truth in what he said that it's tearing you apart, then it's something you shouldn't ignore. Even if you never did either of those things again, it wouldn't diminish your power. You would have fewer developed skills available, but that would only be until you've picked up something else to channel your magic into. What I think more than anything is that you let your power define you, and you might need to let go of that. You're more than your magic, Aren. It's a tool, it's not who you are."

"Then who am I? If I'm not a member of the ruling family of Tyrea, if I've let go of some of my greatest powers, if I can't claim to have a home anywhere, and I've lost everything I once owned, what's left?"

It said something about my state of mind that I didn't hear Kel approaching. "Are any of those things the reason Rowan loves you?"

I didn't answer. I couldn't.

"I'll tell you, then," he said, and dumped a pile of dry wood on the rocks. "It's not for your magic, whether it's dark or light. It's certainly not because you're a good person. No offense."

"None taken." At best I was moving toward becoming a neutral person.

"Actually," he said thoughtfully, "I don't know what she sees in you."

Cassia grinned. "I do." Kel rolled his eyes, and she laughed. "Really, though. She sees your potential, Aren. You're intelligent. You're loyal--that's why it was so hard for you to defy your brother. You care about her, and about the people of your country. If you didn't, you'd be content to let Severn have his throne. You'd be on your way across the sea, out of his reach. You aspire to be something better than what you are, even if you have no idea how you're going to do that." She glared at her brother. "*That* is what she sees in him."

"I knew that." Kel set up wood for the fire, which I lit after a few attempts. "Well, that's new," he said. "Easier than a wet flint, isn't it?"

I frowned at the pathetic flames, then offered a wry smile to Kel. "It's really the thing that I'm most proud of learning over all these years."

Kel laughed. It was comforting to be surrounded by happy people, even if I didn't feel it myself.

"This is not the end for you," Cassia concluded. "You're having a hard time right now because you're letting go of a lot of things. You'll find your way."

"Thanks, Cass."

She shrugged. "I do what I can. What would you say to scouting ahead before we lose the light?"

It sounded like a fine idea to me. I went and transformed, something I was still sure I could do without hurting anyone. I flew over the land, looking for signs of people or dragons, enjoying the evening breeze ruffling my feathers. When I spotted dark spots on the ground over the next hill, I flew toward it.

A jumble of buildings set in a rough square pattern around an open space came into view. A proper village, and more than we'd seen before. I wheeled before anyone saw me and went back toward my friends.

Chapter Twenty-Three

Rowan

I sat on my bed and picked a string of tough, overcooked beef from between my teeth. I'd have complained about it, but that was the only bit of meat I'd found in the bowl of thin soup the sour-faced guard had dropped off for supper. That, a few slices of stale bread, and water in tin cups made for a sad meal, but one I finished quickly.

My churning thoughts hadn't allowed me to sleep much the previous night. I was exhausted, and ravenous.

My cellmate ate more slowly, sipping elegantly from his bowl, taking small bites of bread as he sat on the stool he'd once again brought out from his corner. I supposed it made sense to take one's time over things here. There wasn't much entertainment provided.

At least the headache was gone, though my mind still felt sluggish, like every thought had to be pried out of thick, sticky mud. My companion had asked me about my past and how I came to be arrested, and I'd given the barest skeletons of answers, telling him about the trouble with controlling my magic and about Callum's betrayal, but nothing about Aren or Belleisle. I'd asked him a few questions and got nothing in return.

"Tell me more of this binding," he said.

"It's been on me since I was a baby. I don't remember it happening. It was effective enough that I didn't know I had magic in me, but it gave me terrible headaches all my life."

"And how was it broken?"

I opened my mouth to answer, and hesitated. Trusting people had earned me nothing but pain recently. For all I knew, this man could have been planted in the cell to draw my confession out. He could be a captive, as he'd said, but trading my story for his freedom. He wouldn't learn anything important from me.

"Someone convinced me of my magic," I said. "I was in danger. The magic broke free and saved me."

He sat still as a stone, empty bowl resting on his knee, apparently deep in thought. "And it didn't kill you. Interesting. You said you've had some trouble controlling it?"

I nodded. I'd said that much, though no more.

He moved then, though only to lean forward and fix his gaze more firmly on me. "It's a horrible thing that was done to you. I saw the effects of bindings when I was young. Terrible." A devious smile touched his lips. "But I think your luck may be turning, my young friend."

"You still haven't told me your name."

"Nor have you told me yours," he pointed out, and set his bowl on the floor. "It's hardly relevant. Listen carefully. I want you to use magic."

"What? But you said the walls—"

His smile softened. "Please. It's only a theory, something I've been thinking about since you mentioned bindings yesterday."

"Please explain first." I wasn't about to risk harm to myself just so he could get some excitement.

"Very well." He stood and paced as he spoke. "Think of this. Your magic matured with you, but was trapped within you. It was reared in secret. In darkness. Oppression. It's free now, but uncontrollable. Do you see?"

I almost did. "You think the walls are like a binding? But outside of me?"

He crouched, and his expression became animated for the first time. "It works well enough on those whose magic has never been bound. I cannot use magic in here. But yours may have adapted."

I thought that through as he waited, tapping his heel on the floor. "You're saying my magic is like...like a person who was raised in a cave with no light. It became accustomed to the darkness, but never escaped it. Not until a few months ago."

He nodded. "Go on."

My magic tingled through my limbs as though excited by the idea. "And when a person like that was exposed to the light, it would be overwhelming, but a little darkness would help her adjust." Hadn't Griselda suggested something similar? Contain it a little, and practice. The idea had frightened me at the time. Now, I had nothing to lose.

He seemed pleased that I understood. "Try it. Please."

I laughed nervously, unsure of how else to react. It seemed a risk if I thought he was trying to trap me into a confession. But then, I was already in prison. After the letters I'd sent to Callum, how much deeper could I really dig that hole? And if there might be a chance I could help us escape, I had to try.

"If you insist," I said. "What shall I try?"

"What can you do?"

"Nothing. I thought I told you that."

He frowned. "You said you had trouble controlling it. That's not the same as not being able to do anything."

"I'm sor—" I squared my shoulders. *I'm not sorry.* "It's complicated. I'm figuring it out. Will you help me?"

He pursed his lips and nodded. "Very well. Try to direct your magic at me."

I stepped away from the walls and raised my hands, unsure of how else to do it. *Go,* I told the magic.

Just not too much. I gasped as it welled up in me, and I sensed the resistance of the walls that contained it. They seemed to be responding, fighting back. My magic gave a push of its own, filling me, but it felt smaller than it had at the school. Weaker. The lamplight flickered, and the already chilled air grew icy as I pushed to release it.

Too much. Panic wrapped cold hands around my heart. *You'll kill someone.*

Before I had a chance to form another thought, I instinctively clamped down, dampening the magic as effectively as any binding could have.

The old man sighed. "It was there."

"I know."

He tapped a finger against his chin and forced a hard smile. "We'll try again."

Something in his tone caught my attention. "Where in Darmid are you from?" I asked. "Your accent is strange to me." He'd been trying to cover it up, to speak like the guards he'd been around the past few years, but I'd just caught the hint of something foreign, yet familiar. My mouth went dry. "You're not from Darmid at all, are you?"

"No," he whispered. "You don't get many Sorcerers like me around here, do you? Call me a political prisoner."

"How long did you say you've been here?"

"Too long." He sat on his stool again, and his shoulders slumped. "Tyrea. I'm from Tyrea." It sounded like he was testing the feel of the word on his tongue, as though he hadn't spoken it in ages. "Tell me, have you heard news from there?"

I tried to decide what I could tell without giving myself away. "Well, Severn is—I don't know what he's calling himself, but he's in charge, and is collecting magical talent from everywhere, taking people to Luid and I think building an army."

My companion rubbed a hand over his chin. "Any

other news from the royal family?"

"Yes..." My skin prickled. I knew who he was. Impossible that I should have been the one to find him, but I had no doubt. I'd have seen it sooner, had my mind not been so groggy.

It seemed I should feel more frightened than I did, after everything I'd been told about Ulric. Aren's father. "News about your other sons, you mean?"

His hand dropped from his face. He nodded. "Have you heard anything of them?"

"You might say that. I've spent some time with Aren in the past few months." I bit my lip to distract me from the memory of him. "He's the one who saw my magic, who convinced me to try to escape the binding."

A faint smile touched Ulric's lips. "I see."

I thought he did see, perhaps more than I wanted him to. "Severn was planning to use me for something. He tried to capture us, and that's when the binding broke."

He folded his hands in his lap. "I'd heard from another prisoner that there had been trouble between them. Just a rumor, really. No one here seems to know anything about Tyrea. This falling out was over you?"

"In part. I think Aren was ready to get away from your family, anyway. Dealing with me just forced him to move."

Ulric, the rightful king of Tyrea, settled back into the chair. "I'm well aware of the mess I left behind. I've made mistakes, I won't deny it. When did you say you last saw Aren?"

"A few weeks ago. A little more, maybe. How did you get here? How did the Darmish capture you?"

He shrugged, as though such a massive event meant little to him. "I trusted the wrong people." He seemed to be attempting to pierce me with his dark gaze. "And my other sons?"

"I don't know. Aren didn't really talk about

them."

He nodded. "Well, thank you for sharing what you know."

Could this truly be the father Aren had spoken of as a cold, hard, uncaring man? The man who'd had his innocent wife executed, who had allowed his youngest child to be turned into a heartless killer by his oldest, not caring at all about what happened to Aren as long as his family remained in power? He seemed a bit stiff to me, intimidating at first, but not at all the monster I would have expected. This couldn't be the same man. And yet the longer I looked, the more I saw it. The sharp gaze, the predatory focus when something caught his attention, even the line of his jaw were all familiar to me. His youngest son had inherited all of it.

I'd found a powerful ally, or a powerful enemy, depending on how I approached this. And given that we were both prisoners...

"I'm sorry you've been trapped here." I chose my words carefully. "I think your country has missed you."

He smiled sadly. "But not everyone. Aren told you about me, I suppose?"

I didn't return the smile. "He did."

"I'd like to see him again. And the others. I made—"

"Mistakes, I know. You said." I winced inwardly. It wasn't like me to be so cold to a stranger, but I couldn't forget what Aren had told me. I couldn't pretend that all was well and time had healed his family's wounds. Some, I suspected, were too deep to ever recover from.

He looked away. "Yes. Well, thank you for the news. Would you be willing to try your magic again now?"

I knew I needed to, but when I reached for my magic, all I felt was exhaustion. My power still seemed small and far off. Not ready.

"Might I rest, first?"

"Of course." He stood, and picked up his stool. "I'd like to work on it soon. I don't know how long you have before they take you away, but with some training we might make something of you."

I hated to think what that might entail, given what I knew of the man. Still, he'd behaved decently enough so far. I nodded.

"Thank you, Miss." Ulric walked away.

"Rowan," I called after him. He turned.

"Pardon?"

"That's my name. Rowan. I know your name, it seems fair that you know mine." I wouldn't be friends with the man, but we could work together and be civil.

He held his free hand to his stomach and gave a small bow. "Thank you. And you may call me Ulric. If you need anything, I'll be in my little corner."

He turned away again as I curled up and laid my head on the thin pillow.

If I recalled correctly, he'd been missing for almost three years. Three years, and the most powerful Sorcerer ever to live hadn't managed to escape. But I would find a way. I had to.

Chapter Twenty-Four

Aren

We rose early and set off for the village, expecting to find the idyllic-looking rural community I'd seen the evening before. Instead, we found the place in turmoil. People leaned out from the windows of their stone-walled houses at the outskirts of town, yelling in Cressian accents so thick I found it hard to understand what they were saying. Others ran from door to door, spreading news, gathering a crowd that headed toward the square I'd seen the night before.

We'd passed the outer buildings of the town before a large man in blue coveralls with a pitchfork resting over his shoulder noticed us.

"Not a good time to visit, strangers," he called, sounding suspicious but not hostile.

"What is it?" Cassia asked, and stepped toward him. "Is it a dragon?"

The man looked twice at her before answering. "No, miss. Local trouble, and soldiers—emissaries, they call themselves—from the south causing additional problems."

Cassia tossed her hair back over her shoulder and pasted a look of sweet concern on her face. "That's terrible. Why are they here? Are we in danger?"

"It's nothing to worry about, miss. Same as it is everywhere, them thinking they have a right to every powerful Sorcerer and Potioner we've got. It's just complicated now. Town business, though, and I shouldn't speak on it. You understand."

"We were looking for lodging. What town is this?" Cassia asked.

"Arberg," the man said, looking back over his shoulder, where footsteps approached from around the corner of the building. "I'd suggest moving on down the road. Trint might be a better place for you, and you'll make it there before nightfall." He drummed his fingers against the handle of the pitchfork.

"Thank you," Cassia said, and came back toward us. The man stared at her as she walked away. He saw me watching him and shrugged, then went back to his post at the front of the building.

Kel and I followed Cassia into a narrow alleyway between houses, away from the commotion.

"So what do we do?" Cassia asked. "Move on? He said Trint's just down the road, and that's where your uncle said to go. But then, what's to say they stayed there? I'd have moved on if I were your mother. Made myself disappear, changed my name and my daughter's. If the soldiers are here for someone with magical gifts..."

"Right," I said. "My mother had no power of her own, so it has nothing to do with her. My father never would have let her take my sister if she showed any sign of talent. It's unlikely that she's a Sorceress. A Potioner, maybe." My mother's mother had been a Potioner. The potential for skill in her children was there.

"Soldiers from Luid could be looking for you, though," Kel said. "Maybe not specifically, but they'll have their eyes open. Might be best to avoid them. It's up to you."

"I suppose we get closer and see what's going on," I said. "We'll stay out of sight and head toward the square to see what's happening."

Cassia and I moved ahead, but Kel hung back.

Cassia turned to him. "You coming?"

He leaned out to look down the street behind us. "I'll catch up. Try to stay out of trouble, both of you."

By the time we'd made our plans, our section of town had quieted. It seemed news had spread quickly, and anyone who was going to the square was already there. Cassia and I stayed close to the buildings and out of sight of the few townspeople now roaming the streets, cutting across alleys and quiet side streets when we needed to, working our way toward the town square I'd seen the night before. When we reached it, we hung back in the shadows of a dark alley between a pair of shops.

The scene we found was nothing like what I'd expected.

The crowd, a hundred people at most, was divided down the middle of the square, and the groups stood facing each other, all clenched fists and angry glances. The larger group was made up of townsfolk, wearing clothing that was plain but well made, suited for work. One of their own stood in the middle, her hands bound behind her back with rough rope, face invisible to us behind the black hair that hung tangled over her face. Her plain, cream-colored dress was stained with dirt—or perhaps dried blood—around the hem, her heavy boots scuffed.

I pulled back farther into the shadows. The other group wore uniforms, dirty with travel, but bearing Severn's flame insignia. There was no reason for them to be there looking for me, unless my uncle had reported me after all.

"Ye can't take her," called an older man wearing suspenders and a collared shirt. "This woman stands accused and convicted of murder in cold blood. She killed her own husband. Poisoned him."

"She kilt my brother!" added a blonde woman. "I told 'im he should never have married a Posh'nur from away! 'e was a good man! She don't deserve to live!"

"And she won't," concluded the older man. "She's set to choose the manner of her death, her own in payment for her husband's, as the law demands. Blood for blood, gentlemen. I don't know how you do it down where you come from, but it's how it goes here. I'm sorry."

A man I recognized stepped forward from the group of soldiers. He was a member of Severn's personal guard at one time, red-haired and frequently smirking, as though everything amused him. He wore the same expression now. Regus the Red, they'd called him.

"Is that so, Mayor? Well, I'm sorry, too, but we're taking her with us. It is unfortunate that we didn't arrive in time to save her husband's life."

"Ye're a year late for that!" the blonde screeched.

Regus ignored her. "If you hand her over quietly, we'll make repayment for your loss as is appropriate. We only recently received word that you had a talented Potioner living in this area, and it took us a while to find her. You should have reported her. You knew that Sorcerers and Potioners were required to register in Luid."

The mayor's back straightened, and his chin jutted forward. "We're not accustomed to forcing people to go where they do not wish, unless they're prisoners. That would have been her own decision. You're too late now, though."

The crowd, which had now grown slightly and included the man who'd stopped us earlier, murmured its agreement.

"Are we?" Regus stepped toward the prisoner, and she stepped back. One of the townsmen standing behind her stepped forward to grab the rope that bound her wrists.

"What do you think, pretty one?" Regus asked. "Stay here and die, or come with us and work for Lord Severn? If you do your work well you'll be taken care of, treated much better than I think you've been here. Hot meals, hot baths, warm bed, challenging work. I guarantee safe passage there, no need to worry about these fellows who are with me—as long as you behave, of course."

She raised her head to look at him, trembling—I thought with fear, but when she spoke, it was rage that burned in her voice. "I'd rather die than serve him." Her skin was pale, and she was finer-featured than the townspeople who surrounded her. She spoke with a slight northern accent, tinged with something else.

Cassia gripped my arm hard, but I didn't turn away to look at her.

Regus drew in a deep breath, and the self-satisfied smirk dropped from his face, replaced by irritation. "That seems to be the choice they're giving you, isn't it? Death, or service."

The mayor stepped forward, and Regus drew his sword and pointed it at the man's chest. "Stay back. This is the king's business now, not yours. We're taking her." He turned back to the woman. "Let me say this again. You either accept our offer, or we assume that you're a traitor and we take you to Luid anyway and have you tried and executed. I promise you will not be allowed to choose the manner of your death, and it is never pleasant in a case like this."

"You can't do this!" the mayor yelled. His face turned bright red. "We have laws!"

"And I have my sword and my soldiers," Regus said, smirking again. "I win. Come on, lads. The lady rides with me."

The mayor continued his ineffectual blustering, but Regus stepped forward and took the rope binding the woman's hands. He pulled her roughly toward him, then dragged her, stumbling, toward the rest of his troops.

"What are we going to do?" Cassia hissed into my ear.

"I don't know." I pulled back and leaned against a stack of crates. "If it was just the townsfolk, I'd be less inclined to intervene."

"Why?"

"They have a right to justice. She killed her husband."

"Oh, like you've never killed anyone's husband, I'm sure." She glared at me with her arms crossed.

"But," I added, "we can't let her go with the soldiers. No one deserves that."

"Especially not your sister?"

The words hit me like a slap. "Are you sure?"

"As sure as I can be without speaking to her," Cassia said. "Something about her tone, her expression. My instincts are usually trustworthy."

I looked again. The prisoner was arguing with Regus, closer now and facing us so that I could see her face clearly. A thin scar marred her cheekbone, and her loose hair gave her a wild look, but with a little cleaning up she might have fit in among Luid's high society. She looked nothing like my father. I tried to remember how my mother had looked, but couldn't. I remembered hair like that, though, black as night.

"I thought a twin would look more like me."

"Wrong kind of twin," Cassia said. "What do we do?"

I crouched again. "We can't let her go."

"Psst." We looked up to see Kel standing at the other end of the alley. "I thought these might come in handy." He held reins in his hand, and when we got closer we found two brown horses and a gray one standing around the corner, docile but alert. He craned his neck to look toward the square. "Should I have taken four?"

Cassia stared at him. "Did you steal those?"

Kel smiled sheepishly. "Would you be disappointed in me if I said yes?"

"Hardly."

"Oh. Well, I was going to, but I changed my mind and left some money in one of the stalls."

Cassia's mouth quirked into a smile. "My dear brother. You'll steal a poor farm-girl's heart, but not a few horses."

He sighed."I thought we weren't talking about that."

I took the gray's reins from Kel. The horses were saddled and ready, and I swung onto the big mare's back. "We need to go before that meeting breaks up and they find their horses missing."

Kel and Cassia mounted, swinging their legs awkwardly over the horses. They moved so naturally on land that I often forgot how unfamiliar much of it was to them.

"We're leaving her?" Cassia asked.

"Temporarily," I said. "There's no way we're going to get her away from a hundred people, with more waiting in their houses to help if trouble arrives. A dozen men will be easier to handle, even if they're armed."

I turned my horse and led the way back through the side streets. With everyone occupied at the square, the roads remained empty.

We urged the horses into a canter and made for the dark forest outside of town, then tied the horses to trees and found a place where we could watch without being seen ourselves.

It wasn't a long wait. The soldiers exited the town, riding horses branded with a flame on their hindquarters. The woman rode side-saddle in front of Regus, struggling to maintain her balance with her hands still tied behind her. Regus was laughing, and had his sword drawn, wet and dark with blood.

"Unbelievable," Kel whispered.

The men and their captive turned south and west down the road, which curved into the woods farther on.

We retrieved our horses and cut through the forest with some difficulty, aiming to find a place where we expected to meet the road. When we did, there was no sign of them. No fresh tracks.

I opened my mind to them, and hesitated as Phelun's words about touching people's minds came back to me.

Don't be an idiot, I told myself. *They're enemies.*

I caught their presence before the sound of hoofbeats reached us. "Off the road," I ordered.

We hurried into the trees. The pine forest was difficult to get through, but the trees hid us well once we got behind them.

Voices and slow hoof beats approached. I reached out again and caught tiny glimpses of the thoughts at the forefronts of their minds as the soldiers came into view. Most of the men were thinking things not worth repeating. A few searched for a campsite. Likely they were all supposed to be doing the same, but we humans are so easily distracted by a fine form and a pretty face.

"It's them," I whispered. "Let them pass. We'll find them when they make camp."

We followed at a distance that allowed me to track them while staying out of sight. I wanted to help that woman—my sister, if Cass was right—but I wasn't going to risk my friends' lives for her.

Their voices became louder as they made camp, calling out to each other. Regus ordered his underlings around, and others shouted to those who had gone to find firewood. Kel, Cassia and I left our horses and moved closer.

"Wait," Cassia whispered, and darted silently back to her horse to take something from her bag. She returned to us, stuffing a long object into her pocket.

"What is it?" I asked.

"Dragon flare."

I'd hoped that most of the men would have

dispersed as they made camp, but they were sticking close, setting up tents and taking food out of sacks. The young woman was in the middle of it all, seated serenely on a tree stump, watching the goings-on around her. I didn't think she was missing much of what was happening, but she didn't appear to see us.

"Still too many," I said. "We could try rushing in, or I could change and attack, but either way I can't handle more than a few at a time. And you—"

"Are probably not much help fighting on land," Kel said. "I know. I don't think they'll agree to move this party to a lake."

Cassia worked the slender item out of her pocket. "People around here use these to draw dragons away from their homes and livestock. Light it up, I'll throw."

I hesitated. If a dragon came, we were as likely to die as the soldiers were. Still, the flare itself would be a distraction that might get us past the soldiers.

"Away from the camp," I said. "Lead them away from us."

I lit the fuse. Cassia took off running, leaping over fallen logs, making more noise than I'd have preferred, but speed was more important than silence. I lost sight of her before the crackling noise started, and a spot at the far side of the clearing began to glow.

"What the—" one of the soldiers said, and several ran toward the flickering light. The brilliant explosion, like a star landed in the forest, threw them back.

"You idiots!" Regus yelled. "It's a dragon flare. Pack up, we're moving out!"

They'd seemed undisciplined, but they managed to pull together enough to begin collecting their startled horses and lowering tents. Regus stood next to the woman, who had appeared ready to dart into the forest.

"Friend of yours?" he hollered, trying to be heard over the roar of the flare.

"Not the kind I would have hoped for," she yelled

back. A dark shape passed overhead, then another.

"Dragons!" Regus roared, and drew his sword. "Get out of here!"

Their discipline broke. Trained soldiers they may have been, but not many people from the south have faced a live dragon, and their training would not have prepared them for this. Chaos erupted, men yelling and running around gathering their things, occasionally crashing into one another, still blinded by the flare. A few took horses and nothing else, and left as fast as the animals would carry them.

The two dragons passed over us again, and a low roar rumbled through the forest.

"I guess the flares work," Kel shouted.

"Where's Cass?"

"There."

She ran toward us, arms flung protectively over her head. She was safe enough. The dragons focused on the men who fled from the site, easy pickings on the road. The larger dragon snapped up several men and swallowed them. The smaller took its time over kills, but didn't stop to eat between them. Rather, it seemed to be enjoying the hunt.

Regus continued to hold onto the woman with his left hand, sword drawn and held in his right. I couldn't fault his courage, but I also couldn't let him keep her. I thought that he'd be as happy to use the sword on her as on the dragons.

"Get her, Kel!"

I changed, letting my clothes fall to the ground in a heap as I transformed and took off into the trees. I dove toward Regus. He saw me, and recognition dawned. He laughed.

He pushed the woman away and held his sword ready. I sheered to the left. He followed, striking out with his sword in a controlled movement. I anticipated it and pushed back at the air with my wings, slowing enough so that his swing fell short, then stretched my talons toward his face.

He screamed. The woman screamed, too, as Kel pulled her away. "Let me go!" she yelled, and he grunted in what sounded like pain.

I ignored Kel's struggle as he hauled the woman away from the fight and toward cover. I slashed at Regus's arms when he threw them up to protect his face, and had to fall back when I lost my momentum. I climbed again, and attacked.

The smaller dragon shrieked nearby, distracting Regus for the briefest moment—less than the time it took to blink, but enough that I was able to wrap my talons around his arm and rip into him. He dropped the sword and swung his other hand toward me, grabbing a handful of feathers as he tried to pull me off. I struck out, snapping at his face, and felt his wrist bones snap between my toes.

The dragon's cry came again, and an open mouth full of sharp teeth appeared behind Regus. I pushed away. Pain screamed through my wings and back as they slammed into the ground, but at least I was away from the dragon. A horrible tearing sound followed, and Regus's body—complete only from the chest down—fell to its knees and hit the forest floor with a soft thud. I fled as the smaller dragon feasted.

I flew toward the sound of the woman's voice, which came from a copse of trees near the road. When I landed, Kel was watching her warily. She glared back at him, chest heaving as she caught her breath. I shrieked, and they looked at me. I motioned with my beak toward the sky. The larger dragon circled overhead, then dropped into the clearing.

"Right, move!" Kel yelled.

The woman tried to run in the opposite direction, but Kel grabbed her and threw her over his shoulder. "I'm so sorry, miss," he called to her. She struggled and kicked, but he was far stronger. He ran toward our horses. I followed, leaping between trees, as they were too close together to fly between.

"Ow! I'm trying to help you!" Kel hollered.

He set the woman down near the horses and took a few steps back, rubbing his arm. Cassia ran up behind us, leading a flame-branded horse with a soldier's cloak and bags still attached to its saddle. "Aren, your clothes," Cassia said, and tossed the heap behind her into the trees.

I watched the woman to make sure she wasn't going to bolt, then went and changed. I didn't want to hurt her, but I wasn't going to let her go if she had information we needed. I took another quick look at her. I'd expected a sister—a twin sister, no less—to seem familiar in some way. I felt nothing.

"It's okay," Cassia was saying when I returned. She glanced back at me and nodded. The other woman just glared. "We saw what they were doing to you at the town. We're trying to help." She paused to catch her breath. "Who are you?"

The woman stood straighter. Cassia wasn't short, but this one managed to look down at her, if only slightly, her gaze sharp and accusing. Kel stared at her, enthralled.

"My name is Nox. That's all you need to know," she said. "I didn't need your help. I could have gotten away without you, or perhaps accomplished something in Luid if they had taken me there. Leave me alone." She seemed to be choosing her words carefully and trying to shed her northern accent. I caught a hint of Belleisle in there, though, which I suspected she'd picked up from her mother.

"You're coming with us," I said. "You owe us answers."

She swung herself up onto the soldier's horse and sat straight-backed and imperious. I mounted my own horse to follow if she bolted.

"I don't owe you anything," she said. Her words were brave, but a tremble in her voice betrayed something else. I opened myself, and her fear and uncertainty flooded me far more intensely than I'd expected. I could easily have slipped into her thoughts, but I closed it off, uncertain as to whether she might be sensitive to magic.

She gave me a suspicious glance. "If there's something you need, you can try to keep up. I'm getting away from here before I get eaten."

I glanced back at the clearing, where the large brown dragon approached the smaller one, intent on stealing its gory meal. Everyone else had disappeared. Cass, Kel and I hurried to mount our own horses to follow as Nox headed back to the road.

"Yeah, she's definitely your sister," Kel said, grinning as we chased her. "This should be interesting."

Chapter Twenty-Five

Nox

"That was incredibly stupid," I said to the three of them, once they caught up with me.

The woman leading them down the road was a stunning creature with clear, bronze-toned skin and hair the dark, glossy brown of the mink that townsfolk trapped in the autumn. She kept her blue-green eyes trained on me without fear or concern for propriety. A huntress, I decided, and certainly not from the northern provinces.

I forced my shaking breaths to become even and waited for my heart to slow. These people had saved me from the soldiers. I should have been grateful for that, but my life had a tendency toward going from bad to worse. Perhaps they meant well, but in recent years I'd misjudged too many people. My husband Denn had sweet-talked me into a marriage that left me bitter, scarred, and empty long before his death. I'd wanted to leave town after his funeral, but the townsfolk needed me. They became friendly. Then rumors started about Denn's death, and they turned on me.

I let my hair fall over my face and glanced back at the others from between locks in desperate need of a washing. Nothing about them said they were a threat. They were clearly fools, if they thought attracting dragons was an appropriate way to do anything but commit suicide, but that might make them more dangerous.

Project strength, I told myself. *If they see weakness, they'll tear you apart.* This was my chance to take charge. No longer would I be the little wife creeping around the house the morning after her husband came home drunk, or the student keeping her talent hidden so as not to rouse her mentor's jealousy. Nor would I be the tiny child swept from her bed in the middle of the night, frightened and crying as she and her mother journeyed to a dark and unpredictable future.

No. From this moment on, I live up to my birthright. I am the daughter of a king.

If I could truly believe that, perhaps I could get out of this alive. How would such a woman act? Strong, I decided. I wouldn't let them see my fear. I would force them to respect me, as few people had before.

I slowed my horse to a walk and patted his neck. He was beautiful, a fine traveling companion and better quality than any nag we'd had when I was growing up. The woman rode past me while the men remained behind.

The soldiers had been bad, but at least I knew what they wanted. What did I know about these people? Unless I was mistaken, the man with the long, dark hair was a Sorcerer, and I suspected he might be a shape-shifter, though I'd missed seeing it in the confusion of their haphazard rescue scheme.

We'd had magic-users in Arberg. None of them were strong enough to try something like that, but they'd thought themselves superior to everyone and considered their gifts far more important than those of a mere

Potioner. My mother said that tended to be the way with powerful folk, especially Sorcerers, and advised me to stay out of their way.

I'd hidden in my attic when the soldiers came to claim them for Luid.

The Sorcerer rode up beside me, and I instinctively shied away. I disliked the cold look in his strange brown-and-green eyes. He appeared healthy in spite of his pale complexion, and was handsome enough in a refined sort of way. Not someone who spent his life toiling outdoors, though judging by the scruff on his face and the dirt on his clothes, he'd been on the road a few days. He appeared strong, if lean, and rode with the same proper form as the soldiers. He could have been one of them, if he'd had the right weapons and uniform.

"Did you not know what that stick was before you lit it?" I asked them. "Or was it your mission to kill us all?" Best to attack first, if only with words.

"We knew what it was," the Sorcerer said, sounding irritated rather than intimidated. "We needed a distraction."

I was right. They are fools. "I'd say you got what you wanted, then. Those dragons were mighty distracting."

He glared at me. "It worked. I don't see any ropes binding your wrists or soldiers chasing you."

He apparently expected some show of gratitude. Not yet. Not until I found out what he and his friends wanted with me. "I would have been fine without you," I said.

The muscles in his firm jaw clenched. *May a windwyvern piss on my head if you ever find me a joy to converse with*, I thought. His presence irritated me for reasons I didn't yet understand. It seemed to come on an instinctual, animal level, and I got the sense he felt the same way about me. He started to say something, but the other man placed a hand on his arm to indicate that he would try to speak to me.

One look at that one told me I had better not let my guard down with him. It would be far too easy to be overcome by his obvious charm. Skin the same color as the woman's, eyes like the depths of a lake on a summer day, black hair that he brushed back from his face in a gesture that was somehow bashful and self-confident at the same time. His smile revealed the hint of a shallow dimple at the corner of his mouth. I glanced lower, taking in the challenge. Broad shoulders, a muscular body obvious even under layers of clothing. Big hands with long fingers gripped the reins in an awkward hold.

I'd always had a weakness for beauty. We saw so little of it in Cressia.

Even before he spoke, this man made the always-charming Denn look like a bumbling youngster at his first town social. I'd be careful not to fall into that trap again. Strong and attractive did not equal kind or worthwhile.

"Miss?" He glanced sideways at me. "Nox?"

I looked away. "Yes." An ugly name, I'd often thought, harsh as the land. I'd forgotten my birth name until my mother reminded me of it, and didn't care to take it back even now. I was Nox, and that was all. One needed a hard name in hard times. Still, this man made it sound almost lovely.

"It seemed that those men intended to hurt you, and that you were taken against your will," he said. "We thought we might help you, and that you might help us."

I gritted my teeth. His tame approach was obviously meant to make me relax my defenses. "Is that so?" I asked. "You'll have to forgive me if I can't be thankful just yet. You see, those soldiers saved me from certain death at the hands of people who I helped for years. I'm sure the soldiers would have liked me to help them somehow on the way to meet their master, who would have used my talents to serve *his* needs. And now you're here, saving me from them, and I can't bring myself to believe you mean well." My words didn't seem to trouble him. "Even if your intentions are good, I've done enough helping over these past few years to last me a lifetime. I have nothing left to offer."

I waited for a clever line about my usefulness, but he didn't offer any. I held his gaze for a moment to show him his overly kind attitude wouldn't weaken me.

He studied me, then smiled. "You're well-spoken for a person from this province. Were you born here?"

That smile made me want to return it. I refused. "My mother was from the South. She didn't raise me to be ignorant. Or a fool." His smile didn't waver in spite of my clipped tone. I sighed. "What is it you want?"

He hesitated. "Aren? What exactly did you want to ask her?"

My heart froze for a beat. "Aren?" No wonder I'd instinctively disliked the Sorcerer. I reined my horse in slightly and glanced over my shoulder at the other man. "Is that your name?"

"It is."

"Tiernal?"

"Yes."

No denial. No apology in his voice. I'd heard many stories about Aren Tiernal, and none of them pleasant. A mind-controller, and he used that skill to support Severn—the man responsible for every loss I'd ever suffered. Aren was said to have no conscience, to think of nothing but serving his father, and then his brother. Charming. Attractive. And a person never to be trusted.

I hadn't heard the stories from my mother. She rarely spoke of him. It broke her heart to think of the son she'd lost, and broke mine each time I realized that I alone wasn't enough for her. It wasn't her fault. Strictly speaking, it wasn't his, but I'd blamed her misery and my own on my father's family for years. Too long for me to feel anything but disgust now that I met one of them.

Family comes from love and experience, not blood. He was nothing to me, and I wouldn't fall victim to his powers. *Never open yourself to a Sorcerer*, my tutor had once cautioned. *Never let him in, never let your guard down.* Perhaps the wisest words the man ever spoken. I hardened myself and closed my heart and my mind as well as I could.

I turned away. "You're a long way from home, Aren Tiernal. Have you come to start a riot somewhere?" He didn't speak, but rode closer again so that the two men flanked my horse on either side. *Strike first*, I reminded myself. *Push him away.* "Our mother was very disappointed in you."

The look that flashed across his features in a brief, unguarded moment would have frozen the heartwood of an ice-oak, but I felt nothing. He probably wasn't used to such an affront. I imagined a prince of Tyrea would be accustomed to deference, or to fear. He wouldn't see either in me.

His beautiful companion turned back and narrowed her eyes at me. Her upper lip lifted in either distaste or anger. She was obviously good friends with my brother, and I assumed more. She dropped back and whispered something to him. He nodded, but that hurt expression never left his face.

What did he expect? He probably didn't remember any more of Magdalena Albion than I did of our father, but surely he couldn't have thought she'd be proud of what her son had grown into. They were all monsters in that family. Monsters who had been given every comfort in life that I had been denied. My mother had clung to the belief that her son, her little Aren, would never turn out like the rest of them.

She'd been a wise woman, and yet a fool when it came to the son she'd left behind.

I turned back to the other man, who I hadn't yet

got a handle on. "I think it's customary for you to introduce yourself at this point. I know who he is. I don't know you or your other friend there."

"My name is Kel," he said. "This is my sister Cassia."

She glared at me again as she masked a long stream of coughs in the crook of her elbow. A nasty sound, dry and barking.

"Thank you." I wanted to ask him more, to find out where they were from, but decided I'd have the upper hand if I didn't act like I cared. I wouldn't be with them long, anyway. "What did you say you wanted?"

We were heading south, through woods I'd searched for herbs many times during summer. They looked different now, with only the beginnings of buds on the trees. I didn't know exactly where I was leading them, but I knew that it wouldn't be back home. I rubbed my wrists, where red rope-burns masked the old scars. *Definitely not there.*

"We were looking for you and your mother," Kel said. "Aren didn't know you were alive until a few days ago."

"No? Would he have come right up and brought us home if he'd known?"

Aren didn't say anything, and Kel apparently had no response.

Too much, Nox. They'll dislike you.

I don't care. I decided I was done with being liked. People always felt they could use and discard anyone who was nice.

"My mother is dead," I told them. "Just over two years now. I was married then, and had moved away. She caught a fever and died before I could get back to do anything about it." Hadn't been allowed to go back, but they didn't need to know that. That part of my life was over.

I'm free, I thought, and a shiver tickled the back

of my neck. *Free.*

"I'm sorry," Kel said, sounding like he really was. "I've heard she was a lovely woman."

"Not so lovely after a few years up here," I said, speaking to Kel, but loudly enough that Aren could hear. "She was a good woman, but she became bitter and hard." I nodded back to Aren. "Is that all you folks wanted? To find out whether he could have a joyful reunion with his mother? I'm sorry if you wasted all this time for that."

Cassia's shoulders pulled up slightly toward her ears, but she still didn't say anything to defend Aren.

Kel looked past me to Aren, who frowned and shook his head. I disliked the way he looked at me now that he'd overcome his shock, cold and closed-off. Arrogant. Judging, and finding me lacking somehow. I'd have been more comfortable with anger.

Cassia coughed again, and waved off a concerned look from Kel.

"I suppose the other question we had," he said to me, "was whether your father had come by here a few years ago, before he disappeared."

I laughed. "Really? Of course he didn't. He shipped us off almost twenty years ago on the whim of that little shit Severn, and we never heard another word from him. My mother always hoped that he'd come for us, maybe when the old queen died. She thought he loved her."

I admired my mother. She'd comforted me even in her distress, cheered me through her own despair, and did what she had to do in order to scratch out a life for us in that godsforsaken land. But when it came to the king, she was blind and broken.

"I think she knew after a decade or so that he wasn't coming, but she still waited." I swallowed back the lump that insisted on rising in my throat when I thought of it. I hated Ulric for that more than I hated him for sending us away. "So the answer is no. I have no idea where he is, or was, and I don't particularly care. May I go now?"

Kel frowned slightly. "Maybe if you stayed—"

"Let her go," Aren said, his voice soft and calm, but cold. He stared at me from behind the strands of hair that fell over his face, all dark eyes and disdain. "If she's not going to help us, we don't need her. She obviously wants to go."

Something niggled at my brain like a thought I couldn't quite catch, and a chill passed through my mind as I realized Aren must be looking in. I gasped and imagined darkness enclosing my thoughts as I turned to him. His eyes widened, and his chin jerked upward. The corner of his lip twitched, though I couldn't tell whether it indicated satisfaction, amusement, or something else.

It didn't matter. He'd just confirmed everything I wanted to hate about him.

"Why would I help you?" I asked. "You had to have known I wasn't going to help Severn. That's what you do, isn't it? Aren't you his oversized lapdog?"

Aren took a deep breath, and any hint of a smile vanished. "If we were helping Severn, why would we have saved you from the soldiers who were taking you to him?"

My stomach dropped as I realized that my fear had made me overlook information. Aren and his friends did seem to be working against Severn. But him pointing out my error only made me like him less. I wanted to work against Severn, but not with them. Not with him. *My dear brother.*

I reached up to push my tangled hair away from my face. "I have no interest in finding my father. I have nothing to say to any of your family, especially the king and Severn. They took everything from me and my mother."

Everything, my mind echoed. *Schooling.*

Comfort. Warmth. I was a princess. I should have wanted for nothing.

"I had nothing to do with your being sent away," Aren said.

"No. You didn't help, though."

"I was four years old when you left," he said, his voice deep and threatening. "I thought my mother dead, and I never knew I had a sister. Why would I have come looking for either of you?"

A cold breeze whipped through the trees, rattling branches and sending a chill down the back of my dress. Kel offered me his jacket, and I refused. Aren's words should have made sense, but it was all too much. Trying to keep him out of my mind, making sense of this new information while still feeling aftershocks of fear from the soldiers and the dragons, either of which should rightly have killed me...

"I don't know or care," I told Aren, just to shut down the conversation. "I can't do this."

My mother had been silent on our history for so many years. All I'd known was how she hated "that horrible boy" who was next in line for the Tyrean throne. She never spoke his name, but she had passed on her hatred of Severn to me as surely as she had her long fingers and black hair. She'd never spoken of Aren, though, until she revealed our secret to me. She'd never wanted me to hate my twin brother.

I did hate Aren, though. I hated him for how much our mother loved him, even knowing what he was. How she nearly died of her grief that first winter in Cressia, how she wished she'd been able to bring him with us. I hated him for having enough to eat, a warm bed, and no fear of people breaking into his home to take whatever they wanted because it was only defended by a magic-less exile and her useless daughter. For the fact that he'd been kept, while I'd been thrown away.

Not that any of Aren's advantages seemed to be

doing him any good now.

Gods and Goddess, I swore at myself, *forget all of that. Focus on the future. Now that you're free, perhaps you'll find your way to Luid, after all, and make something of your life.*

Kel rode up beside Cassia to speak privately. The heated discussion went on for a while. They seemed to reach a decision, and she looked more composed when he left her to speak quietly to Aren. I tried to listen in, but all I heard was Aren saying, "Whatever you think is best. You see her better than I do right now."

Kel came up beside me again. I was growing dizzy watching his movements. "We're thinking that it might be beneficial for you to stay with us for a little longer. These woods are dangerous enough for four people, let alone one on her own."

I tried not to smile at the sincerity and honest concern in his voice. I couldn't help liking Kel, just a little. I'd definitely have to be careful. "I think it might be more dangerous with you people around."

He smiled at that, lips parting to reveal perfect teeth. "You might be right. But I can promise we won't intentionally attract any more dragons. You probably know more about avoiding them than we do, and we'll listen to you. And we have bedrolls to share, blankets, and a few coins." He lowered his voice. "I understand that you and Aren probably have some differences to work through, but you both want the same thing, really. At least, I assume that you want to see Severn removed from power."

"That's one way of putting it." I thought that I'd rather see him castrated and impaled on one of the iron spikes that I'd heard topped the palace walls in Luid, or see him torn apart by a hundred dragonlings. Removed from power would be a start, though, and if Aren wanted the same thing, perhaps we could tolerate each other for that.

Kel held my gaze, and I felt myself responding to something strange and compelling in him. I looked away.

"Fine," I said. "We'll travel together. But if any of you get in my way or try to interfere with me, I'm leaving you to the dragons."

"Yes, ma'am," Kel said, and pressed his lips together to hide another smile.

"Don't call me ma'am."

"Yes, ma'am."

I suspected it was going to be a long ride.

Chapter Twenty-Six

Aren

Nox seemed content to ride in silence through the day, head hung low as though wearing her hair as a mask, shadowing her faint scars and the mistrustful expression she wore. She answered questions from Kel and Cassia in short sentences, never giving more than she seemed to think necessary, never leaving avenues open for further conversation. I shouldn't have faulted her for that. Under the circumstances, I'd have been less trusting than she was.

And yet her presence was like a splinter under a fingernail, irritating beyond what it had any right to be.

I never should have looked into her thoughts. It had only been a test to see whether she was alert to it. But what should have been a quick glance had turned into a fast and unintentional free-fall into her mind that flooded me with resentment, fear, uncertainty, obstinacy, and above all her desire to get away from me. It had been far too easy, as though there were an established connection between us. If I'd had any lingering doubts that she was my sister, that would have ended them. I'd have to be careful not to let it happen again.

I'd broken the connection as quickly as I could, without manipulation. She'd noticed, though, and made a feeble and ineffective attempt to push back. I couldn't blame her for the surge of indignant anger she'd felt before I pulled away, but her attitude toward me still grated on my nerves.

"Hold on," Nox said, and stopped her horse. It was the sixth stop she'd made already, and it was barely late afternoon.

"Have you had that much to drink today?" I asked politely.

Her shoulders stiffened. "No. I just need to stretch my legs."

There was purpose in her steps, though, as she stalked off into the woods, and she stooped to dig a handful of roots out from the dirt beside an oak stump. She paused to scrape lichen off of the side of the rotting trunk beside it and came back to tuck the items into the saddle bags on the fine horse she'd claimed for herself.

She'd obviously inherited a Potioner's talents, and they had to be strong if Severn wanted her. Their skills were nothing like the power we Sorcerers carried in us. Though I'd learned a little about Emalda's talents while I lived at the school, I still found it hard to be impressed by what amounted to glorified cooking skills.

Rowan would have given me hell for looking down on someone with lesser magic, and I felt a flash of guilt.

It's not that, I told myself. *She's unpleasant, and has no information that can help us. She's not an asset, and we have work to do. It's best if she moves on.*

Cassia took a long drink from her water bag, and Kel did the same. I didn't like her cough. Merfolk were hardy, rarely falling ill, recovering quickly from injuries. She'd said it was the air. There wasn't much I could do about that, but we'd need to get her home soon.

"Would it be acceptable to you if we moved on, now?" I asked Nox. Kel gave me what I took to be a warning look. I ignored it.

"Yes. Thank you," she said stiffly. Still afraid. I didn't have to look into her thoughts to see that. She mounted, and we rode on. Kel spoke quietly to her, and I thought I caught her smiling, if only briefly.

So Cressia had been a dead end. I'd learned that my father hadn't killed my mother. Perhaps that would make me less inclined to hate him if we met again, but the news did me little practical good. Nox had no answers, and offered nothing but rude words and another body to keep safe on the road.

At least I had Kel and Cassia. Not so long ago, I'd wanted to be alone and resented having a travelling companion. Now I found myself lonely when left with only my thoughts for company. *Rowan's ruined me,* I thought, not unhappily.

And if I ever want her to ruin me more, I'd better get back to work.

If Xaven had no idea where my father had gone, if Severn had no answers he was willing to give, my task seemed hopeless. I had to accept the fact that he was dead, either by Severn's hand or someone else's. There was no one but me left to challenge Severn for the throne.

Dead weight filled my chest, making it difficult to take a breath. I couldn't. I was trained for killing, for manipulation, and for underhanded dealings with enemies, not for magical combat. I could defend myself in a fight against someone less powerful than me, but Severn knew my weak points. He'd trained me himself, for the most part, and had chosen what I studied in order to make me most useful to him. I couldn't control his thoughts, though I'd have had no qualms about using that skill on him.

Even if I won, what then? I'd drive the country into the ground as surely as he would have, even if my intentions were better.

"You okay?" Cassia asked. Her voice had grown raspy.

"Fine. Just thinking."

She gave me a sympathetic smile. "Tempted to just run away from it all?"

"If I had anywhere to run, I might."

"Well, if you—" She held up a hand and leaned away as a coughing fit overtook her. "Excuse me."

Ahead of us, Nox sighed heavily enough that I heard her. She halted her horse until we caught up. "I might help with that. Can we stop?"

I didn't object this time. It would be an interesting test of her skills. Perhaps she'd turn out to be useful after all.

Cassia shook her head. "Let's find a place to make camp, first. It's getting late."

We made our way off the road to a clearing and let the horses forage. Nox and Cassia stood together and talked while Kel and I cleared a space for the fire.

"Is this cough new?" Nox asked.

"Yes. It's just since we came through Cressia. Something about the air here, I suppose." Cass and Kel had obviously decided not to share their true nature with this stranger.

"May I examine you?" Nox sounded more confident now than she had before. Cassia nodded, and Nox placed her fingertips under her jaw, then on her throat.

Kel coughed. "I'm not feeling so good, either. I might need—"

Cassia cut him off with a dirty look.

"Open your mouth?" Nox peered into Cassia's throat. "Is that sore?"

"I' hee gah hah," Cassia said.

"You can close your mouth."

"It feels all scratched up."

"Give me a minute."

Cassia sat on the ground and watched as Nox went through her saddlebags, pulling out roots, shoots, and new leaves, as well as a dark glass bottle the horse's previous owner had left behind. She opened the lid, sniffed, and made a sour face. "That'll do. Anyone have a bowl? Pot? Something?"

Kel retrieved a cracked wooden bowl from among Cassia's things. Nox took it without a word and got to work, pounding plant pieces with a rock and mixing a splash of the alcohol in.

"This is going to taste horrible," she warned Cassia, "but it'll help."

"What do you think?" Kel asked me, speaking quietly.

"Nice of her to help."

"You hate her, don't you?"

Cassia glanced at us, and I stepped farther away. Kel followed. "Keeping her around seems pointless," I said. "I need to figure out what to do about Severn, not help a runaway from Cressia get back on her feet."

"She's your sister."

I nearly laughed. "Blood doesn't mean much. Most of my worst enemies are family members."

"I suppose that's one way of looking at it. But there's your grandfather. You said he's a good person, and powerful. She has his blood in her, too."

I remembered the hatred in her mind. "I think she's got more of our father in her than she'd care to know. She doesn't want to stay with us anyway. She might be warming to you and Cass, but she wants to be as far away from me as possible."

"You peeked?" He didn't sound surprised. Disappointed, perhaps.

"Only for a moment. I've never felt anything like it. Are the rumors about me truly that bad?"

Kel hesitated before answering. "I don't spend a lot of time on land, normally. My dealings with humans tend to be..."

"Less conversational. I know."

"But yes. Honestly, if I'd never met you and saw

you on the street, I'd turn and run. Give her some credit for sticking around this long. She wants Severn dethroned, too."

"She told you that?"

"Sort of." He smiled as Nox tasted a finger-scoop of greenish goop, made a face, and handed the bowl to Cassia. Cassia said something, and Nox nodded and laughed. "I believe she has personal reasons for hating him."

"Don't we all. I just don't like her, Kel. All I saw in her was fear and hate. That's the last thing I need more of."

He turned his attention to me. "Are you sure that's all it is? No bitterness there over—"

"Absolutely not. That would be childish."

He shrugged, and held back a cough.

"I thought you were joking about that," I said.

"No. It's not as bad as Cassia's, but it's there. We're not built to breathe this way for so long." His smile widened as Cassia offered Nox a more practical change of clothes, and Nox thanked her. "See? She's friendly. Just not with you."

"Kel, are you sure you're thinking objectively right now?"

"Yes. Completely." He leaned forward slightly as Nox bent over to set her bowl down. She pulled Cassia's pants on under her skirt, then stepped behind a horse to slip the filthy dress off and a sweater on.

"Right," I said. "Tell me, what do you see there? Don't tell me you haven't tried to look into her, too."

He turned to face me. "I see more deeply than you do, my friend. You saw her thoughts, her emotions. I can't see any of that, and I'm glad of it. It only confuses matters, and it isn't important."

"It is in my line of work."

"I looked into her eyes, and I saw a person who's struggling, who's frightened, who has no idea what the

Titre

future holds, but who's strong enough to handle whatever comes. She's determined. Look at her now—no one asked her to help Cassia. There's a good heart there. Maybe she's scared to show it, but it's there."

"And?"

His lips twitched. "Fine. She's terribly attractive under the dirt. I can't help it if you people are pretty."

I snorted. "Don't bring me into this. She looks nothing like me."

"Whatever you say. In any case, she's not interested in romance at the moment. At least, I don't think so. She's nice enough, but guarded. She's hurting."

"Wasn't she accused of killing her husband?"

Kel shrugged, and a fit of coughing overtook him. "I think I'm going to find out whether that potion's as horrible as she claims. You coming back?"

"No. I'll look for firewood, thanks."

Nox gave Kel a tight smile as he strode toward them. They'd be better off if I left. I couldn't ask Kel and Cassia to come to Luid with me if I decided to challenge Severn. They couldn't help me there, and needed to get home. Maybe the merfolk would even help Nox.

What I wanted was to return to Belleisle and tell Rowan I'd changed my mind and needed her with me. She'd help. She'd done it before. And if I were honest with myself—not that I cared to be—I just missed her. Severn was right. I'd always had this weakness in me. I missed her smile, her strength, her gentle touch, the way she so often found the words to make me believe everything would be all right.

And if I were to face Severn, I wanted a chance to say goodbye to her, first.

No. Self-pity had never helped anyone. I hadn't asked for this job, but it had fallen to me.

Rowan was safer where she was. She would be fine, whatever happened. As for me, I would accept help from my strange travelling party if they still wished to offer it, and head south. If no other brilliant plan came to me along the way, I would challenge Severn. Alone.

I produced a flame in the palm of my hand and watched it grow.

Time to practice.

Chapter Twenty-Seven

Nox

I went through the rest of the items in my horse's saddlebags while the others set up camp. Cassia and Kel seemed to be feeling better since they'd tried my potion. It was a simple but soothing mixture, and they'd appreciated it. I hadn't examined Kel as I had Cassia. Just looking at him wakened feelings I'd buried years before. Not love, though if he were as kind and good-humored as he seemed, I didn't see how a person could help falling for him. But then, no one I'd ever met was what he seemed. *No*, I told myself, *this is entirely physical*. I was an adult, not some hot-blooded young girl. I could handle myself.

I found a pair of finely balanced daggers amongst the soldier's things. Other than a cloak that smelled like horse and sweat, a tin cup, a water bag, and that bottle of what I took to be home-brewed alcohol, there wasn't much that was useful. Someone else must have carried the food and medical supplies for the party. Pity. Still, the knives would be useful if I needed to do more work along the way, and I still had the horse.

I could sneak away tonight. Leave them. Head toward Luid on my own.

The idea brewing in my mind seemed insane, but I couldn't shake it. I'd escaped death by a matter of minutes back in Arberg. True, if they'd let me choose my manner of execution, I might have chosen poison and come up with something that would mimic death but allow me to wake before they burned my body. Either way, I decided, I was living on borrowed time, and I would use it well.

My mother had told me I was born for great things. Now, for the first time, I realized how true that might be.

I would see Severn dead. The idea warmed me as the sun set and the air turned cold. I would make him pay for what he did to my mother. What he did to me. I'd make him feel the pain of nearly starving in that barren land, of being ripped from my home, of working until the skin of my hands cracked in spite of the healing potions I learned to make. Of every compromise I'd been forced into for survival.

And it wasn't just about me. Severn was bad news for Cressia, and I suspected other provinces. How many times had I heard of magic-users executed for refusing to go to Luid? How many had been taken and never heard from again? Much as I hated my father, the people had tolerated him, and only grumbled about him at tax time. They'd appreciated it when he'd sent crews of soldiers to help dispatch troublesome dragons. Severn did no such thing. Though his army was growing, he didn't spare them for the likes of us. Taxes would rise soon, if the old men in the tavern were correct—and they usually were. We'd see no benefit from it, certainly. And there was the air of fear that had come over the land in recent years...

No, I decided. My mission was not entirely selfish. At least, I could tell myself it wasn't.

I set my things down and watched the rest of the group. Kel said something to Aren, who smiled. I hadn't realized he was capable of it. He still didn't look happy, but it was something. Such a disturbing presence. I wondered how he, Kel, and Cassia came to be friends. Kel seemed to carry peace with him, an ability to remain untroubled in the face of rejection and sharp words that I envied. Cassia was harder, but not unkind once I'd spoken to her.

Aren was less frightening than I'd expected, but no more welcoming, and he frequently seemed troubled or angry. I'd do well to put him behind me.

Unless, as Kel said, his plans truly aligned with mine. I tapped a fingernail against my teeth as I thought it through. If Aren was as hard and ruthless and powerful as I'd heard, he'd be my best chance of seeing my plan through. Kel had indicated that Aren had something planned to bring Severn down, and I would help him with that if I could. But I would also be prepared to do it alone if I had to. I could get information from Aren before I made my own plans. I needed to know about Severn, about what I'd find in Luid. Aren had wanted to use me for information. It only seemed fair that he should offer me the same.

After we all shared a meal of dried meat and fruit, Kel and Cassia unpacked a pair of bedrolls with thick wool blankets.

"It's not enough," I said. "The bedrolls. Even if we take turns on watch, there's not enough for three people to sleep."

"Not a problem," Aren said. "I need some time alone, anyway." He bent to set fire to the wood that he had collected, and did so with nothing but his bare hands.

That's not so impressive, I thought. Given time and the right supplies, I could create a potion to do the same.

Then he disappeared, replaced by a large mountain eagle.

"Oh," I said, actually speechless for once. I'd known he had the skill, but to see it in action caught me by surprise. No potion could do that.

I didn't feel him reading my thoughts, but I'd

have sworn he wore a smug look on his beak. *Stupid, superior Sorcerers.*

"I'll take first watch," I muttered, and took one of the blankets to wrap around my shoulders.

"Works for me," Kel said. "I'm exhausted. Wake me in a few hours. We'll want to get moving early tomorrow."

Aren flapped his way up to a branch of a bare tree and closed his eyes. If he was anything like me, it would be a long time before his thoughts quieted enough to let him sleep.

He's nothing like me, I reminded myself. I reached for the soldier's cloak that had been with my horse's things and placed it over a fallen log. The thing smelled too horrible to wear it, but I needed the warmth. I pulled the blanket tighter around my shoulders, and shivered.

Hours passed, and the stars shifted overhead. My heart quieted as I listened to the forest around me. Most people didn't feel the life in the plants the way I did. They didn't know that the trees breathed slow and deep, didn't sense roots spreading through thawing earth and shoots pushing toward the sky, didn't grasp the depth of life in the smell of decaying leaves, or the magical potential in every living thing. I did. I felt it deep in my bones, as I imagined the great Potioners all did.

I didn't truly know. I'd never met a great one.

Kel rolled over and flung an arm across his eyes, then sighed and sat up. He caught my eye and offered a little smile, then raked a hand through hair that stood straight up in patches. He stood and shuffled closer, stepping over his sleeping sister on the way, then sat next to me. The log bowed under the added weight. I shifted over to make room.

"It's a little early for your watch," I told him, speaking quietly so as not to wake the others.

"I know. I'm awake now, though. I'm still not

used to sleeping in the open air."

"You're accustomed to more comfortable surroundings?" I imagined things in Luid were quite different from what I knew in Arberg.

"In more ways than you know."

I could have gone and taken his bed while it was still warm, but my mind was too awake. We sat and watched the fire together, and I found myself glad of company. He didn't look at me or try to touch me. My wariness relaxed, if only a little.

"So you're a Potioner?" he asked. "What's that like?"

"I don't know. What's it like not to be one?"

He shrugged, and his blanket brushed against mine. "I don't know much about it. I know it's a natural gift, but I'd have thought it required study, the way a Sorcerer has to study and experiment before he can use his magic."

"That's true. My teacher was a male Potioner. Something of a rarity. He thought he was fantastic." I grimaced. "So did I, at first. But he wasn't. He taught me the basics, let me study from the few books he had, but much of his knowledge was learned. A Potioner's power and skill are better measured by what we sense." Gods, how I envied Potioners who trained in Luid under real masters.

Kel tilted his head slightly. "I'm not sure I follow."

I reached out to pluck a short blade of spring grass from beneath us. "What is this to you?"

"Grass. Green. Leafy. Food for horses, maybe?"

"All correct." I pressed my palms together with the grass between them. "It's also a non-magical plant, so I don't feel much from it. But based on my experiences and what I feel right now, I know that it would also make a fine addition to bulk up a healing medicine if I didn't have enough of it. It would spread the potency rather than watering it down, at least to a certain point. It would take trial and error to find that point, but I know it would work."

"How?"

I chewed on the bottom of the stalk. "It's something I know on my own. Instinct." *Just like I know I shouldn't be having this conversation with you*, I thought as my gaze met his again and my heart skipped.

"Fascinating."

I shrugged. "I'd get more from a magical plant. It's a useful skill to have, but it's not like a Sorcerer's magic. Are you reading my mind or something?"

He quirked an eyebrow. "No. Why?"

"You seem to be studying me. You've looked at me that way a few times today."

"I am, but I don't know what you're thinking."

"I've heard Aren can do that. Read minds." I pulled the blanket tighter about my shoulders. "I think he did it to me."

"He can," Kel sighed. He didn't seem to like it any more than I did, and I found myself warming to him further. "I can't. I get a sense of people, but it's nothing that intrusive. At least, I hope it isn't."

"What do you sense in me?"

I thought he'd laugh and humor me, but his expression remained serious as he looked into the fire. "Pain. But also—"

A faint noise cut him off, and we both stood. The sound came quietly at first, but quickly grew louder. Flapping wings, nearly overhead. I hurried to put out the small fire. Aren woke in his tree, and his feathers puffed out. He spread his wings and ascended toward the treetops.

Cassia came to stand with us. "What is it?"

"I don't know," I whispered. "Could be a dragon. Stay quiet. It will be fine."

The sounds grew louder. Not a dragon, though. I heard many wings up there, and dragons were solitary creatures from the time they left their mothers' nests.

Three shapes appeared overhead, then four, then six. Shorter necks than dragons. The legs were long, and thick tails flowed behind them in wavering lines.

"Horses!" I whispered, more for my own benefit than anyone else's. A smaller shape joined them. Aren. The horses went around him, but he harried the lead horse until they dipped lower in the sky and disappeared into the trees.

The rest of us weren't far behind, crashing through the trees in the direction they'd headed.

The herd landed in a moonlit meadow lush with young spring grass, and most of the horses folded their massive, white wings and set to eating right away. I'd heard that they had to eat a lot because they used so much energy flying. Their muscles stood out under their skin, thick and strong, and their winter coats were glossy under the long guard hairs. A small, brown mare with a lopsided white blaze on her face stood in front of Aren. She shook her mane as we approached.

"Humans," she muttered. "You never leave us alone." She lifted her nose into the light breeze that had followed them, then looked back at her herd. She folded her wings neatly and turned to me. "Did you send him up? He's not a proper eagle, you know."

"I'm sorry," I said. "I don't know why he followed you. Please excuse the intrusion. We don't mean you harm."

Cassia had brought Aren's clothes. She motioned for him to follow her into the trees.

That's inconvenient. I tried not to be pleased by that. Pettiness would get me nowhere, but I couldn't help it. Even the greats, it seemed, had weaknesses.

He came back after he dressed and spoke to the lead mare. "I apologize," he said. "You reminded me of an acquaintance of mine, and I wanted to ask whether you knew her. Are you from the Western mountains?"

She shook her head. "Nay. We're from the south, not far from what you call the Silver forest. It's a good place to live. Or was. There are too many humans there now, building houses on our grazing land, and many of them want to capture us and put us to work. They've made a sport out of trying to ride us, and they hold us responsible when one falls to his death. One of my herd should have been killed for it." She nodded toward a white mare. "But we've got her back, and we're not planning on returning to that place. These mountains you mentioned are hospitable to our kind? Where are they?"

"West," he said. "You'll see the mountains, but I'm afraid I can't direct you any better than that toward the other horses. Florizel didn't speak much about her home. May I ask your name?"

"Paerella. Your friend is an exile, then?" The mare twitched her tail and brushed it against her haunches.

"I don't know. She was separated from her herd. She's far from here now." He turned to Kel, Cassia, and me. "You didn't have to come. I'm sorry for waking you."

"That's all right," Cassia whispered, apparently entranced by the horses. The moonlight reflected off their bodies and pale wings, making them seem to glow as they cropped at the grass. A feeling of peace stole over me.

"I was also wondering if you'd tell us whether you'd seen any other humans while you were traveling today," Aren added. "We might be heading in the direction you're coming from, and it would be helpful for us to know what's coming."

The mare snorted. "Humans are everywhere. We passed by humans, and stayed away from them. I couldn't tell you how many or what kind, only that there were too many. A town, too, if you keep going down this road. Not so far."

"Thank you, Paerella," he said. "I'm sorry we have

nothing to offer you in return."

"No, you have nothing we need. You've already told me where to find more of our kind, and that's something. Do you think they'd welcome us?"

"I can't say. Florizel has a kind heart. If the others are like her, I think chances are good."

"Thank you." She dipped her head to each of us in turn, then walked in a wide circle around her little band, nudging a young grey back into place beside his mother, giving a white-faced roan an affectionate nip on the shoulder.

"Do you know what town that is?" Aren asked me as we walked back.

"I think it's Gormen," I said. "We won't find much help there. There's a crossroads, though. We'll need to decide which way we're going." He didn't reply. "Please tell me you know."

Aren exchanged a glance with Kel and Cassia. "We haven't exactly decided yet. You were our best hope for finding the king. As that's failed, we have few other options."

The peaceful feeling left, and I reached up to stretch the tightness out of the back of my neck. "So you have no idea what you're doing. Fantastic." I heard the irritation in my voice that I'd tried to hold back.

Aren heard it, too. He rubbed a hand over his face, obviously annoyed. "I thought of heading toward Luid, to confront Severn directly." Cassia drew in a sharp breath, but said nothing. Aren glanced at her. "Not the best plan, but there doesn't seem to be much point in trying to search the whole damned country for someone who's probably dead." He narrowed his eyes at me and smiled humorlessly. "Unless you have a better idea, Nox? Something more brilliant than what I might come up with?"

He knew I didn't. I set my jaw and didn't respond.

Cassia started back toward camp. "Why don't you

all try to get some sleep? I'll take watch for the rest of the night, and we'll set out towards the crossroads and discuss this on the way."

I hung back from the group, and Kel stopped to wait for me.

"What is it with you two?" he asked.

"It's nothing. I'm just tired."

"Really?"

"No. I'm disappointed that there's no plan. You said I should stay to help, but with what? And he gets my hackles up. It's like—"

Something near the edge of the forest caught my attention. I'd been too distracted to notice it earlier. "You go on ahead." I turned to my right and headed toward the trees. Kel followed, but I didn't turn back. My attention was fixed on a marshy hollow.

The magic was never something I saw or heard. But I knew the field held something useful.

Bog water covered the toes of my boots as I leaned toward the ice grass that thrived in the moist soil. Coated in a white, waxy substance, its thick blades reached nearly to my knees. The plants would have tiny, pale blue flowers in another month, and then fat seed heads. Either would have been more useful in a potion, but the leaves would be good to have. I harvested a few handfuls before Kel's slower steps caught up with me.

I held the grass in my fist, careful not to crush the leaves, and took a few steps uphill. The mare Aren had spoken to glanced over at us and went back to grazing the flatter part of the meadow. The ground rose to a rocky hump here, bare save for lichens and moss. In the shadows at the base I found tiny vines with the beginnings of rounded leaves.

"What's happening?" Kel asked as he crouched beside me.

"Plants. Insects. The majestic dance of life." I looked up from my work. "How did you know I didn't leave because I needed some privacy?"

"I'd have backed off if you'd dropped your pants."
He grinned. "Need any help?"

I teased the vine's roots out of the thin soil and
handed the plant to him. "You can hold that."

He cradled it in his hand as he followed me
farther into the grasses. "I wonder what you'd think of
the plants our healers use back home," he said.

"In Luid, you mean?"

"Oh. Right. Just... they bring in things from other
places, I think. Assume."

I smiled. I hadn't seen him flustered yet. It suited
him.

I stopped to pull a starflower up by the roots. At
this time of year it looked similar to the surrounding
grasses, but contained far more healing power.

"You could visit my home with me some day," he
said. "Our healers might not be exactly what you're
accustomed to."

"Maybe," I said. "But they would work the same
way I do." I smiled. "Kel, are you suggesting you'd like to
spend more time with me in the future?"

"Um. No. Yes?" He smiled bashfully. "Can I tell
you something?"

"Of course."

"I like you."

I knew where this was going. I couldn't let that
happen, much as I'd have liked to. It would only
complicate matters. I gave him a tight smile. "I like you
too, Kel. You've been kind to me."

He sighed. "I don't know how this works, exactly."

"I have a hard time believing that." I looked over
his handsome face and took in the way his shirt clung to
his chest, the muscular forearms that showed beneath his
rolled-up sleeves, and back to his eyes. I wondered how
he would touch me. *Gently*, I thought, *at least at first.*
My stomach clenched. *He'd take his time. He would—*

Kate Sparkes

No.

"Can you stop for a minute?" he asked.

"We should catch up with the others." But I slowed my pace as we headed into the woods.

"Nox, do you ever feel like you don't quite fit?"

I raised an eyebrow at him. "Do you?"

He chuckled. "Let me try that again. In the group of people I..." He sighed. "Never mind. It's not important."

"It seems important to you." He had me curious.

His hands clenched, then relaxed. "It's just that where I come from, among the people in my family, we don't do romantic relationships." He seemed to be selecting his words carefully. I didn't interrupt, though I wanted to run. "I feel different sometimes. I wouldn't mind trying it."

"Kel, you know, relationships are entirely overrated." *Gods, this is awkward.* I found him attractive, had felt my body responding to his glances, but this was something else. Something I wanted no part of—or at least, that was what I told myself. "We only met this morning, and I—"

He held up a hand to stop me. "You're not looking for love. I get that, and it's fine. I like you, though. I enjoyed our conversations today. I'd like to be friends with you." He shook his head and chuckled. "This is horrible. Too soon. Sorry. I wanted you to know that I find you incredibly attractive, and I think you feel that, too."

I nodded. No point denying it.

"But I want more than that, and I wanted to tell you so we wouldn't be confused, and..." He shrugged helplessly. "And now I've made a mess of it."

I bit my lip to hold back a smile. "It's fine. I really do like you, Kel." Had I thought him dangerous before? I could certainly resist this poor man. I reached out to give his hand a reassuring squeeze, and pulled back when the

291

heat of his skin sent a flash of warmth through my entire body. *Maybe not.*

I stepped away to look him over again. "I don't understand how someone like you could grow up without learning how to flirt properly."

His thick, dark eyebrows shot up. "Oh, I can do that. Please don't mistake my awkwardness in this area for ineptitude in any other." A slow smile crept over his lips. "If I wanted a strictly physical relationship, you might just be in trouble, my lovely friend."

I snorted. "You're adorable, but I think I'm safe."

He stepped in front of me, stopping me short. His smile changed, leaving only a confident up-turn at the corners of his lips. He raised one hand and brushed my hair back, sending shivers over my scalp and down my back. He paused, perhaps waiting for my reaction, seeing whether I would back away.

I knew I should, but I didn't.

My mouth went dry as he trailed a finger down my jaw line from ear to chin, barely grazing my skin. The meadow disappeared, and the world condensed to the size of the space between us. His eyes filled with undisguised desire, and my body responded in kind.

Before I could say anything else, he walked away.

"We should go," he called over his shoulder.

"Be right there," I whispered. He seemed to have taken my voice with him.

Chapter Twenty-Eight

Rowan

"Again," Ulric ordered.

I gritted my teeth at the order and curled my hands into fists as I concentrated. The air between us grew hazy and shimmered, but the effect lasted only a moment, then popped like a bubble.

Ulric watched from the wall near the door. We'd been avoiding speaking of personal things, and talk of the world outside had already become far too depressing. His interest in my magic had continued, though, and I'd spent the morning telling him about my experiences with my teachers, hoping he'd see something they hadn't.

"This is all you've managed anywhere?" he asked.

I pulled up the waistband of my pants, which were far too large, even with the belt the guards had provided. "It's actually better in some ways. I don't really have experience with illusions. I just thought I'd try it. At least nothing bad is happening."

He raised an eyebrow. "Preventing destruction shouldn't be your goal. You need to reach far beyond that." He stared at the floor, deep in thought. "Have I told you yet about my near-escape?"

"No." He knew he hadn't. I tried not to feel too much hope. If he'd gotten close on his own...

"It wasn't long after I arrived here. They've become much more cautious with me since then. I managed to hide, to surprise and overpower a guard with physical strength rather than magical, and I made it out of this room. I felt my power returning to me, stronger than it was even before my imprisonment. You know why this would have surprised me?"

"Because there was no magic in the land here for you to draw on?"

"Good. Nonetheless, it became dizzying. Overwhelming. I nearly tore the place down around me in my frenzy to escape, over-using my power, shattering a wall when I meant to break down a door, killing ten men when I... well, I meant to do that. But I didn't expect it to be so spectacular."

I tried not to imagine what that meant.

"I didn't make it, obviously," he continued. "That surge of power didn't last long. I used it up too quickly, too carelessly, and they caught me as I was heading toward the king's offices. Took me down with their own magic, with that potion that holds in our power. Returned me here, made me pay for what I'd done, and made damned sure it never happened again."

"So where did that magic come from?"

"They don't know. They think it was what I had saved up from before. As far as they know, we can't use magic at all in here, but I believe there's a sort of push-back when we get free of this place. Our power bounces back stronger than before, multiplied by restraint, though obviously it's temporary. The greater the pressure, the greater the release. They may have killed the magic in the land, but we are magical creatures ourselves. You see?"

I thought of the night when I'd set my own bound magic free, and nodded. "Makes perfect sense, actually. So you think this is to our advantage? All we need to do is get out of this room without shackles and without them drugging us?"

"Indeed. I think your magic is the key to making

that happen. But my dear, you need to work on control now, inside these walls. Remember, in the wider world your magic is like a massive, untrained dog, and you may be right to fear its bite. Within these walls, it's smaller. Train it now, and it will obey you when it becomes a great, snarling wolf. Understand?"

"I do." Yet my stomach felt like a stone inside of me when I thought of using that power. No, I realized. The fear came when I thought of letting it take me over. What might I become if I lost control of myself? A dark, familiar fear I didn't dare acknowledge hovered at the edge of my mind. Something to do with Aren, with my fear of him when we met. I pushed all of those thoughts away.

Ulric patted my arm, as though we were friends. "So we train you now. You said you thought something happened when you tried a copying illusion?"

"I thought so, but I'm not—"

"Excellent. Try again. If we could work you up to creating images of ourselves running away, or some other distraction, think how that would help. I'm not gifted in this, but you may be."

He seemed far too sure of the wisdom of his plan. All I saw were ways it could go wrong, but we had no other choice. We would escape. We had to.

"Stand in the center of the room and do whatever you did the last time you tried to copy something." He retrieved a sheet of paper from his section of the room and set it on the floor. "Make another one of these, and don't hold back. Let's see what you can do."

My heartbeat picked up. Even standing as far as possible from the walls, I felt their pressure. Still, the magic was there. I didn't know if it was manageable. There was only one way to find out.

I focused, imagined a duplicate paper, and tried to will it into being. The image of bright blood running down Griselda's face tried to slip into my mind, and I closed it away behind a heavy door. Still, my throat tightened, and my heart continued to flutter. The air beside the page flickered, and a shadow appeared, then vanished.

Ulric stepped before me, arms crossed. His frustration was obvious. No more friendly gestures for me. "What, exactly, is the problem?"

"I'm trying!"

"Are you? The power is there." His voice took on a rough, growling sound. "I can feel it in you. You're a true Sorceress, a rare breed of human. Why are you hiding from your gifts?"

"I'm not hiding from anything." I paced the perimeter of the room, testing the boundaries. I felt the push of resistance against my power, and moved away from the walls to enjoy the slight relief.

"Then why are you reining your power in?"

"I'm not!"

"You are!" he roared, and moved closer. I glanced at the door, hoping a guard would come to see what the commotion was about, but none came.

Ulric sneered. "The walls are thick. Besides, they're not listening. They don't care what I do to you in here."

I stepped away, bumped into my cot, and sat down hard.

He bared his teeth. "You're useless."

"I'm afraid!" I hollered back.

"Of what?"

I pushed up from the bed. "I'm afraid of accidentally hurting someone."

"So you said, but that's not the fear that holds you back. Stop lying to yourself."

I dug deeper, past the excuses I'd been repeating for months. It felt as though I was ripping a hole in myself, exposing every weakness I was ashamed of. "There's also the pressure."

He snorted derisively.

"Do you think you're the only person who's ever seen potential in me?" I looked straight into his eyes, daring him to interrupt. Almost wishing he would. "Aren was the first. He saw it before anyone else, before I knew about my magic. Albion sees it, Griselda does, Emalda. Everyone has these expectations." I dropped the volume of my voice, and stepped forward. "I'm terrified of not living up to them."

"That's still not what's stopping you."

My dark, unnamed fear stepped forward, and my breath caught in my throat. "I'm afraid of what will become of me if I fail, and of not knowing who I am if I succeed." The words came slowly. "Every day, I feel my old self slipping away, and it frightens me to not know what I'm becoming. I don't want to be like..."

I stopped myself. It felt like a betrayal, this realization that the thought becoming more like Aren's darker side terrified me. I loved him, yet a part of me still feared him and his power, even as I was ceaselessly drawn to them. "I am changing. I killed a man before they brought me here. With magic. What does that mean?"

"It means you're less of a coward than I'm beginning to take you for, that's what." He shook his head in disgust. "What does it matter now, eh? Poor little Sorceress, with powers the likes of which men have killed for. Perhaps it would do you good to remember that you're as good as dead anyway. What do you have left to fear besides that?"

I froze. "That's a horrible thing to say."

"It's true. They're going to kill you no matter what happens in here. What does it matter now if you succeed or fail? Produce the illusion of a starry night on the ceiling, no one but me will know. Set the room on fire, kill me, I don't mind. I'm as dead as you are." He spat the words out. "With my magic trapped and depleted, I am aging quickly. I will die here, without dignity. At least if you kill me, it might be a death worthy of me."

We stood nose to nose as he glared down at me. I wouldn't look away. "Leave me alone."

"No. At least do *something*, girl. Stop being a waste of breath." His eyes narrowed. "Your teachers have all been too easy on you, myself included. Coddling and kindness aren't getting you anywhere. Do you know how my elders dealt with fear and recalcitrance, or how I dealt with it in my own children?"

Hot anger rose in me with the memory of Aren's stories. "I have a pretty good idea."

He let out a cruel laugh and stepped back a pace. "Did he whine about how hard I was on him? That is, when I could stand to look at something so weak and admit that it came from me."

"Stop." Anger became rage, threatening to push me over the edge.

"No." Though I couldn't feel his magic, something about the vastness of his presence made the hairs on my arms prickle. "You've thought badly of my family for how we use our power, haven't you? You don't fear losing yourself. You fear becoming one of us. But your crime is worse." He took another step back. "This is how we deal with weakness."

He raised his hand and swung it hard toward my face.

I held my ground and braced myself for the blow as I released my magic. A high-pitched shriek filled the room, and a shape appeared between us, surprising Ulric and forcing him back. A familiar form appeared, serpentine neck rearing, jaws snapping and front claws pawing at the air. Insubstantial and smoky, the small red dragon spread its wings to shield me and shrieked again. Barely-visible flames shot from its mouth.

The king rested his hands on his knees and laughed as the flames surrounded him and then evaporated.

The illusory version of Ruby dropped onto four feet and faded as quickly as it had appeared.

"Did I do that?" I reached up to touch the pendant that hung around my neck, hidden beneath the high collar of my shirt. I couldn't have chosen a less likely guardian.

Ulric sobered and studied the empty space where the dragon had been. "You did. Never doubt it."

My legs began to tremble, and I sat on the bed again. "It was beautiful."

"It was acceptable. You'll do better. How did that feel? What were you thinking when it happened?"

"I was a little afraid you were going to hit me. Mostly I felt angry, though." I looked up and met his eyes as the reality of it sank in. "You're horrible."

"It worked, though. You've been allowing emotions to hold you back when you should be using them, using your passion to direct and propel your magic. You say you've accepted your magic, but you have yet to truly embrace it and let it become a part of you. I was certain that if threatened, you would respond appropriately."

"And if I hadn't?"

"Then you'd have a bruised face. Does it matter? It worked."

Rage still seethed within me. "Your methods are reprehensible."

"I know, but you can't argue with those results. Do you see how your power survives the pressure here? Within these walls, you're stronger than I am. Don't fear that. Embrace it."

"You didn't have to do that."

"I think I did. Would you have used your magic otherwise?"

I didn't answer.

He eased himself down to sit on the stone floor

with his legs bent in front of him. "I was raised with the knowledge that I was born to hold a country in my hands. I fought for the knowledge I have, increased my power through whatever means I could, and let nothing and no one stand in my way. I learned to be ruthless when threatened. I learned that fear and compassion and love only got in my way, and I banished them. Those lessons were hard-learned, and I decided to make my sons understand them when they were young."

"That turned out well for everyone."

He frowned. "I don't say it worked as I'd hoped. My oldest living son betrayed me, turned me over to your people so he could take my throne. I have another who lacks compassion and love and fear, but it doesn't seem to have done him any good. Wardrel is a monster. I should have had him killed when I had the chance." He said it as though he were talking about culling an unwanted cockerel. "Dan is Severn's shadow, not a strong Sorcerer, but clever and cunning and well-connected, and he no doubt helped depose me. I thought Aren was the same, though significantly more powerful. The last time I saw him he'd stopped trying to please me and was doing Severn's bidding. Like a dog."

"He broke free of that when he realized what Severn was doing to him."

"That doesn't make him any friend of mine, though." His brows pulled together. "I was a good king. Did he tell you that?"

"He might have mentioned it."

"I brought Tyrea together, got the provinces working with each other, trading. My army secured the mountains against your people and prevented them pursuing their obsessions into my lands. I was on the throne through more of your kings' reigns than I can name now, and I maintained peace. I know now that I made mistakes as a husband and as a father, and I regret them more than I can say. But I was a great king, once."

There was nothing for me to say to that, and we sat in silence as the minutes passed, each one bringing us closer to our certain deaths.

"Will you try again?" he asked. "Without my help, of course. Use your own emotions, now that you know how it feels. Let go of your fear. Let go of your ideas of who you should be and embrace who you are, even if it frightens you now."

"I'm tired." A half-truth. I was still reeling from my anger, from shock that he'd stoop so low, and from the realization of my ability. I had done it. I'd stopped focusing on my magic as its own entity, had let it fill me, and I had done more than I ever thought possible. I needed to make sense of it, but I doubted he'd understand that. "Let me rest. Calm myself. Then I'll try."

"No. Listen to me. You must have anger within you for what your people did to you, what they're doing now. Hatred."

I didn't answer. I couldn't.

He nodded as though I had. "Keep your mind clear and calm. If you can't remove emotion from yourself, at least use it in a way that benefits you instead of holding you back. If we can build up this skill of yours, we might be able to work together and get out of here. Practice now, while your power still fills you. Don't turn your back on it."

His gaze was intense, piercing in a way that I found uncomfortably familiar. I had little hope of encountering Aren's intensity again if I didn't do something to change my situation.

Ulric and I were trapped. We weren't powerless.

I nodded.

He held out a hand. I grasped it, and he pulled me to my feet.

"Good. Again."

Chapter Twenty-Nine

Aren

We reached the crossroads at Gormen late in the afternoon. The entire town consisted of an inn, a butcher shop, a general store, a farrier, and a smattering of small houses spread out along a few narrow roads. The buildings on the main road were well-kept, built of stone with decorative shrubs in front to welcome those who might be tempted to stop and spend the night or their money in town. Few people roamed the streets, but those who did gave us polite nods of welcome.

"Will we stop here?" Nox asked. She spoke to Kel and Cassia. Never to me, if she could avoid it. I'd noticed she seemed more bashful around Kel this morning. She studied him, but never let him catch her doing so. "I don't want to spend your money for you, but a bath and a comfortable bed would be nice for a night."

Cassia pulled out their pouch of coins and examined the contents. "Aren, what have you got?"

"Not much."

She frowned. "Since Kel was so generous about the horses, I think we're going to have to choose between a night at the inn, or supplies, or having something left for an emergency later." Her shoulders dropped. "I'm not sure I can take another night in the open air."

I hated seeing her like that. Cassia had always seemed so vibrant. Indestructible. But though Nox's potion had helped with her cough, she seemed to be dragging herself through each day, forcing each step she took. An inn wasn't a lake, but as Nox had said, there would be a bathtub. A cool soak for each of the mers would do them wonders.

We need supplies, my rational mind argued. *But there is another way...*

Darkest magic, another voice responded.

My chest tightened. No one had ever told me what to do when two opposing courses of action both seemed right.

I cleared my throat, and they all turned to me. "If it's that important, I could take care of things. It's nothing I haven't done before. Maybe I've been looking at this wrong, and—"

"Oh, Aren. No." Cassia rested a hand on my arm and squeezed. "I wasn't thinking when I said that. Of course you shouldn't. We'll make camp on the other side of town, and Kel and I will come back for supplies. We're the least-recognizable of the group."

Nox sat up straighter. "Wait, what could he do?"

We didn't answer her.

As we rode on and searched for a place to sleep, I tried not to let my emotions overtake me. I despised myself for not helping my friends. But then, Kel and Cassia never would have let me use my magic that way for their sakes. And would I have felt any better if I'd done it, knowing that I might be doing unseen harm to innocent people? More than that, I hated myself for caring about it at all. I longed for the days when I'd shut thoughts like this out, followed orders, and had only to think of my goal, not the damage I might cause along the way. The old Aren would have been disgusted by what I'd become.

Forget it, I told myself. *Focus on finding a place to sleep.*

The road was well-traveled in that area and

dotted with campsites. We passed by them and looked for something less visible. Whenever there appeared to be a faint path leading away from the road, one of us would go off to see where it went. Most were game trails, but Nox found one that led to a small clearing behind thick tree cover. She motioned for us to follow, and she and I dismounted.

"What do we need?" Kel asked.

I took Rowan's sea glass out of my coin pouch and tossed the bag to Kel. "Use what you need. Food will be fine. Some extra blankets, another water bag if anyone's selling, and a little grain to add to what the horses are digging up." I could think of other things I'd have liked, but nothing worth spending money on. I had the supplies my uncle had given me.

Kel turned to Nox. "Anything I can bring for you, my lady?"

She tilted her head slightly to one side. "Why, all the treasure in the Diamond Dragon's caves, good sir."

He grinned, and Cassia slapped his arm. "Come on, good sir," she said. "We need to get back before dark."

The playful look dropped from Nox's face, and she stepped back. Conflicted, I thought, but didn't care to check in her thoughts. "Actually," she said, "if they're not too expensive, I could do with a few more bowls, maybe a pot."

"For potions?" I asked.

She didn't look back at me. "For potions, but also for cooking. If anyone here can hunt, I can collect anything else that's edible, and we could make a stew that stretches further than the dry rations we've had so far. Potatoes would be lovely." She looked down at her hands. "And soap."

Cassia nodded. "Agreed on all counts. We'll see what we can do."

Then Nox and I were alone, with no neutral

parties between us. I decided keeping my mouth shut was the best course of action. Everything she did irritated me, though I still didn't care to think about why. The way she talked down to us at first and then won over my friends. The way she held herself, as though she thought herself a true princess instead of a girl brought up in the harshest, least-refined parts of Tyrea—and the way she betrayed that when her accent slipped into a backwater drawl when she let her guard down. The uncertainty that came off of her in nearly visible waves, though she tried to hide it under a veneer of cold confidence.

That doesn't hit a little too close to home, does it?

I shook that thought off, too. Gods, even the way she laid out the bedrolls irritated me. I couldn't remember the last time someone had gotten under my skin like this. Not since childhood.

"Are you going to change again tonight?" she asked.

"I suppose I will, unless they get more blankets. Even then, it's better if you all use the extras. It feels like it's going to be a cold night."

She rested her hands on her hips. "Do you know that by magic?"

"No. There's a chill. It's clouding over. I'm guessing based on past experience and prior knowledge."

"Interesting."

I sighed. "What is?"

"I had heard you were so powerful."

I gritted my teeth. "I am."

"I knew a fellow who used magic to predict the weather. Not a Sorcerer, but he used some magic."

Deep breaths. "We have different skills. It's unusual for a person to master more than a handful. Weather-prediction, while terribly impressive, is not something I have natural skill in, nor is it something I've cared to develop. Does that answer your question?"

"I didn't ask a question."

I narrowed my eyes at her. She stepped back. I couldn't fathom why she'd bait me. To prove I wasn't everything she feared? To prove I *was*?

"We should gather firewood," I said.

Most of the fallen branches were damp with melted snow, but I found a few bits that were dry and snapped them into smaller pieces for burning. *Should have asked Kel and Cassia for an axe*, I thought as I snapped a long stick against the trunk of a tree, the branches of which were covered in tiny pink leaves. They'd grow, widen, take on a richer color by summer.

Heartleaf.

I leaned against the trunk and inhaled the sweet scent of its bark, which would always make me think of Rowan. I let the memories overtake me, just this once. If she were there, she'd have helped me sort through everything. She'd make things clearer. At the very least, she'd help me set my problems aside for a while and rest. She would have faith that things would turn out—or at the very least, she'd smile and pretend she did. My mind calmed. I'd need some of that faith if I were going to move ahead with my plan.

I pushed away from the tree and carried the firewood back to camp.

Previous travelers had cleared a space for a fire and ringed it with jagged rocks, and by the time I got back Nox had cleared the fallen leaves from it. She stood branches in the center of the pit, building a cone shape over a space that held smaller sticks and dried leaves.

She offered a tight smile and wiped her hands on her pants. "Go ahead."

"You've done this before," I observed. I would make an attempt to be friendly. Give her a chance, as Kel had suggested.

"Mm-hmm. We can't all shoot flames out of our bodies to warm ourselves."

I lit the flames, and she pretended she wasn't

watching. "Most of us can't do this on any great scale, either. Magic might not be exactly as you've imagined it."

"Severn can, though?"

"He could have this fire blasting higher than your head in seconds, with no wood to feed it."

Nox's brow furrowed. "What else does he do?"

She looked into my eyes, and a chill swept over me that made the hair on my scalp stand up. I knew it was only because some part of me recalled those ice-blue depths from childhood. We'd played together, I knew that. I'd known her as a servant's child, though I couldn't recall anything else. Really looking at her gave me the creeping sensation of seeing something for the first time, but feeling it's all happened before. Time-doubling. I'd never enjoyed that feeling.

"He's always been interested in fire," I continued. "He's familiar with my magic, and can sometimes find me if I'm not careful about blocking him." At least I'd become better about that. "I don't think he can change forms, but I can't be sure. I managed to keep my skill at it hidden from him for a time. That's the problem. I don't know what he's capable of because we've never trusted each other enough to reveal all of our secrets."

"Probably a wise move on your part." She still seemed guarded.

I took the sea glass from my pocket and rolled it between my fingers. "He's forged a mind-connection with a flying horse, strong enough that he can make it do what he wants at any time. He can use blasts of pure magic to do physical damage." I rolled my shoulders forward and back to stretch out the phantom pain in my scar. "He knows things. Not the way I know them. I can see what people are thinking, but that's affected by holes in people's knowledge or mistakes in their perceptions. Severn...I swear he just knows. I don't know how."

The more I talked about him, the more hopeless the task ahead of me seemed. I stared into the fire. "It's too much," I whispered, though I hadn't meant to say it aloud.

Nox narrowed her eyes. Studied me, though not nearly as warmly as she did Kel. "So that's why you've been looking for our father? Because you can't beat Severn on your own?"

A flash of panic crossed her features, as she apparently realized the sharp sting her insult sent through me. I sat up straighter, ready to defend myself, and stopped. She was rude, and over-confident if she thought she could afford to insult me, but she wasn't wrong.

"Close enough." I leaned my elbows on my knees and tried to let my anger drain away. "Ulric could take his position back without fighting for it, at least in theory. He doesn't have to be stronger than Severn. He just has to get back before Severn can legally declare him dead and his crown forfeit. But I don't think there's any chance of that now."

She kept watching me with sharp intensity that tempted me to peek into her thoughts. "But you have your own gifts. And years of training with great teachers."

"I have."

"What were you saying back on the road about something you could do to get us into the inn? Another magic trick? Conjuring money?"

So she didn't know as much about me as she thought she did. She was feeling me out. Perhaps measuring her own skills against mine. "You're quite interested in magic, aren't you?"

She shrugged. "I'm curious. The magic users I've known weren't capable of much. I haven't seen a lot from you, except—" She stopped herself, crossed her arms, looked into the fire. "Well, the eagle thing is impressive. And the fire. I'd just heard other things. I wonder what our odds are if we go to Luid."

"So you're wondering how you can use me?" I'd seen as much hate for Severn in her as I had for me when I'd slipped into her mind. She saw me as a tool. She had no idea what she was dealing with.

Her lips tightened. "Let's just say I'm interested in your sort of magic. I have experience with potions, and I'm good at them, but it's different."

I smirked. "Quite."

The sharp, offended look on her face pleased me. *And now we're even.* I wasn't about to let her think herself better than me, or insult me. She had no right.

"What didn't you do back at the village? If we're going to work together, I'd like to know."

Work together. As if she had anything I needed.

The peace I'd felt back at the heartleaf tree was gone, pushed father away each time she prodded the open wound of my conflicting desires.

"You wouldn't understand," I said.

"What, because I'm just a common Potioner?"

"It's a long story, and it's complicated."

"Make it short."

I shot her an irritated look, and she turned away. She didn't back down, though.

"Fine," I said. "You know I can see into people's thoughts when I want to."

"I do know. You did it to me, didn't you? I felt it."

I did. I wish I hadn't. "I can also change their thoughts. If I'd gone into that inn, I could have made them think I'd paid for rooms. Made them forget we were ever there." *It would have been so easy*, I added to myself. I remembered how it had helped Rowan and me—and the troubled look on her face when she realized what I'd done. I dragged a hand through my hair. "That's what I was referring to."

Silence followed as she frowned into the flames. I wondered when Kel and Cassia would be back.

"I knew something about it," she said, "though

not how you did it. So why *didn't* you do it?"

I laughed, caught by surprise. "What?"

"We could have had warmth. Shelter. Good food for a night. We could have been clean and sleeping on feather beds."

I stared at her. "A few moments ago you were angry with me for looking into your thoughts. Just observing, not even manipulating them."

"Yes."

"And yet you think it would be fine for me to do worse to someone else's thoughts, to change them, to make a person disbelieve reality, just so you can be comfortable? Are you insane, or just that much of a hypocrite?"

Her jaw dropped. "It's not about comfort! We'd have been more prepared for tomorrow, for whatever half-cooked plan you've got worked up. Yes, I'm angry that you tried to pry into my private thoughts. Anyone would be. But you have skills that would be a great asset to us on what happens to be the most important undertaking in the country right now, and you've refused."

"It would have been wrong."

She let out a derisive snort. "Since when has that been a problem for you or your family?"

"Innocent people could be hurt."

"No one is innocent. Believe me."

"I don't want to be that person anymore." How could she not see the value in that? The struggle? "You obviously hate my family. Your family, technically. Yet you mock me for turning away from them."

She stood to pace back and forth at the other side of the fire. "And you obviously have your priorities confused. You've done this before, correct?"

"Yes."

"It would benefit our cause. You could use this skill to get us fresh horses, better food, adequate bedding, weapons... and you didn't because it would make you *feel bad?*"

Her words cut me. She said exactly what I'd been hesitant to think, had drawn my internal turmoil into the light, and I hated her for it. She spoke like my father, like Severn. I remembered the shock and pain I'd felt with Brother Phelun. The cost of my magic.

"It's wrong," I said, "no matter what the reason for it. Objectively."

"Oh, what a load of..." She stopped her pacing and crossed her arms. "You know, this is the worst kind of self-indulgent stupidity. I shouldn't have expected any better from a spoiled Luidite, but I'd heard you were this terrifying Sorcerer, powerful and ruthless, a fairy-tale monster. I disliked you on sight and haven't found anything to like about you yet, but I thought you were at least the type of person who would be willing to do what had to be done."

"What, so you can have your revenge?"

"Yes!" She paused, unclenched her fists. "But not only mine. This is bigger than me, or you."

"I'm doing the best I can." My mind felt like it was ripping in half. There was the Aren who wanted to rise above the evils of his youth, and the one who understood exactly what she was saying, who wanted to return to his old ways, but for a better cause.

"I didn't think I had enough respect for you to be disappointed," she added. "Apparently I was wrong."

I found it difficult to unclench my teeth enough to speak. "I've spent my entire life living by my family's rules, and they're completely different from everyone else's. I was taught that being loyal to my family and to whoever is in power is the most important thing in the world. So yes, I've always done what was necessary if it meant protecting my family. Anything to further our interests, even if it meant sacrificing my own happiness or the lives of others. I'm not there now, and I never will be again. Do you know what that leaves me with?"

"Please enlighten me."

"Nothing. I know good people, but I don't know how to be one of them. All I can seem to manage is to try not to hurt people, and you can't even respect that."

Gods, I'm pathetic.

"You're not a better person for doing nothing," she said. Her fists clenched again. "I don't think I would have liked you if we'd met before, but at least you would have been interesting and potentially useful. I don't know what you're so melancholy about. You have incredible gifts you're not using, and you think that makes you a better person? You've been given everything in life, and you're wasting it. It's disgusting. At this rate you're never going to find your father, and you're certainly never going to get rid of your brother."

Cold calm descended over me. *Are you disappointed that I'm not the monster you imagined, Nox? You want to see the real me?* I pushed up from the log and stepped toward her.

"You don't understand," I said, clearly enunciating every word. "How could you? You don't know anything about what it means to have real magic, to struggle with the power and the possibilities." I smiled, cold and cruel. "You're just a—"

"Don't you dare say it." Her hands trembled, and her cold eyes burned. "Don't you dare."

My smile widened. Hurting her felt good, as good as using my greatest skills had after months of disuse, as good as fighting. It felt like coming home after months away. "Don't tell me you never think it. That you're never jealous. That you don't wish you had what I have."

"I'd use it a hell of a lot better than you do if I had it." Her eyes shone. Fear? Anger? Or had I wounded her so easily?

Without meaning to, I slipped into her mind. A flood of hatred hit me, along with terror, disgust, and pain. Shock, and a sense of betrayal, though she'd had no reason to trust me. I felt her frustration at having her plans thwarted, her burning need to destroy Severn, her disappointment in me. Beneath that, confusion. She was as shocked by her own words and attitude as I was by mine.

Kel had been right. I saw Nox as a haughty, taunting harpy, but it was an act. A defense.

I pulled back, but too late.

She drew a sharp breath. "You *never* do that to me. Do you understand?"

My elation at gaining the upper hand fled. I'd been running from my gifts for months. I'd wasted my time.

"I didn't mean to," I said. "I didn't before, either, on the road."

She backed away, toward where the horses foraged in the woods, and wiped the back of her hand across her cheek.

"Nox, please."

She ran off as Cassia and Kel returned.

"What's going on?" Cassia asked.

With my storm of anger subsiding, there was nothing left to fill me. *Perhaps that's all I am, in the end.*

I sank back down onto the log as Kel took the horses and went after Nox. Cassia sat beside me and tried to put her hands on me, but I pushed them gently away. "I think I'm in trouble."

Chapter Thirty

Nox

Crashing noises followed me through the trees. I'd thought Aren was more graceful than that.

"I'm not interested in talking," I called back. Gods, that conversation had been a mistake. What was I thinking? I'd tried to project strength, to show I wasn't intimidated by him, and had ended up angry. Disappointed at first, when I realized that he wasn't going to be my path to taking Severn down. He was a monster, no doubt. Cruel. Heartless. Yet he was weak, unwilling to use the powers he had.

He'd called me a hypocrite. Untrue. I was simply determined to see my plan through, to let nothing stand in my way. It seemed I'd failed miserably in communicating that.

The footsteps came nearer. Hoofsteps, too. I pressed on until they caught up and a hand rested on my arm.

"Don't touch me!" I spun to find myself not facing Aren, but Kel. I took a deep breath. Of course he'd be bringing the horses. "Sorry."

"Are you leaving us, Nox?" He sounded concerned. Disappointed, maybe.

"I can't stay with him. I don't understand how you can. He looked into my mind. I felt it. He could have seen anything, *done* anything. I—" I stopped.

Gods, I am a hypocrite. I'd as much as wished that on other people. I still thought it was a mistake for him not to use his gifts, but...*But what? Just not on me?*

This wasn't me. I helped people. Hadn't I stayed in Arberg longer than I meant to, simply because they needed me? Apparently my compassion lasted only until it was at odds with my hate.

Even that realization didn't dim my disappointment with Aren, or my aching need to bring Severn down, a need that seemed to grow each day. I crouched in the dirt and covered my face with my hands.

When I looked up, Kel was watching.

"Are you reading me now?" I asked.

"No. Do you want me to?"

I pressed the heels of my hands to my eyes for a moment. "No. I'm just wondering what you saw in me before. Why you said you liked me."

"Because you have potential, I suppose, under this armor you've put on. You're interesting. Perfect people are terribly dull." We continued walking, and he left the horses with mine and Aren's.

"I'll be sorry to see you go," he added.

"I'll be sorry to leave you," I said, and meant it. "Aren and I can't work together, though. I tried to talk to him, and he...He's horrible, you know."

"He can be." Kel frowned. "He's trying to be better."

"That's what he said. It seems like a terrible time for a crisis of conscience, though."

"Is it?"

"We all have to make compromises to get things done. Everyone knows that where I come from. It's about survival. And that's—" I squeezed my eyes shut.

"What?"

He might as well know. Might make him back away and let me go. And that, undoubtedly, would be best for everyone. "That's why they arrested me. I did kill my husband."

I braced myself for his judgement, his disgust. His regret that he'd paid special attention to me, a murderer.

"I see."

A cricket chirped in the silence that followed. "That—that's it?" I stammered. "You see?"

His half-smile and creased brow made my heart jump.

"That's it. Nox, I won't ask why you did it. You can tell me, if you ever want to. Whether your actions were justified in the eyes of the law isn't my concern. I believe you did what you had to do. You didn't kill him over a petty difference, did you?"

"No." A wave of relief filled me.

"Walk with me?" He didn't wait for an answer, but started into the woods, away from camp. I went with him. At least we weren't going back. The sunlight grew dimmer, and the air colder. I wished I'd brought a blanket.

Kel seemed to be looking for something, and changed course a few times. "What else do you think of Aren?" he asked.

The question took me off-guard. "I'd rather not—"

"Please. I'd very much like for you to stay, and I'd also like for the two of you to get over whatever differences make you hate each other so."

"He hates me?"

Kel stopped walking. "Let's work on your end of this first, shall we? Because the chill in the air between you is making me numb."

"Fine." I tucked my hands under my arms to keep them warm. "I think he's mean. Cruel. I think he looks down on anyone who doesn't have his gifts, even though he's done nothing to earn them. I think he's been spoiled, that he grew up with money and knowledge and training, and he doesn't appreciate any of it. I think he feels sorry for himself, and he's letting that make him weak."

Kel pursed his lips and rocked back on his heels. "Do you know why he's opposing Severn?"

I opened my mouth to answer, and closed it again. I didn't know. I hadn't cared. I'd only been concerned with whether he might help me.

Kel nodded as though I'd spoken. "Aren's life hasn't been easy. He bears scars from his childhood— physical, but also scars that run far deeper than that. His father made his life hell when he was a kid. Ulric ignored him, punished him for anything he saw as weakness, looked down on him, offered no love or comfort. He taught Aren to hate, to revile love and suppress fear, to use cruelty as a weapon and a shield. You and your mother were sent away when you were a child, and you probably had no idea what was going on. Aren was the same age, and he only knew what people told him. He thought his mother, the only person who cared for him, was dead. He wasn't even allowed to be sad about it. He's had a lot of opportunities in his life, you're right, and he's taken advantage of them. Many of the talents he has now didn't come easy to him. He worked hard for them, used every teacher, every book, every experienced magic-user available to him so he could become stronger than Severn—who, incidentally, has tried to kill him several times. Did he tell you that?"

"No." Since I'd learned I had a brother, I'd imagined him living a life of ease and luxury while I scalded my hands in dishwater and wasted my gifts healing infected wounds and curing diseases that foolish people often brought on themselves.

"And for all of Aren's hard work, his father never even noticed him. He passed Aren over into Severn's training when he was old enough, in spite of the attempted murder business, and Severn carved Ulric's lessons deeper into Aren. Your family's a bit of a mess, you know. You've had a hard life, but his hasn't been easy, either."

I pushed aside my irritation at being lectured. It seemed I deserved it this time. "You're saying he has reasons for being the way he is. That doesn't make it okay."

"No, you're right. My point is that he's decided to try to be a better person. He turned on Severn, broke free of his family. He has people, my people included, telling him that the way he uses his magic is wrong. He's struggling. Always has on some level, I think. I believe good will come when he figures out who he wants to be. You don't have to stay to see it."

"But you are."

He nodded. "I'll be sorry to lose you. Though things have been tense when you and Aren are together, I've enjoyed being with you. You're a good sort of person, when he's not involved. Compassionate. Kind to most people."

I wrapped my arms around my waist. "I feel a little foolish. I never thought to ask the questions you just answered."

"Hmm. It might be your blind spot."

"My what?"

He shrugged. "We all have them. Things we feel so strongly about, or have our minds so set on, that they make us act out of character. Had you met Aren under other circumstances, you might not have been so cold to him, and he in return may have been kinder to you. But because of the depth of your hated for Severn and the rest of your family—please, forgive me if I'm stepping too far."

"Not at all." My voice cracked.

"That hatred, and whatever your plans are for Severn, those are your blind spot. When those are in the front of your mind, you don't see other things. Better things, maybe." He cleared his throat. "We all have them. Things that make our tempers flare when they shouldn't, or make us act like fools, ignoring rational thought in favor of following our hearts. It's good to be aware of them."

"Thank you, Kel." I wasn't ready to forgive Aren for insulting me, and certainly not for looking into my mind—even if it had been an accident, as he'd said. But I thought I understood a little better.

He smiled. "You're welcome. Aren can be hard-headed about things, but you two could work well together if you get past your differences. Or your similarities, as the case may be."

I winced.

"You have complimentary gifts," he added. "It's actually quite beautiful. Hunter and gatherer. Sorcerer and Potioner. Nox, don't leave us."

The way he looked at me made my breath catch in my throat. He didn't seem to expect anything, or to be waiting to judge what I said. If I'd told him to forget it, that I'd be fine on my own, he'd likely have wished me well on my journey.

I couldn't stay for Kel, but having him around might make up for any other unpleasantness. I made my decision. "We do have a better chance of bringing Severn down together. And maybe I can come up with a potion to guard my mind."

"So you're staying?" Kel grinned, and more than my heart responded to him.

"I suppose I will. For now."

"Excellent." He chewed his lower lip, and seemed to make a decision. "Want to see something?"

"Um..." I'd heard that before, but he was already walking away. I couldn't help appreciating the view as I watched him go.

"There's a lake somewhere not far this way," he called over his shoulder.

"What? I—"

He didn't stop. I followed, only somewhat

reluctantly. I ignored my mind's warnings and let my interest lead me on. Kel got ahead of me and I lost sight of him in the darkening trees, but it was easy enough to follow the sound of him as he crashed around.

"Wait!" I called, but he kept going. He was well ahead of me when I found his shirt on the ground, and then his pants slung over a tree branch.

A loud splash came, not far off.

"I don't want to go swimming!" I called, and he laughed.

"Just come over here!"

My stomach knotted. Hadn't I thought about this? But he wanted more than I was prepared to offer.

Trees and rocky ledges edged up to the pond all the way around. The setting sun turned the surface of the water a glittering orange.

I pulled my sweater tighter around me. "You're going to freeze!"

Another laugh. "I don't think so. Come closer."

I found him in the water, visible from his chest up, standing on the bottom. No, not standing. He moved slightly, as though kicking to keep himself afloat, but he was too high up for that.

I shivered. "What are you doing?"

He grinned, then turned and dived, allowing a sleek tail to break the surface.

What?

I blinked hard and inched onto the boulder at the edge of the pond, then crouched to peer into the water. Even with the light reflecting off the surface I could see that there was no shallow, muddy bottom below me, only deep water. A face appeared. I yelped and fell backward.

"I'm sorry!" Kel called as he surfaced, clearly trying not to laugh. "I didn't mean to startle you." He rested his arms on the rock I'd been standing on and wiped away the water that dripped over his face from his hair. Now that he was closer, I saw that his skin had taken on a grayish cast. There was no goose-flesh on it, even in the cold air. I was covered in it.

Impossible. This was a creature I'd only heard about in stories back home, but he was real. *Real, and...and Kel.* I searched for words, and found none.

His brows pulled together as he watched my reaction. "You're just startled, right? You're not afraid of me? I never know how to tell people who can't guess it for themselves."

"N-no," I said as I stood again and brushed the pine needles off the back of my pants. My heart raced. "It's a surprise, though. You're a—a mer person?"

He nodded. "Always have been."

"I didn't know you'd look so human," I said.

"Is it a bad surprise?"

"I've had worse." Thinking someone was a good person and finding out he was a good mer-person wasn't such a big difference. Far worse things hid behind human faces. I knelt on the rock and looked down at him. "Is this how you prefer to be?"

He nodded. "Legs can be good. The tail is even more limiting on land than your legs are in the water. I don't mind them, but it gets rather uncomfortable after a while. The air is so dry and insubstantial, and my body feels heavy on land. I like my tail. Having legs is like being away from home."

I suddenly felt shy.

"Can I see it?" I asked, and he grinned again. The muscles of his chest and arms tightened as he pushed out of the lake, and water flowed over his skin in rivers that outlined every hard curve. I tried not to stare.

Aside from his skin tone, his top half looked like a human man, though more enticingly built than any I'd ever encountered. His tail was longer than his legs had been, as wide at the top as a person's thighs and narrowing toward the end, where it broadened and flattened into flukes.

Kel rested his chin on his crossed arms and flicked his tail. "Go ahead," he said, and closed his eyes.

It was completely unlike anything I might have imagined. There was no clear place where man ended and mer began. Lines under his ribs opened slightly when he shifted to make himself more comfortable.

"Is that how you breathe underwater?"

"Mmm."

I reached out, hesitant, and placed my hand flat against his hip, if he could be said to have them at that point. The skin of his tail was smooth, as flawless as his face and the rest of his body save for a scar that stood out faintly, curving diagonally around his side, halfway down. I shifted my weight toward it and trailed my finger over the mark.

"That came from a net," he said. "I was young and didn't know any better. I got tangled, and the rope dug in. It only scarred because I was stuck for so long. We're usually quite hardy."

"That must have been frightening," I said, my voice barely above a whisper. I moved again, and Kel lifted the end of his tail out of the water. I ran my hand over the fluke, which was tough but flexible, then back up the center of the tail toward his back. I felt the bones of his spine there, just under the skin. He shivered, and I pulled my hand away.

"No, don't stop," he said. "It's nice. Strange to have a human touching me when I'm like this, but good."

Good, indeed. I hadn't enjoyed touching another person so much in far too long. I couldn't deny how this excited me.

I put my hand back and continued its slide up his body. It was strange how he became more human closer to the middle. I'd seen drawings of something called a dolphin, a playful creature said to dance in the waves alongside ships and guide them safely to harbor. But the dolphin didn't have the narrowing at the waist, above what would have been his—

I pulled my hand away again. *I touched his butt. I think. Maybe.*

Kel rolled onto his side and looked at me. "Time to get back? You must be getting cold. I know I am."

"I suppose." I actually felt quite warm, and hoped the fading light hid the flush I felt in my cheeks. "I'll wait for you to get dressed."

I took one more look. His front was more impressive than the back, stomach muscles strong from swimming, disappearing into the tail, which was flat and a lighter gray on the underside.

I wonder how—

I cut that thought off before it could take root and walked back into the woods far enough to give him privacy to change and dress. My fingers ached to touch the more human parts of him, but that would have gone beyond simple and acceptable curiosity about an unfamiliar creature and pulled me into the trap of appreciation for everything his human body might have to offer.

I took a few deep breaths and leaned my back against an oak tree, pressing my palms to its bark, calming myself with its steadiness.

A few minutes later Kel appeared, and we made our way back toward the flicker of firelight that showed between the trees. I found I couldn't quite look at him, not while the feel of his skin still lingered on me. The entire incident seemed surreal and dreamlike, and I needed time to think it through.

Before we reached the camp site, Kel took my hand to slow me.

"What?" I stopped, but pulled away.

"I—nothing." He looked down at his feet, then back to me. "You're going to work things out with Aren?"

"I suppose we'll try," I said, "if he's open to it." I owed him an apology, but he'd been cruel to me, too.

"Wonderful."

Just fantastic, I added, and followed Kel back toward the camp.

* * *

Aren and Cassia sat beside the fire. Aren raised a questioning eyebrow at Kel, who shook his head. They had meat roasting over the fire, and a round loaf of bread keeping warm nearby added to the mouth-watering scent.

"It's almost ready," Cassia said. "Aren caught a couple of rabbits. The meat's a bit stringy. We'd have done stew, but we didn't have much to add."

"I'm sure it's fine." I stepped closer and breathed deeply, and my stomach growled. "We'll work on a better meal tomorrow."

"Cass, there's a lake back that way," Kel said. "I already went in, but I'm up for another swim."

Cassia looked from him to me, and then to Aren, who nodded. "All right," she said. She broke off half of the bread, then offered half of that to Kel. "We'll eat more when we get back. Keep turning it so it doesn't burn," she told Aren.

Aren nodded again, and then the mer siblings were gone.

We didn't say anything for a while. The rabbit tasted as good as it smelled, and if the meat was a bit tougher than it might have been in the summer, it didn't make it any less enjoyable. I would have eaten more, but we had to leave enough for Kel and Cassia. My satisfied stomach made me sleepy, but I couldn't rest yet.

"Aren?"

"Nox." He didn't say it as harshly as he would have earlier. I took that as encouragement.

"I owe you an apology. Kel explained some things to me, and I..." It was so difficult to get the words out. "I think I was trying to provoke you earlier. I've resented you since long before we met, for reasons I now understand don't make much sense. I still think you should do whatever you need to do to get Severn taken care of, but I'm sorry I got angry. You're trying to do the right thing."

His lips quirked in a half-smile. "If only I knew what the right thing was."

"I probably didn't help with that, did I?"

"I owe you an apology as well. I've been walking the edge of a cliff, trying to hold my temper, and you nudged me over." He paused. "That's wrong. I could have held on. I didn't want to."

Surprising honesty, I thought.

He met my gaze. "It's frustrating to know that no matter what I do, it's wrong. I was angry with myself and irritated with you. You weren't exactly respectful, but maybe that shouldn't have mattered. I'm sorry I insulted you. I need to control that better."

I had to smile. "We're both terrible at apologies."

"That we are. Also, I really didn't mean to look into your mind. It won't happen again, I promise. I'll be more careful."

"Thank you."

He leaned forward. "I was talking to Cassia, and I realized...It's embarrassing."

"What?" I moved closer and sat down again.

"I'm jealous of you." He reached up to rub the back of his neck. "When I was a child, I spent years wishing I still had my mother. When someone was cruel to me, when they ignored me, when I tried to do something with my magic and failed, I thought about her and wished she was there. I don't remember what she looked like, but I remember her warmth." His voice was steady, but heavy. Grief-stricken. "You lost so much when you left. I know that. You should know that you wouldn't have been given much respect in our family, being what you are. I don't know whether you'd have been acknowledged as Ulric's daughter. People have odd beliefs about twins."

"I see."

"But you would have been taken care of, and safe," he continued, "and I'm sorry you missed out on so much. But you had her. It must have been a hard life for both of you, but a part of me still envies you."

My mother and I struggled so hard for so long, and our lives were difficult. We did have that love between us, though. She kept me as safe, warm and well-fed as she could, and did her best to get me a better education than the other children in our village had. She found books, and she taught me to read and write even when I fought against it. She found a Potioner who would teach me the basics of our art, and we lived with him during my apprenticeship. I didn't wonder until I was much older how she paid him for it, and even then I assumed she was happy with him. She certainly never said otherwise, or made me feel guilty for being a burden, or for being ungrateful for the sacrifices she made. I tried to imagine my childhood without my mother, and a lump formed in my throat. Severn's actions had cost Aren as much as they had me.

"Well," I said, after a few more minutes of silence, "does this make us friends now?"

That seemed to amuse him. "I really don't know."

"What does that say about us? We finally find our twin, the one we should be closer to than anyone in the world, and we hate each other at first sight?"

He smiled wryly. "I think it means we have a few decades of normal fighting to catch up on. And maybe that we both have more of our father in us than we care to admit."

"You hate him too, don't you? Not the way I do, but...I assumed you were looking for him because you wanted him back. Kel said he was cruel to you, though."

"I don't know whether I hate him," he said quietly. "I used to think I did. I certainly don't love him, or like him, but since I found out that he saved our mother, I've been wondering what else about him I didn't understand."

"Based on what I just heard, he doesn't deserve that much consideration," I told him.

"Are you still willing to help if we abandon that little quest and go on to Luid?"

"You want me to?"

He nodded. "I think I do. You already helped Kel and Cassia. And if I ever need someone to have a petty fight with, I'll have my sister around. Might not be so bad, as long as we stop going for each other's throats."

I got up to check on Kel and Cassia's food, making sure it wasn't overcooking as it kept warm by the fire. "At least this way I can keep an eye on you and make sure your plans don't get in the way of mine, right?"

His smile came more naturally than it had before. "Right."

"So how long have you and Cassia been together?" I asked as I settled back onto the ground and fed another log into the flames. "She seems to be a decent person. Competent. Deadly loyal to you, but nice."

He raised his eyebrows. "We're not together like that. We were, once, but no. She's still a good friend, nothing else."

Another assumption proved wrong. "Well, she and Kel seem like good friends to have on your side, anyway. Love is overrated. Friends would be a better thing to have."

"Is it?" He opened his hands, revealing the piece of of glass he'd been toying with earlier. He turned it over, watching the firelight flicker over it.

"There is someone, though, isn't there?" I asked. "Where is she?"

"Belleisle. She's a Sorceress, but—It's getting late,

I'll tell you about it another time. If you want."

Of course she's a Sorceress. That was the sort of person he associated with. "That's fine. I'm sure she's wonderful. You miss her."

He nodded. "She's part of the reason I'm doing all of this. Severn wants me in his service, but he wants her dead."

"Pissed him off, did she?"

Aren chuckled quietly. "Yeah, she really did. She's safe for now, but as long as Severn is in power, and if he's thinking about expanding his empire the way I suspect he is, she's not safe anywhere. Neither am I."

"Again, not what I'd heard about you. How does a killer turn into a romantic in such a short time?"

"I don't know. Maybe I was both all along." He seemed embarrassed by that notion. "Are you disappointed? Again?"

I shrugged. "I'll think about it. As long as she's not the only reason you're doing this, I might not lose all respect for you."

"Because you have so much to begin with."

I laughed.

Kel and Cassia came back to find us setting up three beds.

"Are we all being humans tonight?" Cassia asked. "Three asleep, one on watch? Or do we not need anyone to stay up?"

"I'll change and take watch," Aren said. "I can rest and still warn you if someone's coming. You three share the blankets. Maybe tomorrow night we'll do shifts, and I'll get some better sleep. I'm fine for now."

Cassia rolled her eyes. "You always are." She and Kel finished their supper, and for the moment, we were at peace.

"We should get to sleep," Cassia said. "Gather the horses before sunrise. They're safe out there, aren't they?"

And suddenly there was a horse there with us.

She fell from the sky, landing far less gracefully than the other herd had, coming straight into the clearing and scattering burning logs and embers as she stumbled through the fire, nearly extinguishing it. The stink of burnt hair filled the air. Cassia and I stamped out a few places where blankets smoldered, and Aren went to the horse, which was pacing back and forth, breathing hard, spreading her massive wings and flapping slowly, then pulling them back in. She reared when Aren approached her, then looked at his face and went closer to him.

"Florizel?" He put a hand on her forehead and stroked down to her nose. "Shh, it's okay. What's happened?"

She whinnied, a soft, shuddering cry. The hair at the bottom of her thin legs was singed, and even in the faint light of the fire that Kel was rebuilding I could see that her feathers were un-groomed and her hide scratched and dirty. Remnants of an arrow's shaft protruded from her rump.

"Aren," she said. "I can't believe—I was going to get help when I saw the other horses, and they said they spoke to a bird-man, and I—" The whites of her eyes showed, and she paced away from him again, swishing her tail frantically. "Aren, it's Rowan. The men have Rowan. Bad men."

"What?" Not despair in his voice. Anger. His expression became keen and predatory, and any hint of humor had disappeared. He had changed completely and become the fearsome Sorcerer I'd heard tell of. "Who? Did they come to Belleisle already? Do you know where Severn took her?"

The horse shook her head. "No, it's—I'm sorry. She's in Darmid. Her brother was in trouble, and she was supposed to meet with this hunter she knew, but he brought others, and they took her."

Aren's lip twitched in a silent snarl, but he kept his silence.

"I followed as far as I could, but they saw me, and I had to fly away. They took her to the middle part of the country, to a huge city with a stone building with gates and walls. I don't know what you call it, but I can remember where it is."

Aren took a deep breath and ran his fingers through his hair. "Why would she—never mind. She's in Ardare, then."

"Who's Rowan?" I asked, and they all looked at me. Even the horse. I think they'd forgotten I was there. The look on Aren's face told me who she was. "We should talk about this."

"There's nothing to talk about," Aren said. "I have to go."

"Not alone," Kel said. "We should all go."

The horse—Florizel—stamped a foot. "I can carry one, and barely that."

Aren paced, taking up where the horse had left off.

"Nox is right," Cassia said. "We should talk about this before we do anything."

I nodded. "I understand that you're all worried about this girl, whoever she is, but we're in the middle of something important. We can't drop what we're doing—which we all agreed we were going to make a priority—to go rescue your damsel in distress."

"They'll kill her," he said.

I took a deep breath. "If she's with magic hunters, we're already too late."

Aren glared at me. "We're damned well going to try."

"Are we? It's decided, then?" I took a step toward him. "What happened to us being in this together?" Pain stabbed at my palms, and when I looked down I realized I'd clenched my fists so tightly that my nails dug into my skin.

Kel looked from Aren to me and back, wary, then motioned to Florizel. "Why don't we let this poor creature rest? Let our horses rest, too. There's no point moving tonight if they're all exhausted and we don't know exactly what we're doing. Would you like something to eat, my friend?"

"Thank you," Florizel said. "I'm nearly starved. I ate a little grass back where the other horses saw you, but not enough. It's been slow going. I've had to walk so much." Kel took some grain out of the bag, and she lowered her head. "I'm sorry," she whispered. "I'm so tired."

Aren rubbed his hands over his face, pressing them into his closed eyes. "No, please eat and rest. Kel is right."

I went to my supplies and assembled a combination of ice grass blades, heartleaf bark, and green lichen in a bowl that Kel handed to me without being asked. It wouldn't work miracles, but it would stave off infection and ease the horse's pain a little. I pounded the ingredients to muck and added a splash of water.

"I'm afraid this is going to sting," I told her. The horse looked up from the grain ration Kel had given her and nodded.

I worked the arrow head free. The horse's haunches trembled, but she didn't shy away.

"Well done," I told her, and ran a hand over her sweaty coat as I dabbed a touch of the ointment onto her wound. She flinched, but didn't make a sound.

"Nox," Kel said quietly, "We should talk about this."

"What's there to talk about? I'm sorry his friend is in trouble, but she's as good as dead. This is a diversion from our mission, and I don't think we can afford it."

He frowned. "I understand what you mean. It

seems unlikely that we'll find her, but those hunters didn't kill her on sight. She might still be alive, and we know where she is. And you should know that Rowan is the only person I know of who's come close to killing Severn."

"Really?"

I looked to Aren, who was obviously listening in. He nodded. "Came closer than I ever have."

"Then why didn't you mention this wonderful asset before?"

He moved closer and rubbed Florizel's nose. "I thought Rowan was safe where she was, and I didn't want to bring her into this. She's not ready for this fight. But she could be, if we get her back alive and she gets more training. You're free to leave, if you wish." He looked to Kel as Cassia joined us. "None of you have to come. This isn't your fight."

"It is, though," Cassia said. "We stay with you."

They all turned to me, and my stomach went sour. Every time I thought I was getting a step closer to what I wanted, another door slammed in my face. Whenever I found my balance, the ground shifted.

She'd almost killed Severn. Wasn't that what I wanted?

I finished treating the horse's wound and sighed. "I stay, too." I couldn't keep the bitterness out of my voice. *What kind of an idiot goes willingly to Darmid? To magic hunters, no less?*

Kel and Cassia accepted my answer, but Aren seemed to have caught my tone. Perhaps even my thoughts, though I hadn't felt any intrusion. He gave me a cold look and turned away before I could return it.

I gritted my teeth and fought the irrational urge to lash out at him.

It seemed I'd discovered my brother's blind spot.

Chapter Thirty-One

Rowan

Time passed slowly in the cell, and Ulric seemed glad to have the distraction of a student to work with. He didn't try to frighten me into action again, but I remained wary of him. I couldn't get a handle on the man. He treated me with respect when he seemed to think I'd earned it, and even kindness, but I couldn't trust that his offers of information and books to read after supper weren't just his way of winning me over, of making me useful to him.

I finally understood why Aren didn't trust anyone.

Over the course of a few days, and with rarely a moment to rest, I learned to create faint illusions. I never made anything as substantial as the dragon, but Ulric encouraged me to keep working at it. I practiced closer to the walls, fighting to strengthen my power against their resistance, using the anger that I found was, indeed, burning a hole deep within me, beneath my shame and fear. My control increased, even with interference. Ulric's expression glowed at times when his theory about my binding-crippled magic seemed to be proving itself, and turned to a scowl when I still couldn't manage anything convincing enough to help us.

The guards approached carefully and shackled us every time we left the room, clamping broad rings of the blue metal around our wrists at every bath and toilet break—both of which took place in a much smaller room across the hall with the same walls as the cell. If they so much as sensed a magical threat, they kept needle-like daggers ready, dripping with blue-green fluid that promised pain and suppression of power, either of which would have been an effective deterrent on its own.

"Could we try something else today?" I asked Ulric one morning, cautiously and respectfully.

Ulric closed the book he'd been reading. "Why? You're making progress."

"Thank you."

"It was an observation, not a compliment."

I took a slow breath before I spoke again. *It's just his way.* That didn't mean I liked it, or approved of it, only that I had no choice but to pretend those little barbs didn't hurt until we got out of that cell. I could act strong and insensitive for a time. After that, Tyrea was welcome to him.

"I thought that giving myself a break from illusions and stretching my abilities in another direction might be helpful. I think I mentioned that a few things have happened with water. It seems worth trying."

"Very well," he said, as though he'd only been waiting for me to suggest it. He carried his water pitcher out from his private space—both of them luxuries I'd been denied as a temporary guest—and set the glass container on the floor. "See what you can do."

"Like what? I haven't seen many people do things with water before."

Fire, yes, and to impressive effect. But not water, which seemed a far less useful weapon. Perhaps that was why Ulric hadn't suggested trying it, even after I mentioned my escape from Callum.

"Do whatever you wish," he said. "If it's a natural gift, it should be as simple as breathing. Or it would be, in the outside world."

"So you think I don't have a natural gift? Nothing

is simple for me, even outside."

The hint of a smile passed over his lips. "I think in your case we might not pass judgment on that. You're somewhat unique. But we'll see what you can do."

The panel on the door slid open with a grinding noise that had become familiar to me, and my stomach grumbled on cue. "Step away from the door," a male voice mumbled. "Backs against the far wall. Hands up."

We followed instructions, and the single eye visible in the shadows of the tiny window blinked at us until its owner was sure we had complied. The door opened far enough for the guard to push in two trays of muddy-looking stew and tin cups of water. His head and shoulders poked in, too, and he squinted at the water pitcher in the middle of the floor. "What're you up to here?"

"Drinking," Ulric said. "Talking. Reminiscing about the glories of grass beneath our feet and the sun on our faces. You can't fault us for that." He'd cautioned me to not try to attack, to never let on that I could use my magic inside of the cell. I hung my head and watched the guard from beneath lowered eyelashes.

The guard glowered but left us in peace, locking the door behind him. We ate quickly, and Ulric set both cups next to the pitcher. "How's your magic feel today?" he asked.

I knew what answer he wanted—to hear that I didn't feel it at all, that it was simply there. But I wouldn't lie.

"It feels small," I said, as I had the morning and evening before.

"Where is it?"

"In my chest. My arms. My hands. My mind."

He just shook his head. "I'll be reading if you need me. Go play." He disappeared behind his screen, but sat on his stool and leaned against the wall. I pretended I didn't see him watching.

I tried to remember what Aren and Griselda had told me. *Don't think about it, just let it happen. Don't think about the tool. Focus on the outcome.*

I sat cross-legged on the floor next to the pitcher and studied the liquid within. I'd always loved water. I learned to swim in the river near Stone Ridge when I was quite young, playing in the currents, allowing myself to be swept downstream and fighting my way back. I respected it, too. Twice on my journey with Aren I'd been trapped underwater and thought I would drown.

Water was a gift, and it could be a weapon if I learned to use it as one.

No expectations, I told myself. Nothing had to happen. This was a chance to experience my magic fully. Just for fun. *Might as well have it while I can...*

As I watched, the surface of the water bowed up, reflecting the lamplight in interesting new ways. I concentrated on that, not trying to force anything, but enjoying the effect. I felt an urge to check on my magic, to see what it felt like while it made this happen, and resisted. *There's only the water.*

I nudged it with my mind, and a dimple appeared in the dome shape. I released it, and the surface smoothed, then lifted higher. Panic flashed through me as I recalled the other times my magic had come free. The dead magic hunter. The blood on Griselda's cheek. I closed my eyes. *Not this time. Nothing bad can happen in here. It's contained.*

I realized I didn't want it to be contained. *To hell with everything. I'm dead anyway, like Ulric said. Go on, magic.*

When I opened my eyes, the water rose out of the pitcher, squeezing through the narrow neck and taking on the rounded shape of the vessel again as it lifted into the air. I imagined it becoming a perfect sphere, and the water obeyed.

I laughed, and Ulric stepped out from behind his

screen.

I focused again, imagined a storm of water. The sphere exploded into a thousand droplets that scattered through the air, traveling too quickly for my eyes to follow, until they met resistance from the power of the walls. They slowed and hovered, then drew back and pulled together into a ball again. Sudden exhaustion came over me, and I dropped the water back into the pitcher without spilling a drop.

"Well done," Ulric said softly. He still held his book in one hand, dangling beside him, forgotten. A few pages slipped from the battered spine and rustled to the floor. He didn't seem to notice, or care.

I scooped up the pitcher in both hands and sipped from the rim. Nothing had changed. It was the same water they always gave us, metallic-tasting and never cool enough to be refreshing. I wiped my mouth on the baggy sleeve of my shirt. "How did I do that? I've never...It's never been like that before."

Ulric seated himself opposite me and took a drink. "Control. This is a gift, but you had too much of it before, and too much fear of it. It's exactly as I knew it would be. Your magic needed pressure so you could learn to manage it. Keep that control after we leave this place, and you'll have the world at your feet." Something passed over his expression then—uncertainty, or a realization. It was gone before I could make sense of it.

"What else can I do?" I felt stunned, dazed by what I'd done, not fully able to believe I had done it.

"That's up to you," he said. "Elemental control is a versatile gift. Keep experimenting. Turn it to mist, heat it, try to cool it. Find it in the ground and call it to—" He cut himself off. We didn't speak of the outside world. Not yet. "There's a river nearby. If your power was at its fullest, you might call it."

"To drown us?" I smiled, and he returned it. Cautiously, but looking for the first time like he had some hope of getting out.

"Or perhaps something else," he continued. "I still think illusions are worth pursuing as a means of escape, but we'll add this. Keep up that frightened mouse look around the guards. They're already becoming careless with you." He opened his book and took out another loose page. "I've worked out a map of the compound. It may not be perfect, but I've had enough conversations with folks and read enough to—"

The lock clicked, and Ulric snapped his book shut as the door opened. A guard entered, a woman I only saw when she took me to the toilets and baths. Her stern expression never varied any more than her uniform did, and her demeanor was always cold enough to make me eager to return to Ulric's company. A male guard followed, bearing a long dagger dripping with their illegal potion. Magic to be used against magic.

The woman nodded to me. "Miss Greenwood, you're to bathe now."

"Is it the nineteenth already?" I asked, and Ulric chuckled. It was a bit of a joke that we didn't get out for bathing nearly often enough.

"No. Now, please. King Haleth is expecting you."

My heart froze. When I looked at Ulric, he had a blank, stunned look. I remembered what he'd said about the king.

He tries to be present for executions. My heart raced as though pursued by a fire-breathing dragon. It was too soon. I'd found my magic, but we'd done no training in fighting or defense. Ulric had assumed he'd be with me when we escaped. I was a tool to him, as much as his magic. Honed for his purposes.

No, I thought. *He meant well. He meant to be there to protect me.*

"Please," Ulric whispered. "Not yet. She's only a girl."

The guard sniffed. "Not for me to say. She's been

here long enough. Sentencing don't usually wait this long, especially for a murderer."

Ulric's mouth pulled back in a snarl. I reached over and took one of his clenched fists in my hand. He couldn't fight his way out. One swipe from that dagger would render him useless. They were ready for his anger. Maybe they even wanted it.

"Don't," I whispered. "I'll be fine. If I don't come back, I know you'll find a way out." I reached for the clasp of my necklace. Several hairs had become tangled in the chain, but I hardly felt the pain when I tore them free. "Hold this for me. If you see Aren before I do, please tell him I'm sorry, and..." I couldn't say more.

Ulric clenched his jaw. "I know. I will." I released his hand, and he returned to his sleeping area.

I followed the guard to the bathing chamber. She didn't offer me privacy, but removed my manacles and watched with disinterest as I cleaned myself as well as I could in the lukewarm water. I scrubbed my hair and gasped at the cold as she dumped fresh water over my head to rinse the soap out.

They certainly didn't encourage us to linger in the baths here.

A clean dress awaited me, a shapeless brown thing with black buttons up the front of the bodice as the only decoration. The guard looked away as I slipped into it and tied the strings behind my waist. I reached for my boots, and the guard shoved them away with her foot.

"Disrespectful for a prisoner to be shod before the king," she said.

"I didn't know."

"This must be your first time. Suppose it's your last, too."

I ignored that.

Water dripped from my hair, and dampness spread across my back. I concentrated, and the water pulled back into my hair, then ran in a trail-less stream down my arm to pool into my hand. My hair and the dress were left nearly dry, and I let the water drip between my fingers onto the floor, keeping only a palm-sized sphere in my hand. A useless trick, perhaps, but using my magic comforted me in a way I'd never expected. It felt natural, as Ulric had said.

Perhaps they were going to sentence me to death, but I would face that knowing who I was, without the fear and guilt I'd felt for so long.

The guard thumped the back of my head lightly with a wooden truncheon, and the water bubble burst, soaking my fingers. Apparently, she'd been watching more closely than I realized.

"None of that," she muttered, and pushed me ahead of her. She reached around to the back of her belt and produced the cuffs, which she clamped around my wrists. *So much for them letting their guard down.*

I tried to call the water to follow me as we left the room, but felt nothing.

I hoped the guard would slip in the puddle later. We made our way through the corridor and up a curved staircase, and after a long walk down another corridor we reached our destination.

Haleth, king of Darmid, waited in a small library, seated behind a desk of carved and polished oak. He glanced up when we entered and motioned for the guard to leave. She bowed and closed the door behind her.

The king didn't say anything for a few minutes, but kept reading over a document written on a long piece of parchment as my bare toes grew cold on the stone floor. A fire burned in a small hearth near the desk, but the warmth barely reached me. I took the opportunity to inspect the room. Books covered the walls, their dark spines absorbing much of the light from the lamps, leaving a gloomy atmosphere.

A curtain shadowed the corner ahead of me and to the left. I squinted to try to see into the darkness, and jumped when I spotted a pair of eyes glaring back at me. Sir Dorset Langley stepped farther into the light and stood with his arms folded across his chest, his expression blank below his eyes, saying nothing.

I couldn't look away until the king spoke.

"Dorset, isn't it customary for a subject to kneel before a king?"

Sir Dorset still didn't say anything, but unfolded his arms and came toward me. Before I could move, he reached behind me and bent my wrist forward until my middle finger touched the inside of my wrist, sending a surprising bolt of agony up my arm. I gasped and collapsed to the floor.

"Thank you, Dorset. You may release her." The pressure and pain in my wrist eased, and I felt him move away. He went back to his corner. I stayed on the floor. I wanted to defy them, but there was no point.

I looked up from beneath the veil of my hair, feeling detached from the scene that surrounded me.

The king looked so young. Not much older than Aren, certainly younger than Severn. Haleth had brown hair, and there was nothing striking about his physical appearance except for the jeweled crown on his head and the complex, gaudy clothes he wore. His midnight-blue brocade jacket was held closed with dozens of tiny, gold fasteners that curved from his throat down past where his body disappeared behind his desk.

It must take you an hour to get dressed in the morning, I thought. I began to picture it, then stopped before it could make me laugh. That wouldn't help matters any.

He wore heavy jewelry, gold necklaces with multicolored medallions strung on them. The library was no less ornate, swathed in leather and velvet and complex wood carvings. It nearly brought my headache back just to look at it. I supposed it was opulence, though why anyone would aspire to it was beyond me.

"So, then," Haleth said. "Rowan Greenwood?"

I didn't answer until Dorset Langley leaned forward again, and I nodded.

"Formerly of Lowdell, correct? Near the Eastern border."

I nodded again.

"You left your home and went to Tyrea with one of King Ulric's sons, did you?"

How to answer that? It was technically correct, but left out everything important. "It's part of the truth, sire. I don't imagine you want to hear the rest."

"The details don't matter," he said. He moved to a green, velvet-upholstered armchair, one of a pair that occupied the space in front of me. He didn't invite me to sit in the other, or to stand.

"Now, while you were there, you...'discovered' that you had magical abilities?"

"Yes."

Dorset Langley stepped toward me again, and I flinched in spite of myself. "Your Highness," I said, and he stepped back again.

It's a dance, I thought. *One step forward, one step back, hurt the girl, swing your partner.*

Fear was creeping up on me, confusing my thoughts. I paused to steady my voice before I answered. "I learned that I've had magic in me since birth, Your Highness. Someone put a binding on me to hide it, and it almost killed me."

"Who did this?"

I'd made things bad enough for my family without this added to it. "I don't know," I lied. "Aren took me to find help, and in the end the binding broke itself. The magic wasn't my choice, or anyone else's. Your magic hunters know that, even if you don't."

Haleth sighed and drummed his fingers on a small table. "Well, it's a pretty story, isn't it? Convenient for you, who stands accused of witchcraft, of treason and blasphemy, selling your soul to the devil in Tyrea to gain these powers. I'm sure you'd like us all to think that this was something you couldn't help, but we know better. Dorset here has heard a similar story from many in your position, though I suspect with rather less help from Tyrean royalty. Tell me, did you go to the prince because you wanted magic, or did he talk you into it?"

"I've already told you how it happened. He recognized what I was and wanted to help me. Why don't you believe me?"

There was a long pause, then, "Dorset?"

He stepped forward, and before I could add a "Your Highness," he delivered a stinging slap, catching the side of my head and my cheek with the flat of his hand, sending me sprawling on the stone floor. My ear rang, and I tasted blood when I licked my lips. It took me back to the night I faced Severn, the pain and the certainty I'd felt that I was going to die, and my body trembled.

I took a few deep breaths and forced my muscles to still, then pushed myself back to my knees. I would not let myself cry.

Haleth sat impassively through all of it, appearing bored. "We'll take that as your confession, then. You are aware, I'm sure, that the sentence for your crimes is death, to be carried out immediately." He waited for a response. I didn't give him one. "Do you have anything to say to that?"

"No, Your Highness."

He raised his eyebrows and looked to Sir Dorset.

"No one has come forward to speak for her, my lord. None to corroborate her story, none to object to the sentence. These are the gravest of crimes. The punishment is fitting."

"Not to mention the insults to your own family, Langley?" the king asked, a hint of derision in his voice.

Sir Dorset glowered at me. "As you say, Your

Highness. She was to marry my son, and instead ran off with an enemy of our people who threatens your position and your land. Her life is an insult to everything we hold dear."

Haleth propped his head on one hand. "And yet, the fact that she spent time with the prince could make her useful. If we were to make a bargain, her life in exchange for what could be valuable information..."

Langley's jaw muscles flexed visibly. "If I may speak plainly, sire, it's not something I would offer to her. She can't possibly know anything of Severn's plans. If she does, she'll have told the old man. It would be my pleasure to question him again."

"Thank you, Dorset." Haleth looked at me. "Still, we could use her to get to him. Surely Aren Tiernal would be worth her life, at least temporarily. He has more to answer for than she has. Her execution could wait."

I should have stayed silent. "You'll never find him. He knows better than to come here for me, and I don't know where he is."

"Would you tell us if you did?" the king asked. "Would you tell us what else you know of Tyrea, of Severn's plans? Of Belleisle? I understand you've spent time there."

"I'll never tell you anything."

A smile played at the corners of Sir Dorset's mouth, and his eyes glowed with victory.

I'm going to die, I thought. My parents weren't going to come and plead for my life. I would never see my magic grow to its full potential. I'd never see anyone I loved again.

I tried to hold it back, but a tear slipped out of my eye and fell to the floor in front of me. "I would never betray any of them." My voice was strong and clear in spite of the despair that made the rest of my body feel so weak. "I don't think you'd let me live even if I did. Your Highness."

"Do you want to die, Miss Greenwood?"

"No, Your Highness."

"I thought not." He motioned for Dorset Langley to come closer, and whispered into his ear.

Langley shook his head. "It's too great a risk."

"Still, we haven't had someone as strong as her to try it with, and she's behaved herself well enough thus far. She'd be an excellent subject. If you succeed with her, it could theoretically work with anyone."

Langley turned back to me and folded his arms across his chest again. "I can't keep you from offering, sire."

Haleth nodded. "Miss Greenwood, a final offer to spare your life."

He leaned back in the chair and crossed his legs, looking as though he was having a casual conversation with an old friend instead of an accused enemy. My heart skipped. I knew what he was going to offer.

"You say you were born with this magic in you, that you had no choice in the matter? I believe those were your words."

"Yes, Your Highness."

"Then I suppose you'd be eager to take an opportunity to have this birth-curse removed from you. If it's not something you wanted, and I told you that there was a way to have that blasphemous power burned out of you, that you could be cleansed from it completely and forever, and you could be a normal member of society...That should be quite tempting, I think."

My mouth went dry. "I think perhaps I haven't been clear enough on some points, Your Highness," I said slowly. "You are correct in saying that I didn't ask for this. It has always been with me, but I didn't know until this past autumn."

Is this more important than freedom? whispered a voice in my mind. *This choice will seal your fate. You could give it up.*

But this is who I am. No more hiding.

"The fact that I didn't choose it doesn't mean that it was unwanted," I continued. "I was terrified when I first learned about my magic, knowing our people's beliefs about it and the penalty for using it here. But I've embraced what I am. What you call a curse, I call a gift. If anyone put this magic in me, it was God himself, and I won't turn away from it. I would consider that as much a sacrilege as you think the magic itself is. I'm afraid I must refuse your most generous offer."

"You would die, then, before you would repent?"

I gritted my teeth. "I have nothing to repent of, Your Highness. Not in this, at least. My other sins are my own concern."

Haleth looked to Dorset Langley, appearing uncertain.

"So be it," Langley said, his voice almost too low to hear over the ringing that continued in my ear. "It was fairly done, Your Highness. You made a most kind and generous offer, gave her a chance at life that most would not have given. She chooses to die uncleansed and unabsolved. You are blameless in the matter of her death."

"That didn't concern me," Haleth said, and the corners of his mouth turned slightly, though I couldn't tell whether it was with humor or distaste. "I swore to protect this land and its people from what she is, I bear no guilt for carrying out my oath. Call the guard back."

Langley walked past me to the door without looking down at me.

"Why don't you just do it?" I asked. My voice felt small, and yet it filled the room. "If it's so important that you take my magic, why not—"

A fist connected with the back of my head, and white light exploded in front of my eyes as I fell forward.

I laughed in spite of the pain. "You can't, can you? You can't take it unless I let you."

Langley's boot caught me in the ribs, and I was unable to say more.

Haleth stepped closer and lifted my face with the toe of his boot. "Langley, will you take care of this now?"

"If it pleases you, sire, I'd like to wait a few days. Much as I'd like to see this prisoner dispatched immediately, it would mean much to my family if my son carried out the order himself. He's taking care of a few things for me at the moment, but has said he'll be back in four days."

"How poetic that he should slay the beast," the king said. "Very well, Miss Greenwood. You are sentenced to die for your crimes against the Darmish people. When Callum Langley returns to the city, you will be bled until the life is gone from your mortal body." He nudged my chin with his toe as though flicking dirt from his boot, and his face became an impassive mask. "You may go."

I tried to stand, and stumbled. My legs tingled as the blood returned to them.

A different guard appeared, a man large enough to half-push, half-carry me back to the blue-walled cell where Ulric waited.

The door slammed closed behind me. Ulric stood still as stone, eyes wide, lips parted.

I don't know what he saw in my face, but his own softened, and he suddenly looked far older than he had before. I forgot that I was still supposed to hate and mistrust him. I fell into his open arms, sobbing. He held me, awkwardly trying to offer comfort while my sorrow poured out, doing his best to act like the father I no longer had.

Perhaps it was the best thing for both of us.

Chapter Thirty-Two

Nox

Cassia pulled her horse to a stop as we reached the edge of the forest. "I'd hoped we wouldn't be seeing these mountains again for a while."

"I know." Kel stopped beside her. The two had led us through the previous day and this morning, perhaps hoping that Aren and I would make conversation. So far we'd managed cordial silence. I wasn't sure whether he was ignoring me because he wanted to avoid slipping into my thoughts again, or because he was still angry with me for not wanting to throw our plans off track to rescue his little plaything. Either way, I would take it. I'd accepted that it would take time for us to warm to each other. Maybe it wouldn't happen at all. In any case, we would work together.

And she might help, I reminded myself. I came back to that each time I grew irritated with this insane mission. *What have I got to lose?*

Florizel snorted and shuffled sideways. "The mountains aren't so bad. I'm not sure how you're all going to make it over, though. I'm not familiar with the passes humans use."

"There aren't many," Aren said, frowning at the mountains as though they'd sense his irritation and open up for us. "There's the main pass that traders take. It's not far from here, but that's heavily guarded. The

Darmish take care not to let Tyrean magic users in. As far as I know, only Darmish traders get by, and Wanderers from Tyrea if they're clever enough to talk their way past and catch the guards on a good day. There will be magic hunters there."

"Can we get around them?" Cassia asked.

Aren took a map from his bag and handed it to her. "Not without abandoning the horses and climbing. The pass is narrow."

"There may be a way around the north end of the range," Florizel offered. "But we'd have to go north, then south, and I'm not entirely certain about that, anyway."

Aren sighed. "We'd waste days finding out."

"Is that all of our options?" I asked. It sounded hopeless.

"How did you and Rowan get out the first time?" Cassia asked.

Kel had filled me in on what he knew of that story—or as much as he'd thought Aren would want me to know. I'd begun to suspect that this was common among mers, or at least this little family of them. Cassia never gossiped or speculated, either.

"South," Aren said. "Around the bottom of the mountain range." He took the map back, opened it further, and pointed. I looked over his shoulder. The land narrowed here, creating an isthmus connecting Tyrea and Darmid, across which spread the mountains. I looked up at them again. These were old mountains, covered with trees up to their rounded tops, with bare patches showing where the rocks had eroded. Not pretty. Not as impressive as the ones in the north. Still a formidable challenge.

"It sounds like that's the way to go," I said. "Is it guarded?"

"Not as heavily," Aren said, and handed me the map. "When we came through, we passed one guard station. I think any traders heading to or from the south shore of Darmid go by ship, not by land, so it's not as busy."

"Sounds perfect. We can't be too far off from there now, can we?" It certainly felt like we'd been travelling long enough.

Aren exchanged a glance with Kel, then cleared his throat. "It's not that simple. I have obligations that way."

I sighed. "Please tell me you didn't leave some poor Darmish girl with a baby and run out on her."

Kel snorted. "Not that kind of obligation. Aren, you should tell her."

Aren cleared his throat. "When Rowan and I were trying to get to Tyrea, I made a deal with a dragon. She let us live after we found ourselves in her cave, and in exchange we promised that we would go back and tell her how our—" He at least had the sense to look embarrassed. "How our story turned out."

"You..." I sputtered, struggling to find words that would at least keep my jaw from hanging open. "I'm not even going to ask how people *find themselves* in a dragon's cave. Let's just say that it happened. You don't make a deal with a dragon. It's foolish. Dangerous. Stupid!"

"And I suspect more so to break a promise to one," Aren said quietly.

Kel winced at the sound of my teeth gritting together. I dismounted so I could walk while I thought, making a tight circle around the group. "You southerners really don't know anything, do you? You can't do something like that. She has to be an old dragon to have conversed with you at all. Even older to have let you go. There's always a trick. Tell me, did you negotiate how you'd get out after you delivered on your end of the bargain?"

"Not that I recall."

Cassia's skin turned ashen. "Even I know that's

bad."

"So she's got you under her claw if you step one foot in her territory again. But it's that, or facing magic hunters." I rubbed my forehead, where tight pain throbbed. "The only thing worse would be if she had young. They get moodier then. Even less predictable."

Aren grimaced. "About that..."

"No. No, no, no."

"We'll take your advice on this, Nox," Aren said. "You grew up in Cressia. You know far more about dragons than any of us. I've read about them, been on a few hunts. You lived with them, or close enough to it. What do you suggest?"

I stopped and turned slowly toward my brother. No sarcasm in his voice this time. No challenge. I smiled slightly in spite of my irritation. "Are you suggesting, Sorcerer Prince of Tyrea, that a lowly Potioner from the provinces might be able to give you advice? That I might know better than you?"

He shrugged, but his hint of a smile reflected my own. "Seems like a reasonable suggestion."

"He's right," Kel said. "Cass and I know sea serpents, water dragons, deep-sea monsters, and a little bit about what we've met on land, but you're the closest thing we have to an expert right now."

I don't care what Aren thinks about me, I reminded myself, but satisfaction swelled in my chest. True, he still wasn't giving my potions-related skills the respect they deserved, but acknowledging my expertise in this was certainly something.

"You know, it's about time you figured that out," I told Aren. My smile disappeared. "What were the terms if you didn't return?"

"Death. Though we didn't say when we'd return. If we avoid her lands, she never has to know we were here."

I'd never been one to back away from a challenge,

but this one would be more difficult than most. I was a healer, not a defender, and certainly not against dragons. I could put something together to keep them away from a farm temporarily, but I couldn't fight one off. Aren couldn't, either. Not with magic, and not alone.

"We should try the main road," I said. "In case there's a way we can get the horses through. It will slow us down too much if we abandon them, but it still might be a better plan than visiting a dragon."

Florizel lowered her head. "I suppose flying each of you over's a bad idea then, as well."

"We'll keep it in mind," I said. "We should keep the horses if we can. I'll try to think of something to help with the dragon in case that doesn't work."

Aren nodded. "If you think it's best. If we continue on this way, we'll reach the road within the hour."

Cassia rode next to me as we followed Aren through thin tree cover at the edge of the forest, heading south, parallel to the mountains to our west. "We could scout," she said.

"We? As in you and me?" I asked, and she nodded.

"If anyone sees us, they won't detect magic in you, correct? Not like they would in Aren. We can't send Florizel around those people."

"What about Kel? You two seem to work well together."

"We do. He's been distracted lately, though, and he's not the most graceful creature on his feet. You and I would get closer without notice. We'll just see how things look, whether there's a way we could make it through."

"Sounds like a good plan." I didn't point out that Cassia was heavier on her feet than most women of her size and build. It seemed so obvious now that I knew what she and Kel were, but I'd written it off as clumsiness before.

Aren and Kel reluctantly agreed when we shared the plan with them. "You'll be careful?" Kel asked.

"Of course," Cassia answered, though he'd been looking at me when he spoke. My face flushed.

We left the horses and made our way toward the pass, a deep V in the otherwise solid wall of the mountain. A river coursed through it, flowing beside the road into Tyrea. Cassia looked longingly at the water, but we didn't stop. Instead we stuck to the low parts of the uneven ground and tried to make ourselves invisible among the sparse tree cover. The road was empty, and all seemed quiet.

"Maybe it's not as bad as Aren thought," I said softly.

Cassia looked back over her shoulder and stumbled over a hummock of grass. "That seems like an imprudent thing to say."

"My words won't change what's ahead."

She shrugged, and carried on. I grabbed handfuls of plant matter as we passed. Firegrass, simpkin's bow, the buds of the nightflare flower. All familiar. All worth keeping handy. If what I'd heard about Darmid was true, the magic in the plants over there would be less than what I was accustomed to working with in Tyrea.

We stayed away from the road and headed toward the face of the mountain and the forests there. The slope at the bottom was shallow enough, but I lost my breath before we'd climbed far.

"What now?" I whispered.

"Stick together. Get closer. See what we see." She tripped again, and I caught her by the arm before she fell.

"Thanks." She grimaced. "What was that I was saying about Kel?"

We continued upward and south until we reached the pass and looked down on the river, the road, and the mass of people swarming around a small collection of wooden buildings. Cassia crouched behind a log, and I joined her.

"What do you think?" she asked. "Is this better than the dragon?"

I watched the people, and my stomach sank. Some of them appeared to be merchants waiting to get into Darmid, and most of them had set up camp near the river. It didn't look like anyone was getting through. There was no way we'd get in that way. Men in blue uniforms in varying shades roamed among the people, picking through carts of cargo, searching tents, each man paired with another wearing charcoal gray.

"Are those magic hunters?" I asked.

"I don't know." Cassia's brow creased. "Kel and I were fortunate enough not to meet any when we were in Darmid before. I'd like to keep it that way, if possible. They might be a little quicker than you were at catching on to what we are." She said it kindly enough, and I smiled.

"Yes, I should have figured it out the first time you tripped over your own feet. Must be hard when you're not used to them." I clucked my tongue softly. "Poor, helpless creatures."

She flashed a quick grin at me and went back to watching the people below us.

This is how friends speak to each other, I realized. Little barbs, but no sting to them, and meant kindly. The thought warmed me. I'd never had that sort of easy, playful conversation with anyone who I wasn't flirting with.

I turned my attention to the pass itself. The sheer sides wouldn't allow us to trek around the encampment, and the mountains were too steep to avoid the pass completely.

Cassia grabbed my arm and pulled me lower behind the log. Below us, one of the blue-clad men was pointing in our direction, speaking to another.

"Did he see us?"

She shook her head. "I don't think so. He's not raising an alarm. He might have seen something, though."

The fellow and his companion started toward the side of the pass, walking slowly, but with purpose.

"Time to go." Cassia held onto my arm as we moved away from them and back down the mountain, and we sprinted when we reached the foothills. She didn't trip this time.

I looked back several times, but saw no sign of anyone pursuing us. We stopped to catch our breath when we got back to the horses.

"So," I panted. "We need to figure out what to do about that dragon." I stood up straighter, then mounted my horse. The others did the same. "You said she has young?"

"Three," Aren said. "Tiny, though. In a pool of water."

"How long ago was this?"

"Back in the autumn."

"They may have grown. Give me some time to think."

They obeyed. No one said a word to me as we crossed a wide road and followed the foothills south. Aren spoke quietly to Florizel, and she flew away, presumably taking a route over the mountains where there were less likely to be humans watching.

Later, we rode uphill into the trees, finding and quickly leaving a road that was far narrower and more poorly kept than the other one had been. Ahead, the end of the mountain range sloped into forested land, presumably toward the ocean. We dismounted and led our horses through the trees, then rode across uneven, rocky ground. Smoke rose from the other side of a small hill, near where the road would have taken us. In the distance, someone whistled a cheery tune, and someone else hollered for him to shut up.

Aren looked toward the noise. "That's the guard station. I think it's the only one on this road."

"Is that it, then?" I asked when we were well away from it. "Are we in Darmid?"

Cassia shivered. "I don't like it here."

I didn't, either. There was something wrong with the air, something that had been creeping up on us since before we crossed the border. No, not the air. "It's true about the magic here, isn't it?"

Aren turned back to me. "You can feel it, too?"

"I can, thank you. Just because I can't channel magic like you can doesn't mean I'm not as accustomed to its presence as you are." I paused and corrected my tone. I had to stop taking everything he said as an insult. "So they do kill off the magic here?"

He nodded and turned forward again. I rode beside him as we made our way through the shadows of low mountains that forced us to continue south and into a forest.

I tried to remember anything useful that I'd learned about dragons and their young, and asked Aren more questions as they came to mind. Dragons had never been a particular interest of mine, but Aren was right. Where I came from, knowing about them and their habits was the difference between living or becoming someone's meal.

Their young grew in great bursts, depending on what their caregivers fed them. That, in turn, depended on what food was available, the season, and whether the mother thought they were old enough to handle their own size and ferocious power. If we were lucky, this ancient mother would have decided to keep her dragonlings small for longer so that they could mature mentally. They rarely did, though, as the mothers needed to eat eventually, and rarely left their lairs without the young. They'd have fed on her treasure first, and meat later.

We'd know soon enough.

My hopes sank as the land changed again and we rode over burned fields. This would be the edge of the dragon's territory, and she had clearly been out.

"We should stop," I said. "If we get any closer to the heart of her lands, she'll sense you. Or she will if she's as old as you indicated, Aren."

He nodded and led us toward the shelter of the forest next to the burned fields.

The horses were as on-edge as the rest of us. Florizel landed nearby and trotted to catch up. "This place makes me nervous," she said.

I placed a hand on her neck as I'd seen Aren do to comfort her. Her coat was softer than a land horse's, and when she didn't startle at my touch, I ran my fingers over it. "It's all right. The dragon won't be back if everything is dead here. It will be somewhere else, looking for fresh meat."

Kel grunted. "I think that would be more comforting if we weren't fresh meat ourselves."

Aren grinned back at him. "You're not regretting your offer to come with me, are you?"

Kel straightened his shoulders and looked at me. "Not entirely."

Heat crept into my face. I hoped it didn't show in the sunset.

"Oh, for the love of Dryess," Cassia muttered, presumably referencing some mer deity I was unfamiliar with.

We made camp, and I continued to consider the problem. If Aren's description had been accurate, we were dealing with a hornback, a strong and clever beast, but not suited to night hunting. With any luck, even if she somehow sensed Aren, she'd wait to see if he came to her. Still, we didn't build a fire. No sense in tempting her.

Strange that she'd let Aren and Rowan go. I'd heard of dragons developing human tendencies before, but I was certain it hadn't been compassion that made her release them. It had been curiosity. I hoped Aren was thinking about a way to use that, or something else, to get out of there. My concern now was the young ones. Even if they weren't huge, they'd be vicious, and wouldn't give second thought to attacking. Aren had magic, and we had a few small weapons, but if we attacked the young ones, the mother would roast us.

If we can just deter them...

"There's no chance we can get by without her knowing, is there?" Aren asked me.

"I wouldn't try it. She might let you go far enough that you thought you'd escaped, and then roast all of us."

His shoulders slumped. "I thought so. I wish Rowan were here."

"Why?"

"She's the one who talked her out of eating us last time."

So she'd escaped a dragon's cave and nearly killed Severn. Something told me there was no chance of this person being as impressive as Aren seemed to think she was, but I held my tongue on that. He was opening up to me. I'd take it, and reserve judgement on this wonderful woman. If she managed to dazzle her way out of prison, then I'd be impressed.

While the others got things set up, I sorted through the herbs and various supplies I'd picked up that day. I'd organized everything else and packed it carefully into my horse's saddle bags, with the plants layered between strips of cloth I'd torn from the soldier's cloak. I took the cleaned rib bones of the trout Cassia caught the day before, rabbit fur, starflower stalks and nightflare, all of the firegrass I'd collected, several of the cloth strips and a few other items, and excused myself.

It's difficult to work without proper equipment, but I would manage. I moved far from camp and set the ingredients out in a clearing lit by the full moon. I tested them, holding them in my hands, smelling them, taking them in. The plants I'd picked in Tyrea maintained their power here. The other items would work no matter what. They had no magic, only useful properties.

Starflower to entice, firegrass to inflame—or so I hoped. A dragonling might be immune. Still, it was our best shot.

I'd only need one more ingredient. I brought out one of the daggers that my unfortunate soldier friend had left behind.

"Can I help?" Kel's voice drifted from the trees behind me.

"You're getting quieter," I observed, and turned to him. "I barely heard you coming."

Kel stood up straighter. "I'm working on it. I don't think I'll ever be as graceful on land as I am in the water, though. What are you doing?"

"Trying to be prepared. You might not want to see this."

The shadows covered much of his face, but I caught the concerned furrow of his brow. "Do you want me to leave? Whatever it is, I can handle it."

The firm set of his jaw and the look in his eyes told me he wasn't lying. I wondered what he'd seen in his life. Such a strange man. I couldn't deny I was glad to have his assistance and his company. Something about him calmed my mind, even as his presence tended to do the opposite to my body. I could ignore that, though.

"You can stay, if you want to," I said. "Hold the bowl for me."

He stepped into the clearing and cupped the bowl in his hands, holding it out from his body. "Like this?"

"Perfect."

I tried to roll up my sleeves. They were too tight. The whole sweater would have to go. I thought about asking Kel to look away. I didn't want to complicate things further.

Don't be silly, I told myself. *You're both adults. He's seen more, and probably prettier.*

Kel's eyes widened as I pulled the sweater over my head, leaving me in a thin under-shirt in the cold woods.

I waited for his gaze to return to mine. "Don't you merfolk go around without shirts on all the time underwater?"

"Yes."

I raised my eyebrows, and fought back a smile when his eyes wandered again.

"It's just different with you," he said. "It's fine. Carry on. Please."

I took a deep breath and traced the tip of the dagger over the skin of my arm, trying to decide on the best spot to get what I needed while doing the smallest possible amount of permanent damage. I settled on the back of my forearm and stroked the tip of the dagger gently over my skin once, twice, three times, building my nerve.

"Use my blood, if you want," Kel said.

"No. Thank you. I've had worse injuries."

"So have I."

The sharp blade burned as I made a shallow cut into the skin high on my forearm that didn't produce nearly enough blood. I cut deeper on the next pass, carving into my flesh. I gasped, and tears forced their way out of my eyes. I bit my lip and tasted blood. But I got what I needed. Dark fluid dripped over the curve of my arm and into the bowl. I flexed my hand, encouraging the flow to continue until blood filled the bottom of the bowl.

"Help. Please." I nodded toward the pile of cloth. Kel set the bowl on the ground and sorted through the strips, holding them to the light, rejecting the ones with visible dirt on them. I chewed on a stalk of nightflare, which made the inside of my mouth tingle pleasantly as my saliva wakened the tough material and brought out the magic in it.

I looked up at Kel. *How would he react if I kissed him right now,* I wondered, *when it would be unlike anything he's ever felt? When it—when I—could be something truly special?*

I took the plant material from my mouth and placed it on top of the cut on my arm, where the bleeding had already slowed. Even without time to prepare a proper healing potion, this would at least keep infection away. The last thing this group needed was a member of our party falling ill over a little injury. Kel had said that mer folk healed quickly, and Aren had his magic to protect him. As the weak link in our chain, I would have to be more careful.

Kel had lost the twinkle in his eye that usually said he didn't take life too seriously.

"It's just a scratch." I held my arm out, and he wrapped the cloth strip around. Tight, but not constricting. Secure. It could have done with stitches, but going without wouldn't kill me.

What's one more scar, really?

"I'm not going to ask whether that was necessary," Kel said, still not smiling. "You know your business."

"So what's wrong?"

"I just didn't realize your work could require that."

"Most people don't. I'll be fine. Thank you for your help." I needed to pull away, to finish my project before my blood congealed in the bowl, but I couldn't look away from his eyes. They looked black in the shadows, but burned with an emotion I couldn't identify. His gaze flicked down to my arm, and he lifted it gently in his hands.

He bent over in a slight bow and kissed the bandage over my wound.

I pulled my arm away and crouched to pick up the bowl. "What was that for?"

I added the rest of my ingredients to the blood, crushing soft bones with a rock, grinding tough plant materials, mixing it all into a messy clump. Not even Kel's distracting presence could keep my instincts and training from finishing what I'd started.

He watched with interest as I added grass to the mixture and spit into the bowl to add moisture. "Isn't a kiss supposed to make an injury better?" he asked.

"Maybe for children. I didn't realize mer-folk did that, too."

"Oh, we're quite enthusiastic about kissing in any form." His expression remained serious.

My fingers tightened around the cloth I'd picked up, and trembled slightly as I laid the strips out in a starburst pattern, criss-crossing in the middle, and scraped the blood mixture onto the center. It took me longer than it should have to tie the knots in the top that held it closed. When finished, it looked like a lumpy ball that had been kicked through a dirty street by too many children. I wished I had enough materials to make more, but this would have to do.

I left the bundle resting on a fallen tree and stood. I struggled to think of a clever response to his comment about kissing, and couldn't. "What else are you enthusiastic about?"

He couldn't keep that smile away forever. "Oh, so many things."

Gods, that smile. Confident, kind, persistent but never pushy...everything that Kel was, himself. Everything I could want, really. But I couldn't open myself to that. I'd been hurt by love before, and I had another mission now.

My eyes stung. *I don't want that to be all I am. And I don't want to turn him away.*

I'm free, I reminded myself. *My life is mine. Not*

Denn's. Not Severn's. Mine.

Perhaps I couldn't offer him everything he wanted, but I might share in his enthusiasm.

I stepped closer and reached up to place a hand on the back of his neck. I breathed in the scent of his skin, slightly salty even after weeks away from the sea. "Show me," I whispered, and closed my eyes.

He wrapped one arm around my waist and slid his other hand up my back, tangling in the hair above my neck. I stiffened, then relaxed as I opened my eyes and saw the concern in his. Such a small reaction on my part, but he noticed. I bit my lower lip, and relaxed. His lips brushed against mine, gentle for a moment before his arms tightened around me and the kiss deepened. His tongue brushed against my lips, testing and teasing. I wrapped my arms completely around his neck and pressed my body hard against his as I responded.

Gods, it's been too long. Too long since I'd felt desire this thick, this fluid, this consuming. I grew dizzy, and realized I wasn't breathing.

A cold breeze swept through the forest, rattling the branches overhead, and I realized I was also still not wearing much on top. Kel released me for long enough to open his jacket, and I slipped my arms around his ribs. He wrapped the fabric as far as it would reach around me and pulled me close again. Not into another passionate kiss, but to rest his cheek against my hair.

An unexpected pause.

"Kel," I murmured against his shoulder. "Is everything okay?"

He drew in a deep breath and let it out slowly. "I honestly don't know. I feel strange. Like I'm dying, but in a good way."

I slipped one hand under his shirt, tracing my nails over his skin, and he shivered. He was amazing. Perfect, really, unless he was the cleverest liar I'd ever met. But I couldn't give him what he wanted. I needed to be free to sacrifice anything to bring Severn down, and Kel deserved better than something temporary, to be brushed aside when duty called me. He deserved love that was complete and unreserved in a way I felt incapable of.

I knew I should pull away and tell him this wasn't going to work. Better now, before either of us got hurt.

And then Kel tilted my face toward his and kissed me again. A sweet, simple kiss, but filled with longing and promise.

If only it were a promise I could accept.

Chapter Thirty-Three

Aren

I remained awake most of the night, as though by keeping on guard I could watch for dawn's approach and prevent its arrival. When I closed my heavy eyelids and tried to find sleep, it fled from me. What I found instead were racing thoughts. Memories lingered just out of reach, taunting me.

Did Rowan bargain for future escapes? I thought not, but wished I could remember. I knew the dragon would.

Someone sighed. Nox, I thought, probably sleeping no better than I was. She'd said she came up with something for me to take in with me. Not a weapon, exactly, but something to distract a dragon if the need arose. Surely she wasn't worried about me. She hadn't wanted to come here to begin with. If I got eaten, she'd be free to carry on with her own plans.

I won't get eaten, though. I'd get out. I had to. If I didn't, Rowan would surely die.

I would approach the dragon as a rational creature, I decided. One could never reason with a young dragon, but Ruby wasn't like them. She could speak. She could reason. I suspected she felt emotions, but it would never do to appeal to them. It would be an insult to her to even acknowledge that they existed.

The sky turned purple, then faintly pink. I rolled

over to block out the light. *Not yet.*

The trouble was, everything rested on the whims of a creature that by rights should care nothing for the life of a short-lived creature like myself, any more than I cared that the rabbits I hunted wished to go on living. I would be an amusement, or a meal. Perhaps both.

The dragonlings would only see me as the latter.

Kel rose first. "You awake?" he asked.

I opened my eyes to see his bare feet in front of my nose. "I seem to be."

"I'm going to find somewhere to swim. Don't leave without me."

I nodded. We couldn't afford many delays on this journey, but I didn't mind a short one that morning.

Kel soon returned to find the rest of us packing our things. "There's a deep river not far off," he said, "if anyone's interested."

Cassia and Nox brightened. Nox dug through the bags for a bar of soap as Kel gave directions to Cassia. He watched the pair until they disappeared into the forest.

"What's going on with you and Nox?" I asked.

He grinned. "Don't tell me you're getting protective of your sister. I think we should be long past that, given your history with mine."

I smiled back, glad for a reason to do so. "Not at all. I suspect Nox knows exactly what she wants, and if that means you, I wish you the very best of luck."

"You still don't see it, do you?"

"No," I admitted. "She's turned out to be more helpful than I expected. She cured your cough, and she patched up Florizel quite well." At this, the flying horse glanced up, then went back to grazing. "We've had a few moments when I thought we understood each other, but she's still so abrasive."

"She's hurt," Kel said. "Over the past twenty years, you've built up your armor to protect you from the slights and pain that your family inflicted on you. She's had to defend herself from other trials, maybe more than we'll ever know. She's serious about destroying Severn, no matter what it takes, and maybe that makes her less willing to compromise and make nice. But she has a good heart. A strong one. When she lets her guard down, she makes me laugh. When she's wrong, she admits it and tries to change. Do you know how admirable that is? How difficult?"

"I'm somewhat familiar with the challenge."

"And gods, she's attractive."

"I understand."

Kel gave me a sly glance. "That little scar on her lip makes me wonder whether she'd like to—"

"Enough!" I winced. "I said I wasn't going to be protective. I didn't say I wanted to talk about it."

His smile turned distant. "She's been telling me a bit about being a Potioner, and it's fascinating. Did you know she does most of her work by instinct and by feel? It's magic, really. Just not the same as yours, or mine."

"No," I admitted. No one I knew had ever treated it like more than a learned skill. Perhaps Emalda did, but I'd never spoken to her about it.

"She can't talk about these things with you," Kel continued. "You two seem determined to hate each other. One step forward, fourteen back."

"All I want is Rowan, alive. I'd put up with a hundred Noxes if it meant I could do that. Especially if her help means getting out of the dragon's cave alive. Did she say exactly what she had in mind for that?"

He shook his head. "I helped her. I didn't ask a lot of questions."

Florizel led the horses back from their night in the woods, and Kel and I tacked all four up. We were finishing when Nox and Cassia returned.

"Feel better?" I asked.

"Much," they both replied.

Nox squeezed a stream of water from her thick

hair. "I've needed that for ages. Are we ready to go?"

"I think it's time to leave whether we're ready or not," I told her, ignoring the way my stomach turned at the thought of going deeper into the dragon's territory.

We rode on, away from the burnt fields and buildings, back into the woods. I couldn't say they were familiar. Rowan and I had been walking quickly in the opposite direction last time I'd passed through this area. I'd been burning up with anger, distracted by thoughts of how I'd convince her of her magic, too absorbed in that to note landmarks. I recognized the gentle curve of this last mountain before the sea, though. The dragon's cave was in the side of it.

Not far, now.

My fear faded, turning to numbness. There would be no turning back.

I stopped when we reached a place that did seem familiar. We had stopped here after we fled the cave. "I'll go ahead on foot now," I said. "Hang back, and stay away when you see me go into the cave. If things go badly, or if there's even a hint of trouble, you should all run. Nox, you said you had something for me?"

"I have." Nox dug into her bag and pulled out a large, bloodstained ball of cloth. She sniffed at it, wrinkled her nose, and held it out to me. "Just—wait, I can't." She pulled it back before I could take it.

"Can't what?"

She sighed. "I can't let you go in there alone. You'll never get out."

"I appreciate your confidence in my abilities." We both spoke in low voices, though I suspected the dragon already knew we were there. "What about you?" I asked. "Do you like *your* odds?"

"I like my odds of seeing Severn dead better if you live, and I wouldn't be going with you if I didn't think we have a chance if we do this together. I was thinking about it last night. Many older dragons have an affinity for damsels, and from what you've told me, I'm guessing this one is no exception. I'm not sure I qualify, but it might be the key to getting you out of there." She dismounted, and Kel followed suit.

"Nox," he said, "can we speak privately for a minute?"

She gripped the cloth bundle tighter in her hands. "I have to do this."

"I know. I wouldn't ask you not to. Just give me one minute."

She led the way into the forest. Cassia brought her horse up close to mine.

"What do you think of that?" I asked as we watched the pair disappear behind a boulder.

Her lips tightened. "I don't know. I worry about him. He has a tendency toward attachment, always has. It's not normal for us. Everyone back home knows how he feels about this sort of thing, and we respect it, but he knows it's not going to happen with a mer." She shook her head. "I want him to be happy, but this...Aren, he can't let it happen with a human."

"It may be too late."

She shrugged. "I don't know. He doesn't talk to me about it. I hope he can to you. You've been there."

"He can if I make it out of that cave alive."

She glared at me. "You'll be fine. Nox will be fine, and Kel will be happy, at least for now." She ran her fingers through her still-damp hair. "I fully expect you to come out of there with the dragon tamed and ready to give us all a ride to Ardare."

I snorted. "Let's just try for alive, shall we?"

Kel and Nox returned. Her face was flushed. He looked worried.

"Everything all right?" I asked.

Nox glanced at Kel, then me. "Yes. Let's go."

We left our horses with the others and walked through the woods. Cassia and Kel followed at a good distance, as I'd asked. No one spoke, and not even a bird chirped in the trees overhead. Nox ran her fingers over deep gouges in the bark of an oak tree and shivered. "We're close."

"No," I said quietly. "We're here."

The low opening in the rock appeared unchanged except that the ground in front had been cleared of the debris I remembered from before. Ruby and her brood were indeed going in and out of the cave, and responsible for the destruction we'd passed.

Nox reached for my hand. "Not to get cozy. I just..."

"I know." I gave her fingers a reassuring squeeze, and for the first time wondered whether having her in my life would have made it better through all the lonely years. "It's going to be fine."

We stepped into the shadows of the mountain and into the cave's low, gaping mouth. Warm air surrounded us as we crept down the passage that led to the main cavern, and dim light showed the way.

"She's here," I whispered.

Nox motioned for me to go forward.

A deafening noise somewhere between a shriek and a roar echoed down the passage.

"I think they're expecting us," Nox said, and pushed me behind an angle of rock that jutted out into the passage. A moment later a blast of fire shot past us— small, but hot enough that I broke into a sweat.

"Thanks," I said.

"Yeah. Any ideas on how we're going to make it the rest of the way without getting cooked? We can't go back now."

"Not really." I stepped out from behind the rock. "Ruby!" Another shriek answered me, and a scuffling noise, followed by a yelp.

"Well," said a rough voice that sent shivers rippling over my skin. "I had begun to think you weren't

Kate Sparkes

coming back."

"May we enter? Or will your young attack?"

She let out a low, purring sound. "I think I can hold them back. Come."

Nox's face paled, but she set her jaw and stepped out from behind the rock. I was glad to have her with me, and perhaps she was right in thinking that a feminine presence would help. I only hoped she wouldn't say or do anything that would put us into more danger.

The cavern had changed little. The shallow pool that the dragonlings had been resting in was nearly empty, and two dragons the size of ponies sat at their mother's back feet. Both were the color of pale cream, with translucent wings and red eyes. The larger of the two hissed at us, and one of Ruby's massive, red forepaws clouted it over the head.

She was no less impressive this time than she had been before—red scales glowing with a dull light, sinuous body curving around the back of the cavern, gray spikes gleaming down the length of her spine, wings of the same color folded neatly.

Not everything was as I remembered, though. She held her head a little lower, and she was missing a small patch of scales on her side. One of her many horns had broken half-off.

She shifted to lie on her belly like a cat, leaning forward on her elbows, and stretched her neck toward us. Her nostrils widened as she inhaled a breath large enough that it pulled Nox's hair forward. Nox winced, but held her ground.

"That's the wrong one," Ruby observed.

"My sister," I said.

The dragon blinked slowly. "Where's the other girl? Rowan? I wanted her to come back." She let out a hot breath, and I became light-headed.

"She would if she could," I said, and wished I'd thought to take a drink to wet my mouth before we entered the cave. "She's been captured. We're on our way to get her."

"Are you? Interesting." She didn't sound particularly interested.

Keep her talking.

"Your young have grown an impressive amount since I last saw them," I said.

That comment seemed to please her. "Indeed, they're doing well. They've nearly destroyed my treasure stores and the animal population around here to do it, but that's as it should be. We don't waste time like your species does." She cocked her head to the side. "On with the story, then. Tell me what happened after you left my cave, until right now. And I warn you, I'm not in a generous or receptive mood. If you displease me, I will consume you."

Nox sat in the mouth of the tunnel, and I stepped farther into the cavern and took a seat on the rock where I'd found Rowan on our first visit.

I looked at the dragonlings again. There had been three before. No wonder Ruby wasn't feeling generous, if something had happened to the third.

Rowan would have done a better job of it. Thanks to the numerous times I'd already told the story, I was able to recall events and many things people had said along the way, but I still did little more than summarize. Ruby listened. She interrupted occasionally to ask questions, or to order more details about things like the Grotto, or what types of food had been served at the banquet we'd shared with the merfolk there. She was particularly interested when I reached the part where Rowan's magic broke free, and chuckled when I told her that the scale that Rowan had claimed as her prize from Ruby had probably saved her life when it happened.

"Oh, that's good," she said. "That's perfect. I was so angry with her for not taking my treasure, but this worked out well. Quite fitting." She snorted, and the dragonling on her left reared up on his hind legs and whined.

Ruby swatted at him again, but he ducked under her claws and leapt toward us. Perhaps Ruby could have stopped him, but she didn't try. She only watched.

Nox was ready. In a swift motion she pulled out the bundle she carried and tossed it in front of the dragonling. He squealed and let out a flame, but chomped down on the ball instead of me.

The dragonling chewed on his prize, seemingly content, and then wailed. Tears streamed from his eyes, and he darted to what was left of his hatching pool and doused his snout in the water.

Ruby turned slowly toward Nox. "You came prepared."

"I did. He'll probably have some pain in his mouth for a few days, but it won't kill him."

"Hmm. That might teach him a much-needed lesson about obeying me." She turned back to me, as though nothing had happened. "What happened then?"

I kept an eye on the dragonling and his sibling as I spoke, but neither chanced another attack. Ruby had never seen Belleisle, so she ordered me to describe it and the people there in great detail. I couldn't tell her anything about Rowan after I left the island. Though she listened, Ruby didn't ask for many details about what I'd done since then.

"Now, the people who took Rowan—what do you know of them?" Ruby asked.

"Magic hunters," I told her, and she growled. The room became warmer.

"I could have guessed," she said. "They killed my littlest one. Why shouldn't they take the only human who ever interested me? I was looking forward to her visiting again. Not that I care about her, mind you." Ruby stretched and arched her back, spread her ragged wings, and flexed her claws. She sighed a great, hot breath and laid her head across her wrists.

"It's a terrible thing, isn't it? Look at me. I'm a dragon, I shouldn't mourn so. The loss of a dragonling is to be expected. I've lost entire clutches of eggs in the past. I've lost young ones. I don't even know where any of the previous ones are now. And yet this one...It shouldn't matter, but it gives me pain. I dislike it." She looked back at the other two young dragons, then laid her head down again. They tilted their heads to the side in unison, and the less aggressive one peeped softly.

"I've lived too long," Ruby said. "It's not right for a dragon to be this way. It's shameful, and I shouldn't even know what shame is. Once these two complete their training and are ready to leave me, I think that's the end. I can't allow this to continue."

I glanced back at Nox, and was shocked to see compassion written on her face.

Ruby noticed it, too.

"Don't pity me, human." She growled, and the dragonling who hadn't tasted Nox's defense pawed at her leg in excitement. "I won't tolerate it."

"No," Nox said. "I admire your strength. It's easy to bear a loss when it doesn't matter to you. To carry on after one that wounds us so deeply takes courage."

"Courage. Another human concept," Ruby said, but the anger faded from her eyes. "I suppose it took that for you to come here, eh?" she asked me.

"Pleasant as this has been, I can't say I didn't think about avoiding you."

One corner of her mouth twitched upward. "I imagine you did. So what to do with you now? Our previous agreement is concluded. You have delivered what your friend promised, though I can't say it was as enjoyable as I'd hoped. My half of the agreement was completed when I let you go the first time. What's to stop me from eating you now?"

"I don't know. You've already said you don't care

what happens to Rowan, so I know you won't release me to help her. It's too bad, though." I smiled as I realized she'd given me an out, perhaps intentionally. "You know, Rowan could have told that story better. She still might, some day, but only if I get her away from those magic hunters."

"Do you really think you have any chance of helping her?" Ruby asked. "They're strong, they're smart as humans go. They're mean, and they hate what she is. You think she lives still?"

"I hope."

"Ah." Ruby raised her head and waved a clawed hand at me. "Hope. I'm not that far gone yet. Still, I suppose there's a chance. A small one."

"You could help," I said. "Help us get her back, take your revenge on the magic hunters."

She bared her teeth as she chuckled. "Oh, human. No. As much as I might enjoy attacking a city, that would be the end of me. That time will come soon, but what would become of my dear little ones? They've not finished learning to hunt, and they're quite helpless. Perhaps if you'd come to me in a few weeks. Unfortunate timing, you see."

I nodded. "If you won't rescue your storyteller, perhaps you'd at least let us try."

Ruby drummed her claws on the cave floor. "You'll report back to me?"

"If I'm alive to do it, and if we're able. When the story is over, of course, which might take some time, and providing you'll let us go after that."

The dragon's eyes flicked from me to Nox, and back again. She appeared amused, if only slightly.

"Very well," she said. "Go. You'd hardly be a meal for me, and the young ones have eaten recently. I can't say what sort of mood I'll be in next time, but I'll consider your request. And I—" Her lips scrunched up, as though she'd tasted something far worse than what her

375

young one had eaten. "I wish you good fortune, if you believe in such a thing."

"Thank you."

The dragon's eyes narrowed, and the corners of her mouth curved slightly. "Will you take a prize this time? I'm afraid I have no scales loose to offer."

"Thank you, but I'm afraid I'm going to have to decline," I replied, and returned her smile. "You've already been too generous."

"Go, then," she said, and the expression erased itself from her face. "This has been somewhat amusing, but I'm tired. I'll keep the little ones back for a short while, but I'd leave the area quickly if I were you. They want out for some air, and they do love a pursuit."

Nox backed slowly out of the cave, and I followed. Both dragonlings shrieked as we disappeared, and I covered my ears to block out the echoing noise.

"Thank you," I gasped as we emerged into the sunlight. "That potion...contraption...whatever it was—"

"Later," she said. "Just run."

We did, pausing to collect our horses and our friends, and raced off down a dragon path and a road that were all too familiar to me. Memories flashed in my mind—bodies hidden, questions answered, the horrible way that Rowan had irritated me when we first rode this path.

I'd have gone back in time if I could, taken the journey again if it meant more time with her. *We'll have that again*, I told myself. There were adventures ahead, once we got her out of Ardare.

I just hoped we weren't already too late.

Chapter Thirty-Four

Aren

Everything felt wrong on the journey from Ruby's den toward Rowan's hometown. Trees that had once been clothed in autumn's riotous colors now burst with green buds. Landmarks I recognized—the port town where I'd made the most fateful decision of my life, the place on the road where Rowan had fled from my attack—felt wrong, more dull than I remembered them. I'd felt urgency and excitement then, as I did now, but everything had lost its edge.

That, or I had.

We stopped at a crossroads. A wooden sign pointed to Lowdell in small letters and Ardare in larger ones, both in the same direction. I'd forgotten that if we came this way, we'd have to pass through the town where Rowan's parents lived.

Nox took the lead, with Florizel and me behind. Florizel had suggested a disguise for herself. It worked reasonably well, though the piled blankets and assorted bags weighed her down, and she became nervous and startled easily after a few hours of not being able to move her wings. She wasn't happy about being tied to my horse, either, but we had to maintain appearances. She was a small packhorse, nothing more.

"Is there a way we could go around the town?" I asked Kel.

"Cass and I could swim the ocean," he said, "but not you. This was the only road I saw leaving the area when we were here before. We could brave the forest on the landward side of town, but it'll slow us down significantly."

"No more delays," I said.

"Then we go through town and keep our heads down."

We didn't speak further until the town came into sight an hour later. Lowdell sat on grassy land that sloped toward the ocean and featured tidy wharfs where fishing boats rocked on low waves. A pleasant enough spot. Not wealthy-looking, but the buildings were well-constructed, and if I recalled correctly, Rowan had mentioned a fine library and a busy downtown. Taller buildings clustered around the wharfs, while wood-paneled homes dotted the land outside of the town center, with the spaces between them growing wider and less consistent the farther out they were. The ones closest to us had large yards and gardens, and were separated from each other by a sea of waving grass. All were within walking distance of downtown, but those on the outskirts had an air of solitude about them.

Nox and Kel fell behind, riding close and speaking quietly to each other.

"I hope we don't meet Rowan's father again," Cassia said as we approached the first of the houses. "That's their place, there."

I slowed my horse and brought her to a halt. The house didn't look like anything special, white-washed clapboard with a neat little fence around the property and a small carriage house or stable in the back. No sign of anything growing in the rock-bordered garden. One of the front windows was cracked in a radiating pattern. I had trouble picturing Rowan in such an unremarkable setting. But then, she hadn't grown up there. Her parents had sent her away to a place where no one could see what she was.

"Maybe we should stop. I want to speak to her mother."

"Aren," Cassia said cautiously, "what exactly do you think that's going to accomplish? I told you, they're not interested in talking. If they didn't want us there, they definitely won't want you."

"I want to know whether they're aware of what's going on. Florizel said Rowan's mother had sent her a letter, that Rowan was bringing medicine for her brother. I want to know whether they truly know what's happening."

"Even if the letter was genuine, she had nothing to do with this," Cassia said. "That woman didn't want any harm to come to her daughter. She's heartbroken. Let's leave her alone. Please."

"I suppose we could ask Nox about that sick brother."

Cassia shook her head. "I know Rowan would probably want us to, but we can't risk it. What if someone in that house betrayed us?"

"Do you think that's likely?"

"No," she said as Kel rode up beside us. Nox remained behind, looking for something in the grass. "Not at all. Rowan's father was quite angry about everything, but at worst, I think he wanted to forget about Rowan and move on with their lives."

"You say that like it's not a bad thing."

"It could be worse," Kel observed. "Why, does that make you angry?"

It did, more than I wanted to admit. "You know how I feel about what her parents did to her."

Cassia gave me a stern look. "So I'm going to ask again. What do you hope to accomplish there? Do you want to see whether they're the monsters you've made them out to be in your head? Find a way to make them feel worse about what's happening? Because I don't think that's possible. You might make things far worse for them if anyone else finds out you were there, but I don't think this situation can hurt them any more than it already does."

"I don't want to hurt them."

That was a lie. Perhaps they were punishing themselves for what they'd done, but they couldn't possibly be hurting as much as they'd hurt Rowan. I wanted them to feel the physical pain she'd endured every day for most of her life. I wanted them to know how it hurt her to be reminded of the fact that her family and friends hated what she was, that her parents were ashamed of having produced a monster.

I could make them feel her pain. I could get into their weak, magic-less minds and manipulate their emotions so that they felt that rejection the way she did. But even if I hadn't been having doubts about using that skill, Rowan wouldn't have wanted me to use it on her parents. In spite of their rejection, she loved them.

I once told her that she was too trusting, and that had turned out to be true. She was also too forgiving. That had worked in my favor. I only hoped it wouldn't end up hurting her more.

"What, then?" Cassia asked. "Why do you want to do this?"

"I want to know whether they knew she was coming back, whether Callum talked to them before he sent his letter. Whether they've been notified of where she is, been allowed to visit her in prison or speak on her behalf. Anything that might help."

"I am sorry I lost the medicines," Florizel muttered, though we'd agreed that she shouldn't speak even when we didn't see humans around. "Rowan said he might die. She was so worried."

"It's fine," I said as Nox rode up. "Rowan's first concern would have been you getting away, not the medicine. Do you remember what was wrong with him?"

"No."

"What's that about medicine?" Nox asked.

"Rowan's brother is ill," I said.

"Are you asking me to—"

"No. We need to move on." I wanted him to live, if only for Rowan's sake, but Cassia was right. It was better if no one saw us, and we wouldn't likely learn anything that would help Rowan even if we did stop. My petty curiosity would have to remain unsatisfied.

Nox bit her lip. "I could if we had time," she muttered, but said no more about it. It seemed that leaving skills unused troubled her as much as it did me.

Florizel returned to her usual silence as we followed a bustling main street that took a curving track past a shipping yard, a market, and a stately court building. We passed several winter-faded wanted posters ordering that Rowan or I be turned in for a reward if seen. I didn't worry. The likeness in the picture was terrible. People always had trouble remembering me, especially if I knew they'd seen my face.

Several people gave us appraising looks as we passed. Though I'd packed my cloak away, our clothes weren't quite right for this country. There was little we could do about that now. At least Florizel didn't seem to be drawing particular attention.

A shop's bell tinkled behind us as we passed, and sharp footsteps hurried over the cobblestones.

The steps slowed as they reached us, and a short, slim woman with graying hair came into view beside Cassia, who now rode ahead of me. Cassia leaned down slightly as the woman said something. The woman veered off and held the skirts of her black dress high over her ankles as she climbed the wide steps of a stone building with marble statues in front, as though she hadn't even seen us.

It put me on my guard immediately, but Cassia didn't seem frightened or upset. She spoke to Nox, and they led us up a side street, avoiding the town square that had just come into view.

"What was that about?" I muttered to Cassia, just loud enough so she could hear.

"Just wait," she replied. "Don't talk here."

The street led us out of the busier part of the city and into a pleasant parkland of low, grassy hills. No one was there but us and an old man preparing garden plots next to a pond. He didn't look up as we passed, but packed his things and left. As soon as he was gone, Florizel began consuming the tender shoots that poked out of the dark soil.

"Can we speak now?" I asked.

"That was Rowan's mother," Cassia said. I looked back over my shoulder, though I knew I wouldn't see her. "She owns that shop, and saw us pass. She remembered me and Kel. I hope no one else did."

"And?"

"And she wishes to speak with us."

"I see."

"Aren," Kel said, and gave me a warning look.

"I'll be civil. And brief." I couldn't promise any more than that.

A few minutes later the woman approached. I saw the resemblance between her and Rowan, though this woman's demeanor was closed off in a way I couldn't imagine seeing in Rowan.

"Mrs. Greenwood," I said, and we all dismounted.

She stopped a short distance away from us, smoothed her skirt, tucked a few graying hairs back behind her ear, and walked closer. "You came back," she said to Kel and Cassia. "What's happened? Is something wrong? Where's Rowan?"

"I think Aren might be the one you want to talk to about that, ma'am," Cassia said.

I handed my horse's reins to Nox, who was eyeing the plants sprouting in the gardens. "Don't get too comfortable," I told her. "We might need to leave quickly."

I motioned for them to give us space. Cassia and Kel started toward the pond, but Nox didn't move. She frowned and rubbed a hand over her face. Kel turned and watched her, hiding a smile behind his own hand.

"Ma'am, is your son still sick?" Nox asked.

Rowan's mother seemed surprised. "He is. Did Rowan get the letter I sent?"

"It seems so. What's wrong with him?"

Mrs. Greenwood—Lucilla, if I recalled correctly—described the symptoms, and Nox frowned. "I can prepare something for him while we're waiting."

I wondered whether that counted as disobeying my order about not getting comfortable, and realized that it didn't matter. Nox was along on my mission, but she didn't see me as any sort of authority figure. She would do as she pleased, and for once, I didn't mind.

"It won't be as good as what Rowan was bringing," Nox continued, "but it will strengthen him and help his body fight off the sickness. Bring the fever down."

Lucilla started at the sound of her daughter's name, and hesitated. I didn't pry, but opened myself. She was afraid, and likely with good cause. Still, she nodded and shook Nox's hand. "I'd appreciate it more than I can possibly say. You are too generous. Too kind."

"Some people seem to think I am." Nox tilted her head. "There will be magical plants involved. Is that a problem?"

Lucilla's smile faded. "Won't be the first time I've tried to use magic to save one of my children. I only hope it works out better this time."

"Very good. Give me ten minutes."

"Too long," I said.

Lucilla bit the inside of her lip. "If you can't, it's fine. I'm sure our doctors will...Well." She shrugged. She obviously knew they couldn't help Ashe any more than they had Rowan.

I sighed. "Ten minutes. No more, please."

Nox led our horses away. The others joined her, leaving me alone with a woman I'd despised ever since I figured out what she'd done to Rowan.

When I looked back at Lucilla, she had retreated a few paces and was staring at me.

"You're the one who took her away," she said, her voice soft.

"Yes."

Vertical lines formed between her eyebrows. "How dare you come here? Where is she?" I left myself open, and a swirl of confusion, anger and fear jumped out at me. "Tell me!"

There was a time when I would have been angry with her for demanding anything of me, and for doing it so disrespectfully. That was when I'd thought myself someone important.

I took a deep breath. "Yes, I took your daughter away. But I didn't force her to go anywhere. I think Kel and Cassia might have mentioned that the last time you saw them. Rowan sent you a letter explaining the rest?"

She nodded. "Not telling me everything, I suppose."

Gods, I hope not. "Enough that I think you know this isn't all my fault, though. The binding that you had someone put on her was killing her, but it's gone now. She's been trying to use her magic, but it hasn't been easy. She's lost many years of learning opportunities, and I think she's still ashamed of her power."

"So she's like you now? But she's safe?" She smoothed her hair behind her ear again, though it hadn't moved, and offered me a seat at the opposite end of a bench from where she seated herself.

"As of the last time I saw her, she was. I've heard otherwise since."

Her expression grew tight. Pained. "What?"

I wasn't going to reveal a bit of our plans until I was sure we could trust her not to alert anyone in Ardare. I glanced back over my shoulder. Nox was hard at work.

"First, please tell me what you want with us," I said. "Quickly. Time is short." Then I'd decide what to tell her.

"I want my daughter back." Lucilla's voice trembled. "But I can't have that. So I want to meet the man who took her. I want to know where she is and what's happening. I want to know that you and your friends aren't lying to me about everything that's happened."

I bit back my irritation and tried to speak calmly. I'd get further that way. "You have no reason to trust me, I know. But you might consider the fact that I'm here right now, trying to help her."

She rested her forehead in her hands. "If you knew the things I've heard about you...You can't imagine how terrified I was when I heard. It was unbearable when I thought thieves took her on the way to Ardare, but it was somehow worse when I found out that she was with you."

"There were worse people she could have been with. I've done my best to keep her safe and help her."

Her laugh came out strangled. "I couldn't have known that, could I? News from your country gets to ours slowly, if at all. And then the letters came, and I was so relieved that she was alive, even if she was angry...But our lives have fallen apart. I know that's not Rowan's fault."

"You blame me, then?"

"I blame you for taking her, for interfering in her life."

"For saving her life?"

She shook her head and turned her chin defiantly up at me, an expression I recognized. "You can't know that. We were managing her pain with medicines, and she'd have had even better doctors when she moved to Ardare. The best alive."

"They'd have discovered what she was."

Lucilla squeezed her eyes closed, deepening the fine lines at the edges. "I know," she whispered.

Her arguments rang false even to her, I realized. She just needed to speak them aloud.

"I did try." She tugged at her dress sleeve. "When I found the proposal letter from Callum in her room, I decided to tell her about the binding. I had kept the secret successfully for so long, but I couldn't let her marry a magic hunter without knowing. Maybe she'd have changed her mind. She left before I could tell her, and I didn't have a chance..." The fire went out of her eyes. "I do blame myself. I don't know what I could have done differently, but this all began with a decision I made. I know that."

If she was looking for absolution, I was in no position to offer it. She seemed genuinely regretful, though. I couldn't condone her choices, nor could I condemn her for them. I let go of my desire to hurt her. Cassia was right. This woman was hurt enough. Sorrow and loss swirled around her like shadows.

I wouldn't pry into her mind, but I would trust her, at least a little.

"Is Callum still coming around here?" I asked.

"Not since Rowan's letters came. And then out of nowhere he showed up at my door, offering to send a letter from us to Rowan along with his. I thought it strange, after all that time, and he seemed so on edge. I said so to Rowan in my postscript, told her it would be best to leave him alone. He was hurt so badly by all of this."

I could hardly feel sympathy for him. I hoped it *had* hurt him. It obviously hadn't changed him for the better.

She smiled sadly. "Again, that's my fault, but I don't know what else I could have done. You can't know what the last twenty years of my life have been like, waiting for someone to find out what I did. You didn't see the look on Callum's face when he stood at our door holding his letter, when I tried to explain that I thought she was as good as cured."

"The letter he sent to Rowan asked her to meet him at the border. He apparently offered her safe passage here, to see you. Did you know about that?"

"What? No. What happened?"

"I don't know, exactly. I wasn't there when she got the letters, which I'm guessing no longer contained your warning. I know that she came back. She met Callum in a small town in the mountains, hoping she could explain the truth about magic to him and bring medicine for her brother. There were magic hunters waiting for her."

"No." She clapped her hands over her mouth, covering everything but her tear-filled eyes.

"They took her to Ardare. I hoped you'd have more information."

Rowan's mother wiped her eyes. "I can't believe he would..." She shook her head. "Yes, I can. What's happening now, do you know?"

"No. They took her over a week ago to what was described to me as a large stone building with water around it. We came as quickly as we could, but I don't know what they've been doing, whether they held a trial, or—"

"They held her trial while she was away. They convicted her of treason, blasphemy, and conspiracy against the crown." She pulled her sleeve down over her hand and wiped her eyes in a child-like gesture. "Rowan and I had so many fights over the years, so many problems. She probably told you that. But I love my daughter. You must get her out of there before they kill her."

If they haven't already, I thought, and my stomach tightened. "We'll try. I don't know what else to tell you. I'll do anything I have to, if there's any way."

She took a deep, shuddering breath and looked up at me again, narrowing her eyes slightly. "Will you? Anything?"

"Yes."

I looked toward the pond again. Nox held up two fingers. Kel shrugged.

"I feel I should ask you what your intentions are for my daughter, Mister Tiernal," Lucilla said, and gave me that sad smile again. I suspected she wore that expression frequently. "This is ridiculous. I thought that if I ever met you, I'd do my best to kill you for what you did to my family, to my daughter. But it's true, isn't it? She said that you were her friend, in her first letter. In the second one she said she loved you. Do you feel the same about her?"

"Yes." I admitted it without hesitation. "As for my intentions, I suppose that depends entirely on Rowan, doesn't it?"

"You do know her, don't you?" Her smile brightened, then faded. "I should have known her better than I did. Tell me, is she happy? Or rather, was she the last time you saw her?"

The unspoken question: *Do* you *make her happy?*

"I think she was, sometimes. She didn't have the pain anymore. She was learning things she's always been curious about. She made some friends, but it wasn't always easy for her. And she missed you. She worried about all of you. She wanted to talk to you, to find out exactly what happened to her when she was younger. She tried to understand why you did it, but it hurt her." Though I was no longer interested in making this woman suffer, I wasn't going to spare her anything, either. "It took her a while to accept that what she is isn't a bad thing."

She looked away. "It is here."

"Then it's probably a good thing she won't be staying in this country any longer than she has to."

Lucilla nodded slowly. "I can't say that I'm happy about any of this. I appreciate that you've been helping Rowan, but I'm not comfortable with her relationship with you. I'm sorry. It's just not what any mother wants for her daughter."

"No. I wouldn't have recommended it, either." I still wasn't convinced I was the best thing for Rowan, but I'd be hers as long as she cared to have me.

"But you'll be good to her?"

"I've been doing my best." I didn't know what else to tell her. Now wasn't the time to worry about whether or not I could make Rowan happy or help her reach her potential. For now, I had to focus on keeping her alive. "I should be going. We could be running out of time."

Nox hurried over and handed Lucilla a bundle of grasses and assorted plant material, braided together and tied around the ends with purplish roots. "Here, ma'am. Simmer this in fresh cream until the dried seed-heads there turn green. Mind you don't boil or burn it. It will help."

"Thank you, my dear. I can't say how much this—"

Nox waved off the thanks. "It's what I do." She walked away, leaving Lucilla looking bemused.

She turned back to me. "Will you take a message to Rowan?"

"If you have something to say, I'll tell her."

She hesitated. "Tell her...Tell her that I'm sorry. For everything. Tell her that I did what I did, the binding and keeping her condition a secret, to protect her. It wasn't because I hated what she was. If there had been another way, I'd have taken it. I wanted to tell her, but the time was always wrong. Tell her that I love her.

Please."

I stood to leave. "I will. Is there anything else?"

"Only that Ashe misses her, and has never stopped loving her through all of this. He was ready to go over the mountains looking for her when she first disappeared. He talks to her in his sleep sometimes, since he's been ill."

"She misses him, too. I'm sure she'd want to send her love."

She stood as well, and smoothed her skirt again. People don't often surprise me, but Rowan's mother did. She stepped away, then turned back and wrapped her arms around me, squeezing tightly.

"Thank you for taking care of her," she whispered. "Please give her that. I didn't do it often enough when she was with us."

Her eyes took on a sharp look as she caught sight of something behind me, toward town. I turned to see the gardener we'd passed on the way into the park. Alone, but definitely watching.

"You should go," Lucilla said. "Now." Her lips formed a hard line. "I'll take care of him if I can."

I leaned in closer and spoke quietly. "You should leave town, as soon as possible. You, your husband, any other family members who might find themselves in a difficult situation if things go badly with this rescue. Or if they go well, for that matter."

She thanked me and hurried back toward the retreating gardener and the little town that now hated her family. As the rest of us mounted and fled the city, I committed Lucilla's message to Rowan to memory.

I only hoped I'd have a chance to deliver it.

Chapter Thirty-Five

Rowan

"Time's up."

"Not yet." I sat up on my bed, where I'd been taking a break from practicing hand-to-hand combat training with Ulric. Without weapons, we'd been limited in what we could practice, but I'd learned to throw a punch, how to ground myself and balance, and how to dodge an attack.

Ulric's demands had only increased now that we'd been given a few more days together. I wasn't complaining anymore, but the constant mental and physical demands were exhausting me. I'd pushed through it again and again until I'd collapsed.

"Now, please," he said. "Tonight's the night."

My heart stopped, then thumped as it caught up to itself. "No. Tomorrow. Langley said four days. We have one more until they come for me."

"Exactly. They'll be prepared for us to act when they come to take you away. I don't know how much they know, but they must suspect that we've been working on something during all this time we've been together. You've been careful to show nothing?"

I looked away. "One of them saw me playing with water in the baths. It just happened. Nothing big. They can't know what I can do."

His face took on a pinched look. "Very well.

Nothing else?"

"No." I lowered my voice. "So we act tonight, then, when they bring our food?"

"Unless you feel prepared to blast the door down."

"No." We'd discussed it as a training possibility. I had blasted a hay bale once, and had pushed a man hard enough to crack his skull. Ulric thought the two events were related. I thought they were accidents caused by my panic and lack of control. In any case, I hadn't succeeded in doing anything further with it in the cell, even when Ulric threw books at me to try to provoke the reaction.

I'd given him permission to try it, but still resented the bruise I'd gotten on my shoulder.

"What's our plan?" I asked.

He motioned for me to stand, then went to his sleeping area and came back carrying his pillow and bedding. He arranged them beneath my blankets. "They've seen you resting," he explained. "But this time, you'll actually be hiding next to the door. As soon as they open it, you go. Defend yourself if you have to, but don't attack. You're not ready for that. I'll run, too, as soon as the guard is distracted by you."

"They'll stop you."

"We'll have to risk it. If we can just get away from these damned walls, I'll be able to defend us. I do have some strength left in these old bones."

I sat back down on the edge of the bed. "What do I do then?"

"Conserve your energy until I tell you to act. Be prepared to create illusions when you have the power for it. Copies of us. But not until I give the word."

I couldn't help wondering, still, whether I was a true partner in this. Something in his tone made me think he'd be happy as long as he got out, even if that meant leaving me to the guards as a distraction.

"How will you defend us?" I asked. "I'm curious

about your skills. You know mine so well." He'd never told me what he could do, always avoiding the question.

"I'll do what I need to."

"Please. I'd rather not be startled by anything when we're trying to get out."

He sat next to me on my bed, careful not to crush the hidden pillow. "The ground may tremble."

"What?"

He smiled, though his expression remained tight and guarded. "The stones would obey me if I told them to crumble on our heads and kill everyone. I won't say I haven't been tempted on occasion to do it, though they would crush me as surely as anyone else. I may disappear, but only briefly."

"That's impressive."

He waved my comment off. "Just something I was training myself in before my unfortunate disappearance. I'm not sure I'll be able to pick it up again after all this time, or how reliable it will be."

"Anything else? Turning into a bear?"

He shifted away from me. A slight movement, but I noted it. "I draw strength from enemies."

The room seemed to grow colder. "Just enemies?"

"It's nothing to be concerned about. It's limited. I can only draw from one person at a time. I'll take on his physical strength as he loses it. As soon as I let go, he'll get back whatever I haven't used up."

I tapped a finger against my knees, a gesture that conveyed far less agitation than I felt. Magic wasn't the only thing I'd learned from Ulric. "And magic? Can you draw that power as well?"

"Yes. It's irrelevant, unless any of them have hidden power. I won't use it against you."

I imagined myself drained, left to those dogs while he took my power and ran.

Don't be stupid. He wouldn't have spent all this time training you to control your power if that was his plan all along.

"Are you sure you'll be able to manage it?" I asked. No harm in reminding him that he might need me. "How long ago was your last near-escape? Since you practiced magic?"

He shot me a dark look. "Years since I've managed much. There's magic in me. I feel it when I step away from the walls. I believe that the push-back effect will come again, increasing my power when I leave this place."

"But you're not certain."

"No. All of this is unprecedented, as far as I know. We have no choice but to try. Together. Gods, what I wouldn't give for a clock. You'd better go to the door. Any more questions?"

I moved to the door and leaned against the wall next to it. "Which way do I run once I'm out of here?"

"Turn right. Keep going. I'll catch up."

"And if you don't?"

"You remember the maps I showed you? The passage past the—Hush, now."

The little window in the door hissed open next to my head. "Backs against the wall." A man's voice.

Ulric moved to the far wall as he always did. Hands up. No sign that he planned anything.

"What's wrong with her this time?" the guard asked.

Ulric shrugged. "Your walls give her headaches. She'd move her bed away from them, but you've so kindly bolted it to the floor."

The window slid closed. Ulric and I exchanged a glance. His brows knit together.

It's taking too long.

No backing down, now.

The lock turned. The door opened.

I ran.

The guard held our supper trays in one hand and

his blue-dripping dagger in the other. I threw a shoulder into his as I darted past. He stumbled and fell against the door, pushing it fully open. From the corner of my vision I caught sight of Ulric moving toward us, and I ran, darting to the right and leaving the room behind. Within a few paces, I felt my magic growing, infusing me.

"No!" Ulric's voice rang through the corridor.

Sounds of struggle, scuffling and thumping, came behind me. *Damn it.* I stopped. Maybe he had planned to use me, or abandon me. I wouldn't do the same to him. If the guard had caught him...

A sharp pain ripped through my arm as I turned. When I looked down, blue-green fluid intermingled with my blood. I stumbled, dizzy.

No.

A half dozen guards congregated outside the cell. Most were busy with Ulric, but a few had their eyes on me.

I fought the potion, called my magic and pushed it from me. It left, but had no effect on anything. I fell to my knees and cringed as pain swirled behind my eyes, and I felt my magic being pushed back into me.

We were too late. They'd been ready.

I forced my eyes to open. A soldier lay on the ground, bleeding from the head. His bow lay beside him, and his remaining arrows lay scattered over the floor. They had Ulric, though. The handle of a dagger protruded from his thigh. Drugged, surely, or he'd have fought them off. Ulric slumped forward, held up by a guard at each elbow. He looked up at me.

"Go!" he hollered.

I crawled away and forced myself to my feet. The corridor spun around me. I was away from the cell, but for all I could use my magic, I might as well have been entombed in its walls. Torchlight burned my eyes.

Footsteps echoed behind me, approaching far more quickly than I could run. I glanced back. A soldier ran at me, sword drawn. I stumbled and hit the floor hard, scraping the skin of my hands on the rough stone floor.

I pushed myself up on my knees and closed my eyes, waiting for the fatal strike.

I'm sorry, Aren. I tried to come back to you.

"Hold!" Not Ulric's voice this time, but a familiar one, big and booming.

Tears gathered between my lashes. I bit my lip and held them back. *Not in front of him.*

Dorset Langley caught up with us.

"Orders are death if they try anything," the soldier said.

"I'm changing the orders," Langley replied. He grabbed my arm and jerked me to me feet. Cold metal snapped around my wrists. "My son is on his way into town as we speak. He's going to take care of this one."

"If you say so, Sir." I didn't look up, but heard the bemusement in the soldier's voice. "What of the old man?"

"I'll make sure he gets his punishment. After. Drug him, lock him in the cell. I'll come back. I've been waiting a long time to be allowed to do this."

The barely-concealed rage in his voice made me fear for Ulric. I might be fortunate enough to have a quick death. My cellmate would surely not have the same.

Langley grabbed me by the jaw and forced me to look at him. "She's still awake. Dose her again."

"Please," I groaned.

"We don't have much left," the soldier said, but I heard his garments shifting as he reached for something. "If we give her more, we won't have him knocked out. I'd suggest—"

"I don't care what you suggest." Langley nearly snarled the words. "I'm tired of seeing everyone underestimate this girl. Put her out. Callum will arrive in the next few hours, and we'll be rid of her. Leave the old man shackled, and leave him to me."

One more try. I jerked away from Langley, then called to my magic and drove it forward with my fear and my anger.

Nothing happened.

I hit the floor, unable to balance. Pain burst in my arm, burning through my body.

Langley delivered a sharp kick to my ribs and leaned in. "I'll see you soon, Miss Greenwood."

Chapter Thirty-Six

Aren

I set the fire burning low and hot before Florizel and I left the group the following night, right after sunset. We'd camped in the woods, hidden in the forest on a bluff that overlooked the city and the surrounding lands. Any closer to Ardare and we'd have been in a farmer's field, our fire announcing our presence.

Maneuvering around the horse's massive wings and mounting without a saddle was awkward, but I managed. I clamped my legs tight behind her wings, as she instructed, and she trotted through the woods until she felt accustomed to my weight.

"Are you sure you can fly with me up here?" I asked.

"Yes. I took Rowan and her things across your country. I can take you over the city and back. Do you think it will help?"

I reached down and scratched the place where her left wing connected with her body, and she shivered. "I do. We'll be much better prepared for whatever comes next if I've seen where they're keeping her, but I can't afford to use more of my magic than I absolutely have to."

Here in the heart of Darmish land the magic was thin and insubstantial, and I doubted it would restore me quickly if I used up my own stores. I would have to ration that power carefully.

Florizel raced down the hill, spread her wings, and lifted off. I leaned in close to her neck and wondered how Rowan had ever found the courage to do this with nothing to save her if she fell. The land stretched out below us, dimly outlined in the cloud-diffused moonlight. The city lay straight ahead, a wall of black behind which lights shone—streetlamps, windows, a lone sentry's lantern bobbing across the top of the wall.

By the time we reached Ardare, I felt more settled on Florizel's back. Though I was accustomed to flying, my stomach turned every time I looked down. It felt wrong to fly so high in my human body.

Don't fall, I reminded myself. *Don't waste magic.* I tightened my grip in her mane.

Florizel reduced her altitude as we passed over the wall, keeping near the low clouds while allowing me to see. The buildings below us were packed tight into the city as though huddled together against the dangers of the world outside, leaving little room for streets or open spaces. Most citizens were staying indoors, out of the damp weather, but a small group had gathered on one corner. Several men cheered two who circled one another, lashing out in uncoordinated punches as they wobbled drunkenly over the stones.

Not a city on high alert. Not yet, at least.

A moment later we were past them, flying over a section of the city made up of tall buildings and a maze of narrow streets. We moved toward a wide, dark space. The river. A massive structure rose straight out from the middle of the water, lit by blazing torches along the tops of its walls and on the towers at each corner.

"That's the place they took her, there," Florizel called back. "Shall I get closer?"

"Please. But try to stay out of their light."

Florizel flew upstream, following the course of the wide river that wound its way through the town and under its walls. The structure below us connected with the rest of the city via a wide drawbridge. A pair of closed doors in another section of the wall led directly into the river, doors extending below the surface of the rushing water, with no landing area in front of them. I saw no other way in.

Florizel pulled up and we flew higher, farther from watchful eyes below as we passed over. This wasn't a single building but a thick, five-sided wall surrounding a yard dotted with more lanterns. Paths criss-crossed it in a star pattern, meeting in front of a few small buildings constructed of stone. Windows in the walls cast their glow on the yard, but it was still difficult to see much detail. The walls themselves were as wide as houses, and likely contained rooms of their own. A proper fortress.

Then we were past it, and flying over the river.

"Go around again," I said.

Florizel turned.

I had just leaned back to get a better look at another set of water doors when someone whistled below, sharp and piercing. Florizel shied and darted higher into the clouds. I tried to hold on, but lost my grip on her mane, and she was gone. The fall sucked the air from my chest as I plunged head-first toward the river. I gritted my teeth and used a portion of my remaining magic to transform. My clothing fell toward the water, and I dove to catch my boots in my talons before they splashed down. I caught one, but the other hit the water hard, sending up a loud splash.

I veered away from the river as a beam of directed light moved over the space where my boot had disappeared. The light swept back and forth over the water's surface, and I circled overhead, waiting to see whether we'd been spotted. This body's night vision didn't allow me to see much. I hoped the view from the tower wasn't any better.

After a quick scan of the surrounding water, the light disappeared, and everything in the fortress returned to quiet. If the whistle had been a warning, they'd decided it was a false alarm—or so I hoped. I lifted higher into the air where Florizel circled, watching for me.

"I'm so sorry," she whinnied.

I couldn't answer, but turned back toward camp. She followed as we passed over winding residential streets with dark spaces I took to be yards and gardens—a luxury in a city such as this. I wondered whether Rowan would have lived there if her life had taken a different direction, if she'd never met me. Whether that would have made her happy.

Perhaps, until her magic killed her.

Kel, Cassia and Nox all stood and hurried toward Florizel as she landed, riderless, near the fire. I took another pass over the area to search for threats while she explained what had happened, and when I returned, Kel had pulled out the last of the spare clothing for me to wear. No coat, and I'd have to rely on thick socks to protect my feet, but at least I wouldn't have to roam the city naked.

"Aren, I'm so sorry," Florizel said again when I returned from dressing. "I thought they saw us, and that you had a better grip."

"It's all right," I said.

Nox had been keeping occupied sharpening her daggers. She put them away, then turned to frown at me. Her lips pinched into a thin line, and she pulled me away from the group.

"How much do you have left?"

"Enough. Don't worry about me."

Her expression tightened. "What happens if you use it up?"

"I won't have any left." I smiled. I couldn't let her see that for the first time in my life, I was concerned about losing my power. In truth, I'd felt some loss after

401

just two transformations, like a section of my spirit had been carved away, far worse here than I'd felt it elsewhere in Darmid.

She folded her arms across her chest. "Very funny."

"I'll be careful."

She looked back at Kel and Cassia, who were still talking to Florizel. "I assume you have vast stores of magic, being who you are and all. I just want to know that you're not going to be left defenseless when we're in the middle of enemy territory."

"I'm hardly defenseless. I have trained in non-magical combat."

"I'm sure. But it's always been a game to you, hasn't it? You've had your magic to fall back on." She paced a few steps away and turned back to me. "I want you to be careful."

"Because of your mission?"

"No. Yes, but...take care of yourself. I'm just starting to get used to you."

I smiled reassuringly and thumped her on the shoulder. "Likewise."

Florizel approached me. "Are you taking the horses into the city?"

"I hadn't decided. They'd make for a faster escape, but I'm wary of taking them when we might need to hide, and they won't do us any good once we reach the river. What do you think?"

Her eyes widened. An ear twitched. "I...me? I suppose I'd offer to keep them for you, should you leave them outside of the city. The big forest starts not far from the southern wall, I could hide them there. Let them forage. Make sure they're ready to go."

"Thank you."

She lowered her head. "You won't think me a coward for not coming to get Rowan?"

Nox patted the horse's neck. "You'd be doing a

great service by keeping the horses ready for when we all come out."

Perhaps Kel was right about Nox. She cared. She wanted to help, to heal. She'd got me out of the dragon's cave. I couldn't blame her for hating our family and therefore being afraid of me. *Hard as a stone and stubborn as an ass, but...*

"What are you looking at me like that for?" Nox asked.

"Nothing."

She shook her head and went back toward the fire.

We slept for a few hours and rode for the city at midnight, avoiding the main road and approaching the forest by way of several farms' back fields. Florizel wore her disguise and walked with us. Bats swooped overhead and a dog barked in the distance, but otherwise the world was still.

Florizel led us through the forest until we reached a road that cut through it. "I'll take the horses back into the trees a little," she said, "in case anyone comes by way of the road." She pawed at the ground with a forehoof. "If you could just leave them able to forage, I think they'll be fine with their saddles on. You're sure it's good for me to stay here?"

I looked toward the city, which we were close enough to that I heard the rush of the river as it passed under the wall. "I'm sure. Thank you."

Nox tucked her daggers into sheaths at her waist, and Kel and Cassia took their hunting knives out. I did the same, and wished for a more substantial weapon. When my uncle had asked whether I needed anything, I hadn't expected to be caught without my magic.

"What kind of travelers are we?" Cassia asked as she hung the strap of a small bag across her chest. She took items from the larger saddle bags to fill it. Flares, an extra knife, bandages. "Who approaches a city at this hour?"

"I don't know," I said. "We might have an easier time if we wait until morning."

Kel nodded. "Those farmers must bring goods to market in the morning. We could slip in with the crowds."

"And be slowed by them," I said. "More people about means more eyes on us, even if they're not paying any particular attention. Right now we might need to deal with one or two guards at the gate. In the morning there will be more. More people to make our escape difficult, as well."

Nox bent to tighten her boot laces. "Guess we go now, then," she muttered, and stood. "How will we get past those one or two guards?"

They all looked to me.

My body suddenly felt far too heavy, weighed down by the choice. Become a better person, the one everyone seemed to think I was capable of being, or use my darker gifts to accomplish something truly important? Idealism, or need?

I reached into my pocket to feel the comforting shape of the sea glass Rowan gave me, wanting only to touch it, to draw strength from a reminder of her. It was gone, washed away by the Darmish river.

I wouldn't lose her, too. I straightened my shoulders, looked toward the city, and moved my moral line back.

"I'll take care of the guards."

"If you're sure," Cassia said.

I nodded. "They're enemy soldiers, and this is a battle. If it's an unfair fight, so be it. I'll make it so they don't alert anyone, and they'll forget us."

I would allow myself to turn this far toward my darker self. No further. As long as no civilians were harmed, I wouldn't allow myself to feel guilt over fighting against those who actively oppressed magic.

With that decision, I felt myself come alive. Excitement like I'd felt when I twisted the minds of Severn's sailor and fought the men in the woods flooded through me. I kept my expression neutral, but my heart raced. I wanted this, and badly. Darmish soldiers deserved no better than having their minds warped and broken, but I would hold back for the sake of my friends.

And what does that say about me?

I decided it didn't matter now.

"This is an interesting turn-around for you," Nox said.

I sighed. "Why—"

Kel cut in. "Perhaps we could leave conversation about Aren's sliding scale of morals for another time. The night is passing."

We approached the city by way of the road. Stones bit into my feet, but I kept up a steady pace. If this was the worst injury the night brought to me, I'd be thankful.

A single gatekeeper snored in his booth, muddy boots resting on top of a tiny, paper-covered desk. We might have slipped by had the metal gate not been locked. I rapped on the window, and he snorted.

"Hullo. Stop, now. State your business."

Sleep-addled minds are as easy to read and manipulate as inebriated ones. I was in his thoughts before he so much as focused on our faces. "We have business here," I told him, and searched his thoughts for a legitimate reason to let a small group into the city at night.

Visitors. Off to care for family in the south end, sick with this damned ague that's brought half the city and three quarters of the king's guard down. Idiots for coming into it. Had a hold up back on the road, couldn't make it before nightfall. Robbed. Will file a report in the morning. Looking forward to resting tonight.

"That will do," I told him. "You'll remember it?"

"Yes." He spoke in dull, emotionless tones. I hadn't let him become frightened or excited. I pushed him toward irritation at having his nap interrupted, and his facial expression shifted, eyebrows bunching, mouth narrowing.

Cassia turned away.

"And our paperwork was in order, of course," I added.

"Yes, yes," he said. "If you don't mind, I've got my own papers to attend to." He stood and unlocked the gate. "Have a lovely evening, and best of luck to you. Apothecary's got a little something to rub on your hands to kill the sickness. Nasty bug, that."

"We'll keep that in mind." I planted the image of an older man in his mind, his middle-aged son, and their wives. Unremarkable folk he wouldn't be able to describe in any great detail. "Have a pleasant evening."

No one raised an alarm.

We moved into what I took to be the industrial section of the city. Low buildings surrounded us, forges and carriage makers and a host of dirty, unmarked buildings. Few homes, if any, and fewer prying eyes. I didn't trust our luck.

"Which way?" Kel asked.

"Toward the river."

The buildings around us changed as we moved on. Wooden buildings several stories high rose over us, looming, watching our passage with dark, empty eyes. Light was scarce, save for a few lamps lit on corners, and those dimmed by fog.

We followed signs pointing toward "GENERAL COMPOUND—COURTS, HOLDINGS, BATTERY." The journey seemed to take forever, but the sky was still dark and the city quiet when we reached a sheltered walking path beside the river. We followed it upstream until we stood directly opposite a set of water doors in the walled compound. From this lower angle, the structure loomed higher and more imposing than I remembered. The water split into the two man-made canals that flowed around the building. Not a long swim, if we had to do it, but the water would be frigid.

"Not promising, is it?" Nox observed, as though she'd been reading my thoughts. "This whole town gives me chills. Ugly, too." We followed Kel and Cassia into the shadows of the giant trees at the edge of the river. Nox shivered as she looked at the water, then again at the compound. "I don't see how we get in. Could you make the guards think that we're supposed to be there?"

"Yes. But I'd have to get close enough to them, and it's nearly impossible to manipulate a mind if I don't have a person's attention. I can't influence them through the door and make them open it. Once they see us, they'll raise some alarm. We'd have to get in and incapacitate them, or they'd have to come out."

"But you would do it?"

"They're no different from the guard at the gate." I silently cursed Phelun, the mer elders, even my grandfather—everyone who had helped create the niggling doubts at the back of my mind that dumped cold water on my desire to do my work. "It's just a question of getting in. The front gate will be the most heavily-guarded. That leaves the water doors."

Kel cleared his throat. "You might have friends who could help with that."

A wide grin spread across Cassia's face. "Aren't you glad you brought us?"

"No," Nox said. "Isn't that dangerous?"

"It'll be fine," Kel said, and took her hand. "All we need to do is get the door open for you."

"And get rid of the guards first, not knowing what's waiting in there." Nox shot me an angry glare, then looked back at Kel. "I need to talk to you. Alone." She stood and pulled him away.

"I didn't try to stop you going into a dragon's

cave," he muttered, but followed.

"Should have seen that coming," Cassia said.

"Do you think she'll try to hold him back?"

She shrugged. "She likes him. A lot. Obviously she doesn't want to let him risk his life for someone she's never met. You're willing to let Kel and me go into this because you know what's at stake. She has no reason to care what happens to Rowan, and a lot of reasons to be concerned for Kel."

My intent seemed so selfish when she said it that way.

"I'm willing to let you go because it's your decision," I said, "and because you both seem confident that you can do this. I hope you know that I'd never trade your lives for anyone else's, or expect you to do this for any reason other than wanting to help Rowan. This isn't what you agreed to help me with when we met in Cressia. I'm more thankful than I can say that you care enough to be here. Rowan will be, too."

Cassia turned away to study the lamplight reflecting in the river. The breeze lifted her hair, gently brushing it back from her face. "What if we're not doing this for Rowan? What if it's for you?"

I reached for her hand, and she turned back to me. Her hesitant smile brightened the shadows of the park. "Don't get me wrong, I adore Rowan. She's a lovely person, and I consider her a friend. I mean, for her I've given you your space on this journey instead of inviting you into my bedroll at night to keep me warm. But you and I go way back, and we've got a lot of good memories. You've been a great friend to me and a better one to Kel, excepting a span of seven years or so. And I..." She swallowed hard.

"What?"

"You know that we don't have romantic attachments like you do, my stupid brother notwithstanding. But what you and I have is different from what I have with anyone else. You're a friend in a way that's deeper than I'm accustomed to. I don't love you, but I do." She shook her head. "That makes no sense, I know. I just want you to know why we're doing this. Your mission to remove Severn from power is important to our people, but it's more than that. Kel and I just don't want to lose you."

I swallowed back the lump in my throat. I'd never considered the idea that friendship could be as deep as any other kind of love. It was true, though. I cared more for Kel and Cassia than I did my own family.

"I don't know what to say."

She smiled and squeezed my hand. "There's nothing to be said. Nothing changes."

"I couldn't have wished for better friends. I hope I'll be able to repay this some day."

She gave my fingers another squeeze, released them, and reached back to twist her thick hair into a knot at the back of her neck. "I'll tell you that unless your sister is far more persuasive than I think she is, Kel and I will be going into the river and opening that gate for you. And for Nox, if she's going to join us."

"I am," Nox said as they appeared from the deep shadows. "Kel thinks that he needs to do this." She still held his hand tightly.

"But you don't have to," I told her. "As you've pointed out, Rowan's capture isn't your problem."

"And as I've also pointed out, I think you have a better chance of succeeding at anything if I'm along. It worked in the dragon cave, and if it means that Kel is more likely to get out alive, then I'm coming."

"Thank you. All of you. Kel, Cass, what's next?"

"Now you wait here," Kel said, "and Cass and I go do what we do best. We swim, we wait for that door to open, and we go in. When we open it again, you follow."

"We swim?" Nox asked.

"Is that a problem?" Kel unlaced his pants and let

them fall to the ground.

Nox looked away. "No, I can swim." Her voice sounded strained. "But I don't enjoy it."

"A perfect match," I muttered under my breath. Cassia was the only one who heard, and she tried not to smile.

I joined Nox in looking away when Cassia pulled her shirt over her head, but caught a good glimpse of smooth skin and the curve of a breast as the fabric whispered over her head.

Good memories, indeed. I was glad to have them, but all I wanted now was to have Rowan back in my arms. Cassia left her clothing, but took her bag and slipped Kel's hunting knife into it, along with her own things. She tightened the strap over one shoulder and under the other arm to hold the bag tight against her ribs.

Kel and Cassia took advantage of the shadows as they approached the water, then slid into one of the few sections of the river that wasn't dimly illuminated by the park's lamps. All Nox and I could do then was wait.

Chapter Thirty-Seven

Aren

Every noise in the park seemed to announce our presence. A cat ran out from the bushes and between Nox's feet, and she clapped her hands over her mouth to hold back a gasp. She took several deep, shaky breaths. "I think I'm going crazy."

The leaf-covered ground soaked my socks and sent up the musty scent of decay. I crouched, trying to keep warm but unwilling to sit in case we had to move quickly. It was cold enough next to the river that I could barely feel my toes.

Should've made the gate guard give me his boots.

"I'd keep an eye on Kel for you," I told Nox, keeping my voice low. I still wasn't comfortable with her going in there.

She shrugged one shoulder. "Pathetic as it sounds, you're the only family I have, and those two are my only friends. I can't let you all wander off to your deaths without joining in, can I?"

"At least you won't be lonely."

"Yeah. Well, your girl had better be pretty amazing if I'm going to risk my life to get her out of there."

"She is."

As the minutes crept by, my doubts crowded close.

We must be too late. This is all for nothing. They've had her a week. This is suicide. Why should more people die just because I can't live without her?

I forced my mind to be still. My focus needed to be on the present, on being aware of danger and doing what I could to keep my friends and my sister safe.

It's insanity. Leave now.

The flickering light across the water picked out the outline of a small boat containing a single cloaked figure, rowing with strong, steady strokes, cutting through the water toward the door directly opposite us. The whisper of the oars moving through the water and the lamplight reflecting off the low waves would have been a peaceful sight at another time. Now every rock of the vessel set me more on edge.

Nox's nails dug into my arm through the fabric of my shirt. The doors opened outward, slowly, pushing against the current of the river. Light shone out and the boat passed through. The doors closed behind it as slowly as they'd opened.

"Where are Kel and Cass?" Nox whispered.

"Inside, I hope." They should have gone in under the boat when the doors opened.

Minutes passed before a crack appeared between the doors, a thread of light on the dark wood. It stopped, then opened a little more.

"Come on," I said to Nox, and tucked my knife into my belt. "I don't think we're going to have much time."

I slipped feet-first into the water, holding my breath to keep in a gasp. The water was so cold that my skin burned from it. Nox removed her boots and jacket and lowered herself into the water beside me. Air hissed between her teeth.

"I can't do this." Her teeth chattered. "We'll never make it."

"Yes, we will. Keep moving." I pushed off from the

edge and moved toward the middle of the river, angling upstream to compensate for the pull of the current. My hands and feet had gone numb before we were half-way across, and when I looked for Nox, she had fallen behind. She kept her face above water, but barely. A ripple on the surface covered her nose, and she sputtered, splashing. I reached for her and forced my fingers to clamp onto her wrist.

"Keep moving," I repeated.

Magic warmed my body. The cold still bit painfully into my skin, but I felt warmth deep in my muscles, keeping them from seizing up. I tried to hold it back, to save the magic for later, but couldn't. This was survival, and beyond my control. I took advantage of it and pulled Nox closer, dragging her along with me. She kept kicking, kept fighting her way through the water. I couldn't imagine what a struggle it was for her.

I felt the drain on my magic again. I'd never had to measure it before, and had no way of knowing what I had left. I only hoped that, like physical strength, I would find that I had more than I thought when a crisis arose.

I pushed harder through the water. The sooner we were out of the freezing river, the sooner my magic would stop trying to save me from it.

The doors were halfway open when we reached the wall, and we passed between them, our heads just above the water. If there were enemies waiting, their spotting us wouldn't be any worse than staying outside to drown. Twin walkways lined the indoor canal, and torches burned at regular intervals along the walls, giving off both a stink of oil and a promise of warmth.

The doors closed behind us, with the sound of trickling water tapering off as they sealed. I pulled Nox toward the walkway to our left and grabbed the slippery stone edge. She gasped as Kel pulled her out of the water. His hands grasped my wrists. I wrapped my hands around his forearms, and he hauled me up.

The air inside the wall was significantly warmer than the river, but I still shivered.

Kel stood with his back to the wall, looking down the short entry passage. At the end of this space, the canal appeared to continue to the right, following the inside of the wall. The boats would come in the door, then have to make the sharp turn to whatever lay beyond. I looked back toward the door. Here, in the outer edge of the wall, narrow slits in the stone offered a limited view of the water and the shoreline beyond.

Kel rubbed his arms under the blanket he had draped over his shoulders. He wore another wrapped around his waist, taken from the pile beside a wooden wheel that opened the doors via a system of pulleys. Another, identical wheel sat on the walkway on the opposite side of the canal.

Two men were tied together next to it, dripping wet, with rags stuffed in their mouths. They glared at us, and one began struggling when he saw us looking, lurching side to side and straining against his bonds.

"Enough," Kel said to him. "They're not going to hurt you, as long as you cooperate." He picked up the pile of blankets, then draped several over Nox's shoulders and handed the rest to me. "Are you two all right? I'm glad you came when you did. The water makes the doors heavy. I think opening them's supposed to be a two man job, but Cass isn't back yet."

"Is she all right?" I asked, though he didn't sound concerned.

"She was a few minutes ago."

I shook open a blanket and used it to absorb what water I could from my clothes and my hair. The magic that continued to heat the blood in my veins wasn't nearly enough to dry the clothes that stuck to my clammy skin. I walked in a circle, moving my arms until my body warmed itself and I felt the magic was no longer helping. My socks squelched beneath my feet, and I stopped to take them off.

"Is Cassia coming back?" Nox asked. "Should we look for her?"

"She went after the guy in the boat to make sure he wasn't coming back. These two were easy enough. I don't think they expected to see a naked woman pulling herself out of the water after that boat passed. Put them off their guard a bit."

I snorted. "Just a little?"

The men on the other ledge continued to glare.

Cassia rounded the corner and walked toward us. "You people are so predictable."

With her hair tied behind her neck, every toned curve of her body was visible. I couldn't blame the guards for being distracted. She stepped around a coiled rope and accepted the blanket I held out for her, wrapped it around herself, and tucked a corner into the top to hold it in.

"I got him after he grabbed me. I hit him pretty hard and tied him up, but I think he's going to be okay."

Nox shivered, and Kel sat down and wrapped his arms around her. She leaned into him. "Those guys don't look too happy. What's next?"

"Getting you out of those wet clothes," Kel said.

Nox grinned in spite of her chattering teeth. "Nice try. Really, though. What are we going to wear? We can't go walking around in blankets, even in the middle of the night. Someone's going to notice."

We all looked at the bound men, and I noticed for the first time that they weren't dressed as soldiers or guards. They wore plain civilian clothes in two different color palettes. Workers, not soldiers. I reached out to their minds to see who they were—it never took much digging to learn the basics of a person's identity. They didn't even seem to feel me looking. One was a blacksmith, longing to be home in bed before an early morning in his shop. The other was a baker, afraid for his life.

A baker, for the gods' sake.

The blacksmith shook his head hard and drew his legs tight to his chest.

Cassia frowned. "That would have been too easy. I never thought I'd have trouble getting a man out of his clothes."

"This is up to you, Aren," Kel said, barely speaking above a whisper. "Are you going to convince them to do this quietly, or are we going to have to fight them for it?"

This far and no further, I had told myself when I used my talents against the guard at the gate. *Enemy soldiers only.* But these men weren't. Rowan had almost left me once when she found out I was manipulating people like these. Emalda had forbade me to use my powers against this sort of person, and though I'd resented her rules, I'd begun to understand her objections, and Albion's, and Rowan's. My gift was a powerful tool, and a terrible one.

The younger-looking one, the baker, pushed the rag from his mouth and gagged as it dropped into the river. "Please. I have a wife and kids. Don't hurt me."

"Calm down," I told him. "If we intended to kill you, we'd have done it by now. That's not to say we won't, but if you help us, things will go easier for you."

A tear trickled down the man's face. "I help you, I hang. Kill me if you have to. At least that way my family will get—" He sobbed as the larger fellow jerked around to deliver an elbow to his ribs.

"Shut up," I told him, keeping my voice low.

His sobs turned to wails. Nox shifted her weight nervously, and Kel glanced down the short corridor.

"Shut up!" I ordered again, then lowered my voice as he complied. "Do they always have city folk manning the doors here? Are they so desperately in need of bodies?"

Neither answered, but their thoughts were there, ready to be taken. To be manipulated. To be changed.

Darkest magic, brother Phelun's voice whispered in my mind.

For Rowan, I answered. *Time's wasting.*

And with that thought, I understood. Black and white bled together in my thoughts. Dark magic and light, right and wrong, heroic intentions and villainous all melded, and I decided that it didn't matter. I would see this through. I'd sacrifice my soul to the tortures of every imaginable Hell and break every person who stood against me if it meant getting her back. If that made me a monster, so be it. I would use my dark gifts wisely, but I would embrace who I was, goodness be damned. A sense of balance I'd been missing for far too long returned to me.

I dug deep to sense the baker's answer to my question. He flinched.

Doors usually manned by trained guards. They're short-staffed tonight thanks to the illness in the city, and all the guards on duty have been called to an execution on short notice.

My heart stilled. "Who are they killing?"

His body struggled, but he couldn't defend his mind. *Sorceress. Damned if I know who, or care.*

"How do I cross?" I asked. Kel took a board off of the wall and lowered it to span the waterway. I stood and left the blanket behind, and crossed toward the men.

I focused on the baker first. He glared defiantly at me. There was no way to make this easy or subtle, to simply change his thoughts. He was already fighting, struggling to close his mind against further invasion. I forced my way in, snapping his attention away from his surroundings, leaving him dazed.

The smith turned away and squeezed his eyes shut, as though that would protect him from whatever I had done to the baker. His thoughts swirled in a dozen directions, every word and image stained by fear and anger. It was a more difficult connection to make, but soon his mind calmed and became as blank on the surface as the other man's.

I motioned for Cassia to join me, and she undid the ropes that bound them. They sat there blinking at us, helpless and docile.

"That's really...I'm going to go." Cassia's voice shook. She hurried to cross the water to get away from me. It would have hurt if I'd let it. Instead, I focused on slipping back into the guards' thoughts, making them remove their own clothes and hand over everything we needed, puppets in my control. They kept their underclothes, if not their dignity.

Perhaps I should have given them a few bruises and the memory of having fought valiantly, but there was no time and not enough magic to waste on such things. I took the clothing back to the other side and handed the baker's things to Nox while Cassia went back and tied up the now-compliant men.

"They'll be all right?" she asked.

"They'll be fine," I said. I hoped it was true. Though Phelun's voice had been silenced, his words and my grandfather's still resonated in my mind. I'd done what I had to, but I felt shame rising in me.

Life was so much simpler before I cared.

Kel offered me the smith's larger clothes, and I refused. "You and Cass are somewhat more conspicuous in what you're wearing," I said. "I'm just a little damp." That was a lie. My clothes were still dripping, but there was nothing else to be done. I'd simply have to keep moving.

Kel said nothing as he dressed. He and Cassia didn't look at me, or at the guards. I told myself their fear didn't matter, but felt the sting of their silence. Nox laid a hand on my arm and squeezed. When I turned to her, she offered a reassuring smile that betrayed no disgust, no horror. A hint of pride, perhaps, and understanding. I didn't look closer lest I slip into her mind again, but I nodded my thanks.

Saving Rowan was the right thing to do, but that didn't make me feel better when I looked across the water and saw the pair of men staring at the walls with blank minds and empty eyes.

I did the same to the third guard, who sat just around the corner, and was relieved to find his mind easier to access, requiring less magic. I wasn't getting any back. This fortress was a dead space.

Judging by how quickly my power was depleting, I decided I couldn't afford much more manipulation of anyone who was going to resist me. Certainly not a transformation.

"Which way?" Kel asked.

"I don't know. Hold on." I returned to the first pair of guards, both of whom still sat back to back, contented enough with their lot. I might not have enough power left to wrestle another mind into submission, but I'd use these.

My stomach turned as I called silently to the baker, the one who had been crying earlier. He'd seemed at least somewhat knowledgable. "Do you know where they're performing the execution?" I asked quietly. I could have just searched for the information, but speaking the question aloud brought the answer to the forefront of his mind.

"Oh...this way." He crossed the plank and started toward the junction inside the wall. Maintaining my hold on him was far easier than establishing it had been, but still I felt my hold slipping, again and again. Each time it did, he stopped moving. Stopped thinking.

Don't worry about what you've done, I told myself.

"Don't worry," the man echoed.

Kel took a sharp breath and shook his head.

"Don't mind me. Takes some getting used to."

Our hostage took us left, away from the indoor canal and up a short set of steps to a wide corridor that followed the path of the wall. Widely-spaced torches left broad and deep shadows. The hall was empty, save for the tension among my friends that hung thick in the air. Every noise, every air current that made the torch-light flicker set us more on edge.

We passed wooden doors, all of them closed.

"What are those rooms?" I asked.

"Mostly staircases up," the baker said. "I don't think much happens on this level. Entrances. Exits." He reached up to scratch his arm, though I hadn't told him to do so. He looked back at me and his eyebrows pulled together in confusion.

Not yet. I dug deeper into his thoughts, and his expression flattened. We needed to get rid of him, though. I wouldn't be able to hold on forever.

"Where are we going, exactly?" I asked him.

"There." He pointed at the wall, toward what would be the interior of the structure. The courtyard. "Way across, but that's all I know. Come here." He moved to a door and batted a hand against the wood panels. Kel leaned against it, listening. The latch clicked softly, and Kel pushed the door in to reveal a dark stairwell. A window on the far wall, too narrow to climb through, showed a view of the yard, distorted by old glass. Lights still flickered out there, but otherwise the place seemed quiet.

"They might be done," our captive said. "I hope so. Once they're done, maybe I can go home."

Kel stepped between me and the guard before I could react.

"I'm not going to hurt him," I said. "Not more. You're sure that's all you know, friend?"

"Yes."

I dug deeper in his thoughts, just to be sure, and

ignored memories of his family, his friends, his life. All of it was irrelevant. There was nothing more there about the fortress.

"Leave him," I said, and turned to go.

He tried to follow.

"Stay."

He blinked at me, and moved again toward the door.

"Go ahead," I told the others. Cassia listened at the door, then hurried out, followed by Nox and Kel.

I gathered my magic.

"You deserve far worse than this," I whispered, and stepped into the corridor, pulling the door shut behind me. I sent a blast of magic into the lock, jamming it. Smoke rose from the door handle, and I hissed as I pulled my hand away. Blisters formed on my palm.

A faint knocking came from the other side of the door as we walked away. At least he'd stopped crying.

Cassia looked back over her shoulder.

"He'll recover," I told her.

"Are you sure?"

"No."

We stuck to the shadows as well as we could, though there was no sign of anyone else roaming the corridor. The baker had said they were short-staffed, but someone would be around, and they'd show up the moment we let our guard down.

Nox drew her daggers as we stepped into a dimly-lit alcove and stopped.

"Are you any good with those?" Kel asked her, his voice barely a whisper.

"You don't last long up north if you can't defend yourself. I'm not completely useless without my potions." She gave him a cocky little smile and tossed a dagger in the air. It rotated once, and she caught it neatly by the handle. "Didn't see that in me, did you?"

"You're full of surprises."

Torn

"Stop it," I muttered. If we got out alive, they'd have time to flirt later. If they kept it up, they'd get us all killed.

Nox darted across the hall and flattened herself against the wall. With her dark hair hanging over her face and the gray clothing she now wore, she blended in with the deep shadows. "I don't see anything."

I started to let my awareness out, and hesitated. Even with that, a skill I'd been using for years and that hardly required any effort from me, I felt an instant drain on my magic. I was pulling from a nearly-empty well now, thanks to my transformation earlier in the night and everything that had followed.

I nodded to Nox, and we moved on.

Around the next corner, we came to a doorway leading out into the courtyard. I crouched and crept to the window. A group of men stood outside a door on the adjoining section wall, talking and laughing. No tension in their postures, no sign that they were waiting for a fight, and yet all appeared to be armed.

Kel knelt beside me and looked out. "What do you think?"

"That's probably the way we want to go."

"That guy couldn't tell you anything else?"

"No. But it fits. If all of the staff here are involved, they're waiting for something before they can go ahead."

"Of course."

I knew he was thinking the same thing I was, that it was just as likely they were standing around because the job was done.

"You should all stay here," I said. "I appreciate your help. I couldn't have made it without you. But this is too dangerous. If you—"

"Please, gods, no speeches," Nox groaned under her breath as she stepped to the window. "Don't be a stupid arse. We'll watch your back in case—Aren, the guards are moving."

She didn't have to tell me. I saw. The door behind them opened, spilling a rectangle of bright light into the shadows of the yard. Someone leaned out, and the men all straightened their shoulders and placed their hands on their weapons. The door closed again, leaving the soldiers to guard it.

My muscles tightened. My breath slowed.

Time's up.

My friends followed me out the door, weapons ready. Long, dewy grass chilled the bottoms of my feet and re-soaked the hem of my pants, and the chill in the air would have had me shivering had I not been warmed by the fire building inside me. Calm descended over my mind as I calculated attack angles. No magic this time.

Cassia grabbed my arm. I stopped. She loosened the strap on her bag so it hung lower and pulled out a long dragon flare and a flint, both of which had been wrapped in cloth. She covered her eyes, then checked to make sure we all understood.

Gods bless you, I thought.

Kel placed a hand on my arm and leaned in. "We'll keep them out of the way. You get in there, and we'll follow."

"Thank you," I whispered.

To think I'd once preferred solitude.

We moved forward again. Cassia put the flint to the flare and scratched. Nothing happened.

I motioned for her to hold out the flare. Nox narrowed her eyes, and I wondered whether she could feel my lack of power as she felt it in the land. Surely not. She was only a Potioner, and we barely knew each other. Still, she seemed concerned.

As was I. Still, I turned my back on the guards and managed a weak flame. The flare burst to bright life, and Cassia threw it in a long, spiraling arc at the guards.

"What in God's name is—" one of them managed before the flare brightened further. I squeezed my eyes closed. Even with my hands over my face, the brightest moment of the flare's burn cut through, leaving me blinded. As soon as I could risk opening my eyes, I ran forward, squinting against the flickering light. Kel took out one guard with a solid punch to the jaw that the man didn't see coming. My mer friends may not have been trained to fight on land, but they would manage.

I hit the door with my shoulder before I saw it, pulled back on the handle, and was relieved to find it unlocked. I ducked into another empty corridor, closed the door tight, stood with my back to the opposite wall as I waited for the white spots to fade from my vision. Sounds of battle continued outside the door—thuds, grunts, a groan. No warning shouts, though. I hoped that meant my friends would take the guards down before they had a chance to call more.

This hallway was narrower than the last one, with doors along one side that might have led to rooms, or simply to more staircases. No sounds betrayed human presence. I moved forward, listening at each door. Nothing, save for the sound of water dripping somewhere ahead of me, counting off the seconds.

Too late. You're going to be too late.

Finally, muffled voices reached me. I pressed my ear to the smooth wood of the door, but heard only mumbles. Two men, I thought. The creak of another door opening, and a dull click.

The mumbling continued, but only one voice spoke. I adjusted my grip on my knife and pressed down on the latch to open the door. The voice inside stopped. Footsteps approached. I flung the door wide and leapt into the room, knife ready.

The first thing to catch my eye was the tall, broad, brown-haired man who jumped back as the door swung open. He had his own knife in hand, and slashed out. I ducked, and slammed the door behind me. A sharp pain stabbed into my left foot, sending a bolt of agony up the length of my leg. I ignored it.

The next thing I noticed was the red-haired figure lying motionless on a hard table in the corner, gagged and bound, clad in a blood-stained white dress and familiar knee-high boots. The beginnings of a bruise covered one side of her face, surrounding cracked skin over her cheekbone. Dried blood trailed from her nose to her lip and from above her hairline over her temple. A fresh trail of glistening blood flowed from a shallow cut just below her collarbone.

My opponent tried to circle behind me. I tore my eyes away from Rowan and spun. The other man didn't speak, but I knew well enough who he was.

Callum Langley.

"You're done here," I told him.

"Not quite." He swallowed hard and stepped backward toward the table. His eyes darted toward the other door, set into the wall to his left. "Just give me a moment."

Rowan's eyes fluttered open and widened. I looked away from her and tried to keep his attention on me. He lunged forward, bringing his knife toward my throat. Instead of jumping back, I spun sideways and delivered a punch to his jaw. The knife glanced off my arm as he stumbled, drawing blood but not doing nearly the damage he'd intended. I grabbed for his weapon, momentarily forgetting the burns on my left hand—and the fact that my magic wasn't healing them. I winced and flung the weapon aside. It skittered under the table.

Callum regrouped quickly and ran at me, hunched forward, and his shoulder collided with my stomach, forcing me back until my head connected with the wall. Everything in the room doubled before my eyes. I brought my own knife up behind him and slipped it upward under his ribs. Not deep enough. He gasped and jerked away, and I pulled my blade free.

He backed away, hands open, inviting me to come

at him again, and moved toward the table—and toward a set of knives I hadn't spotted hung low on the wall, long and cruel, and I assumed deadly sharp.

A line of blood dribbled from his lips, but he didn't seem to notice. He glanced back at Rowan, whose eyes had closed again. Drugged, I supposed.

I stepped forward, and my leg buckled under me as pain from my injured foot shot upward again.

I couldn't get to her before he would.

Langley reached for a knife. In one motion he pulled it from the wall and raised it, then brought it toward Rowan's throat as I lunged toward him.

In an instant, Rowan's eyes flew open, she tucked her legs up to her chest, and she kicked out with both, catching Langley in the stomach. He stumbled backward, turned, and caught himself—but not before I buried my knife in his chest and pushed upward into his heart. Hot blood flowed over my hand, and I released the knife.

Langley stepped back, an expression of shock on his face. "How dare you?"

Someone pounded on the door I'd entered by as Langley backed toward the other. His legs bent, and he sank to the floor. He turned to Rowan.

"I never wanted this," he choked, and collapsed. I waited. He didn't move.

Rowan moaned. I limped to the table, where she tried to push herself up. Her hands, I saw now, were not bound by rope, but by broad, blue-metal manacles that reached high on her forearms, attached by a chain to the wall. I pulled the gag from her mouth and sat on the table. She appeared dazed. Drugged. She collapsed against me, sobbing, and I wrapped my arms around her.

My head felt weightless, my thoughts muddled. All I understood was that I'd found her. Nothing had ever felt so real and important as she did then, pressed against me. Her body trembled, and I held her tighter, though my arms were no more stable. I ran my hands over her back, touched her hair and her face until I'd convinced myself she was alive.

"I thought I'd never see you again," she said, and leaned back. Her eyes searched mine, then looked me over, drinking me in. "I never should have left Belleisle. I'm so sorry."

"What have I told you about apologizing?"

She laughed softly, and another tear rolled down her cheek. I reached up to tangle my fingers in her filthy hair, and pulled her into a deep kiss. She leaned in, pressing her lips so hard against mine that I thought they'd break. She tasted like blood and tears, and nothing had ever been so sweet. Danger and death surrounded us, but seeing her again, having her close, cut through all of it and strengthened my body and my spirit. Even if I died in that compound, at least I would be with her.

But by the gods, I would fight to get us out.

The chain behind her rattled. "I want to touch you," she murmured, and pulled back. "And I want these off."

"Will he have the key?"

She looked past me to the body on the floor. "I think so. Be careful."

The door to the hallway opened, and I jumped to my feet. Pain seared through my leg again, and I still felt light-headed from the knock against the wall, but I would fight again.

Kel stepped in. "Sorry we took so long. One of them tried to run toward a warning bell, but we— Rowan."

"Hello, Kel." She smiled again, though her chin trembled. "Gods, it's good to see you."

The corners of Kel's eyes crinkled. "You curse like a Tyrean now."

She shrugged. "I know I don't belong here. Might as well move on, right?"

I rolled Langley onto his back and searched his

pockets. A small ring held several keys, which I tried on
Rowan's shackles. One opened the lock that fastened the
chain onto them, releasing her from the wall, but nothing
worked in the tiny lock on the cuffs.

"I might have something," Nox said. I turned to
see her and Cassia in the doorway. They stepped further
in and closed the door, and Nox held up a set of keys.
"Courtesy of one of the lovely gentlemen out there."

A fresh cut marred my sister's forehead.

"Everyone all right?" I asked.

"Never better," Cassia replied, and forced a smile.
"But I think we should get out of here."

A bell clanged outside.

"Definitely time to go," Kel agreed, and slipped an
arm around Rowan's waist. "You need a hand?"

Rowan glanced back at me as we all moved into
the hallway. She frowned as she saw me limping. "What's
wrong?"

"Nothing. Keep going. I'm fine."

We headed back toward the door to the
courtyard. Nox tried keys in the shackles until the lock
clicked and the metal clanked to the floor.

"Thank you." Rowan rubbed her wrists. "Who are
you?"

"Long story," Nox said, and stooped to pick up the
shackles, which she strung through her belt. She turned
to the door. "This way. We'll go the way we came. We'll
get lost otherwise."

Rowan hung back "No." She squeezed her eyes
shut, and appeared more focused when she opened them.
"We need to get away from here, but we can't leave. Aren,
your father. He's here. He's been here the whole time,
but they're going to kill him. That way." She nodded
further down the corridor. "Down below."

"My father?" I wasn't sure how to react to the
news. My father, here. I'd given up on finding him, and
for days my thoughts had only been with Rowan. And

she'd been with him. A chill came over me. *We almost waited for morning. We almost let both of them die.*

Cassia looked uncertain. "We're going deeper into the fortress?"

"This is what we came here for," Nox said softly, addressing Cassia. "Aren and I are not leaving. You and Kel take Rowan and go." She pulled a dagger out of her belt. The other was gone. "We'll be fine."

Rowan shook her head. "I can't go. I have to show you where Ulric is. He might be hurt. I can't leave him here." She looked back at the room I'd found her in. "Dorset Langley has been with me since they took me from the cell, but he left just before Aren came in. He's gone to finish Ulric, I know he has. Please."

A shout of alarm echoed through the corridor. Rowan's lips pressed into a thin line. She seemed to be growing stronger every second. "Come on," she said, and led us past the courtyard door. Her steps faltered, and Kel caught her.

"Thanks," she said. "The shackles kept my magic from getting that stuff out of my blood, but I think it's getting better now." Her steps slowed, and she touched her fingertips to her chest. "He was right. It does come back stronger."

I had no idea what she was talking about, but the awe in her voice told me it was important. I only hoped whatever it was would heal her quickly.

I stayed at the back of the group, keeping up as best I could. I was able to move quickly as long as I didn't put my full weight on that leg, or my foot flat on the ground. When I paused to check the wound, I found a deep puncture, only bleeding slightly, but the flesh around it was red and swollen. I'd had worse injuries before.

The corridor turned into a steep staircase leading underground, curving under the courtyard. I lost track of the turns we made, but Rowan seemed sure of where she was going.

We stopped in front of a heavy-looking door with a metal pull on the outside and two keyholes.

"That's not good, is it?" I asked, nodding at the locks.

"I don't think so," Cassia said. "I'm guessing that none of the guards carry both keys. I might be able to unlock one." She found the key to fit the upper lock quickly enough, but nothing for the lower.

Rowan looked at me. "Can you?"

Footsteps echoed from farther down the tunnel.

I closed my eyes and tried to pull magic into myself. There was nothing in the area except for what I felt burning in Rowan, stronger than I'd ever felt it before. In fact, hers seemed to be growing. "I don't think I can."

Rowan closed her eyes. "I think I could right now," she said, "but I don't have the skill." She looked to me and stepped closer. "What's wrong with your magic? I felt it when you kissed me. I mean, I didn't." Her eyes filled with concern. "Did they catch you? What did they do to you?"

"Nothing. I've been using a lot of it, that's all, and there's nothing here to replenish it. How is yours so strong?" She practically glowed with it.

She glanced at Nox, then back to me. "Long story." She frowned. "I'm going to try something. Griselda asked whether you'd ever tried to take my magic when we—" She bit her lower lip. "Never mind the explanation. I'm going to try to give you some, since you seem to be empty."

Before I could reply, she placed both hands on my neck and pulled my face toward hers. As she pressed her lips to mine, warmth flowed from her and through my body, thin sunlight burning through my veins. Magic. Hers felt different from before, sure and ready and powerful. Confident. Something had changed in her.

She pulled back. "Well?"

I felt the magic rushing to my injured hand and foot. Before it could be used up I touched the lock, and it cracked inside the door, which swung open onto a well-lit room with blue walls. I tried to hold Rowan's magic in reserve, but couldn't stop its healing.

I looked behind me. Bloody footprints trailed down the corridor. Perhaps the magic knew best. It was fading already. Using itself up.

I followed Rowan into the room. She moved quickly, gracefully, as though she hadn't just been drugged and nearly dead. Her bruise, which should have been darkening, had begun to fade.

At first I didn't recognize the man who stood in the center of the room with blue shackles around his ankles. He appeared dazed, but competent enough. His hair was whiter than when I'd last seen him, his face more lined. His expression remained blank as he saw me. My heart pounded from dread as much as excitement at finding him at last. He'd brought that reaction in me since I was a child.

"Hello, Aren," he said, voice catching as he spoke.

I forced myself to look him in the eye, as an equal. I would not let him underestimate and dismiss me again.

"Hello, Father."

Chapter Thirty-Eight

Rowan

Aren's new friend unlocked the shackles around Ulric's ankles, then stepped away as though retreating from a hungry wolf. I left Ulric and his son to enjoy their reunion in peace. I forced myself to move slowly, though everything in me wanted to run from that cell. I moved down the hallway a few paces and crouched with my back against the wall. We all needed to be alert, keeping watch. But it was too much, too fast. I rested my face in my hands, just for a moment.

I'm supposed to be dead.

I'd thought I *was* dead. I'd tried to find peace even as I slipped repeatedly between pain and drugged oblivion, tried to accept my death, to die well...and then Aren was there. Seeing him had surprised me as much as seeing a unicorn roaming the halls would have. I'd thought he was a ghost, and both of us dead, and had for a moment been glad that at least we were together.

Then he'd kissed me, and he'd felt so warm, so solid. I'd felt his heart pounding, and mine, and it had broken me.

I took a deep breath and touched my fingers to my lips, pressing hard as though it would hold back the emotions that still threatened to flood me.

Forget the past few hours. Forget the weeks in the cell. Forget the fear. Move forward.

At least Dorset Langley wasn't in the cell, though that did leave me wondering where he'd gone.

I pushed my back against the wall and stood. A bell clanged, calling whatever troops might be in the area to arms. We needed to go, now. The soldiers had to know where we were, and they'd come soon.

Kel approached. "You're missing an interesting family reunion in there. Awkward, actually." He glanced down the hallway, listened, looked back the other way, and leaned against the wall beside me. I noticed for the first time a deep gash on his forearm.

"You should take care of that," I said.

He shrugged. "Nox will patch me up once we get out of this pit." He looked me over and frowned. "You're okay, right? They've been treating you well?"

"Could have been a lot worse. Hours alone with Dorset Langley weren't pleasant, but I guess he kept me safe from the other guards until Callum got here." I wanted to say *to finish me off*, and couldn't. Even now, after his knife had been nearly at my throat, I couldn't believe Callum had wanted me dead.

Kel reached out to run his thumb over my cheek, where the pain from Sir Dorset's last attack was receding. I closed my eyes and saw Langley's anger, felt the sting of every injury I'd been awake for.

The other woman stepped out of the cell and cleared her throat. Kel's hand dropped. "We should be going," she said, and glared at me as she passed.

"That's Nox," Kel said.

"We sort of met. Who is she?"

"Aren's sister." Kel pushed off from the wall to follow Nox, joining Ulric and Cassia.

I didn't move. "Aren doesn't have a sister," I said, too late for Kel to hear.

"That's what I said."

I turned to see Aren emerging from the cell, still limping. He gave me a pained smile.

I turned to look again at the retreating woman. "She...how..."

Aren draped his arm across my shoulders and pulled me close. "I'll explain everything later."

We moved down the corridor, heading in the same direction I'd gone when called to the king's offices, and when I'd tried to escape. Aren leaned on me, and I took some of the weight off his leg. "What happened to you?" I asked. "You look terrible."

"The very words I've been waiting to hear from your beautiful lips since I left Belleisle." His smile faded. "It wasn't easy getting in here. I'll be fine."

"Will you? What about your magic?" Something had seemed off when he first kissed me, but I'd been too drug-addled and shocked over seeing him to place what the problem was. Even after, I'd thought that perhaps the drug and the manacles had suppressed my own magic enough that I couldn't feel it. But I was sure, now. When I'd tried to share my magic, I'd felt almost nothing in him. A breeze where there had once been a blizzard.

He set his jaw in a determined look I knew all too well. "It will recover once we get back to Tyrea. Even just away from this cursed city. I don't know how you survived this for so long."

"Your father's been enduring it longer than I have."

Ulric turned back and glared at us. "If it's not inconvenient," he said, "please consider shutting up."

The words stung, and Ulric's tone more so. *Don't be sensitive*, I chided myself. *He wants to get out of here alive.* I nodded, though our voices hadn't been any louder than our footsteps.

With every step he took away from the cell, Ulric stood straighter. Every time he glanced back over his shoulder, he appeared to have become younger.

At least there's that. I felt the push-back effect he'd described in myself. My magic seemed ready to overflow, and I almost felt that if I didn't use more, I would burst from it.

And, I added to myself, *that much power might not be a good thing.* I'd learned control in the cell, over smaller amounts of magic. Trickling stream magic, as Ulric had said. This would be a flood again, and floods could kill.

I stopped, pulled Aren aside, and kissed him again. He didn't object. The magic refused to leave me this time. It felt like I was trying to cram my foot into a too-tight boot. Though Aren could surely feel my magic, I couldn't pass much of it on. I held him tighter, focused harder, and then focused on him instead of the magic. Something happened, though I didn't feel much impact on my own power. My headache returned, and subsided as I stopped trying.

I released Aren, frustrated. There was a time when it might have worked, when my magic would have flowed from me and healed his wounds.

He looked a little brighter when he pulled away, though I couldn't tell whether it was the magic or the kiss that had done it.

"Did you get anything?" I asked, barely mouthing the words.

"I did, a little." He smiled faintly. "You should hold onto that, though. You'll need it."

We moved forward, and he leaned on me less. *I'll do that a thousand times,* I decided, *if that's what it takes to get him out of here.*

Shouts echoed behind us, sounds of panic and frantic orders. We all quickened our pace, and I stole glances over my shoulder. My heart raced, and my face broke out in sweat.

Faster. Don't be caught. Not again.

Footsteps clattered, accompanied by the clanking of light armor. Ulric stopped and turned, and a terrifying grin spread across his face. His eyes sparkled with malice like I'd never seen in him. Terrifying as it had been, he *had* only been acting when he threatened me.

"Down," he ordered. We obeyed.

He closed his eyes. "Oh, that's better." He turned his gaze on me, and I shivered. "Do you feel it?"

I nodded, but couldn't hold back a frown. He'd changed, become a stranger, and not one I trusted as I had the man in the cell who had thrown himself into danger to save me.

Or to use you, I thought again. *You'll never know.*

Ulric laughed deep in his throat. "Watch, and learn."

A dozen guards rounded the corner. Ulric raised his arms, swept them wide over his head, and pushed his hands forward. There was nothing to see, no wind or temperature change to feel, but every hair on my body stood on end as the force passed over us.

The invisible power caught the guards, knocking them off their feet and throwing them back. The ones in front screamed. I caught a glimpse of bright blood and looked away. I didn't need to know what he'd done.

Ulric roared into the silence after they fell. "Gods, that feels good," he said, louder than I'd have dared. He moved past us toward the soldiers. I didn't move. I couldn't.

You'll have to use your magic for the same purpose some day, I thought. My stomach churned at the thought. I'd killed before, but not intentionally. This was far beyond anything I'd imagined in the days when I dreamed of fairy tales and innocent magic.

Ulric handed Aren a long dagger he'd pulled from one of the fallen soldiers. I noticed that Nox carried a similar weapon, sheathed at the small of her back. She went to the men to pick up a second blade, and tested its weight and balance. Kel looked back toward the bodies and away, appearing nauseated. It seemed he and Cassia were content with the hunting knives they held in their hands. The weapons were perhaps not ideal for combat, but they'd obviously served well so far.

Ulric hefted a heavy iron rod in one hand and a short sword in the other, then turned and continued his determined march through the gradually narrowing tunnel. The rest of us followed.

Kel took Nox's hand. "That was interesting use of magic."

"I'm not sure *what* that was," she replied.

"If it gets us out of here," he muttered, "I'll call it a miracle."

"Changing your mind on magical force?" Aren asked.

Kel looked back, as did Cassia. "Necessary evil, maybe?" He said it jokingly, but there was something deeper there.

Aren smiled sadly. "Maybe that's it."

We reached an opening in the wall on our left that contained the curving stone staircase I'd taken to my audience with Haleth. Torches burned bright and hot leading up the stairs. The tunnel we were in seemed unused past that turn-off—unlit, cold, and dirty. Ulric paused, then placed one foot on the bottom stair.

"I thought the way out would be underground," I said. In fact, I knew it. He'd never fully explained the route, but I knew from his notes that this wasn't the way.

Ulric's hands balled into fists, and the air crackled again. "It is. But they're here. Haleth and Dorset Langley." He spat the names out. "The king wouldn't have attended a messy execution himself, but taunting me afterward would have been too sweet for him to miss. If I were alive, of course. That would have been up to Langley."

"He didn't come to the cell, did he?" I asked.

"Not yet."

I swallowed back the dry lump in my throat. "He could be anywhere. Waiting."

"He knows you'll come after the king," Aren added. "This fortress may be short on troops tonight, but that's where they'll be waiting. Too many even for you to handle, and I can't help. They'll kill you."

Ulric's lips pulled into an animal snarl. "I don't care, as long as I kill the two of them first. We'll see if the gods are smiling on me tonight." He started up the steps.

"Then Severn wins," Aren said, barely loud enough for Ulric to hear. He leaned against one of the cold, stone walls. Ulric hesitated.

I climbed a few steps toward him. I'd faced death already that night. I could take his anger. "If you're not going to come with us and take your throne back, Severn keeps it, and the rest of us will join you in death before long. The country will fracture, more people will die, and it will be like you never accomplished anything at all, good king."

His lip curled in distaste. "Are you using my words against me, girl?"

"They're all I've got. Sir."

It was a close thing. He kept his cold gaze glued on me, and I took a step back when I realized he was calculating whether he might have enough power to win if only he stole mine. I had no doubt he could do it, that he would be too strong for me to fight it, even if I knew how. No, the cellmate I thought I knew was gone. He looked at Aren, frowned, then turned to Nox. Something passed over his face then, though I couldn't place what it was. Not a softening, but a change.

He flexed his hands and stepped down the stairs without another word, and strode confidently into the darkness of the tunnel ahead.

"Is he always like this?" Nox asked Aren.

Not always, I thought.

"Yes," Aren said. "He's not accustomed to being told what to do."

"I meant his magic," she said.

"Oh. No, not as I remember. He's an incredibly gifted Sorcerer and has had centuries to develop his gifts, but I've never felt power on this scale. I don't understand it. There's so little magic here."

A deep scowl-line formed between Nox's blue eyes. "You ran out, didn't you? That's why you look like shit."

"I'll live."

"Let me know if it gets worse."

"I don't think you can do anything now."

She sighed. "I know. But you might need me later."

"About Ulric's magic," I said. They both looked at me. Kel and Cassia were too far ahead to hear. "He calls it a push-back effect. He's stronger now than he's ever been, but it won't last long."

"All the more reason to hurry," Nox said, and rushed ahead to speak to Cassia, then Kel.

The shadows grew deeper until I couldn't see my hand in front of my face. The air became colder and wetter, and though I saw nothing, I felt water in the walls, seeping down them, dripping over rough, moss-covered rock. My connection to water felt as sensitive as new skin. Somewhere nearby, there was more. Much more.

A soft glow appeared ahead, and I realized it came from Ulric. He held one hand in front of him, and a ball of soft, white light hovered over it. The ceiling had become lower as we walked, held up with wooden beams. Aren and Kel had to stoop slightly each time we passed one to avoid hitting their heads.

No one asked exactly where we were going. No one dared.

The passage curved to the left, following the shape of the fortress above. The river flowed beyond the walls. A need to respond to it rose in me, and I pushed it aside. If I so much as acknowledged my magic, I'd probably call the river and break the walls, flooding the place before we could escape.

I thought I heard footsteps behind us again, and stopped. Only the soft patter of dripping water and the footfalls from the group ahead remained.

"Are you getting anything?" I asked Aren. "Sensing anyone?"

"No. Couldn't if I tried. Why, are you?"

"It's nothing. I just want to be out of here."

Ulric stopped in front of a rough, wooden door to our right—the wall holding back the river. He tried the handle, then gathered his magic and blasted through. A draft of dank, cold air washed over us as the old wood crumbled, and we stepped into a narrow tunnel made of stone. The beams supporting the walls and ceiling here appeared half-rotted, and the walls themselves were in need of maintenance, dotted with loose stones. Moisture gleamed off of every surface as Ulric's light passed. In the shadows, something scurried away.

"What is this?" I asked.

"Escape passage for the king," Ulric said without looking back. "Or it was for a former king. I don't know how many people remember it's here, but they'll figure it out soon enough. Keep moving."

The river's power reverberated through me as we followed the downward-sloping tunnel under it. I'd never felt such a connection through my magic, such a need to respond.

Aren stumbled and caught himself, then motioned for the others to keep going. Kel turned back, took off his boots and wool socks, and offered them to Aren. I thought Aren would refuse, but he accepted them and slipped them on.

Ulric waited, arms folded in front of him, not saying a word. As soon as Aren was standing straight again, Ulric moved ahead.

Kel wiggled his bare toes and kept walking,

untroubled by the cold and the damp. Nox shivered, and Kel put an arm around her. She leaned in and reached around to touch the handles of the daggers at the back of her belt. She interested me. She seemed competent, and Kel was obviously fond of her. Cold, though, at least when she cared to look at me. I'd ask Aren about her later.

And if I didn't get a chance to do that, it wouldn't matter, anyway.

The ground beneath our feet sloped upward as we reached what I felt was the middle of the river, and we climbed slowly toward the city on the other shore. The walls gradually stopped their weeping as the ground leveled out. Aren moved slowly, but steadily.

Ahead, Nox stopped and waited for us. She narrowed her eyes in the dim light, taking in Aren's appearance and gait.

"You fool," she muttered, but with as much concern as irritation in her voice. She pressed a hand to his forehead, and frowned. "You did use up your magic, didn't you?" He didn't answer, and she offered him an arm, which he refused. "Aren, have you ever been ill before? Feverish? Had an infection?"

"Nothing serious, no. Don't worry. I just feel a little weak now. Strange." He kept walking, with a grim expression of determination pasted to his face.

"That's not a good thing," Nox said, keeping pace beside him. "Your body has never had to heal without magic, has it? It's never been without that protection. Some sickness, or whatever you've done to your leg...Something is racing through you at ten times the normal speed."

Aren's brow creased. "This information is only useful if there's something we can do about it right now. Otherwise, moving forward should be our concern." He spoke in tight, clipped syllables.

"I might be able to slow it, once we get back to our

things."

Aren leaned down to massage his thigh with one hand. "That will be wonderful, if we get there. Just keep walking. Please."

Kel looked back. "For the sake of all your gods, man. Here." Before Aren could object, Kel threw an arm around his waist.

"You're not carrying me," Aren said.

"Wouldn't dream of it."

Aren put an arm across Kel's broad shoulders, and they walked that way until we'd caught up with Ulric and Cassia.

We reached the end of the tunnel, a solid brick wall. Ulric felt around, frowned, and looked up, holding his light near the ceiling. A rusted padlock dangled from a cobwebbed wooden panel overhead.

No one asked Aren to try breaking the lock. Kel released him, and Aren rested against the wall. When he looked back at me, his eyes seemed unfocused, if only for a few moments.

Ulric saw it, too. Based on what Aren had told me of his father, I didn't expect him to show compassion, but concern wouldn't have been out of place. It was irritation I saw there, though, and my shoulders tightened.

Aren saved us, I thought, wishing Ulric could hear. *If he has no magic, it's our fault.*

Ulric studied the lock, then slipped the iron bar he carried into the shackle of the lock and twisted hard, cracking the time-weakened metal. The lock fell toward the floor, and Cassia snatched it out of the air before it could clatter to the stones at her feet. Ulric reduced his light to a dim glow that barely illuminated our faces.

Kel stretched his arms over his head and pushed the panel up slightly. We waited, all of us listening for any sound that would indicate that someone was waiting for us. There was nothing, and no light came into the tunnel from above.

"Let me," Nox said. Kel eased the door closed, and crouched. She climbed on his back, then pushed herself up to balance her knees on his shoulders. He stood slowly as she tangled her fingers in his hair to keep her balance. If it hurt him, he didn't show it. She adjusted her weight, released him, and pressed her hands to the filthy wood.

She pushed up and peered out into the darkness above.

"Well?" Kel asked.

"Nothing. Boost me up."

He held her ankles as she stepped onto his shoulders, then released her as she disappeared through the trapdoor, leaving it open behind her. Soft shuffling noises drifted down. Nothing urgent or concerning, but Nox didn't indicate what was happening. Minutes later, a rickety wooden stepladder descended. Nox leaned down into the tunnel.

"Come up," she whispered, so softly that understanding her was more a matter of lip-reading than listening. "Douse the light, be silent."

Ulric went first, followed by Kel, who reached back to help Aren. I followed, and Cassia came after and pulled the ladder up behind her.

The little room was dark, save for the glowing outline of a door on one wall that barely cast enough light to see by. Not silent, though. Muffled voices reached my ears, coming from whatever room lay beyond the door. The air smelled dusty and slightly spicy. As my eyes adjusted, I noticed boxes and barrels in the corners. Shelves covered the wall opposite the door, stacked with glass jars and bulging sacks. I stepped closer, careful to make no sound as I crept across the rough wooden floor. The sacks made soft rustling noises when I touched them. Onions.

We were in a store-room. Cassia ran the toe of her boot over the trapdoor, which had disappeared seamlessly into the wooden floor as soon as she closed it. "Someone else must know about this tunnel, and where it comes out," she said, addressing Ulric. He grunted softly, but didn't answer.

Nox looked over the shelves. She seemed disappointed by their contents, but took an empty sack and slipped a few items into it.

Ulric came closer. "What time will it be now?" he asked Nox, still barely whispering.

She shrugged. "I don't know how long we were in that fortress. If it was only a few hours, we'll be in the early morning. So either the people out there are early risers, or—" She nudged a keg of ale with her foot. "This may be an alehouse, and those good folks are just closing up for the night. I suppose you want to blast your way out?"

I winced. He wouldn't appreciate that.

"We'll wait," he said. "If no one has followed, perhaps we've found good fortune. Drawing attention to this place will not help us. But if those people aren't in bed in the next few minutes, we leave. I'll not give the city guard time to set up outside if they do know about the tunnel. And if anyone walks into this room, that will be their bad luck."

I stepped away, and Ulric grabbed my arm. "Are you ready to fight?"

"I am."

"Where are you going now?"

"To check on Aren." I fought to keep my voice quiet. "He's not holding up well."

"You'll keep your magic to yourself, though." An order, not a question. "I feel mine draining already, and I have to conserve. Save yours. We'll need it."

"Aren needs it."

His fingers tightened, digging into my flesh, and he pulled me close enough that I felt his breath in my ear. "If you can't use it responsibly, I swear I will." He let me lean away. "It's not personal, Rowan. You've heard, I'm sure, that I'm a driven man. You've been a valuable ally, but I will not allow you or your sentiment to stand in my way. Understood?"

I glanced around. Nox had moved on to another shelf, and if she heard, she didn't seem to care. Everyone else was too far away to be listening in, though Aren watched from his seat on a box in the corner.

"Understood."

Ulric crouched on the floor next to the door, sword in hand.

Aren moved to the side so I could sit beside him. "What was that about?" he asked.

"Nothing."

He leaned back against the wall and closed his eyes. "You were stuck in there with him, weren't you?"

"They only have one cell to contain magic. It wasn't so bad. Mostly. I learned a few things about magic. Controlling it. Aren, you need more."

He shook his head. "No. Whatever this push-back thing is, keep it. We're not out of danger yet."

"If yours burns out, you could lose it forever."

He smiled a little. "You want to fan my flames, Miss Greenwood?"

I looked back at Ulric, who watched us intently from the corner. I rested my head on Aren's shoulder and tried to relax. No intense connection. Nothing to arouse suspicion. But I let my magic go, imagined it swirling around us and flowing into him.

"Don't try anything unfamiliar," Aren said. "Don't want to burn the place down." But he sat up straighter, as though he were getting something. I kept trying.

I stopped as the lights went out in the other room. Stairs creaked, and then the building was silent.

Ulric pushed the swinging door open, and we crept through a large room filled with tables, some with benches beside, others with chairs set upside-down on top. The ash-blackened hearth gave off the scent of wood smoke, and I wished we could stay and light a warm fire, just for a few minutes.

The sky outside the windows showed not deep night, but the purplish light of pre-sunrise, painted in light strokes with streaks of cloud. The city would wake soon.

Ulric hesitated at the main entry door, made sure we were all with him, and eased it open. He stepped outside and motioned for the rest of us to wait. Aren pulled me aside and kissed me again, long and deep, then rested his forehead against mine.

"One for the road," he explained.

"We're going to get out of here alive." I almost believed my words.

"I love you, you know."

I smiled and wrapped my arms around him. Nothing had ever felt so good as having his body pressed against mine again. "I love you, too." The words seemed inadequate, but I didn't know what else to say.

Ulric waved for us to follow, and we left the safety of the building. The streets were quiet at that early hour, but not empty. A cart creaked over the wide cobblestone street, drawn by a big bay horse that plodded along, head down. His master affected the same posture, and didn't seem to notice us. We crossed the street and headed into the shadows of a long alleyway between wood-shingled buildings that rose two stories overhead, with lines of laundry criss-crossing between them. I didn't recognize this portion of the city, but sensed the river ahead, calling to me.

"We'll go back by way of the river," Aren said. "Our horses are waiting in the forest outside the gate."

Ulric paused. "How did you get past the gates to get in?"

"I manipulated the guard."

"And you can't do that now."

"No. But we think there will be people coming and going from the market, if we want to try to duck out then."

Ulric crossed his arms. "There won't be anyone coming or going if they issue a city-wide alert."

"Why haven't they?" Cassia asked, frowning. "They must know we've gone."

"Hmm. Keep walking." Ulric pressed on, and we climbed over a low gate in the alley. A growl rose from a wooden crate to our right, and a thin dog covered in patchy white fur emerged, teeth bared. Cassia turned and hissed at it, cat-like, and the dog retreated into its shelter.

"Never cared for dogs," she commented. "Dirty things."

I supposed they didn't see many of them where she came from.

We reached the end of the alley and stepped into the thin morning light. Beyond a broad road and a widely-spaced row of shacks and wooden docks, the churning gray river flowed. Rowboats in an array of colors bobbed on the water, which seemed to be at flood levels, nearly overflowing the banks.

Ulric turned toward the river, then halted.

A dozen guards in dark blue uniforms and bright armor emerged from behind a nearby building. I turned to run back into the alley. Eight more men blocked the other end, approaching slowly and cautiously, picking their way around the debris and laundry. The dog barked, then yelped in pain.

I gripped Aren's hand, but released it as I remembered the small amount of fight training Ulric had provided. *Keep your hands free. Be prepared to move.*

My magic welled up, ready to act, if only I could find my focus. I pulled in a long breath and let my power infuse me, then stepped further from the alley, keeping the wall of a red-brick building at my back, moving toward the cover provided by a stack of boxes. The others followed—all except Ulric.

Deep in the city, a bell clanged.

Ulric stepped toward the soldiers in front of us. The soldier leading the group, a tall and muscular fellow with bright red hair sprouting from beneath his polished steel helmet, gasped and collapsed. Ulric kicked him in the face, sending a spray of blood over the street as three more men rushed forward. Ulric moved like a man of twenty years rather than several hundred, with speed, grace, and strength I hadn't seen in him before. His sword flickered through the air as though weightless, taking down man after man in the tight group. He held the iron rod in the other hand, fending off enemies who dared try to avoid his blade. When a fellow larger than the first approached, Ulric's eyes lit up. He stole that one's strength, and the mountainous man fell to the ground.

The first one he'd done it to stirred and pushed himself up, having regained what was left of his strength, but seemed unable to do much after the kick to the head.

It all happened so quickly that I had trouble following it, let alone reacting. A mesmerizing dance of pain and death, played out in moments.

Ulric disappeared.

He'd warned me to expect it, but I gasped. His clothes had disappeared with him, but not his weapons, which seemed to move through the air on their own, slicing and jabbing. Ulric reappeared mere seconds later, but he had made his way to the rear of the group. He caught their attention, and they turned, providing a chance for the rest of us to move.

I spun to look back again. The soldiers in the alley were almost on top of us. Cassia and Kel stood closest to them, weapons drawn. Kel made for an imposing sight with his broad shoulders and determined glare, and Cassia no less so in spite of her slim build. Still, we were outnumbered, out-trained, and under-armored.

We needed to run, but a pair of guards blocked the way to the river.

Where did they come from? They seemed to be emerging from the city's walls like cockroaches.

Above the sounds of battle, a muffled snapping sound reached me. A shadow passed over us, but was gone before I looked up.

No distractions.

I couldn't close my eyes this time, but watched as the two soldiers approached. I released my magic on a wave of fear and desperation, but directed it with my determination that we would not die here. I called to the river. It felt heavy, like I was trying to lift the earth itself, and wilder than the water in the cell or the baths. I clenched my jaw and pulled harder, straining the muscles in my neck and shoulders with the effort as I wrestled a force of nature far stronger them myself.

The water obeyed. A great wave of it rose above the banks of the river, carrying a red rowboat with it. Pain shot through my muscles in a great spasm, and I released the wave. It crashed down over the guards that stood ahead of us. The boat landed on one, pinning him to the ground, opening an escape route.

"Go!" I yelled. Nox, Kel, and Cassia sprinted past, heading for the river. Aren lagged behind.

I fit my body to the shadows and glanced back. The other soldiers had emerged from the alley. Four came toward us, though none seemed to have his eye on me. The others went to help with Ulric, who was facing off with the one soldier still standing there. The king had done well, but his former enthusiasm had left him. His shoulders heaved with his breath, and his sneer at the oncoming soldiers was more grim than threatening.

Nox broke ahead of the group, racing for the docks, a Darmish soldier on her heels. He lunged and tackled her to the ground. Kel thundered toward them, followed closely by Cassia, then Aren, limping as quickly as he could. I called again to the water, gathering my strength, unsure of how to act without hurting my friends.

Kel attacked, shoving the soldier off of Nox, burying his knife in the man's side where his armor gapped. Nox climbed to her feet and turned to me. Her eyes grew wide, and her dagger flashed in her hand. I gasped and ducked as the blade spun through the air, straight at my head.

A strangled sound behind me told me that the dagger had found its mark, and that it was a good thing I'd reacted quickly.

Cassia yelled. A guard had her backed against one of the sheds. The twin blades he held were no larger than her hunting knife, but his arms were longer, and she couldn't get close enough to attack. She feinted toward the road, and when he moved to block her—no, I realized, to toy with her—she threw herself into the river. The guard dashed off into the darkness between two fishing sheds.

At least she can swim, I thought, and then wondered how true that was if she couldn't get her pants off and transform underwater. Odds had to be slim that they practiced swimming in their human legs.

I caught up with Aren, and Ulric ran toward us. "Tell me you can all swim," he said as he reached me and Aren.

"Sort of," Aren said, and glanced at Nox, who was headed for a green boat. She held a hand above her eyes, watching for Cassia.

Ulric sent out a blast of magic over his shoulder, and someone screamed—the last man standing from the group he'd been fighting. He leaned forward to rest his hands on his knees. His arms trembled.

The soldier who had been after Cassia darted out from his position between the sheds and ran at Nox.

Aren took off toward her, more slowly than he usually ran, but from a closer position than the guard had started from. He reached Nox first and pushed her out of the way, into the river, just as the guard reached them.

Aren grimaced as his leg buckled under him, and my heart jumped into my throat. He pushed off from the wet ground, feet slipping in the mud beside the river, and knocked the soldier off-balance.

The soldier brought his knife over his head and down, plunging it deep into Aren's shoulder.

"No!" I screamed, and pushed off from the wall to run to him. Ulric grabbed me and threw me back, away from Aren. He roared and sent out another blast of magic that I felt burning through my body, though I hadn't been the target. The soldier fell in a pool of blood before he could strike at Aren again. Half of the soldier's head had vanished, or been blown off.

Ulric stumbled sideways, but caught himself.

I fought back tears and ran toward Aren. In my peripheral vision I saw Kel dive into the river after Nox. They resurfaced and swam to join Cassia farther out.

"Aren!"

He knelt on the ground, one hand clasped over his shoulder. Blood flowed freely from between his fingers. "I'm fine."

"Stop saying that. You're not fine!" I braced myself in the slippery mud and pulled him to his feet.

"Rowan," Ulric gasped as he caught up, and gestured back over his shoulder.

Despair filled Aren's eyes as he looked, followed by a grim look of determination. "They've roused the sick ones."

I turned. At least twenty fresh soldiers had arrived. Some appeared to be only halfway into their proper uniforms, moving out of time, as though they hadn't quite wakened from the sleep they'd been pulled from. Still, they were too many. Far too many. Cold calm radiated from my chest and through my body as hope fled.

But not everyone had to die.

"Get into a boat, now," I ordered. "Both of you. Grab Kel and Cassia and Nox. I don't know how good any of them are at treading water."

I looked back at the river in time to see several guards leap into a white boat and row toward them.

"No," I whispered, and called the river again. My hands trembled, though I couldn't say whether it was from fear, rage, or the shock of seeing Aren injured. Whatever it was, I used it as Ulric had taught me, to propel my magic.

The soldiers' boat rocked, but still moved ahead. I pushed harder, willing the strength of my magic to make the river's might my own. The waves rose up. The boat capsized, and the soldiers in their heavy armor disappeared.

I looked to Kel, Cassia, and Nox. They were weathering the waves, but wouldn't last long.

"Get in a boat," I repeated. "Now!"

Aren started to object, but Ulric grabbed his arm and pulled him toward the water. They climbed into the green rowboat. "Get in!" Aren called.

I looked back at the street. There were at least fifteen guards left, and likely more on the way as soon as they'd been roused and assembled. Unless I sank every boat on the river, they'd be after us. Even then, they'd come. "Go! I'll hold them off."

Aren climbed out of the boat, and Ulric pulled him back in with one hand as he untied the boat with the other. I gave the water a gentle push, and it carried them toward the middle of the river, where Ulric pulled Nox in and reached for the others. I wouldn't risk pushing them more. Still, the current was strong enough to carry them, and they had oars.

I took a last, quick look at Aren. He'd slumped

back against Kel, but kept his eyes on me.

Their only chance for survival, Aren's only chance, was for me to keep the soldiers occupied. At least now it wouldn't be a great tragedy if I hurt anyone while I experimented.

Magic still roared within me, though it felt calmer now. Smaller, perhaps, but I didn't want to focus on it to find out how much I'd lost already.

Calm. Steady. The power is yours. I stood firm in the muck of the riverbank, watching the assembling soldiers as they stepped around the bodies in the street. My heart pounded, but did not race. My breath strengthened me, and my magic infused my limbs and my mind, lifting me as though I might fly away.

I called to the water upstream. It came, and stacked into a shimmering wall that rose over the roofs of the sheds, then higher than the roofs across the street, broad as a barn, obediently remaining behind the river's banks, waiting for my permission to move. Pride swelled in me at the sight. *Gods, it's beautiful.* A lake's worth of water, and still building.

There was no time to enjoy my victory. Soldiers clanked toward me, approaching cautiously, swords drawn. I reached over my head and behind me, as though I could grab hold of the water, and brought my hands forward in an arc as I darted into the shadows next to a shed to shield myself from the wave.

The wall of water obeyed, crashing forward and down over the street and the soldiers, landing like a rockslide. Though the wall of the shed sheltered me from the worst of it, I felt the crushing blow, and panic rose in me as my feet left the ground, swept up in the massive wave that swirled over the road and between buildings. Water filled my mouth and my nose. A moment later my feet found the ground, and I fell to my knees in the mud. I gasped a breath of wet air and stood. My skirt clung to my legs like a wet sheet, and I pulled it free.

The soldiers had been knocked off their feet, hit harder by the wave than I had been, but most were stirring, a few lifting themselves off the soaked ground.

I pushed sopping hair out of my eyes, flicked a strand of seaweed off my hand, and readied myself again. The magic definitely felt less now, though still greater than what I was accustomed to. I could manage my trick once more, and give the others time to escape.

A shadow passed over again. I'd have looked up, but a soldier had found his feet. He charged at me, disarmed, but heavy and strong and well-armored.

A white and grey shape fell from the air, landing on him, pinning him to the ground.

"Florizel!"

She whinnied and delivered a kick to the soldier's head that seemed more out of panic than strategy, then hurried toward me.

"Get on!" she cried. I didn't hesitate. As soon as I'd found my seat, I felt her muscles quiver, ready to take off.

"Wait," I said. If we just flew off, the soldiers would turn their attention back on the boatload of enemies that had just escaped. "Give me a moment."

Florizel whinnied, but stood her ground as the soldiers climbed to their feet.

I reached deep inside of myself to find something more peaceful than rage to drive me. I pictured Aren, remembered my shocked joy at seeing Kel and Cassia again. Remembered the school. Belleisle. The people there who made me feel like I was enough just as I was, but who believed I could be more. I remembered love.

And I called the river.

It rose again, not as a towering wall, but as a thick fog that rolled over the banks to surround us, closing over our heads and those of the soldiers.

"No one move!" someone hollered.

One more thing, I begged my dimming magic.

Just this, and then we can rest.

I took in a deep chestful of the river-scented fog, and I imagined.

When the fog cleared, a half-dozen more Florizels and Rowans surrounded us. Florizel shied, and the others all did the same. I patted her neck, and my illusory sisters copied my action. Had I been more experienced, they might have acted on their own. Several of the illusions seemed real and solid. A few were clearly illusions, if good ones, and one was barely there at all. It would have to do.

"Now!" I said, and Florizel didn't hesitate. She reared up and wheeled to face an empty section of street, and she ran, wings flapping hard, and lifted into the air. Her ribs heaved under my tightly-clamped legs, and her shoulders flexed and released with the beating of her wings.

"Over the river!" I called. She complied, passing over the water, heading downstream. "Other way!"

I wouldn't follow the others. Not yet.

She turned. The illusions behaved just as we did, surrounding us as though we were a flock of great birds. I patted the right-hand side of Florizel's neck and she veered that way, wheeling back over the soldiers in the street below.

An arrow arced toward us, released by one of the recently-arrived troop members, and shot straight through the Rowan next to me.

At least we've got their attention, I thought. I indicated that Florizel should fly for the fortress upstream, and she complied.

They would be preparing their troops at the compound, too, if they had any left. With any luck, if we flew high enough, they'd think my rescuers had brought a herd of flying horses with them, and we were escaping that way. They'd follow us. By the time anyone told them any different, my friends would be safe.

Florizel flew well, weaving and darting high over the water. "Higher," I called. "Over the walls, just so they see us."

The bell still sounded inside the fortress. A dozen soldiers raced out over the drawbridge and halted as they caught sight of us. Dorset Langley led them, clad in his gray magic hunter's uniform. He watched in silence as we flew over the fortress.

From the wall to our right came a volley of arrows. Florizel shied to the left. I held on, but cried out as a searing pain sliced through my left arm. Something fell to the ground below us—a pike, perhaps. I glanced at my arm. The blade had sliced through the sleeve of my dress, but with the wind whipping the soaked fabric about, I couldn't see much aside from blood. The fingers of my left hand weakened and lost their grip on Florizel's mane, and I couldn't afford to let go with the right to put pressure on the wound.

"Shit," I gasped.

Florizel stretched her neck out long and pushed harder through the air.

I remembered Aren's body trying to heal a similar wound, and failing. My magic alone wouldn't be enough. We'd have to land as soon as we knew the soldiers were no longer following.

The illusions around us faded as we flew toward an unfamiliar forest, and magical warmth built in the injured muscles of my arm as white spots appeared before my eyes.

Do not faint, I ordered myself. *Not this time.*

A horse screamed somewhere far behind us, and someone shouted.

We flew on.

Chapter Thirty-Nine

Nox

Ulric and Cassia grabbed the oars, though they seemed unnecessary. The river's current pushed harder than I remembered from when we swam it farther upstream, and we seemed to fly over the surface. Cassia used her oar to paddle while Ulric used his as a rudder, steering us to the middle of the river. I looked back, but couldn't see anything past the buildings that now crowded the banks.

"We can't just leave her," Aren said. He sat on a white canvas tarp in the bottom of the boat with Kel, leaning against his friend's back, feet resting on a fisherman's wooden tackle box. "There had to be twenty of them back there. She's not ready for that."

"She's more ready than you think." Ulric scrambled to hold on to his oar as a sudden surge of water pushed us on again. A dozen more boats had broken their moorings, and drifted toward us. Cassia used her oar to push them away when they got too close. "If we go back now," Ulric said, "she's dead, and so are we. Let her do this."

Aren slumped lower, and I moved cautiously closer to him. The boat heaved, and I dropped on to the seat nearest him.

"What happened back there?" I asked, and he pulled down the collar of his shirt. A knife wound penetrated the back of his shoulder, clean but deep. I poked at the skin around it, and he winced. "I can take care of that when we get back to our supplies." Barberry root would stop the blood flow, but I still didn't have anything to stitch it with. We had to get him back to magic, and hope he recovered.

Aren just grunted and let me poke some more. He leaned his head back and rested it against Kel's shoulder.

"Here," Cassia said, and tossed me her bag. "The bandages will be soaked, but there might be something you can use."

"You did amazing things back there," I said softly, not wanting Ulric to hear me offering reassurances. Aren didn't need our father judging him as any weaker than he already was.

"Not much good now," he responded, and closed his eyes.

I unrolled a long strip of cloth and squeezed out as much dampness as I could before I pressed it hard against the wound. Unsanitary. He'd need something to fight infection later.

I rested a hand on his brow, which felt warmer than before. I'd never seen a sickness take hold so quickly.

Ulric caught my concerned look. "Can you patch him up?"

"I'm not a physician or a healer," I said without looking up. "But I'll do what I can."

He grunted. *Disapproval. How unexpected.*

"She is a healer," Aren said, and placed a blood-spattered hand over mine, just for a moment. "A fine Potioner, even with limited supplies. I have complete faith in her ability to keep me alive until my magic returns."

My heart swelled. I knew it was foolish, but hearing those words from him, who such a short time ago had thought my talents worthless, meant a great deal to me. I squeezed his fingers and put Ulric out of my mind.

"What about your leg? That could be the source of the sickness, if you've got a cut there."

The boat pitched. If I'd had anything in my stomach, it would have gone overboard.

"I stepped on something sharp," Aren muttered. "It's nothing."

"Look alive," Ulric said. "Wall's approaching. Pass me that." He motioned toward the canvas sheet that Aren and Kel sat on.

I looked ahead to the wall. It spanned the river, but with a great deal of clearance beneath. A few tiny figures dotted the top—guards, but not many. It seemed they hadn't received word of our aquatic escape. Perhaps Rowan was doing her job back there.

"Lie down," Ulric ordered, and opened the tarp over us, careful not to let it flap around and draw attention. "The river will have to carry us through. No one move."

The boat was small, but we made ourselves fit. Ulric took the space behind the boat's rear seat, leaving the rest of us in the center section. Kel lay on his back, Aren beside him. Cassia pulled her oar in and fitted herself between them, and I lay on top of Kel. He wrapped his arms around me, and we all helped hold the tarp down. It stank of rotten fish, a fact which didn't help my motion sickness.

The heavy fabric shifted in the breeze, and something heavy knocked into the side of our vessel. I bit my lip to keep back a loud gasp. *Just another boat.*

"Do you think they spotted us?" I whispered.

Cassia shifted to make herself more comfortable, and the boat rocked. "I guess if they start shooting, we'll know they did."

I narrowed my eyes at her. "Don't say things like that."

She winked. "I thought you weren't superstitious."

"I'm also not stupid."

"Hush," Aren whispered.

I closed my eyes. My mind drifted with the uneven rocking of the boat, anchored by the steady beat of Kel's heart under my ear. We passed into shadows. *The wall.* Kel's arms tightened around me, and I held my breath as I waited for arrows to fall, for someone to shout a warning.

Light came again, filtering through the holes in the heavy fabric, and I released my breath.

"Don't move yet," Ulric ordered. He said nothing else until several minutes later, when the boat jolted and the bottom grated over rocks, then stopped. He lifted a corner of the tarp and peered out.

"All ashore," he said, and we hurried out onto the pebbled shore of the river, which had become wide and shallow. Trees lined the edges, shading us again. I took the tackle box and followed the others into the trees.

Behind us, the city was still visible, brightly lit by the sunlight.

"It shouldn't be far back to the horses," I said. "Aren, can you walk?"

"Of course." He limped behind the rest of us, but kept pace. Cassia hung back, but he refused her help.

"Stubborn, isn't he?" I asked Kel.

"Yep. Seems to run in his family."

We hurried through the woods toward where we'd left the horses. The four were there, saddled and ready as Florizel had promised, but the flying horse herself was gone.

I turned to Ulric. "I don't suppose one of your magical skills is communicating with animals? I'd like to ask where our other friend has gone."

He frowned. "No."

Perhaps he expected a more respectful tone. He was, after all, my king, and had just showed incredible power in getting us out of the city. Growing up in Cressia,

I'd never been taught awe of royalty, but had he come to town, we'd have been expected to show respect. I just couldn't manage it. Not now. I'd have expected to feel many things when meeting my father—anger, perhaps, over what he'd done to my mother. Fear, maybe. Relief at having found him, which had been my goal since I decided to work with Aren.

All I felt when I looked at him was emptiness.

"We should wait," Aren said, and sat on a moss-covered rock. "Rowan will never find us if we go too far, and Florizel might be coming back from wherever she went."

I exchanged a glance with Kel. He shook his head slightly.

"Who's Florizel?" Ulric asked, and Aren explained.

"If we stay here, near the city and the road," Ulric said, "the wrong people will find us, and there will be nothing left for Rowan to come back to. If Rowan gets away from the city, she'll find us somehow. But safety will be her first concern. She's a clever girl. She won't lead them straight to us. We need to leave. Now."

I fixed the tackle box to the back of my horse's saddle. Much as I wanted to see whether there was anything in there I could use to stitch Aren's shoulder up, we didn't have time. Still, I took a moment to dig out the barberry roots I'd picked up in Tyrea. Nightflare would have been better, but I hadn't found any since I'd used it up on myself.

"Chew this," I told him.

He didn't comment on what would have been a horribly bitter taste, or give any reaction except to hand it back to me when he'd finished. "Was that supposed to help with the pain?"

"No." I pulled his collar open, removed the bandage pad, and pressed the crushed, wet roots into the wound. Aren hissed. "That's a deep cut. This will constrict any blood vessels that are still open, and promote healing." I re-bandaged the wound to hold the plant material in place. "Keep that there until I tell you otherwise. Come on."

He didn't move.

"Aren," I said, and stepped toward him. "Get up."

"Rowan will be fine," Kel said. "She always is, right?"

Aren looked up. "What if she's not?"

"Then she's not," I said. "Ulric is right. If something happens to her, you staying here and waiting for the Darmish army to come and get you isn't going to help her. If she dies—"

Aren winced.

"If she dies," I repeated, "it will be because she decided to risk her life so we could get away, so you and your father could finish what you set out to do. If we get caught, her sacrifice is a waste. And if Florizel left, she had a good reason for it. We should do the same."

Aren's hands clenched into fists, and the muscles in his forearms tensed as he glared at me. He was ready to fight. He'd never attacked me, but I'd seen that look on too many faces to mistake it for anything else. I stepped back, ready to use Kel as a shield.

Aren climbed to his feet, then turned to adjust his horse's bridle and prepare it for riding. "Come on, then."

I turned back to my own horse, only to see that Ulric had taken it for himself. Kel mounted his horse, then offered me a hand up so I could ride behind him.

"That was harsh," Kel said quietly as we rode into the woods, following Ulric and Cassia, with Aren trailing behind.

"It was honest. You know as well as I do that what she did helped us, but it was incredibly dangerous. I want her to find us, but I'm not going to give Aren false hope if it will get us killed." I glanced back. Aren rode with his shoulders slumped, but with his eyes fixed firmly ahead. His skin was far too pallid, his eyes too pained.

"We need to get Aren somewhere he can rest," I added. "He's going to collapse soon, and I want to be as far from the city as possible when he does."

I was wrong about that. Aren kept his jaw set and his eyes forward as he rode on through the morning. We came to a wide stream at mid-day and stopped to water the horses. They seemed nervous without Florizel's presence.

My stomach grumbled. We'd dropped the bags of food we'd taken from the tavern, which left only the little bit of dried food we had in our bags, at least until I had time to search the forest for something fresher.

"Too bad there won't be any fish here," Cassia said.

I agreed. Still, I went to the tackle box. No needles, but the fishing line would do for stitching, if I snapped the barbed end off of a hook to pull it through. It wouldn't be pretty, but it would work.

"Aren, let me see your shoulder."

He pulled his hair aside, and I peeled back the bandage. The bleeding had stopped. "Lucky you," I said. "I'm not going to stitch at this point. How are you feeling?"

"Like something that came out of the back end of a large dragon," he admitted.

It had to be bad if his answer wasn't *it will be fine.* "We'll get you something to bring the fever down as soon as we stop for the night. Is the magic any better?"

He shook his head.

I was about to order him to take his boot off when Ulric told us to move on.

We left a false trail leading into the forest on the opposite side of the stream before returning to it and leading the horses upstream. Water splashed over our boots and wet the hair on the horses' legs. The day was growing warm, and the cool water was welcome. Kel was still barefoot, and Cassia took off her boots as well.

Ulric breathed deeply, presumably enjoying the first fresh air he'd had in years, and he seemed to grow stronger with every step—nearly as quickly as Aren was faltering. My brother hid it well. If I hadn't known better I'd have said he was only tired and preoccupied with thoughts of Rowan. He still had that glassy look to his eyes, though, and he walked with a pronounced limp, leaning on his horse. He struggled to re-mount when we left the river and turned east, but refused help.

By the time Ulric decided it was safer to stop and make camp than it would be to continue into the evening, Aren was shaking, barely able to hold himself up.

We set up camp in a shallow indentation next to a low escarpment that wound through the trees. It wasn't perfect shelter, but it cut what little wind there was and gave us a feeling of security. We built a good fire, lit this time by Ulric, and I prepared a stew with the supplies we had left. We shared out our bedding as best we could. There wasn't nearly enough. Aren wouldn't be transforming that night, and we had an extra body.

Darkness settled over the forest as we finished setting up camp. Aren sat and talked to Ulric for a while, trying to agree on where we'd go next. They must have decided that they needed rest more than a decision, because Ulric went and lay down near the fire, and Aren settled down on his bedroll and pulled his boots off. I crouched beside him.

"Show me that leg now," I said. "No arguments."

He looked annoyed—still thinking about what I'd said earlier, I supposed. His expression softened. "Thank you. I don't think it's much. It wasn't bleeding too badly even when it first happened."

"Give," I said, and he extended his leg toward me. The light wasn't good, but I could see well enough. The skin around the deep puncture wound had become swollen and red, and felt hot when I touched it. I pulled back on the skin, and Aren groaned. There didn't appear to be any debris in there, but the puncture was deep.

"Stupid Sorcerers," I muttered. "You really haven't ever had to worry about infection, have you?"

"What?"

I shook my head. "When an average person gets a wound like this, he ends up with an infection like the one you've got brewing here. It's poisoning your blood, and far worse than it would in a person who didn't usually rely on magic. We should have treated this hours ago, escape plans be damned. Judging by the fever you're running, you're lucky to be conscious. You have no magic protecting you, and your body has no idea how to function without it. For all we know, you've also picked up whatever sickness that gate guard was telling us to avoid."

He swallowed hard. "I hadn't thought about that."

"Of course you hadn't." I thought it through. "Unless anyone you fought was ill, it's probably just the infection from your foot. But I can't know."

"Can you do anything for it?"

"I could cut off your leg. How would that be?" He didn't react, and I sighed. "I'll get something together for you. It would be better if I were at home, with proper equipment and suspension fluids. This will be primitive, but it will help."

He lay on his side with one arm under his head and closed his eyes.

I was looking through my things, trying to find the stokeweed I was sure I'd picked back near the dragon's cave, when a rustling noise in the dark forest stopped me. I wasn't the only one who heard it. Kel, Cassia and Ulric leaped to their feet, and even Aren sat up and watched closely.

An indistinct shape moved toward us, ghostly in the dark forest, broken by the shadows.

"Florizel?" Cassia whispered, and stepped

forward. Aren sat up straighter.

The horse's head hung low, and she held her wings high over her back like a swan. When she lowered them, a smaller form came into view, slumped over her withers.

Aren stood and moved unsteadily toward them, stumbling over his feet in his rush to reach Rowan.

Rowan lifted her head from Florizel's neck. "Sorry we took so long." She slid down from the horse's back and landed awkwardly. "We couldn't see you until you lit that fire. Poor Florizel has been carrying me all day." She took a few unsteady steps toward us. "Do you have anything for her to eat?"

"No grain left. The horses have been having some luck foraging around here, though," Cassia said, and touched Florizel's cheek. "What happened?"

The horse didn't answer, so Rowan did. "She flew into the city and saved me. Dropped out of the sky, took out a guard, and carried me away. I'd have been doomed without her."

"As we would have been without you," Aren said, and took Rowan into his arms.

I turned away. Rowan's presence grated on me. It seemed she was every bit as impressive as the others said—or at least she'd become so, once she'd pulled herself together after Aren rescued her. She'd done a fine thing back in the city, and had no doubt saved our lives. But it was her fault we'd been in that danger to begin with, a fact which I suspected no one would bring up. No one ever did to people like her.

I went back to my bags to find something that might restore a horse's strength more quickly than food and rest alone. Starflower, perhaps, though I needed that for Aren's potion, too. She could have a hint of fireweed in the morning after she slept, but it would keep her awake now.

But if I also gave her this slip of cowberry...

I carried a few items back to Florizel. Aren and Rowan had moved away.

"Abandoned you, did she?" I asked, and set the plants down. Florizel nosed at them, but didn't eat.

"I told her to go," she said. "It was so brave, how she stood up to those guards back there. She needs to rest."

"You were brave, too." I pulled a cloth from my pocket to rub the sweat and dried blood from her coat. I didn't see a cut anywhere. Not her blood, then. "You saved Rowan's life."

Florizel sighed and leaned into my touch. "I wasn't brave. I was terrified. I heard the bells coming from the city and knew you all must be in trouble. I wanted to fly far away."

"But you didn't. You flew into danger."

"I hated it. I could never do it again. I still want to flee, even now."

I patted her neck. "I think you might be the bravest of us all. Eat, please. Take care of yourself."

She nodded, and I left her to her foraging.

Rowan accepted what little food was left in the pot. She and Cassia sat with Aren while she ate, and spoke quietly. She didn't seem to want to talk about what had happened. "We held their attention," was all she said. The skirt of her dress was torn shorter than it had been before, and she'd wrapped the missing fabric around her arm in a bulky bandage that was stained through with fresh blood in several places.

"That's filthy," I said. "Better change it before you end up like him."

I went back to preparing the salve I'd been planning before Florizel and Rowan showed up.

Kel followed, and watched while I pinched leaves, stems and roots into a bowl. "I hope this one doesn't require a blood sacrifice."

"Not a sacrifice. An ingredient. I didn't realize it

would bother you that much to see blood."

"It only bothered me because it was yours," he said softly. I looked up, and he reached out to brush away the hair that hid my eyes.

I leaned in to his touch, and he cupped my cheek in his hand. I only took a moment to enjoy the fact that we were alive and together. Much as I wanted to just collapse, there was work to be done that only I could do. Kel sat nearby while I prepared the mixture and went into the woods with me as I searched for moss. I set the bowl next to the fire to let the components of the salve warm and combine, and went to check on Aren. He was asleep, but his breaths were shallow and quick.

"He said you could help him?" Rowan said, barely glancing away from Aren.

"I'm going to try."

"That's good. I can't. I used to be able to heal things like this, but that talent is gone now." She chewed her lip. "I can't even give him any more magic so he can heal himself. I tried, but I think mine is all busy with this." She gestured to her arm, which she'd unwrapped. The wound had obviously been severe, a deep gash that cut from the outside of her elbow to the front of her shoulder in a ragged line. She'd lost a lot of blood, if what I'd cleaned off of Florizel was any indication, but the wound had almost pulled together, even without stitches. It probably wouldn't even scar. I envied her that.

"I didn't have time to properly introduce myself," she went on. "I'm Rowan. Aren said you're his sister?"

"That's how it looks," I said. "I'm sure he'll tell you the whole story."

"I got most of it from Cassia just now. Aren's not talking much." She hesitated. "Is he going to be okay? I've never seen him sick. Hurt, but he gets over that quickly. Usually." She sounded nervous.

Good. Again my intense dislike of her flared up. She deserved to be worried. *Calm down, Nox.* I knew I was being irrational, but was too exhausted to care.

I pulled the thin blanket up over Aren and stepped back. "He got a nasty wound on his foot when he was running around barefoot and in wet clothes, looking for you. The infection is raging through him already, and getting worse. He's used up his magic reserves, and hasn't been getting enough sleep since he found out where you were. It was too much, and he's worn down. There's not much magic around here to help, either."

She closed her eyes. "It's better than it was at the compound, but you're right. Barely any."

"You were born here?"

"Not here, exactly. East. But in this country, yes."

"That's what I meant."

I walked away and she followed, brushing pine needles off what was left of her skirt. "You don't like me much, do you?" she asked, not sounding hurt by it.

I shook my head.

"Why?"

"Why do you care?"

"I'm just curious."

I took a deep breath and released it slowly as I turned to face her. "You didn't see Aren's face when he heard that you'd been taken. That was the most afraid I've seen him since we met. Even when we went to visit your friend Ruby, he wasn't terrified like he was at that moment. He thought the magic hunters were going to kill you, and I think that would have killed him. He risked his life, and mine, Kel's and Cassia's, to save you from a situation you got yourself into. Now he's hurt and sick and not able to fix himself, and it's your fault." My vehemence surprised me, as did the way my voice caught in my throat. I couldn't possibly care so much for my brother. And yet, there it was.

"I never should have come back to Darmid," she said quietly. "I know it was stupid. My brother was sick, and I thought Emalda's potions were his best hope."

"You thought you'd be able to say hello, drop off some magical medicine, and they'd let you go again?" Perhaps she wasn't as smart as Aren seemed to think.

She pressed her lips together. "I wanted to believe that. I haven't always been on the best terms with my parents, especially my mother. This could have been a better way to end things with them, and I just wanted that so badly." She looked at my brother again. "I never meant to hurt anyone. Especially not Aren."

I sighed. She'd done what she thought was right. Even if I thought her decision stupid, she'd done it for good reasons. I couldn't say I'd have done differently. Still, I needed to clear the air between us.

"Of course you didn't. You just cared about your family," I said. She looked at me warily. "Let me tell you something. That man over there, the one you didn't mean to hurt? He's the only real family I have. We've had a rough start, and I wanted to hate him as much as I did my father and the others. But I can't. He's trying to do great things, but he was willing to throw it all away for you, to save you from your own foolish mistake."

Rowan winced. "I understand. You love him. So do I."

Do I? I might not have gone so far as to say that, but it seemed Aren was becoming another blind spot for me. I'd have to watch that.

I softened my tone. "What you did saved us, and I want you to know I'm grateful for that. I can respect it. For what it's worth, I'm glad we have you and Ulric on our side for whatever comes next. Don't worry about whether I *like* you. It doesn't matter."

She met my gaze again. "Fair enough. If you can help Aren, you'll have my respect, as well."

"I'm working on it." I went back to the fire and stirred the salve. The surface bubbled, but felt barely warm when I tested it with my finger. That meant the ice grass was working, and would help to draw out any dirt or brewing infection in his blood.

"I'm going to need fresh bandages," I told Rowan. She was giving me extra space. "Something cleaner than what you found for yourself."

"I've got it," Cassia said. "Though we're going to run out of blankets soon if we're not careful." She'd torn an entire cotton blanket into long strips. "At least spring is here."

I soaked a patch of moss in the pungent herb mixture, which had reached a sticky, syrupy consistency while it sat by the fire, then folded pieces of leaves and roots inside of a strip of cloth and took all of it to Aren.

"You awake?"

He opened his eyes half-way. "Close enough."

He'd grown warmer since I'd last checked on him, and his foot was still swelling. I washed it as well as I could with the water I'd boiled earlier and pressed the moss and the salve-pad to the puncture. Aren drew in a sharp breath, then relaxed as Rowan sat beside him and took his hand.

Cassia handed me another bandage, and I wound it around Aren's foot and ankle, binding the other items to him. The salve would work its way into the hole in his foot. It would sting, but it would work. I felt it as much as I knew it. "If the fever's not better by morning, I'll see if I can find something to help," I told him. "It's too dark to see now."

"Thank you," Rowan said, and yawned. She lay down beside Aren without letting go of his hand. "Let me know when it's my watch."

"Don't worry about it," Kel said. "We're going to need an early start anyway. Cassia, Ulric and I will take watches tonight. You focus on healing, and if you can give him any more magic when that's done, so much the better."

Kel handed something to Rowan—a necklace. "Ulric said this is yours."

She thanked him, and tucked it into Aren's other hand.

"What about me?" I asked. "I can stay awake, too."

"Not tonight." Kel took my hand to lead me to a place away from the fire's light where he'd set up a bed. "You've done your part today, more than once. Come on, I'll tuck you in."

Kel lay down, arms open. I hesitated. I cared for him, more than I wanted to. Spending a night next to him would only make it worse. And yet I wanted this, wanted to wrap myself in this strange, brave, loyal and kind person whose laugh made me forget my pain.

"Come here," he said, and smiled. "I have no nefarious plans, I swear."

I returned the smile. "How do you know I'm not coming up with some terrible ideas of what to do with you?" I sank to the ground and stretched out with my back to him, facing the fire, using his arm as a pillow. There was barely enough room for both of us, but we were able to share blankets this way. It felt right. Natural. And for once, I didn't want to run from it.

"How's this?" he asked.

"I've had more comfortable pillows," I said, "but I think this is the best."

He wrapped his other arm around my waist and pulled me closer, fitting his body around mine.

Ulric waved toward the fire as he went to his own bed, and the light burned lower. Cassia sat near Florizel. Kel and I might as well have been alone in the woods.

"This whole journey has been insane," he whispered into my hair. "Exhausting. Dangerous. Can I say that and still be happy that you're here with me right now?"

I twisted my fingers between his and squeezed. "I'm glad you're here, too, even though I know you'd be better off at home."

He shifted his weight, pressing his hips against my backside. "Nox, what is this that's happening with us?"

"I don't know." My heart pounded in my ears. I wanted to let go, to fall for him, but I still feared it. "Do we have to decide right now?"

"I wouldn't mind knowing."

I pulled Kel's hand up, closer to my chest. His fingers traced gentle circles over my ribs, trailing up to the exposed flesh where the top of my shirt was unbuttoned, floating over my curves. I closed my eyes and enjoyed his undemanding touch. My body yearned for more, but there were so many other things to consider.

After my husband died I decided that I was done with love for good. It wasn't long before some of the other men in town started giving me that look. It seemed no one expected a long mourning period, and certainly I wasn't supposed to want to live on my own for long. We hadn't had any children. I was barely even considered used goods. But I wasn't going to take someone into my bed or my heart simply because it was expected. I felt nothing for those men, and knew that none of them would be any better than what I'd already had.

Kel was different in so many ways. What I felt for him was confusing, frightening in its intensity. I just didn't know what to do with it.

"I've been many things to people in my life," I said softly. "Daughter, student, nuisance, wife. Murderer. I'm not any of those things to you. You're my friend."

"I am."

"And you want more."

"I do. More than I've ever wanted anything. I feel connected to you like I haven't to anyone else. Ever."

"Does that scare you?" I asked.

"Yes. A lot. But I want it, too."

I rolled over to face him and touched my fingers

to his lips. I'd become accustomed to being alone, and so many of my plans depended on my being dispensable. We had Ulric, but he hadn't made it to his throne yet, and Severn still lived. I needed to be willing to do anything to bring him down, to make him pay. Even if it meant sacrificing my own life.

But when I looked into Kel's eyes, I found myself wanting something more peaceful and beautiful. The two desires would tear me apart if I let them.

I will decide. Soon.

I moved my face closer to his. "I want more, too, but I'm not sure how much I can handle. Everything is so complicated."

The compassion in his eyes nearly brought tears to mine.

"You let me know." His lips brushed against my fingers as he spoke, and I moved them up to smooth the tension from his brow.

He pulled me into a kiss that washed my other concerns away, if only temporarily. I pressed my body to his, relishing emotions and physical desires I'd thought dead until I met him.

Kel pulled away and raised his head to kiss the hollow behind my jaw. I shivered.

"Go to sleep," he said. "I'll still be here in the morning."

"For how long?"

"How long do you want me?"

I tucked my head under his chin. "For this moment," I mumbled as I drifted away. "And the next one." I yawned. "And the next..."

Chapter Forty

Rowan

"Aren," I whispered.

He opened one eye. "Is it time to go?"

"If you're able. Drink this."

He took the hot tea that Nox had brewed and sipped it, then grimaced. "This is terrible."

"It's blue pine bark," Nox informed him. She stood behind me with her arms crossed, obviously trying to appear annoyed, and failing. She was probably as relieved as I was to see him looking better. "Keeps fevers down, eases pain." I moved aside so she could examine him. "That's about all I can do for you now, save for changing those bandages."

He didn't protest when she unwrapped his foot and pressed freshly brewed potion onto it. Nox had been up before dawn, brewing whatever she could find to keep us all going. I'd been unable to sleep most of the night, and had watched her work. She moved with purpose and certainty, never hesitating in the tasks she'd set for herself. Even if she wasn't going to be a friend to me, I was glad to have her with us.

"How's your arm?" she asked.

"Not bad." I lifted it and moved it around. It was still stiff, but I wasn't about to complain. I was alive, and everything was working. I'd had far worse pain.

I would have liked to talk to Ulric about the flood

of magic, about his own experience when we left the cell and what he expected to happen to us now, but he was no longer the man I'd met in the blue room. The mellowing effects of captivity were gone. I now saw the tyrant who Aren had told me about, cold and calculating, uncaring and focused entirely on strategy. He was speaking to Kel now, gesturing toward Aren as though he were an inconvenience rather than the catalyst for our freedom.

Aren stiffened slightly as his father approached.

"Will you be able to travel?" Ulric didn't crouch to speak, but looked down his nose at Aren.

"I will."

Ulric tapped a foot on the needle-strewn forest floor. "We'll get you back to Tyrea, and everything will be better. Once your power restores itself, things will be as they should." He gave me a strange look, then turned on his heel and left us.

"Was that supposed to be encouragement?" I asked.

Aren quirked an eyebrow over the top of his cup as he sipped at the potion again. "That's about as good as it gets. He might actually be concerned. It's hard to say."

We needed to move, but I ducked under his arm to rest my head on his chest. "I missed you. I'm sorry I was so stupid."

"Don't worry about it, okay? You're safe, and I'm going to be fine. Besides, your misjudgment of Callum led to us finding my father. We'll call it even."

My stomach filled with ice, and I tensed at Callum's name.

I felt Aren's shoulders drop, and he put his arms lightly around me. "Do I need to apologize for that?"

"Please, no. Never. You saved my life. It's just a bit of a shock to me. I've been imagining you both as separate parts of my life, never to meet again. The fact that he came back into my life was my fault. His death was his own doing, and his father's. Callum might have been a different person if not for Dorset's influence. I don't think he wanted to hurt me, but he thought he had to."

"Family can be hard to escape."

We both turned toward Ulric, who was now speaking to a confused-looking Florizel. Aren chuckled under his breath at them, and it turned into a cough. "We'd better get moving before this gets worse again."

Florizel gathered the horses, and in a few minutes, we were loaded up and on the move. Nox and Kel rarely left each other's sides, and when they did, warm glances flew between them across the campsite.

The woods were quiet, bright, and sunny, but there was nothing relaxed about our progress. Every snap of a branch set us on edge, ready to defend ourselves.

We swung wide around Ardare, staying to the woods, and our progress was slow. As we moved east, aiming for the north end of the isthmus, the ground beneath the horses' hoofs became rougher, with more stone protruding from the ground. The area was unfamiliar to me. We wouldn't be passing through Lowdell. I wouldn't see my family. I looked south, toward an ocean I couldn't hope to see from here.

"They'll be fine," Aren said softly. "We went through there. Your family is safe, or they were a few days ago. I told your mother they should leave."

It took me a moment to process the idea of Aren and my mother in the same place. Again, two halves of my life colliding. My chest tightened. "Did you see Ashe?"

"No. But Nox prepared something for him. She's a good Potioner." He lifted his leg in the stirrup as though testing its strength. "A miracle worker, really. He'll live. You'll see him again, some day."

I blinked back tears. "I'll have to thank her later."

He nodded. "Your mother sent her love. And her apologies."

I closed my eyes. "Thank you. Tell me more later?" I couldn't talk more about my family. Not yet. Not when the knowledge that my mother still loved me made me feel as though my heart might rip in half. *Safety first. Then comfort.*

The lay of the land forced our path to twist and turn as we rode on. Holes appeared in the ground, surrounded by lips of uneven, pockmarked stone. Caves, perhaps a network of them. They reminded me of our journey to Belleisle, though I didn't expect we'd encounter any cave fairies while still on Darmish land.

Though the route would keep us away from most human civilization, I couldn't help thinking that even here, someone had to be watching. The back of my neck prickled, but though I checked over my shoulder, I saw nothing.

Aren regained his strength as we traveled, and told me more of what had happened on his journey. I suspected he was leaving things out, but hearing about the Dragonfreed brothers and his visit with Ruby was enough for me. I was glad he'd had friends with him for most of it. Kel and Cassia joined in the conversation a few times, but for the most part it was just the two of us, riding at the back of the group.

We stopped for a meal and to make camp in a cave-dotted meadow. The mountains were in view, but we'd never make it before nightfall. Florizel flew toward them to scout as much as she could before sunset.

"Do you feel that?" Aren asked. He dismounted and stepped toward the trees. He breathed deeply and spread his arms wide. When he turned back, his dark eyes shone. "It's stronger here. I don't think they've destroyed as much of the magic in this area. It's coming back to me."

"Good," Ulric said. "Can you do anything?"

Nox crossed her arms and glared at him. "Other than perform what amounts to a miraculous healing on himself? His magic is working. He's walking. It's amazing."

Ulric turned to her with an identical expression. "Avalon, I—"

"That's not my name anymore." Her lip lifted in a sneer. "I left that in Luid when I was a child. I have no desire to take it back." Kel placed a hand on her arm, and she shook him off.

Ulric pinched the bridge of his nose. "Very well. Nox. I understand that you have problems with me—"

"I'll have a lot fewer when you start showing respect to the people who saved your life." Nox turned away and went to her bag to find her dagger. She stalked off into the woods in the direction Florizel had taken the horses, and Kel and Cassia followed her.

"I didn't mean it that way." Ulric turned back to Aren. "I simply wondered how quickly you were recovering. Rowan, too."

"As I said, it's coming along," Aren said. "I don't think I can do anything impressive now, but I'm healing, and I'll try to be aware of anyone coming."

They both looked at me.

"I feel drained, actually, but it's getting better the closer we get to Tyrea," I said. "It's coming back. Starting to feel almost normal." I grinned. I had to. "Except that I think I can control it now."

"Good. That's good." Ulric seemed about to say something else to Aren, but instead walked away and looked at the mountains.

"Don't feel too sorry for him," Aren said. "He'll figure out his place with us."

I took Aren's hand and squeezed it. "I know. But he did help me, so much. Things are strange now, but maybe he'll come around."

He smiled down at me. "You seem different."

"Yeah?"

"Less afraid. Stronger. I mean, I—" He looked

away, sheepish. "I loved you before you had control of your magic." When he met my gaze again, his eyes held a flicker of the heat I had missed so much. "But there's something incredibly attractive about you as a true Sorceress." He spun me around and into his arms and leaned in to catch my lips with his. I pushed up onto my toes, unable to get as close as I wanted to, pulling away only when I couldn't breathe anymore. He stumbled slightly on his bad leg as he stepped back, and grinned.

"You've changed, too," I said. "I don't know what it is. It's good, though."

His smile faded. "I'm not sure good is the right word." He ran his fingers through his tangled hair and looked out over the land that stretched away from us, back in the direction of Ardare. "I don't think that's what I am."

I began to object, but he stopped me. "Let me say this. I know you don't approve of some of the ways I use my magic. It was quite clear the first time I told you about the mind-control that you were horrified by it. Perhaps rightly so. You're not the only one who feels that way. It's a terrible power, and one I once used recklessly for purposes I should have thought to question. When we went to Belleisle, I agreed to give it up, at least temporarily. Between Emalda and my grandfather, the mer-folk and brother Phelun, I became convinced that it was dark magic. Wrong. And maybe it is. But when it came down to a choice between using dark magic and losing you, there was no question in my mind or my heart about what I had to do."

"Aren." I reached for his hand again. "I'm glad you used it. I'm beginning to understand that everything's not as black and white as I once thought it was."

He smiled slightly, but regret remained in his eyes. "I need you to know that I'm never going to be a white knight. I know there's darkness in me, and in my power. I'm not going to fight it or hide it. But I think I can use it for better purposes than what Severn planned for me. I will try to be wiser about it, but I will use every one of my talents if that's what it takes to accomplish our goals. Even if people get hurt. Does that still bother you?"

My heart swelled. I reached up to tuck his hair behind his ear and traced my fingernails over the warm skin of his neck. "No. There was a time when it would have, but you're right. I've changed. When I thought I was never going to see you again, I didn't only miss the parts of you that are easy to accept, or the parts I'd have chosen to take home to meet my family. I wanted everything. Even the parts that make me uncomfortable. Even the things that frighten me." I gave him a shy smile. "Didn't I tell you I liked your claws? Maybe this fairy tale ends with the damsel in love with the dark prince, not the white knight."

Aren took another deep breath of the cool air and pulled me close again. "You know I—" His expression turned sharp, and he looked toward the forest. "Where are the others?"

Nox appeared from the woods, running up the hill toward us, out of breath.

"Where are Kel and Cassia?" Aren asked her.

"Back by the river," Nox gasped. "They got away downstream. Soldiers sneaked up on us when we were watering the horses."

Ulric's mouth pulled back in a silent snarl, and he stepped forward. The ground beneath us vibrated. I grabbed Aren's arm.

"He can control it," he whispered.

Five soldiers in a tight pack ran out of the trees. The ground stilled, and Ulric continued toward them in slow steps, arms outstretched. The rumbling started again, and the soldiers' steps faltered. They stopped.

The ground beneath them opened with a deafening snap, swallowing every one of them as a cave cracked open. When the ground stilled and the dust settled, a muffled groan rose from an elongated space like a mouth in the earth. Tendons in Ulric's neck stood out as he lifted his arms again. The cave ceiling collapsed, leaving a deep, rocky crater.

Ulric took a few steps toward us, then fell to his knees. I ran to his side and knelt in the grass. "Are you all right?"

He reached for my hand, and I helped him to his feet. "I'll be fine," he said, though he looked dazed. "It's been a while since I've used as much power as I have today. I think...I think I should rest." He moved bent-backed toward a patch of longer grass. "That action requires such power, you see. I could do it once. Three years is just—"

His eyes closed, and he collapsed onto his side. "Nox!" I called, but she was already there.

"Go," she said. "I'll handle this. Find the others."

I turned to see another soldier charging Aren. He wouldn't be able to use magic to defend himself.

I stepped forward to help, but at that moment my nightmare appeared from among the trees. Dorset Langley rode toward us on a white stallion, sword drawn, grinning as though his senses had left him completely. His wild hair and wide eyes did nothing to lessen the effect.

"There you are!" he yelled, eyes on me.

I stepped back.

"You little bitch," he continued in a more conversational tone as he dismounted. His horse shuffled away, tossing its head nervously. "You ruined everything. My family is a laughingstock. Did Callum tell you that? He might have redeemed himself if he'd stepped in and finished you, but no. You and your friends and your magic go free while he grows cold in the mortuary. I won't allow you to leave. You won't live while he rots." He snarled. "This ends now."

A cracking noise, and the man Aren had been fighting dropped to the ground. Aren limped toward us, and Langley pointed the sword toward him without looking away from me. "You're next," he said. He pointed the sword at my heart. Not touching, but within lunging distance.

I held my ground. "I don't think so."

"Rowan, step back," Aren said.

"No." I called on my magic. True, it wasn't as strong as it would be when we reached Tyrea, but it would do. My magic had been born in these lands, and grown up in isolation. I could work with this.

Something else rose in me, along with my magic. I saw the faces of the prisoners who had passed through my father's courtroom, the faces on wanted posters of those accused of possessing magic. Callum, who should have been someone's prince charming, but had been twisted into a villain by his father's lies. My cousins, who had likely died for the same reason I should have. Rage tightened my hands into fists, but I held back.

"Are you going to bring me down with a clever illusion?" Langley asked, and laughed. "Lovely trick, that."

"No." I turned my focus inward and attempted to capture what I'd felt when I played with the water.

That feeling of power and control clicked into place. A grin spread over my face, baring my teeth at the man who had taken so much from so many. "You knew. All this time, all those deaths...You knew. You're the king's adviser. You could have stopped all of it. And yet you continued the lies, the killings."

"I did, and with pleasure. We do have standards to maintain." In a lightning-quick motion he swung his sword at me. I darted back, but he caught the front of my shirt, and the tip of the blade raked across my ribs. He kept moving, ready to swing again.

No.

Langley drew a sharp breath as his muscles became rigid, halting his motion. I caught sight of Aren hurrying toward us, and I held up a hand to stop him. I could handle this. And I would.

The air grew cold, and water droplets beaded on Langley's skin, soaking into his clothes. Not sweat, but the water from within his body, called by my magic. I directed it toward the ground, where it gathered in a hollow in front of him. The tiny puddle frosted over as the temperature dropped, a consequence of my experimentation.

Control, I reminded myself, but found I no longer feared the effects of my magic. I would deal with them as they came.

A vein throbbed in Langley's forehead, and his limbs trembled as he drew several sharp breaths. He tried to lunge at me again, but his skin tightened so that he could hardly move. The puddle grew.

I stepped away from his sword and walked in a circle around him. His eyes rolled to follow me, and he fought to turn his head.

You are becoming what you fear. There's no turning back from this.

I forced the thought away and focused instead on my anger, which fueled my power.

"I don't know whether I can give it back," I told him, and nodded toward the puddle. "I could try. You might survive if you ride away now, get back to your doctors in the city. Leave us. A day is coming when magic will return to Darmid. Do you feel it?" He didn't answer. I leaned closer to speak into his ear. "I have no desire to kill you, in spite of everything. But I leave it up to you."

That was a lie. A massive, terrifying part of me wanted him to die.

"Go to hell," he gasped.

"After you."

"Rowan," Aren said behind me, in a low, calm

voice. "I'd be pleased to take care of this for you. One more life on my ledger is nothing."

"Thank you, but no. I owe him this, on behalf of my people."

Langley's eyes still moved, absorbing the sky and the mountains, straining to take the world in.

I called the water. Pain shot through my muscles, perhaps reflecting a portion of what he felt, but I didn't stop. Sir Dorset's once handsome face pulled in on itself, and his lips stretched back over his teeth. His eyes sunk into his face as he pitched forward, landing with a splash in the shallow pool at his feet.

Dead.

The silence of the forest was broken only by the sound of Nox retching into the bushes. My stomach turned. I felt feverish. Numb. The strength drained from my legs, and Aren stepped in to let me lean against him.

"Sorry," Nox said as she approached. "I didn't expect that." She nudged the body with her boot. "Bastard deserved it. You okay?"

I nodded. "Go find the others," I told Aren. "We need to get out of here."

I sank to my knees, and Nox sat beside me.

"I've never killed anyone on purpose before," I said.

She rested a hand on my shoulder. "I did, once. It wasn't like I thought it would be."

"No?"

"No. It was easier."

I couldn't turn away from the body. *You did that,* my mind whispered.

He deserved it, I replied, emotionless.

No one deserves that.

I couldn't bring myself to shed any tears for Dorset Langley. There would be time for reflection later, for second-guessing. For guilt. At that moment all I wanted was to leave that mess behind me.

I forced myself to look away, and rested my face in my hands.

"You did what was necessary," Ulric said. Nox and I both turned, and he stumbled toward us. He crouched and placed a hand on my shoulder. "You saved us. You're a warrior, Rowan. Be proud." He frowned as he said it, but his words sounded sincere. "You did well."

I didn't answer. I couldn't.

Chapter Forty-One

Rowan

The magic around us grew stronger as we rode through forests that lay outside the reach of Darmid's magic hunters. Aren grew stronger with it, seeming to come back to life as we rode. He spoke quietly with his father, and laughed with his friends. I had never seen him so relaxed. His work was far from over, and there was still danger all around, but he was alive, and grateful for it.

Ulric rode Dorset Langley's horse, returning Nox's to her. The north end of the isthmus required us to ride up a steep incline as the cliffs reached to the water's edge, but Florizel found us a good route, and we made the passage more quickly with her help than we ever could have without it.

I tried not to think about what I'd done. Survival was the thing now. That, and gratitude for my life and my freedom. Even that seemed dull, though, and I plodded through the days hardly speaking to anyone. They didn't try to force me. Not even Kel, who always seemed to be up for conversation. I woke frequently from nightmares of Langley's withered face and my countrymen's hate-filled stares. I slept next to Aren, who woke with me and ran his fingers through my hair until I slept again, but even he couldn't save me from this.

Still, the horror eased as time passed. While I couldn't let go of my conflicted feelings about what I'd done, I began to adjust, to feel more like myself.

Once back in Tyrea, we left the mountains behind us and rode south and east toward Luid. I'd never noticed the ambient magic when we were in Tyrea or Belleisle before, but now I felt my body taking it in like a beggar at a king's feast. Spring had begun to unfold in earnest, turning the forests greener seemingly by the minute. Birds flitted through the trees, calling out and fighting their tiny battles over nesting space.

On our third day in Tyrea we found a deep lake where Kel and Cassia could swim and the rest of us could wash the dirt and sweat from our bodies and our clothes. I laughed when Kel splashed me with his flukes. The world began to feel right again—at least, until we dried off and I started thinking about what lay ahead.

Cassia rode beside me later that morning, silent. I realized that it was the first time she'd approached me since the border. I'd been too distracted to notice.

"Do you hate me now?" I tried to smile at her as though it were a joke, but I knew how they felt about people using magic as a weapon.

"No. Do we hate Aren for things he's done that we can't condone?"

"I suppose not. But you think it was wrong of me to kill Langley."

She tossed her wavy hair over her shoulder. "You did what you felt you had to do. You were protecting the rest of us, and he was an enemy who had hurt you before and intended to do so again. I would never say you were wrong to defend yourself, and the rest of us. I hope you don't feel guilt over that."

"So it's only the magic that bothers you?"

"The magic." She seemed deep in thought, and I left her to it.

"It's difficult to explain to someone who didn't grow up in our world," she said at last. "Magic is a tool. It's a part of us, as much as it is for you, but we only use ours on ourselves. It heals us, and allows us to change our form, but that's all. We don't manipulate the world around us. More importantly, we don't use it against one another. We believe magic is a blessing, not a weapon."

"So you think I was right to defend myself, but not to use magic to do it? He would have killed me otherwise. I had no weapon. No fighting skills."

"I know. Rowan, I can't tell you that I approve of what happened back there, but I never want you to doubt my friendship. We just...My people see things differently. Aren learned years ago that we have to agree to disagree on that, even as we try to open each other's minds to different ways of thinking. We don't try to force him to change, and he doesn't use his power against us. Ever. No matter what."

"I wouldn't, either."

She smiled. "I know. It's awkward though, isn't it? Disagreeing on something so vital?"

"A little."

"We—our people, not just me and Kel personally—we fear death by magic more than anything. Call it superstition, call it self-preservation, it makes no difference. Have you heard stories about what happens when a mer dies?"

I thought back through the few stories I'd read about them. "Something about turning to sea foam?" I asked, feeling stupid for even saying it.

Her smile warmed. "That's how it appears to land-bound folk. In reality, our physical form disappears when we die. It's how we know our spirit has been set free. But when we die by magic..." The smile vanished. "Our bodies don't disappear. It's as if they're anchored to this world by the magic. We can't tell whether those that die that way have had their spirits released, or whether they're trapped there in a rotting body. It's dying with a curse on you. It's—" She saw my horrified expression, and reached out to take my hand. "It's not the same for your people. I wanted you to know why it's hard for us to see things like what happened back in Darmid, why our elders are so wary of Aren. And I want you to know that you don't need to feel guilty on our account, whatever our views are. Kel and I are more open-minded about these things than some, and we're not going to judge you for it. Not yet, anyway." She winked, but tension remained between us.

"That makes no sense. But thank you."

"Thank *you*. It's good to have you back, and I'm glad you've got your magic now. And everything." She gave me a half-smile and rode ahead to speak with Kel.

Aren took her place. "Everything all right? You seem better today."

"Pretty near. Every time I push one concern aside, another one pops up to take its place. Nothing that's your problem."

"Tell me."

"I'm worried about my parents and Ashe."

"Aah." He thought for a moment. "Well, Nox was confident that her herbs would help him, and we told them to leave town."

"You said that. I hope they listened. My father might not be so keen on the idea. I can't help wondering what will happen to my aunt and uncle and the others at Stone Ridge. Maybe nothing, but I can't know."

He winced. "Please don't say you're going back to check."

I swallowed back a lump in my throat. I wanted to go. My family at Stone Ridge—Ches and Victoria, Della and Matthew—had raised me. My parents had a warning to flee, but what of the others?

"I suppose I need to let go and accept that I don't belong in Darmid anymore. I just wish I knew where my home is."

Aren smiled, broad and warm. "Your home is with me."

My heart stumbled over itself. "Sounds like a good plan. Speaking of plans...Where to now?"

"We'll try to get to my uncle. If we can't make it there, we try for Belleisle and regroup. My father has never been welcome there, but Albion's not a fool. He'll see that having Ulric back on the throne is the best thing for all of us."

The road curved away from the foothills, through a grassy plain and into a thick forest. Branches crowded overhead, and bushes tangled beside us, forming a loose tunnel as we rode. Ulric slowed his horse and waited for the rest of us to catch up. He looked to Aren, who had a familiar, eagle-sharp look in his eyes.

"I don't feel any people," Aren said, "but something isn't right."

Ulric sat up straighter. "Severn?"

"No. I'm not sure what it is."

"Stay on guard. Aren, Rowan, no magic if we can avoid it. It's best no one knows who we are if we meet thieves, or even other travelers. We can't trust anyone."

We kept to our previous pace, though it was difficult for me not to urge my horse into a gallop. The woods could have come from a storybook, one of the dark, haunted places where witches and wolves dwelt. Branches rubbed together in the wind, creaking and groaning. Though it became darker as the afternoon wore on, no one mentioned making camp.

As we came around a bend in the road, a dark-clad form dropped from the canopy onto Ulric's horse, landing behind Ulric. The horse reared, but the man held on and produced a knife, which he held to Ulric's throat.

"Quiet him!"

Ulric steadied the nervous horse and turned it to face us. "You don't want to do this, friend," he said. A bead of blood appeared at his throat. "This will not end well for you."

"No?"

At least two dozen men materialized from the trees around us. Cassia gasped, and Nox pulled her dagger. Florizel reared, kicked out a forefoot at the man closest to her, and took off into the sky before anyone could grab her.

My magic boiled up inside me, but I held it quiet. I felt Aren's power crackling in the air as he fought his instincts. If these people had magic in them, they would feel his if he tried to read them or control them, and I suspected there were too many for him to handle alone. He looked to Ulric, who gave his head a tiny shake. Aren frowned, but his magic quieted.

A lanky, bearded fellow in an incongruously jaunty cap stepped forward and grabbed the reins of my horse and Aren's.

"What brings you our way?" the stranger asked. He spoke calmly, obviously not intimidated by us.

"Just passing through," Aren said. "We have nothing of value."

"Ah, of course not. We'll have to check, of course." His men began sorting through our bags. "I'll like your friend to drop her knife, lest we have an accident with the old man."

Nox seemed to consider her options, then growled and dropped the dagger onto the road. One of the men scooped it up and tossed it to their leader. He examined it and nodded his approval as his companions came back with Nox's herbs, the food we'd gathered along the way, and what little else we had.

"I thank you," the leader said. "And lest you think us common thieves, please know that you are contributing to a worthy cause."

"Really." Aren hardly sounded convinced.

"Oh, yes." The man tipped his cap, twirled a finger through his beard, and drew a long sword that could only have come from one of Severn's soldiers. He held it steady and looked down the blade, meeting Aren's eyes as he pointed it at him.

A few of the others laughed, but their leader remained serious. "Our mission is simple," he said.

"And what's that?" Aren asked.

A slow grin spread across the lead thief's face. "Death to the monarchy."

Aren and his father exchanged another look. "An impressive mission," Ulric said to the thief. "We wish you well."

The thief straightened his cap and motioned for us to dismount. "Perhaps your horses wish to join our ranks, eh? Perhaps you will move on without trouble. And if not..." He shrugged and wiggled the sword again.

"Wait!" A child's voice called out from the woods.

The thief winced. "Go home!"

A small, whitish-haired form stepped out from the bushes. "It's okay," she said, and the crew's leader lowered his sword. "I know those two."

"Patience," I gasped. I barely recognized the girl. I'd last seen her when Aren and I had first traveled to Belleisle, back in the autumn. Then, she had been leading the other Wanderers' children in games and organizing a play to entertain us, carefree and lively. That child had disappeared. She seemed older now, and far more serious. Her hair had been cut to her shoulders in a ragged line, and she walked with a slight limp. She came and stood beside my horse and looked from me to Aren with one blue eye. The other was gone. Only a sunken mass of scarred skin remained.

Her lip trembled, but her voice remained firm. "You guys had better come with us. I have a lot to tell you."

{The End}

Dear Reader,

Thank you once again for joining me in this journey! I hope you've had a good time. I know I have, and I'm so happy you came along.

If you enjoyed this book, please consider leaving a review on e-book purchasing sites and/or on Goodreads—they really do make a difference to a book's chance of success. Your recommendations to friends, family, teachers, students, garbage collectors, pet-sitters, and lawyers help tremendously, as do book mentions on Facebook page posts. When you recommend books you love to people who buy them, it makes it possible for authors to continue producing high-quality work for you to enjoy.

For information on upcoming releases, previews on cover reveals, chances at advance review copies of future books, and more, join my infrequent but always fun mailing list!

http://mad.ly/signups/96420/join

You'll also be the first to hear release news about the conclusion of this little story.

And with that...

Watch for Sworn (Bound Trilogy Book 3), coming soon

Much love,
Kate

About the Author

Kate Sparkes was born in Hamilton, ON, but abandoned the mainland to live near the ocean in Newfoundland, where she spends way too much time looking for merfolk. She lives with her wonderful husband, two children, many fuzzy things, and an office full of dragons.

For more information on upcoming releases, sign up for the newsletter
(http://mad.ly/signups/96420/join),
or visit Kate online:

Blog: www.disregardtheprologue.com

Facebook: www.facebook.com/katesparkesauthor

Twitter: @kate_sparkes

Instagram: @kate.sparkes

Acknowledgements

Massive thanks, first, to you. The people who purchase, read, and review these books make it possible for me to live in a fantasy world of my own creation, struggling with words and ideas every day, in order to take you all on dazzling adventures. Your support means so much to me.

To my alpha and beta readers: KL Schwengel, Shannon Andrews, Katelyn Lowden, Scott Holley, Annette Flick, and Alana Terry... you make this possible through your encouragement and your gentle (and not-so-gentle) criticism. You are a part of this book's lifeblood. Thank you. And to Krista Walsh, thanks for the hand-holding, the guidance, and the shoulder to cry on. You get it, man.

To my editor, Joshua Essoe: Thanks for the honesty and the assistance, and for always encouraging me to grow as a writer.

To AM Liebowitz: Thank you for the copy-edits and for catching those last few typos. Well... we'll hope they were the last.

To Ravven: You're some kind of magic-worker. Thank you for another incredible cover!

To Cal and Glenda Sparkes: Thank you for letting me work in the Princess room (and at your table... and in the guest room...), and for your love and support. My mom told me to marry a guy whose parents I loved. Mission accomplished.

To my parents: Thanks for introducing me to books, for encouraging me to do what makes me happy, and for deciding against tossing me out with the garbage when I was a cranky baby. You're rockstars. I love you.

And finally, to my husband and my children... thanks for letting me get 'er done. I know your lives would be easier if I didn't have this crazy obsession, but I hope they're better when I'm living my dream. I love you guys so much. You're my favourite people.

Also By Kate Sparkes:

The Bound Trilogy
Bound
Torn
Sworn (coming soon)

* * *

Short Stories
The Binding (A Bound Trilogy prequel)